RELATIVE TRUTHS

VALERIE S ARMSTRONG

Order this book online at www.trafford.com
or email orders@trafford.com

Most Trafford titles are also available at major online book retailers.

Printed in the United States of America.

ISBN: 978-1-4907-1835-4 (sc)
ISBN: 978-1-4907-1838-5 (e)

Trafford rev. 10/31/2013

 www.trafford.com

North America & international
toll-free: 1 888 232 4444 (USA & Canada)
fax: 812 355 4082

Author of: Livvy

No Roses for Abby

Follow the Butterfly

Looking for Lucius

Dedication

In memory of my dear friend, Maggie Ross, an avid reader, who encouraged me to continue writing. This one's for you, Maggie.

Acknowledgements

A special thank you to my friend, Eileen Usher, who did an excellent job of editing the manuscript. Also, to Michael Fedecky for his help in designing the cover.

Chapter One

Charlotte Hamilton rolled over in bed, slowly opened her eyes and tried to adjust to the sunlight streaming through the windows. Adam must have opened the shutters when he left earlier that morning but then she remembered he was away and not expected home until the weekend. She should have been used to waking up alone by now but she really missed snuggling up beside him and sometimes, when he was in the mood, they would end up making out, even on a weekday when there was really no time to dilly dally.

Some of Charlotte's friends considered her to be the consummate Stepford wife but she resented the implication, insisting she had a mind of her own and truly enjoyed cooking, cleaning and all of the other chores most women she knew thought of as grunt work. She had even gone to George Brown College and taken a culinary arts course so that she could experiment on her family with all the new varieties of foods available. Adam was so impressed with Charlotte's ability in the kitchen that he never hesitated to invite people over for dinner, even at a moment's notice.

She sighed as she threw off the pale green coverlet and looked around the room. This was her favourite place in the house, except for the kitchen, and she had spent countless hours making sure everything in it was perfect, right down to the pale apricot lampshades and the olive wing chairs flanking the fireplace. They had moved onto Highland Avenue right after Tyler was born and she still couldn't believe she actually lived in such a beautiful house. After being brought up most of her life in a small semi-detached home just north of the Bloor viaduct, it had taken her a long time to get used to having five bedrooms, four bathrooms and a pool in the back yard.

She was still day dreaming about the day they moved in when she felt something heavy land on her feet. It only took her a second to realize it was Zoe looking for her breakfast. Charlotte, like her mother, had always loved cats and, on their first wedding anniversary, Adam presented her with an adorable Persian kitten they named Sheba. When Sheba died, at the age of eighteen, Charlotte was heartbroken but three months later Adam smuggled Zoe into the house and there was no turning back. Charlotte crawled to the bottom of the bed, ruffled the soft tortoiseshell hair on Zoe's head then looked into her eyes and whispered, "What are we going to do today?"

Later, after Charlotte had padded downstairs to the kitchen and filled Zoe's bowl, she stood looking out of the window and pondered the question again. What was she going to do all day? She worked at the reference library two days a week and was usually thankful for all of the time she was free to do whatever she liked but, on this particular day, she was feeling somewhat lost. Adam was in Montreal on business; Tyler was taking a break from university backpacking through Europe with two friends while Alexa, their youngest, was visiting with Charlotte's mother at her home in Cabbagetown. Alexa claimed she liked to visit Nana because they always went to neat places to eat and she liked helping her in the garden. Charlotte suspected what Alexa really liked was being just a hop, skip and a jump away from all the trendy shops and sometimes she would come home with a new outfit, compliments of Nana.

Charlotte poured water into her new Keurig coffee maker, added a k-cup of dark roast coffee, shook some cornflakes into a bowl and covered them with a small amount of milk. She was a creature of habit and ate the same breakfast nearly every single morning. Even on weekends, when she prepared a full meal for her family, consisting of eggs, bacon, sausage, home fries and toast, she only indulged on special occasions such as an anniversary or a birthday. While she ate, she stared out of the sliding glass doors leading to the back garden and wondered what Adam was doing. She was never really content when he was out of town and lately it seemed to be happening more often. It wasn't that she didn't trust him; in fact, she thought he was the most honest and sincere person she had ever known and couldn't imagine him ever doing anything to deceive her. This trip away seemed particularly prolonged but he was collaborating on the design of a new school being built in the Westmount area of Montreal and had to attend all kinds of meetings with city officials and the school board. When Adam was in town he often worked long hours but at least he was close by at his office on Bay Street. Sometimes they would have lunch together at one of the popular restaurants in the financial district or Charlotte would make an excuse to drop in for a short visit. It made her feel important when she walked into the offices of Carter and Hamilton, Architects. The staff always greeted her warmly and she was particularly fond of Adam's assistant, Diane, who had finally married the man of her dreams after dating him for eight years and now had a two year old son she doted on.

Charlotte slid open the glass doors and wandered outside with a second cup of coffee. She loved to walk in the garden early in the morning and it was already warm with very little breeze. It had been an exceptional summer and, so far, July temperatures had been well above normal. There were several trees bordering the wide flagstone pathway leading down to an expansive lawn and a kidney shaped pool and, against the back fence, a structure which looked like a very large doll house. Charlotte smiled when she thought about Alexa and how she used to spend hours playing in this house while Tyler preferred to spend most of his time in the pool. She missed them both so much and wished they were little again so that she could pamper them. She had always wanted to be a mother and willingly gave up pursuit of her career as a physiotherapist the first time she became pregnant.

She was watching a flock of birds, who had just settled on the branches of one of the trees, and was still daydreaming about the past when she thought she heard the telephone and hurried back to the kitchen but, before she got there, the ringing stopped. She checked for messages but there were none so, assuming she must have imagined it, she put her dishes in the sink and climbed back upstairs to take a bath.

Soaking in a hot tub was one of Charlotte's greatest pleasures and today was no exception. It was the one place where she could truly be alone and not be disturbed. Sometimes she would read for half an hour or even longer, occasionally adding more hot water, but at other times she would just lie back and relax every muscle in her body. Today she wasn't in the mood for reading and even relaxing seemed to be evading her so after ten minutes, she stepped out, dried herself on one of the ultra-thick towels and after applying body lotion, walked naked into the bedroom. Her reflection in the full length mirror on the closet door caught her eye and she paused to take a good look at herself. At forty-two and the mother of two children, her body was in excellent shape. She was five feet six, had always been slim and today she was no more than five pounds heavier than when she was a teenager. She wasn't really into exercise but she spent a lot of time on her feet and occasionally indulged in yoga classes but she was well aware she inherited most of her physical attributes from her mother. She stepped closer to the mirror and examined her face, scrubbed clean and without the benefit of make-up, apart from tiny crow's feet at the corners of her eyes she knew she could pass for thirty-five, if not younger. Again, she had her mother to thank who, at seventy-four, had hardly any wrinkles and only a smattering of grey among her shoulder length blond hair. Charlotte's hair was almost identical in colour, straight as a die and fell below her shoulders. She had worn it that way for years and only on rare occasions would she sweep it up on top of her head or attempt to turn it into a curly mop, usually without success. Just at that moment she heard the telephone again and this time there was no mistake. She ran around to the other side of the bed and picked up the phone from the night table, "Hello?" she said tentatively and slightly out of breath.

"Hi, honey, what are you up to on this lovely morning? I hope I didn't wake you."

It was Adam and she was smiling as she answered him, "Adam, how lovely to hear from you. Actually I've been up for a while."

"And where are you now?"

"Well, I just had a bath and you caught me naked in the bedroom."

"Too bad we don't have Skype. I miss you honey."

"I miss you too and I can't wait for you to get back on Friday."

There was a pause and then, "That's why I'm calling. There's been a bit of a snag with the permits and Sam's flying out tomorrow to help sort it out. We probably won't be through until about six on Friday and it will be too late to drive all the way home, so I'll be bringing Sam back with me on Saturday morning."

Charlotte tried to keep the disappointment out of her voice, "Oh, that's too bad. I was hoping we could still have dinner at Le Paradis on Friday but I guess it can't be helped."

"Sorry, hon, maybe we can go on Saturday night if you don't have other plans."

"No, I haven't made any but we'll wait until you get home to decide, you may be too tired after the long drive."

"Where's Alexa? Is she still at your mom's?"

"Yes, it's awfully quiet here all on my lonesome. I may go over there later to see what those two are up to."

"That sounds like a good idea. Look, sorry to cut you off, I just wanted to know how everything was. I guess I'd better go, I have a lot to get done today."

"Adam wait, did you call here earlier, I thought I heard the phone?"

"Yes, but I hung up after three rings in case you were still sleeping."

"Oh, I was in the garden and couldn't get back in the house fast enough. Anyway, I should let you go and get on with your work. Take care of yourself. I love you."

"Love you too, bye honey."

Charlotte replaced the receiver and searched through her closet for something to wear, all the while thinking about Adam and anticipating having to spend Friday night alone. Things must have gotten pretty complicated for Sam to fly to Montreal. Sam was the Carter half of Carter and Hamilton and someone she admired. He and Adam had become partners almost ten years earlier, two years after they had worked together on a project and something just clicked. Sam was twelve years older than Adam, had been married for thirty years and had two young grandchildren. To Charlotte, he was like a great teddy bear, over six feet and two hundred and fifty pounds with red hair and a remarkably boyish face. He was one of the kindest people she had ever met.

She selected a pair of navy capris, a white tee and her favourite canvas Keds and quickly got dressed then it was back to the bathroom to put on her make-up and run a comb through her hair. Even on a quick trip to the grocery store, Charlotte always made sure she was presentable, another trait she got from her mother who wouldn't be seen dead on the street without her lipstick. Meanwhile, Alexa, who had just turned fifteen, had absolutely no interest in putting, what she described as, goo all over her face and, like all of her friends, preferred the natural look.

Moments later, Charlotte was backing her brand new green Acura out of the driveway and onto Highland. She then turned south and continued to drive through the meandering streets of her Rosedale neighborhood, an affluent area of the city, with mostly large single family homes and an abundance of trees. She passed Branksome Hall, the exclusive all-girls school where they had decided to send Alexa and Charlotte couldn't help thinking how fortunate her children were to have a father who insisted they get the best education he could afford. She wasn't sure they really appreciated it but they were both good students and seemed to have some rather lofty ambitions. Tyler wanted to be an archeologist and spend most of his time digging for artifacts in Egypt, hoping to find a monumental discovery, while Alexa was leaning towards becoming a pediatrician. It all made Charlotte feel a little inadequate as she had quit high school at sixteen and took a job working as a bank teller for two years before enrolling in classes to study physiotherapy. Her mother had brought her up alone from the age of six, after her father died in a freak drowning accident while sailing on Lake Ontario with a friend. John Fleming was a loving husband but he had no head for finance and carried no life insurance. Despite having a steady job as a graphic artist, Nancy couldn't afford to send her daughter to college.

Charlotte was headed towards Cabbagetown, which laid claim to being an area with the largest number of preserved Victorian houses in North America. Her mother had bought a house there just after Charlotte married Adam and had made the last mortgage payment on her sixty-fifth birthday. Since then, she had continued to work full time until two years earlier but now she worked two days a week from home and with the income from investments, her pension, and part-time earnings, she was very comfortable and completely independent. She had never remarried, and although she had been involved in several relationships over the years, nobody could take the place of John.

As Charlotte turned the corner onto Salisbury, she could see both her mother and Alexa were already at work in the front garden. She could only see the tops of their heads, so she assumed they were planting flowers or pulling weeds and when she pulled into the driveway they both looked up with anticipation. Charlotte poked her head out of the car window and grinned, "Surprise, surprise!"

Alexa jumped to her feet while Nancy sat back on her heels and smiled, "Mom," Alexa called out, "we didn't expect to see you this morning."

Charlotte got out of the car and embraced Alexa, "Hi sweetie, I was feeling a bit lonesome so I thought I'd come and see what you were doing."

"Nana and I were dead-heading some of the flowers."

"I can see that," Charlotte remarked walking over to her mother and helping her up. "Hello, Mom," she said giving her a hug, "how are you? Is your ankle still bothering you?"

Nancy waved her hand in the air, "It's just fine, I think I must have twisted it the other day but it's better now. Anyway, what are you doing here so early?"

"I was telling Adam, I was feeling a bit lonesome. The house is awfully quiet when I'm there by myself."

"When's he coming home?"

"Not until Saturday now, Sam had to fly out to take care of some issue with the permits so he's being delayed."

"Oh, that's too bad but you'll have him back for most of the weekend. Why don't we go inside and I'll make some coffee?"

"That would be lovely. Come on sweetie," she said to Alexa as she put her arm around her and followed Nancy into the house.

Charlotte was greeted by the two most important residents when she set foot inside the door, Nancy's two cats. Both females, Gypsy was as black as night while Luna was as white as a fresh layer of snow. Charlotte bent down to stroke both of their heads as they vied for attention by rubbing against her legs. "Aren't they sweet, Mom?" Alexa asked. "Maybe we should get a companion for Zoe."

Charlotte deliberately chose to ignore Alexa's remark and continued on through the entry hall to the kitchen where Nancy was already filling the coffee percolator. "Sit down," Nancy said, "coffee won't be long and I got some wonderful molasses cookies at a shop in the Distillery district if anyone's hungry."

"I'm always hungry, Nana," Alexa responded.

Charlotte laughed as she looked at her daughter perched on the edge of her chair watching her grandmother pile some cookies onto a plate. She had always had a good appetite but was as slim as a reed and the envy of her best friend, Hildy, who gained a pound if she so much as looked at an ice cream cone. Even when puberty kicked in, other than developing two rather indistinct bumps on her chest, she maintained the same boyish figure. Alexa was grateful she was able to consume all of her favourite foods in great quantities and not gain an ounce but she secretly wished for a little more curves like her mother. Other than being exceptionally slim, she had the same shade of blond hair as Charlotte and although not quite as attractive, her eyes were the most startling shade of blue and were her best feature. Today she was wearing a pair of shocking pink shorts and a teal blue tee which accentuated the tan she had developed from spending many hours in the sun.

Nancy placed the cookies on the table and Alexa immediately grabbed one and bit into it, "Mmmmm Nana," she said licking her lips, "this is really good." Charlotte shook her head, "You won't be able to eat any lunch if you fill up on those now."

Nancy chuckled, "I don't think that's going to be a problem. I think your daughter has a hollow leg."

"Are we going out for lunch today?" Alexa asked.

Nancy nodded, "Yes, if you like, dear. We could go to one of the places down at Harbourfront and then take a look at some of the shops."

"Oh, that would be great, Nana, I love it down there. Are you going to come with us, Mom?"

Charlotte thought for a moment and then answered, "You know, I think that would be really nice, I'd love to come with you. You don't mind me tagging along do you, Mom?"

"Of course not, I love spending time with the two of you but before we go we have to finish up in the garden. You can come and help if you like. I can give you some old cotton shorts to put on so you don't get those pants dirty."

After an hour of dead-heading, pulling weeds and planting three tomato plants it was time to get cleaned up and head down to the lake. They decided to take Charlotte's car and then she would drop Nancy back later and take Alexa home with her if she hadn't already decided she wanted to stay another night. On the drive Charlotte was about to ask Alexa what her plans were but before she got the chance Nancy said, "I hope you don't mind, dear, but I'd like Alexa to stay over for another day. She said she would help me with the back garden too."

Charlotte glanced at Alexa, who was lounging in the back seat, "My, oh my, you're very industrious. What happened to Hildy? Aren't you going to spend some time with her this week?'

"No, she's gone up to the cottage with her family and won't be back until next Tuesday. Why can't we get a cottage, Mom? It's so much fun up where Hildy is, they swim and take the boat out and they have cookouts too. I love it, especially at night when everyone gathers around the campfire. Sometimes her Dad tells ghost stories and it gets really creepy."

Charlotte glanced across at her mother and rolled her eyes, "You know why, Alexa. Your father often has to work on a Saturday and it would be too far to travel for just one day. I don't think you're really hard done by. Last summer Nana took you to Florida for two weeks and the summer before that we were in Italy."

Alexa slumped down in her seat, "I know, but this time I haven't been anywhere."

Nancy shook her head, "I think you should be grateful you get so much time off. Why don't you call some of your other friends? What about the little Chinese girl you used to chum around with?"

"Sunny? She's Korean, not Chinese. Anyway, she went back home with her mother to visit her grandparents."

There was silence for a few moments and then Nancy looked back over her shoulder at Alexa, "I have a suggestion but your mother has to agree to it."

Alexa sat up and leaned forward eagerly, "What is it, Nana? Are we going somewhere?"

"Well, I'm going to Victoria in a week or two to visit Peggy and if you like, you can come with me."

"Oh, Mom can I go?" Alexa asked shaking her hands with excitement. "Please say yes, I like Aunt Peggy and Nana told me she lives right on the beach. Please, Mom, please say yes."

"How long will you be gone?" Charlotte asked without taking her eyes off the road.

"Two weeks for sure, maybe a little longer. I'll have to make sure it's okay with Peggy first but I'm positive it will be."

"I think I need to discuss it with Adam first."

"Why?" Alexa cried out. "Dad won't mind."

Nancy looked at Charlotte and raised her eyebrows. "I think Alexa's right, Adam will probably be pleased she's away enjoying herself rather than moping around the house."

Charlotte hesitated then nodded, "Okay, you can go, but I don't want you paying for her air fare, Mom, we'll take care of that."

Nancy didn't get a chance to respond because Alexa was too noisy whooping and cheering.

Lunch at Pier Four Storehouse and exploring all the unique Harbourfront shops made for an enjoyable afternoon and by the time Charlotte dropped Nancy and Alexa back in Cabbagetown, she was feeling rather mellow. It was only when she got back to the house that she felt the loneliness start to crowd in again. Thankfully, the very next day she was due to work at the library and then only one more day to get through before Adam would be home. Later she made herself a light supper then poured a glass of Chardonnay and stepped out into the garden. It was still very warm so she walked over to the small bench, under the shadow of one of the maple trees, and sat down. She suddenly felt really sad because she knew she was losing her children. Tyler had always been a bit of a free spirit and she had almost become accustomed to his thirst for travel. Although, still only nineteen, he had spent the last four summers away from home, whether camping in Algonquin, exploring Vancouver Island or backpacking in Europe. Alexa, had been more of a homebody but recently she seemed restless and Charlotte was beginning to feel the effect. She had no concerns about her daughter spending time with Nancy, she knew her mother always took great care of her and she was very fond of Peggy. Nancy and Peggy had been best friends for over forty years and when Peggy married her second husband and moved to Victoria, Nancy really missed her. They only saw each other briefly when Peggy would come back to visit her children but after her husband died, they really connected again, mostly by e-mail or telephone, and then Nancy flew out to Victoria and fell in love with the place.

Thinking about her mother's best friend caused Charlotte to think about her own closest friend, Jodi. She had known her since high school and while Charlotte had spent twenty one years in a happy marriage, Jodi had divorced her husband after three years and never remarried. She had been involved in a number of relationships, had a successful career in real estate and seemed happy enough but Charlotte couldn't help wondering if she really missed having children. On the two or three occasions they had talked about it, Jodi insisted she wasn't cut out to be a mother and was quite content to spoil Alexa and Tyler, or her own sister's three youngsters. Two weeks earlier she had left Toronto to visit her parents in Halifax but she was due back the next day. Charlotte decided to call her on Thursday night to see if she would like to go out to dinner on Friday. Hopefully she would agree and that would take care of another lonely evening, the one she was supposed to spend with Adam.

Chapter Two

Thursday seemed to pass in slow motion. Even the hours at the library appeared to crawl by and Charlotte was grateful when it was time to leave. That evening Nancy brought Alexa back home, stayed for a cup of coffee and then left to go shopping with her next door neighbour. For most of the evening, Alexa either had her cell phone to her ear or was texting while Charlotte sat in the family room with Zoe on her lap and read the James Patterson novel she had been trying to finish for almost a month. She was feeling a little better after calling Jodi and confirming their dinner date the following day but there was something about the conversation that bothered her. It had all seemed a little rushed and she got the feeling Jodi was somewhat subdued and not her usual bubbly self. When Charlotte asked if anything was wrong Jodi claimed she had to unpack and get some laundry done and suggested they catch up at dinner, but Charlotte wasn't really buying it.

Jodi lived in a townhouse on Mutual Street so they agreed to meet at Byzantiums in the neighbouring gay village area. At six o'clock, Charlotte was already seated at a table near the window and sipping on a glass of Zinfandel when she saw Jodi crossing the road towards her. In appearance, she was the complete opposite of Charlotte except for her height.

Voluptuous, with a dark complexion, brown curly hair and brown eyes she was rather flamboyant and had a unique sense of style. This evening, she was wearing a multi-coloured maxi-dress with green stiletto sandals and Charlotte suddenly became very aware of her own simple white shift, relieved only by a strand of amber beads and two-inch white pumps. She had to admit to herself, she felt rather plain.

The two women embraced and Jodi remarked, "You've got some sun, it looks good on you."

Charlotte smiled, "Thanks, I was helping Mom with some gardening during the week and we spent some time at Harbourfront. How about you, tell me all about your visit home."

Jodi was about to reply when the waiter interrupted them. She ordered a glass of Merlot then picked up the menu. "Did you pick something out yet?" she asked.

Charlotte looked puzzled, "We've got lots of time. Let's just relax for a while before we eat. I want to hear about your trip. How are your parents?"

Jodi put down the menu and took a sip of wine, "They're both fine and really happy they moved back east. Dad always wanted to go back to his home town when he retired and now he's taken up fishing while Mom's involved with some local choir group. She always fancied she could sing so now's her chance to prove it."

"What about Greg? Is he still travelling a lot?"

Jodi hesitated then lowered her eyes, "Yes, he just got back from New York. He was at a conference."

Charlotte reached across the table and grasped Jodi's hand, "You seem upset, is something the matter with your brother?"

Jodi shook her head, "Let's eat first and then we can talk about Greg."

Charlotte withdrew her hand and picked up the menu, "All right, we can do that," she said reluctantly. "Is there anything that appeals to you?"

Both women opted for shrimp cocktails then veal scaloppini with mushrooms and Marsala cream sauce. There was little conversation while they ate and Charlotte could feel the tension. She rushed through her meal and could hardly wait for Jodi to finish eating so, when she finally set her knife and fork in the middle of her plate, Charlotte said, "Why don't we have another glass of wine?"

Jodi nodded and beckoned to the waiter then excused herself to visit the ladies room. By the time she came back, the dishes had been cleared, the wine had been served and Charlotte was on the edge of her seat. Jodi had only just sat down when Charlotte leaned across the table and asked in almost a whisper, "So what's going on, Jodi, the suspense is killing me?"

Jodi gave a deep sigh, "You may not like what I'm going to tell you."

Charlotte frowned, "What do you mean. I thought this was about Greg, what does it have to do with me?"

Jodi paused as she picked up her wine, "I'm afraid this has a lot to do with you and I guess there's only one way to tell you and that's straight out. Greg saw Adam with a woman."

Charlotte shrugged, "So, what's the big deal. Maybe he was with a client. I told you on the phone he was in Montreal working on a project. It could have been someone from the school board. Anyway, I thought you said Greg was in New York."

"I did, and that's where he saw Adam."

Charlotte shook her head, "That's impossible, he hasn't been to New York for over a year. Greg must have seen someone who looked like Adam."

"He swears it was Adam even though he didn't get a chance to speak to him."

Charlotte felt her blood pressure start to rise, "Well, he has to be mistaken. I'm telling you, it couldn't have been Adam. Where did Greg actually see this person by the way?"

"He was at the St. Regis Hotel. Greg was having a bite to eat with a couple of people he met at the conference. They were in the King Cole Bar and when he glanced up he saw Adam leaving with a woman. He said there was no doubt it was Adam but he was a little surprised at the way he was dressed. Greg didn't think he was the jeans and black leather type."

Charlotte waved both hands for Jodi to stop, "This is ridiculous, Adam never wears leather, in fact he doesn't own anything in leather so it couldn't have been him."

"So I guess you don't want to hear about the woman he was with?"

"Well of course," Charlotte shot back sarcastically, "I suppose you're going to tell me she was some young bimbo in a mini skirt with her boobs hanging out?"

"On the contrary, Greg said she was a very attractive, elegant woman with black hair, very slim and wearing a black cocktail dress."

"I see, and pray tell me, why didn't Greg talk to Adam?"

"Apparently he never got the chance. By the time he got over the shock of seeing him and raced to the door of the bar, they were nowhere to be seen. He even went out to the lobby and checked outside the main door of the hotel in case they were already on the street."

"Well, it's hard to believe Adam's got a double but I guess everybody has one somewhere. I think you should tell Greg that Adam was in Montreal and he obviously made a mistake."

Jodi sighed, "Okay, if you insist but . . . ."

Charlotte cut in, "I do insist and now let's talk about something else."

By the time Charlotte left the restaurant to drive home, she was still feeling tense. She had attempted to make small talk, telling Jodi about Alexa's upcoming trip with her mother and Tyler's latest adventure but it felt like there was a cloud hanging over her head and after she left Jodi on the corner of Church Street, she was anxious to get home. All sorts of scenarios danced through her head as she drove north towards Rosedale, none of which made any sense. It couldn't possibly have been Adam and she made an effort to try and put it out of her mind.

Nancy had come over to keep Alexa company and was surprised to see Charlotte arrive home a little before eight o'clock. She was in the hallway when Charlotte came through the front door, "I didn't expect to see you so early. I thought you might go somewhere else after dinner."

"Where would we go, Mom?" Charlotte asked putting her purse on the hall table and kicking off her shoes.

"I don't know; a movie or maybe a walk through Yorkville. It's such a lovely evening; a walk would be really pleasant."

Charlotte walked past Nancy into the kitchen, "I'm going to make some coffee, would you like some?"

Nancy stood at the doorway and frowned, "What's happened, something's upset you."

Charlotte shook her head, "Nothing's happened, Mom. Where's Alexa?"

Nancy walked over and placed her hand on Charlotte's shoulder, "She's in her room listening to some music. Now tell me what happened, I know something's wrong."

Charlotte stopped what she was doing and leaned back against the counter, "Jodi claims Greg saw Adam in New York with a woman."

Nancy paused and then started to laugh, "That's funny, Adam with another woman. You don't really believe it do you?"

Charlotte looked annoyed, "I don't think it's funny but no, I don't believe it. Greg made a mistake; it was just someone who looked like Adam."

"Did he talk to him, by any chance?"

"No, look Mom, sit down and I'll tell you exactly what Jodi told me."

A few minutes later Nancy got up from the table, "I hope you're not going to let this bother you. On the one hand, you say you don't believe it was Adam but, on the other, you are obviously concerned. I think you should just forget about it and whatever you do, don't mention it to Adam. There's no sense in stirring up trouble."

Charlotte nodded, "I know you're right, Mom. Don't worry about me, I'll be just fine. Why don't you pop upstairs and say goodnight to Alexa before you leave?"

"I will, dear, and you try and relax. Watch a little television, go to bed early and before you know it Adam will be back."

"Okay, Mom, thanks a lot," Charlotte said as Nancy ran up the stairs to Alexa's room.

Charlotte poured herself a glass of wine then went into the family room. Five minutes later she heard Nancy call out goodnight and then heard the front door close. She felt so much better after confiding in her mother. Nancy always seemed to be able to put things in perspective. She settled down on the sofa and was searching for the remote when Alexa came bounding into the room, "Hi, Mom, watchya gonna watch?" she asked.

"I have no idea," Charlotte replied. "Why don't you have a look and see what's on?"

"I already know Jane Eyre's on the movie network, can we watch it?"

"I didn't know you were a big fan of the classics."

Alexa giggled and then, in a creepy voice, said, "I love all the dark, scary movies like Jack the Ripper, Dorian Gray and all that stuff."

Charlotte laughed, "So now I'm just finding out I have a ghoulish daughter. Today is full of surprises."

Alexa didn't catch on to her mother's remark. She just threw back her head and howled like a wolf and when Charlotte looked at her in alarm she just grinned and whispered, "Jekyll and Hyde."

Chapter Three

Charlotte awoke on Saturday morning after a restless night's sleep. Both she and Alexa had gone to bed right after the movie ended but it took her a long time before she actually drifted off and, an hour later, she was wide awake. Adam had called earlier just as she was slipping into her nightgown but their conversation was brief as he was with Sam and having a nightcap before heading off to bed himself. She couldn't help thinking about him and wondering if he was actually capable of cheating on her with another woman. She had no reason to believe he had ever been unfaithful but he was forty-four years old and maybe there was such a thing as a mid-life crisis. There was no doubt women found him attractive; he was tall, still in good shape, with only a touch of grey in his full head of brown hair and he was even more handsome than the day she met him. He could also be very charming, rarely talked about himself and always showed an interest in other people.

Charlotte thought back to the first time she ever laid eyes on him. It was at a party following an exhibition of Henry Moore sculptures at the Art Gallery. They weren't even formally introduced; she literally bumped into him as she was stepping back to get a better view of a reclining woman cast in bronze and, when she turned around to apologize, something clicked. Two weeks later, they were almost inseparable and, during that time, Charlotte discovered he had been an only child but, unlike her, he had never known his father. He'd been brought up in Ottawa and at the age of nineteen, when he left home, his mother married a dairy farmer and moved to Napanee. Mary McLeod was a not a woman many people could relate to. She was secretive, judgemental and had a quick temper. Charlotte only tolerated her for Adam's sake and did her best to avoid her. The family only saw her on rare occasions and, during those times, Charlotte got to know Ray McLeod and really enjoyed his company. It was a complete mystery to her why this mild mannered man with a rather wry sense of humour ever married Mary in the first place. Ray had two children of his own but they were grown and, they too, avoided Mary as much as possible. It made Charlotte even more grateful for her close bond with Nancy and the knowledge that, although lonely at times, she had enjoyed a happy childhood.

Adam wasn't expected home until after lunch. He had mentioned they would be taking their time driving back and would probably stop for a late breakfast on the way. This gave Charlotte time to tidy up, do a little shopping and bake Adam's favourite dessert, chocolate pecan pie. By nine o'clock, Zoe had already appeared in the kitchen peering into her bowl and emitting a few pitiful cries before it was refilled while Alexa was nowhere to be seen. That suited Charlotte as she wasn't really up to entertaining Alexa and hoped she would stay in her room for at least another hour. It was eleven before she eventually arrived downstairs aroused by the aroma of something delicious baking in the oven, but she had to settle for cornflakes and sweet tea before Charlotte hustled her out of the door to accompany her to the Summerhill market. After shopping, they decided to have lunch at Caffe Doria where they both ordered Panini sandwiches stuffed with mozzarella, tomatoes, prosciutto, and roasted red peppers.

"I don't know how you can eat that, you just had breakfast two hours ago," Charlotte remarked.

Alexa rolled her eyes, "It was only cornflakes, Mom."

"I know, sweetie, but you can't expect me to cook eggs and bacon when you get up so late."

"If Dad was here you would have cooked it for him."

Charlotte sighed, "Not if he came downstairs when it was almost lunchtime. By the way, he should be arriving home by noon; will you be there or are you planning on going anywhere this afternoon?"

"No, I won't be home and I won't be having supper either. I was talking to Joanie earlier and she invited me to a pool party. Her Dad's having a barbecue later and all the kids will be staying for that."

"Oh, it sounds like a lot of fun. At least you'll only be down the block. Remember, if it's dark when you decide to leave, I want you to call Dad and he'll come and walk you back. I don't want you walking by yourself."

"I know, Mom, you always tell me that."

Charlotte reached over and grasped Alexa's hand, "Yes, I know I'm a nag but you're my precious girl and I wouldn't want anything to happen to you."

Alexa slowly withdrew her hand and looked around her to see if anyone was watching, "Oh, Mom, you're such a mother hen."

Charlotte chuckled, "Where did you pick up that expression? I love you and I don't care who knows it."

Alexa leaned across the table and whispered, "I love you too but don't tell anyone."

Charlotte just shook her head and grinned, "You are priceless, young lady."

Back at the house, Alexa changed into her two-piece blue swim suit, slipped on a pair of shorts, cuddled Zoe and hugged Charlotte, then sailed out of the front door singing happily to herself. Charlotte watched her until she was out of sight and smiled. She really liked Joanie's parents, Rolf and Annette Erikson. They had been neighbours for several years and had two children, both boys, one fourteen and one eighteen. Charlotte suspected Alexa had more than a neighbourly interest in eighteen-year-old, Joshua.

At two o'clock, she was already dressed in a pair of white capris and a canary yellow halter top anxiously waiting near the living room window. Her mind started to wander again as she gazed out onto the street. What was she doing hovering, half hidden behind the drapes; she had never done that before? She felt like she was spying as though she expected Adam to drive up with some woman sitting beside him. She really needed to get a grip on herself unless she blurted something out and accused him of the unimaginable.

By three o'clock she was pacing the living room when suddenly she heard a car pull into the driveway and quickly ran down the hall and threw open the front door. It was Adam looking windblown in his new Tesla Roadster convertible. He had always loved cars and he'd come a long way from the tiny red Volkswagen Beetle he'd owned when she first met him. He looked up at her and grinned as he came to a stop and stepped out onto the driveway, "Hi, honey, you look nice," he called out as he retrieved his suitcase and laptop from the trunk, "sorry I'm a bit late."

Charlotte smiled as she waited for him to climb the steps, "What kept you?" she asked as she leaned forward to kiss him on the cheek.

Adam dropped his bags and took her into his arms, "Is that all I get, a kiss on the cheek?"

"No, of course not," Charlotte answered taking his face in her hands and kissing him fully on the lips.

"That's better. I've been waiting for that for days."

Charlotte pushed him away playfully and turned her back on him, "Well if you come inside, then maybe you'll get some more."

Adam picked up his bags and followed her inside then dropped them at the foot of the stairs. "Where's Alexa?"

Charlotte took his hand and pulled him into the living room, "She's at the Eriksons' at a pool party and she won't be home until this evening."

Adam frowned, "I hope she isn't walking home after dark."

"No, I told her she had to call and you'd go over there and walk her back."

"I see, so how would you like to spend the afternoon, Mrs. Hamilton?"

Charlotte pulled him down onto the sofa, "How about snuggling up right here? I've really missed you."

Adam chuckled, "Well that would be nice, but it's too great a day to spend indoors. Why don't we have our own pool party? I can mix up some margaritas and we can relax, have a swim and, then later, order in a pizza."

"Oh, so you don't want to go out to dinner?"

"Not really, honey. I'm a bit tired and, in any case, shouldn't we be here for when Alexa calls?"

Charlotte sighed, "Yes, I guess you're right. By the way, you still haven't told me why you got home so late."

"Oh, right. Well, I had to drop Sam off and, when we got there, Eleanor was out front working in the garden and insisted I come in for a drink."

"Didn't you tell her I was expecting you?"

"No, I didn't, I thought I'd only be there about a half hour but we got to talking and, before I knew it, an hour had gone by."

"And how is Eleanor these days?"

"She seems fine and she invited us to dinner next week so that we can meet their new grandson. Vanessa's flying in from Calgary with the two children and staying for a week."

"Oh, I would love to see the new baby and speaking of babies, you know our baby girl will be sixteen next month. This is a special birthday so I want to have a party and invite a lot of people, not just family and a couple of friends."

"I think that would be great, honey. Have you given any thought as to what we should get her as a gift?"

"Well, she was mooning over a Tissot watch the other day when we were in Birks. It's expensive but it's something she'll have for a long time and, at the same time, it's practical."

"You do whatever you think best." Adam remarked as he got up from the sofa. "I'm going upstairs to unpack and put on some shorts and then I'm going to make those margaritas."

Charlotte looked up at him as he walked away, "Aren't you going to tell me about your trip?"

"Later," Adam called out as he kept on walking.

They spent most of the afternoon sunbathing poolside sipping on ice cold margaritas and munching on nachos which Charlotte had liberally covered in home-made guacamole. They talked some more about Sam and his family, then Adam filled her in on the issues with the school board while in Montreal but she was more interested on what he was doing when he wasn't working on the project. It got to the point where Adam looked at her and frowned, "I feel like I'm getting the third degree here."

Charlotte was quick to shake her head, "No, no, I was feeling a bit lonely while you were gone this time and I kept wondering what you were up to, that's all."

"Well, I've told you. It's always the same when I'm working on a project. When the day is over, which is usually pretty late, I eat supper, go over my notes, watch a little TV and go to bed. Now, if you've finished grilling me, I'm going for a swim."

Charlotte reached across to grasp Adam's arm as he jumped up but he was too quick for her and seconds later he was diving into the pool. She was shocked at his reaction but angry with herself for causing it. Why had she interrogated him? Were the seeds of doubt implanted in her mind? Was he capable of cheating on her?

Adam swam several lengths of the pool then walked up the steps at the shallow end and came back to where Charlotte was sitting. He picked up his towel and wrapped it around his torso then looked at Charlotte and said, "I think I'll go indoors for a while, the Blue Jays are playing the Red Sox this afternoon."

Charlotte stared up at him, knowing he was annoyed, "Okay," she said quietly, "you go ahead. I'm going to stay out here a bit longer."

Once alone with her thoughts, she began to wonder why Adam had been so defensive? Did he have something to hide? After a while, she knew what she had to do. She had to put all of the negative thoughts out of her mind and trust him just the way she had in the past. She couldn't bear it when he was annoyed with her and she was determined to make things right.

Chapter Four

Charlotte decided to remain in the garden hoping by dinnertime Adam would be in a better mood. He rarely showed his temper but when he did, it was usually with good reason. A half hour later, beginning to feel the effect of the humidity, she jumped into the pool and managed to swim five lengths before rolling onto her back and gazing up at the clouds which were beginning to gather overhead. It only took her a minute to realize being in a pool if there was a storm wasn't a very good idea and she quickly climbed out, retrieved her towel and ran into the house. Adam was lounging on the sofa in the family room with a beer in one hand watching the baseball game. "I think there's going to be a storm." Charlotte remarked as she came through the door. "I'm worried about Alexa, she shouldn't be in the water if there's lightning"

Adam looked up, "Are you sure? There was hardly a cloud in the sky when I came indoors."

"Well, there is now. Why don't you check the weather station and see what the forecast is?"

Adam sighed as he picked up the remote and switched to CP24. Just as Charlotte had expected, it showed a storm was expected early in the evening. Adam quickly switched back to the baseball game, "I guess you're right," he said nonchalantly. "I'll go after this inning is over."

Charlotte bit her tongue and went upstairs to take a shower and change. She hoped, by the time she came back downstairs, Adam would be gone.

At just before six it was raining heavily, lightning could be seen in the distance and the rumbling of thunder could be heard. Adam had left almost an hour before and Charlotte was pacing the living room again. Fifteen minutes later he came through the front door, soaked to the skin, without Alexa. When he saw the questioning look on Charlotte's face, he held up one hand with palm facing forward, "Don't worry," he said, "all the kids are in the house."

"So I gather she won't be home for dinner?"

"No, I said she could stay. There was quite a crowd there and I didn't think it was fair to make her come home."

"I see, I guess that's okay as long as you go back and get her later. I bet she was pleased to see you, you were gone quite a while."

"Actually we only spoke for a few minutes. I watched the end of the game with Rolf."

"Well, you'd better get dried off. You're dripping all over the floor. While you're doing that I'll get on the phone and order a pizza. Do you want your usual?"

"Yes, that's fine. Just make sure they don't forget the anchovies this time."

The rest of the evening seemed just like any other Saturday. They usually stayed home and watched a DVD or occasionally went to the movies. Charlotte had always loved sitting in a dark theatre looking at the giant screen. There was something about the atmosphere that was so much more appealing than watching a movie at home. One of her favourite things growing up was her weekly trip to the movies with Nancy and, every now and again, they would still get together if there was something showing that piqued their interest.

At ten o'clock, Charlotte began to get anxious because it was still raining heavily and Alexa hadn't phoned. A few minutes later, just as she was about to voice her concern, Adam's cell phone rang and she overheard him tell Alexa he was on his way. "I think I'll come with you, "she said.

"That's not necessary, honey," Adam replied. "No sense in both of us getting wet."

"But I'd like to come. We can take the big umbrella."

"Really Charlotte, you're acting a bit odd today. I can go by myself; I don't need my hand held."

Charlotte immediately felt her blood pressure start to rise, "Just go," she said abruptly.

After Adam left, she tried watching the latest news report on CNN but she couldn't concentrate. Suddenly she realized she hadn't seen Zoe for hours and wondered if she'd been left outside. She started wandering through the house calling her name even checking in the cupboards, where Zoe would hide whenever there was a storm, but to no avail. In a panic, she ran out into the garden, ignoring the fact that she was immediately soaked through, and started calling Zoe's name again. She began searching frantically under bushes and the patio furniture and as she got close to the barbecue, which was covered by a large tarp, she heard a pitiful cry. Bending down and peering under the tarp, she finally spotted Zoe looking wet and bedraggled and shaking with fright. She couldn't coax her out and finally had to grasp her front legs and pull her out. Gathering her in her arms, she ran back into the house just as Adam and Alexa walked through the front door. Alexa screamed when she saw her mother cradling Zoe, "Oh, heavens, what happened, Mom?"

"She got left outside in the storm, poor baby. She's shaking like a leaf."

Alexa came forward and reached out, "I'll take her," she said. "You go and get dry, Mom."

Charlotte handed Zoe over and walked right past Adam and up the stairs. Adam didn't seem to notice. He turned to Alexa, and stroked Zoe's head, "I'll get you a towel to wipe her off. She's had a bit of a scare but she'll be okay. She just needs to get warmed up and if you give her few treats, she'll be as good as new."

Alexa smiled, "She's already purring, Dad."

"I wish everyone around here was as easy to please."

Alexa glanced at her father and frowned, "Is everything okay, Dad?"

Adam smiled and put his arm around her, "Everything's just fine."

Charlotte didn't see any point in changing her clothes again, so she slipped on her nightgown and a robe and then padded back down to the living room. Alexa had already gone up to her room and taken Zoe with her and Adam was watching a wrestling match on television. "Would you like something to drink?" she asked.

Adam hadn't heard her come in and looked up in surprise, "Oh, hi," he said then held up a bottle of Heineken, "no thanks, I still have half a beer."

Charlotte hesitated, "Well in that case I think I'll go up to bed. Will you be long?"

Adam kept his eyes on the screen, "What? Oh, I don't know, this is a good match. You go ahead and if you're asleep I'll try not to disturb you."

Any other time Charlotte would have come up behind him, linked her arms around his neck and whispered, "You can disturb me any time you like," but somehow, tonight, she didn't think he would react the way she wanted him to.

Chapter Five

Over the next two weeks, life appeared to settle back into its normal routine and then Alexa was off to Victoria with Nancy and Adam announced he had to return to Montreal for more meetings on the Westmount project. Charlotte suddenly realized she would be alone again for at least four days while Adam was away. "Do you really have to go?" she asked, the night before he was due to leave.

Adam frowned at her, "Of course I have to go. This is my job. It's not like I've never been out of town before. What's wrong with you lately, Charlotte?"

Charlotte shrugged, "I don't know. I guess I just feel a bit restless. Tyler's not here and now Alexa's away for the next two weeks, maybe even longer, I feel like I've got a lot of time on my hands."

Adam suddenly softened and put his arms around her, "Look, I know you miss the kids but one day they'll be gone for good. You need to find a hobby or do some volunteer work. Helping out at the library for just two days a week isn't enough"

Charlotte rested her head on his shoulder, "Yes, I know you're right. I do have Alexa's birthday party to plan but that won't take me too long and then what will I do?"

"Well, you like tennis. You could join the Moore Park Tennis Club. You also love animals, so why not volunteer at the Wildlife Centre?"

Charlotte nodded, "I'll think about it."

Adam released his hold on her, "Promise? I don't want you moping around the house."

Charlotte nodded again, "I promise," she whispered.

The very next morning, just after Adam had driven off, the mailman arrived with a letter from Tyler. Charlotte was puzzled because she had never known Tyler to write a letter. His usual form of communication was texting or e-mail. As she slit open the envelope, she noticed it was postmarked from somewhere in Greece. There was only a single sheet of paper with Tyler's distinct spider style writing covering the entire page. He had arrived in Athens one week earlier, from Rome, and had abandoned the group of friends he had been travelling with. Charlotte was alarmed when she assumed he was now alone but as she continued to read, she became even more concerned. He had met a girl in Florence and claimed she was the most amazing girl he had ever met and they had paired up for the rest of the trip. Her name was Shelby and she came from London. She had been with her sister and two other friends but soon after they met they decided to break away by themselves. So far so good, Charlotte thought, it's probably just a summer romance and when it was time to come home, they would probably never see each other again. She wasn't prepared for what was to come. Tyler was planning to end his trip in London and would be staying until the beginning of September instead of returning to Toronto in mid-August. The rest of the letter was all about Rome and Athens and how excited they were about going to Barcelona to see the architecture.

Charlotte sat with the letter in her lap for quite a while. She knew now, why her son had written rather than phoning. This way, she couldn't argue with him. Even if she tried calling him on his cell phone, she knew he would know it was her and probably wouldn't answer. She thought about calling Adam to see what he had to say about Tyler extending his trip but Adam would most likely tell her not to fuss and let Tyler enjoy himself.

When it came right down to it, Tyler wasn't the problem. She knew she had to accept the fact her children were teenagers and beginning to develop their own ideas about how to live their lives. She had no right to interfere unless she thought they were in danger or going down the wrong path. It was now time for her to concentrate on her own life.

Later that evening, she got a call from Nancy and after her mother put Alexa on the phone and she listened to her raving about Aunt Peggy's place and how pretty Victoria was, she wished she had made arrangements to go with them. She had no idea if Peggy would have been able to accommodate her but they could have worked something out, Anything would have been better than being alone with nothing to really keep her occupied.

Two days later, after spending one full day at the library and the other tending to chores around the house, Charlotte got a call from Jodi. It was just after six o'clock when she picked up the phone and heard Jodi's voice, "Charlotte, it's Jodi," she said rather abruptly. "Are you going to be home this evening?"

Charlotte hesitated and then replied, "Hi, Jodi. Um . . . . yes, I'll be here. Why, did you want to come over?"

"Actually I would like to see you. Have you eaten yet?"

"I just had a salad and some yogurt but if you haven't eaten I'd be happy to make you something."

"No, I had a big lunch and I'm not hungry. I'll bring a bottle of wine though."

"That's not necessary. I have a bottle of Chardonnay chilling in the fridge, if that's okay?"

"I'll be there in about twenty minutes," Jodi responded and before Charlotte could say another word Jodi rang off.

Charlotte stood staring at the receiver in her hand thinking Jodi had sounded rather strange and she wondered why she was so anxious to see her. They rarely visited each other's homes, preferring to go to a movie and dinner together or shopping. Slowly she put the receiver down and checked to see what she had to nibble on with the wine. She found a bag of Tostitos, poured some into a dish, and then opened a can of Fancy Feast for Zoe and refilled her water bowl. After that she quickly ran upstairs, changed her cotton shirt for a sleeveless powder blue top, ran a comb through her hair and touched up her make-up. She was well aware Jodi would probably show up looking like a fashion plate and while she felt she could never compete with her, she always tried to look presentable whenever they were together.

At six-thirty, Charlotte heard Jodie's car pull into the driveway. She didn't wait for her to ring the bell and was already waiting for her at the front door when she came up the front steps. Despite the heat of the day, she was dressed in a pink and white floral dress with a white jacket and looked as cool as a cucumber. "Hi, there," Charlotte said as she embraced her. "You look nice. Did you just come from an appointment?"

Jodi nodded as she followed her into the house, "Yes, I was showing a client a condo at Harbour Square."

"Wow, I guess it's pretty expensive there," Charlotte remarked as they walked into the kitchen.

"Would you believe over a million dollars? But, it's on two levels with terraces on both levels. I'd love to live there one day but I don't think I'll ever be able to afford it."

Charlotte motioned for Jodi to sit at the table while she poured the wine, "You don't mind if we stay in the kitchen do you? It seems a lot cooler in here even though the air conditioner is on."

Jodi looked around her, "Are you kidding? This is my favourite room in the house."

Charlotte brought the wine and the Tostitos to the table and sat down opposite Jodi, "I was really surprised when you called and said you wanted to come right over."

Jodi picked up her glass and took a sip before answering, "I needed to talk to you, Charlotte."

"It sounds serious. Is something wrong? Are you sick? Tell me."

Jodi put her glass down and reached across the table to grasp Charlotte's hand. "This isn't easy," she said.

Charlotte pulled her hand away and laid it against her chest, "You're scaring me. This is bad news isn't it?"

Jodi nodded very slowly, "You remember what I told you about Greg seeing Adam in New York? Well, I saw Adam last night at the theatre with a woman."

Charlotte stared at her in disbelief and then stood up with her hands clenched at her sides. "That's a lie," she cried out. "He's in Montreal so it couldn't have been him."

Jodi got up and started to walk around the table but Charlotte backed away. "Don't." she said holding her arm out with her palm facing Jodi. "Don't come near me. I don't know why you're doing this. I thought you were my best friend."

Jodi stopped moving forward and sighed, "I am your best friend and that's why I had to tell you. I would never lie to you, Charlotte. I was at the Princess of Wales in the orchestra section. We were only about four rows from the front and, when the show was over and we got up to leave, I turned around and saw him. He was about ten rows away with a blond woman. They were exiting the row and he had his hand on her shoulder. We tried to catch up to them but it was too crowded and when we came out onto King Street he was nowhere to be seen."

All the time Jodi was talking, Charlotte stood motionless but breathing heavily. Then, when Jodi paused, she sank down onto a chair and shook her head. "It's not possible," she said softly. "I spoke to Adam last night. I told you he was in Montreal."

Jodi sat down in the chair next to Charlotte, "What time did you speak to him?"

Charlotte hesitated, "It was around seven-thirty."

"The show started at eight."

"I'm telling you again, he was in Montreal."

"How do you know that for sure? Did you call him or did he call you?"

"I called him, so he had to be there."

Jodi sighed, "At the hotel or on his cell phone?"

Charlotte shook her head as she realized the implication, "No, no, I don't believe any of this. How can you be sure it was him? You never spoke to him and the last time, when Greg said he saw him in New York, he didn't speak to him either."

"I'm positive it was him, Charlotte. The lights had already gone up in the theatre and I saw his face. He even glanced in my direction but I know he didn't see me."

"Who were you with?"

"Rick Morgan. I just met him a week ago so he doesn't know Adam."

"I see. So you're the only one who saw him?"

"That's right and if you think I'm getting a kick out of telling you this, you are so wrong. I know I'd want to be told if I had a husband who was seen out with another woman."

Charlotte stood up, "I think I'd like you to leave now," she said.

Jodi slowly rose from the chair, "Don't do this, Charlotte."

Charlotte crossed her arms over her chest, "Please, just go. I'd like to be by myself."

Jodi picked up her purse and took a step towards her but Charlotte took a step back. "Okay, I'll leave," Jodi said, almost in a whisper, and started to walk towards the door. When she got there she paused and turned around, "Can I call you tomorrow?"

Charlotte hadn't moved but she nodded her head and, after she heard the click of Jodi's heels receding down the hallway and the front door being opened and closed, she fell to her knees and started to sob. A half hour later, she was still there in the kitchen sitting on the floor but she had no more tears to shed. Zoe was lying beside her and, with the innate ability of an animal to sense something was wrong, one of her paws was resting on Charlotte's thigh. She reached over and picked Zoe up then slowly got to her feet and walked out of the kitchen into the living room. She gently laid her down on the sofa then picked up the cell phone, which was sitting on the coffee table. She needed to speak to Adam. With a shaking hand, she tapped in the phone number for the Hilton. He always liked to stay there when he was in Montreal. It was right downtown, only three blocks from the Convention Centre and a short walk to Old Montreal. She glanced at her watch as she waited for the phone to be picked up and saw it was only seven-thirty. He was probably out having dinner somewhere and she didn't want to leave a message but, even if she couldn't speak to him, she needed to know he was there. When the hotel operator answered and she asked for Mr. Hamilton's room, it seemed as though she was put on hold for ever. Then she heard a response she had never anticipated, "I am sorry but there is no Mr. Hamilton registered, Madame."

Charlotte took a moment to absorb what she had just heard, "Adam Hamilton; he must be there. He would have checked in on Monday."

Again the wait seemed interminable and then, "I have checked, Madame, but no one of that name has been registered here this week."

Charlotte quickly cut off the call without another word and dialed Adam's cell phone. The call went straight through to voice mail but again, she didn't want to leave a message. She returned to the kitchen and looked at the two, almost full glasses of Chardonnay, still sitting on the table then, one after the other, gulped them down. A dozen thoughts were racing through her mind. Where was Adam? Did he really even go to Montreal? Was the man Jodi had seen, really him? Why was he cheating on her after all these years? Hadn't they had a happy marriage? Didn't she satisfy him in the bedroom? There were so many questions and no answers and she needed to know the truth. She considered calling Diane to find out if she knew where Adam was. If he went to Montreal, she would have made the reservation for him. Then she realized, if she did that, Diane might want to know what was going on and she couldn't risk it. She got up from the table and took the wine out of the refrigerator. There was still over half a bottle left and she was in the right frame of mind to finish it off.

A half hour later, Charlotte slowly climbed the stairs to the bedroom and without even bothering to remove her make-up, stripped down to her bra and panties and climbed into bed. She was tired and needed a little nap. Later, she would call Adam again.

Chapter Six

Charlotte woke up just after six o'clock, as the sun started to rise. When she opened her eyes, she felt a dull ache in the back of her head and her throat felt like sandpaper. Zoe was sleeping peacefully at the bottom of the bed but was startled when Charlotte suddenly sat up and threw off the covers. That's when she saw she was still in her underwear and it all came back to her. She lay back down again and closed her eyes. What was she going to do?

An hour later, after drifting off to sleep again, she got out of bed, stripped down and stepped into the shower. She rarely took a shower, somehow the effect of water pouring down on her head made her feel violated but this morning, for some reason, it seemed to be the right thing to do as though it could wash all her troubles away.

After drying off and slipping into a pair of shorts and a tank top she blow dried her hair, put on a minimum amount of make-up and went downstairs. Zoe had already preceded her and was waiting patiently in the kitchen for her breakfast. Like a robot, Charlotte filled her bowl then prepared her own breakfast of cornflakes and coffee. After breakfast, she drove to the market, bought some fresh bread and fruit and then returned to the house to get ready for work at the library. She had left her cell phone at home and when she picked it up from the kitchen counter she saw there was a message from Adam. She put the phone down, without listening to the message then noticed the red light on the land-line phone was blinking. There was another message from Adam but, again, she ignored it. She was eerily calm as she put away her shopping and went upstairs to change into a pair of white linen pants and a turquoise cotton blouse. She didn't want to talk to Adam or hear his voice until she could actually look into his eyes. That was the only way she would know if he was telling the truth.

When Charlotte turned the corner onto Highland at just after five, Adam's car was in the driveway. It was the last thing she expected and she wasn't prepared to face him. Rather than stopping, she kept on driving until she came to Rosedale United Church. Once there, she parked the car in the lot and just sat there, not sure what to do. She was tempted not to go home at all until after dark so he'd get a taste of his own medicine and begin to worry about where she was. On second thoughts, she knew she couldn't delay a confrontation with him any longer, so she took a deep breath and drove back to the house.

Adam was in the family room watching the news and didn't hear Charlotte come in. She stood in the doorway for a moment watching him. He didn't look any different, he had the usual can of beer in his hand and his feet propped up on the coffee table. She wasn't sure why she expected him to look different. Maybe he was supposed to have a scarlet letter on his chest. Several crazy thoughts ran through her mind and then suddenly, as though he sensed he was being watched, Adam looked back over his shoulder and saw her standing there. He immediately put down his beer and, jumping up from the couch, started towards her, "Charlotte, honey, I didn't hear you come in."

She just stared at him as he kept walking forward then gathered her into his arms and gave her a kiss on the cheek. She felt herself stiffen and he must have felt it too because he took a step back and frowned, "Are you okay?"

She turned away from him and started towards the kitchen, "I didn't expect you back until tomorrow," she replied.

He caught up with her just as she entered the kitchen door and grasped her elbow, swinging her around to face him. "I called you and left you two messages. Why didn't you pick up the phone? Where were you so early in the morning?"

Charlotte shook his hand off and backed up against the counter, "Where was I? You have the nerve to ask me that?" she said with eyes blazing. "Where were you when I called you last night? Perhaps that's the real question."

Adam shook his head, "When did you call me? I didn't get any message from you."

"It doesn't matter when I called. I asked you where you were. Are you going to tell me or not?"

"I'll tell you if it will make you any happier. I was at Molson Stadium watching a game. The Argonauts and the Alouettes were playing."

"In Montreal?"

"That's where the stadium was last time I looked," Adam snapped back sarcastically.

"I don't believe you. You were here in Toronto. Somebody saw you."

Adam laughed, "Oh, so I drove all the way back from Montreal or I never went there in the first place. Is that what you're implying?"

Charlotte nodded, "Yes, I called the Hilton and you weren't even registered there last night. In fact, you weren't even there all week."

Adam was beginning to get annoyed, "That's because I was at the Omni. There was some film festival going on and most of the hotels downtown were fully booked. Diane managed to get me a room at the Omni at the last minute."

"How do I know if you're telling me the truth?"

Adam started to turn on his heel and walk away, "I'll get you the bloody receipt. Maybe that will convince you."

Charlotte sat down at the table and waited for Adam to come back. When he did, he threw the receipt at her and she looked up in surprise, "Take a look at it," he demanded. "I checked in on Monday and checked out this morning."

Charlotte picked the receipt up and stared at it. The dates were correct and she noticed there was even a charge for a telephone call made in the morning before he checked out. Had he called her from his room instead of using his cell phone? She slowly folded the paper and passed it back to him. "That doesn't explain what you were doing in Toronto last night," she said quietly.

"Are you fucking mad?" Adam shot back. "What other proof do you need?"

Charlotte started to rise, a little afraid, because she had never heard him use language like it before. Adam slapped his hand on the table, "Sit down. We aren't finished here. Who saw me and where did they see me? Come on spit it out, Charlotte."

Charlotte hesitated, "Jodi saw you at the Princess of Wales."

Adam threw up his hands, "Well, obviously it was somebody else."

"What about the last time you were supposed to be in Montreal? Was that somebody else too?"

"What in the world are you talking about?"

"Greg saw you in New York in some bar with a woman. How do you explain that, Adam?" Charlotte yelled.

Adam put his hand on his chest and started to laugh, "You mean Greg, Jodi's brother? This has to be some kind of joke. Was the woman I was with last night the same one I was with in New York?" he asked and kept right on laughing.

Charlotte was furious, "You think this is funny. Well, I don't."

"Ha! So, first Greg sees me in New York and then Jodi sees me here, when both times I'm supposed to be in Montreal. Why didn't either one of them speak to me if they were so damn sure it was me?"

"Because neither one of them was able to catch up with you."

Adam shook his head, "How bloody convenient."

Charlotte looked at him and felt the tears start to well up, "So, you're denying everything?"

Adam started to back up towards the kitchen door, "You're damn right I'm denying everything because it's all a big lie or a figment of their imagination and you obviously prefer to believe them over me." At that he turned and started to walk away. Charlotte reached out her hand in an attempt to stop him but he looked back over his shoulder and said, "I'm going out. Don't wait up for me."

Charlotte buried her face in her hands as she heard Adam pick up his keys from the hall table, open and close the front door, and then drive away.

Chapter Seven

Charlotte heard Adam come in at just after midnight. She had been in bed since nine after pacing the floor, for what seemed like hours, and attempting to call him twice on his cell phone, without success. It went to voice messaging both times. She waited for him to come upstairs but as she watched the minutes on the digital clock advance towards one o'clock, she knew he would not be sleeping in their bed that night. Eventually she fell asleep but awoke several times with countless thoughts racing through her head.

Early the next morning, just before seven, she heard the sound of water running but noticed the door to the en-suite bathroom was wide open. She realized Adam was taking a shower in the bathroom down the hall next to Tyler's room. Obviously he was trying to avoid her but he still had to get dressed for work and all of his clothes were in their bedroom. Ten minutes later, Adam walked through the door, with a towel around his waist, and then proceeded to retrieve some clothes from his closet and from the drawers housing his underwear and socks. As Charlotte continued to watch him through half closed eyes, he briefly glanced over at the bed and then left the room. Half inclined to follow him, she started to sit up but then lay down again. Maybe it would be better if she just let him go off to work and then later, when he came home, they could talk. The problem was; Adam didn't come home at the end of the day.

Charlotte spent the morning cleaning house and making an eggplant and ground beef casserole then after lunch, she drove to the market and picked up a baguette and a chocolate hazelnut flan. Often, on a Friday, they would go out to dinner but she knew that wasn't going to happen so she planned on preparing a special meal that would appeal to Adam. Maybe then, on a full stomach and one or two glasses of wine, he would be relaxed enough to talk to her without getting angry.

By seven o'clock, she knew for certain all of her efforts had been in vain. She tried calling him on his cell phone, but just like the night before, he didn't answer. She had eventually rationalized he had to be telling the truth and whoever Greg and Jodi saw, it had to be somebody else. She had every intention of telling Adam just that, but now the seeds of doubt were beginning to grow again. Where was he? What was he doing?

Just as she was removing the casserole from the baking dish to put into a Tupperware container, the telephone on the kitchen counter rang. Hoping it was Adam, she picked it up and tentatively answered, "Hello." It was Nancy and even though, for a brief moment, she was disappointed, she was happy to hear her mother's voice. "Mom, I was hoping you'd call me today. I've been wondering what you and Alexa have been up to," she said trying to sound sincere.

Nancy sounded really upbeat, "Well, we've been having a great time. We went on a three hour whale watching cruise this morning. We saw a family of Orcas and took a zillion photos. I've never seen Alexa so excited."

"Oh, that sounds incredible. How about Peggy? Is she enjoying having you there?"

"Yes, and she doesn't want us to go home. She really is quite amazing. Even though she has a touch of arthritis, she doesn't let it get her down. We're taking her to dinner tonight at Chandlers on Wharf Street. She loves seafood. Alexa's not quite as keen but at least she likes shrimp."

"Is she there now? Can I speak to her?"

"Of course you can. I'll put her on."

There was a lot of shuffling and mumbling and then Alexa came on the line, "Hi, Mom. I wish you could have been with us this morning. It was the best moment of my whole life when I saw the whales. Aunt Peggy came too. She's so much fun. And guess what Mom? We saw a dolphin and some bald eagles. It's so neat here."

"That's wonderful. Where else have you been?"

Alexa sounded almost breathless, "We went to tea at The Empress Hotel yesterday. I felt like a princess and they had this real china with gold on it and so many pastries to choose from, I didn't know what to pick."

Charlotte chuckled, "I know just what you mean. I went there with your Nana before you were born and it was just the same then."

"Really, Mom? Anyway, I loved it and tomorrow we're going to Butchart Gardens. I'm having a great time here."

"I'm so glad but I do miss you."

"I miss you too. Where's Dad? Can I speak to him?"

Charlotte hesitated, "Your Dad had to work late. I'm sorry, sweetie."

"Oh well, I guess I'll speak to him next time. Do you want to talk to Nana again?"

"Yes please, just for a minute. Look after yourself. I love you."

"Love you too, Mom. Hang on, here's Nana."

A moment later, Nancy was back on the line, "So, dear, what have you been up to?"

"Not too much. It's been a bit boring around here. I've been doing some planning for Alexa's birthday next month. I want to have a party for her as it's a special birthday this time."

"Have you given any thought as to what to give her?"

"Yes, she saw this watch in Birks she really likes. How about you, Mom, do you know what you're getting her?"

"Not yet, but there's lots of time. By the way, how's Adam? Is he back from Montreal?"

"Yes, he came back yesterday but he's working late tonight."

"On a Friday? Goodness that man works too hard. I would have liked to have said hello to him but never mind, just give him my love. We have to go now but I'll probably call you again at the beginning of next week."

"Okay, Mom, bye for now. Love you."

"Bye, dear, love you too."

Charlotte hung up the phone and sat down for a moment. She had wanted so badly to confide in her mother but she didn't want to spoil her holiday. There really wasn't anybody else she could talk to except Jodi, but she was at the heart of the problem. If only Adam would come home. She made herself an omelet and a cup of coffee and sat in front of the television watching an episode of Whale Wars on Animal Planet. She tried to focus on the program but her mind kept going back to the conversation she had with Adam. She thought she had resolved the whole issue and was willing to trust him again but his refusal to talk to her made that almost impossible.

She had just finished washing the dishes and was putting them away when she heard her cell phone ringing. She ran back to the family room, where she had left it on the coffee table, and saw it was Jodi. She wasn't sure she really wanted to speak to her but, after the fifth ring, she finally answered, "Hi, Jodi," she said in a low voice.

"Charlotte, I was just about to hang up. Is this a bad time to talk?"

Charlotte sat down on the sofa, "No, it's okay, I just finished eating. How are you?"

"I'm fine but more to the point how are you? I'm sorry I didn't call you yesterday, Rick picked me up right after work and we went straight to dinner and a movie. I was hoping to catch you on your own. Is Adam around?"

Charlotte decided to tell Jodi everything that had transpired and, when she had finished, Jodi remarked, "So he denied it was him. I'm so sorry about all this. I almost wish I hadn't told you but I couldn't really live with myself knowing he was cheating on you. You deserve better than that after all these years. I really don't understand these men. They hit their forties and they start acting like teenagers. You know, Charlotte, I'm glad I'm not married anymore and I don't think I'll ever get hitched again. I'm not sure I'll even live with anybody. This way I can do as I please and I think I get a lot more respect."

Charlotte had heard it all before. She knew exactly how strongly Jodi felt about being independent and in a lot of ways she envied her but not the fact that she would never know the joy of having children. She was thinking about this when she heard Jodi say, "Charlotte, are you still there?"

"Oh, sorry, yes I'm still here. Zoe distracted me for a moment," she lied.

"Would you like me to come over and keep you company?"

"No, I don't think it's a good idea. Adam could come home at any minute and quite honestly, Jodi, I don't think you're his favorite person right now."

Jodi sighed, "No, I don't expect I am. Look, if you need me, just call. You know I'm here for you. Maybe we can get together next week for dinner."

"That would be really nice. I'll be in touch, I promise."

"Okay. You take care. Love you"

"Love you too," Charlotte whispered, putting the phone back down on the table.

Adam arrived home at just after eleven and Charlotte was waiting up for him. She heard him come in and go straight to the kitchen. This was followed by the sound of a cupboard being slammed and then, what sounded like, a glass shattering. Obviously he was drunk and her first instinct was to run and see if he had hurt himself, especially when she heard him curse. Thinking better of it, she remained in the family room, as quiet as a mouse, hoping he would go straight on up to bed and not really caring which bed he ended up in. Moments passed and then she heard footsteps and suddenly he loomed in the doorway holding a mug in his hand. He looked a little disheveled with his shirt open and his tie hanging loosely around his neck. His eyes opened in surprise when he saw her, "Oh, didn't think you'd still be up," he said, slightly slurring his words.

Charlotte got up and walked over to him, "Why didn't you call me?" she asked.

Adam shrugged, "Didn't think you'd care if I called you or not" he replied.

"We really need to talk but maybe tonight isn't a good time." She started to squeeze past him through the doorway. "I'm going up to bed, are you coming?"

He shook his head, "Nope, not yet. I think I'll stay up for a while and watch the news"

Charlotte started to walk away down the hall, "Well, I'll say goodnight then."

Adam stared after her and then gave a mock salute, "Yes, ma'am. Goodnight ma'am."

Charlotte didn't know how she had the will power to avoid going into the kitchen without checking to see if there was glass on the floor. She was pretty fastidious about her housekeeping and just walking past the kitchen door and climbing the stairs to her bedroom was a challenge but she wasn't going to clean up Adam's mess.

Chapter Eight

For the second night in a row Charlotte had a fitful night's sleep. Adam didn't come to bed and in the morning, when she didn't hear him stirring, she checked Tyler's room but he wasn't there. Becoming a little alarmed she went downstairs to see if he was already up and found him fast asleep on the sofa, still fully clothed and with the television still on. She decided to leave him there, go back upstairs to take a bath, get dressed, and then get on with her day. Later, when she came downstairs and peeked around the door, to see if he was still asleep, she discovered he had gone. She checked in the kitchen and then went to the bottom of the stairs to see if she could hear him. A moment later, she heard him go into their bedroom and assumed he must have taken a shower and was now getting dressed. She raced back into the kitchen and was measuring out cornflakes into a bowl when he appeared in the doorway in a pair of casual slacks and a light blue tee. Charlotte glanced up at him and couldn't help thinking how handsome and refreshed he looked even after a night of drinking. "Good morning," she said, almost in a whisper, "Would you like some breakfast?"

Adam walked over and sat down at the table, "Yes, that would be nice if you don't mind making it."

"How about some scrambled eggs and bacon and some toast?"

Adam nodded and then stood up again, "That would be fine if it's not too much trouble. I'll make the coffee."

"You don't have to; I can manage."

Adam put a hand on Charlotte's shoulder, "I want to do it," he said.

There was an awkward silence as Charlotte prepared breakfast and Adam proceeded to make the coffee. Charlotte had no idea what to say without the risk of starting another fight but it was Adam who started the conversation. They were both sitting at the table, toying with their food, when he looked across at her and said, "I want to apologize for last night. I know I was drunk and probably disrespectful and I don't blame you if you're annoyed. I expect you were wondering where I was. Well, I went over to Sam's. I needed someone to talk to and quite frankly I'm glad I went because Eleanor put things into perspective for me. You have to believe I haven't cheated on you and I never will. This individual Jodi and Greg both saw has to be someone who looks very much like me and I can't blame them for making a mistake, although I'm a bit disappointed Jodi doesn't have more faith in me. Eleanor pointed out that Jodi is your best friend and you've known her since high school. You had every reason to believe what she was telling you and my reacting the way I did was pretty childish." He reached over and took Charlotte's hand, "I'm so sorry, will you forgive me?"

Charlotte nodded with tears in her eyes, "I'm sorry too for doubting you. I should have believed you. You've never given me any reason to think you'd go off with some other woman but I was beginning to wonder if I'd let you down somehow. Maybe you were getting bored with me or maybe you just wanted someone younger and prettier."

Adam smiled and squeezed her hand, "Now I think you're just fishing for compliments. You're not boring and you're even more attractive than the day I first met you. I wouldn't trade the last twenty years for anything and I couldn't wish for a better partner."

Charlotte shook her head, "Twenty-one years."

"Has it been that long?" Adam shot back with a grin on his face. "It seems like only yesterday when I first saw you at the museum."

Charlotte sighed and withdrew her hand, "It was the Art Gallery."

Adam laughed, "I know, I was just teasing you. Look why don't we go out somewhere special tonight for dinner? We'll get all dressed up and then maybe, afterwards, we can take a walk through Yorkville."

"It sounds perfect, I would love that. What are you doing this morning?"

"Well, I know it's Saturday but I need to go into the office for a few hours and this afternoon I'd like to watch the ball game, the Jays are playing the Yankees. What about you, what are you up to?"

Charlotte stood up and started to clear her side of the table, "Well, after I've cleared away the dishes, that is if you ever decide to finish your breakfast, I'm going to the market and then I'm going over to Mom's to water her flowers and check on Gypsy and Luna. Mom's neighbour, Mrs. Walker, has been looking after them. In fact, she's almost been living there. Mom's so lucky to have somebody like her right next door."

"Yes, she is," Adam responded as he shoveled scrambled eggs into his mouth. "That reminds me, where's Zoe? I haven't seen her around this morning."

"Oh, she's out in the garden chasing squirrels. By the way, will you be home for lunch?"

Adam stood up as he finished off his coffee and walked over to the sink, "Yes, I should be back by about one."

By mid-afternoon Adam was settled on the sofa watching baseball and Charlotte was busy baking. After seeing Mrs. Walker earlier in the day, she wanted to do something nice for her, to show her how thankful she was for the way she was taking care of Nancy's cats. She decided to make her some honey rhubarb muffins and take them over to her on Sunday morning. As she stood at the kitchen counter, mixing the ingredients, she couldn't help thinking how normal everything seemed at that moment. The last week had been so stressful and she never wanted to go through anything like that again. She had her husband back and she could hardly wait to go to dinner later. She almost felt like she was going on a date and she planned to wear something special for the occasion.

At seven o'clock, Charlotte descended the stairs wearing a dress that had been hanging in the back of her closet for at least ten years. It was pale green chiffon with spaghetti straps and had been a favourite of Adam's. She was wearing it with strappy sandals and she had taken a lot of time with her hair and make-up. Adam was waiting in the hall for her and looked very dapper in grey slacks, white shirt open at the collar and a black blazer. He glanced up as he heard Charlotte's footsteps and let out a wolf whistle, "Wow, you look fabulous," he said.

Charlotte reached the bottom of the stairs and gave a slight curtsy, "Thank you kind sir," she responded. "Now where are we going?"

"We're going to Sotto Sotto's," Adam replied, taking her arm and ushering her out of the door.

"Isn't that really expensive?" Charlotte asked pulling back a little.

Adam looked at her and frowned, "So? We can afford it and you deserve to go somewhere special. Call it a peace offering if you like."

Charlotte decided not to make a fuss. She realized Adam was trying to make amends and later, after they had finished their meal and were enjoying an espresso and a Grand Marnier, she was relieved she had just followed along with his plans. They were both feeling very mellow. The food had been exceptional and the ambience so romantic, it did indeed feel as though they were out on a date. Adam looked across the table and murmured, "You look really beautiful in the candlelight."

Charlotte smiled, "Do you still want to go for a walk or would you rather go back home?"

Adam grinned, "Is that an invitation?"

"What do you think?" Charlotte answered looking rather coy.

The intimacy between them later that night was both gentle and aggressive. Charlotte couldn't remember the last time she had been more satisfied. If Adam had been trying to make her forget about the tension between them, he had succeeded. Just before she closed her eyes and fell into a deep sleep, she said a silent thank you to whoever was watching over her.

Chapter Nine

By the time Nancy and Alexa returned from Victoria, Charlotte and Adam were back to their normal routine and any tension between them had long been forgotten. Adam had to take another trip to Montreal but it was a flying visit and he left early in the morning via Porter Airlines and was back the same evening.

At the beginning of August, Charlotte finally got a telephone call from Tyler. He was now in London with Shelby and staying with her parents in Chelsea. He sounded very impressed with the family, her father being an eminent doctor on Harley Street and her mother a professor at University College. It was obvious he wanted to stay in London but Charlotte said it wasn't an option. He was due to go back to York University in September to continue his studies and when he suggested he could apply for a gap year and spend it in England, Charlotte had to put Adam on the phone. She gathered from listening to one side of the conversation that Tyler was being stubborn but Adam was persistent and even threatened to cut off all funds if Tyler refused to come back in time. When he eventually put the phone down, he was red in the face but nodded and said, "He'll be here the first week of September."

Two weeks later in mid-August, Alexa celebrated her sixteenth birthday. It was a beautiful summer day and Charlotte had gone all out to make it a special occasion. She spent hours preparing food as well as hiring a caterer to provide all kinds of delicacies. With Nancy's help, they set up buffet tables in the garden and strung up several strings of lights so when it got dark it would look like fairyland. The invitations that went out suggested everyone bring their bathing suit and not to worry about dressing up. Alexa wasn't too happy when she first saw the invitations. She had imagined herself on her sixteenth all gussied up like a prom queen in a strapless gown and heels, especially as she wanted to impress Joshua. Charlotte just laughed and told her he would be even more impressed when she wore her new, and rather revealing, red bikini.

The party appeared to be a great success. All of the young people were having a good time in the pool while the grownups were content to lounge on lawn chairs and sip on beer or wine. Sam and Eleanor were there along with the Eriksons' and two other sets of neighbours and then, an hour into the party, Jodi arrived with Rick. It was all a little awkward even though Adam had promised not to bring up the subject of Jodi's recent revelations but, after she had introduced Rick, it was obvious Adam was keeping his distance.

About an hour after everyone had eaten their fill from the buffet table and Alexa had opened all her gifts, including the Tissot watch which she went into raptures over, Jodi approached Adam. "I guess you're pretty annoyed with me," she said. It sounded more like a statement than a question. Adam just raised his glass and replied, "This is a birthday party for my daughter. I don't really want to discuss this."

Jodi was taken aback at Adam's attitude and hesitated before responding, "You're right, please forgive me."

Adam started to turn away, "Forgiven and forgotten" he said abruptly.

Jodi stared after him as he walked over to the Eriksons' who were in a lively discussion with Sam. She felt thoroughly chastised and didn't quite know what to make of it. Was he guilty as charged and being defensive, or was he completely innocent and justifiably angry?

It was just after eight when the sun started to go down and Nancy noticed Alexa was nowhere to be seen. Most of the young people had taken off their bathing suits and were wearing shorts and tank tops, or tees. She thought Alexa might still be in the house changing but then she noticed Joshua was missing too. She decided to mention it to Charlotte as she was concerned about where they were. Charlotte then asked Hildy and Joshua's sister, Joanie, but they just shook their heads, so she headed into the house and checked in the kitchen and the family room but they weren't there.

She was annoyed that Alexa would skip out on her own party and felt it was disrespectful of her to have abandoned her guests. She felt sure she would find her with Joshua listening to music or playing video games in her room and was prepared to give her a piece of her mind, birthday or not. She went upstairs and when she got to the door and listened, it was deadly quiet. She began to wonder if they were there at all. Quietly, she opened the door and stood frozen in her tracks when she saw Alexa lying on her back with one breast exposed and Joshua practically lying on top of her. For a moment or two she was so shocked, she couldn't move. Suddenly Alexa became aware her mother was standing there and jumped up into a sitting position while pushing Joshua off of her and adjusting her top. "Mom, what are you doing here?" she cried out in alarm.

"I think I'm the one who should be asking that question," Charlotte replied. She looked over at Joshua who was cowering at the far side of the bed. "It would be a good idea if you just went home. Don't worry I won't say anything to your parents."

He rushed past her and out of the door and Charlotte turned back to Alexa, "I'll give you five minutes to get yourself together and then I expect you to go back downstairs and play hostess. We'll talk about this later."

Alexa nodded as she watched Charlotte exit the room and quietly close the door.

Before Nancy left to go home, just as the party was ending, she suggested to Charlotte it would be better not to talk to Alexa about her reckless behaviour until the next day, rather than later that night. At first, Charlotte was reluctant to take her mother's advice but she realized she couldn't be very objective when she felt so shaken up at seeing Alexa in such intimate circumstances. At midnight, when all of the guests had left and Alexa was attempting to sneak up to her room, Charlotte caught up with her and whispered, "We'll talk in the morning."

Alexa stopped, just as she was starting up the stairs, and turned around, "Please don't tell, Dad," she whispered back.

Charlotte just nodded and went into the kitchen where Adam was putting glasses in the dishwasher. He glanced up, "Is everything okay?" he asked. "Alexa didn't even say goodnight."

Charlotte walked over and stood beside him, "She was just tired and a little overwhelmed with all the attention. I think the party went really well, don't you?"

Adam put his arm around her, "It was a fabulous party, honey. You did a great job of organizing everything."

"Yes, but it's been a really long day. How about we call it a night?"

Adam closed the door to the dishwasher. "Good idea. By the way, I'll be up early tomorrow. Sam and I are going to play a round of golf."

"That's perfect because I'd like to spend some time with our daughter."

On Sunday morning, by the time Charlotte got up, Adam had already left. She didn't expect Alexa to show her face for at least another hour, so she had her breakfast, took care of Zoe and then went to do some work in the garden. Finally, at ten o'clock, Alexa poked her head out of the patio doors and yelled out, "Good morning."

Charlotte looked up from where she was digging out some weeds, "Oh, hi sweetie. I'll be right in to make your breakfast."

"That's all right, Mom, I'm not hungry. I'm just going over to Hildy's and I'll be back later."

Charlotte quickly got to her feet, "Oh no you don't, young lady. We need to talk about last night before you go anywhere. Go and put the kettle on for tea."

Alexa rolled her eyes and disappeared inside the house as Charlotte pulled off her gloves and followed after her. Once in the kitchen she asked Alexa to help while she whipped up some scrambled eggs and toast and when it was ready she said, "Sit down and eat and while you're eating I want you to listen to me."

"Oh, Mom," Alexa moaned, toying with her food and not looking up. "Do we have to talk about this? I'm sorry. It won't happen again."

Charlotte sat down on the opposite side of the table, "I know you don't expect me to understand but I do. I was your age once and I know how easy it is to cross that line. Thankfully, even though I was tempted, I was a lot older before I first had sex with anybody."

Alexa looked shocked, "You mean Dad wasn't your first?"

"No, he wasn't. When I was eighteen I thought I was madly in love with the brother of one of my closest friends. I honestly believed we would get married one day and that's why I finally gave in. Making love is a wonderful experience especially when you care really deeply for someone. That's why I want you to wait, Alexa. You'll know when the time is right. Making out in this house is not acceptable under any circumstances and you're fortunate I didn't tell your father about it."

Alexa shook her head, "It's really hard, Mom, I get all these feelings when I'm with Josh."

"I know, but you have to think about the consequences. What if you got pregnant? Have you any idea what it would be like to have to bring up a baby? You would have to drop out of school and you wouldn't be able to go out and have fun with your friends, like you do now."

Alexa paused and then, looking very solemn, she said, "I think I'd give it up for adoption or have an abortion."

Charlotte got up and came around the table. She sat down beside Alexa and put her arm around her, "Oh, sweetie, that would be a terrible decision to have to make and one you might regret for the rest of your life."

Alexa hung her head, "Hildy's mom got her birth control pills."

Charlotte nodded, "I see. Well, it's something we need to consider. Maybe I'll have a talk with Dr. Atkins and then we can decide the best thing to do. Right now, I'm asking you to be very careful. Try and stay away from situations where you're alone with Joshua and then you won't be tempted."

"Okay, Mom. I promise I'll be careful."

Charlotte got up and patted Alexa on the shoulder, "That's my girl. Now, you can go over to Hildy's but be home for lunch. Your father will be back by then and maybe we can drive up to Willow Lake or Port Perry. It's a beautiful day and we can go for a swim."

Alexa jumped up, "Oh, that would be great, Mom. Can Hildy come with us?"

Charlotte grinned, "Yes, she can. Now run along and make sure you're back on time."

Chapter Ten

By the end of August, Charlotte was once again feeling pretty content with her life. She knew any concerns she had about Alexa had been resolved because, a week after the incident, Joshua announced he was involved with Kelly Bedford, the sister of one of his closest friends. Alexa received the news via text message from Joshua himself. At first, she was devastated until Charlotte assured her she was probably well rid of him as he was most likely just trying to take advantage of her.

Alexa was soon distracted from her own problems when, on the first Saturday in September, Tyler arrived home from England. There was a great deal of excitement when they picked him up at the airport. As he walked towards them in the arrivals lounge, Charlotte couldn't help thinking how much he resembled Adam. She noticed it more and more as he got older and he looked even taller than when he left, almost four months earlier. He seemed rather quiet on the drive home and they had to pump him for information about his trip. He claimed he was really tired and would fill them in on Sunday and show them all his photos but Charlotte felt as though he was holding something back. When they got to the house, he declined the offer of anything to eat or drink then went off to look for Zoe and, after finding her and settling her in his arms, announced he was going to bed.

Charlotte looked at Adam and said, "Maybe you should go up and talk to him. Something isn't right."

Adam shook his head, "No, let's just let him get some sleep and maybe tomorrow he'll tell us what's going on."

On Sunday, it was after ten when Tyler finally came downstairs. Adam was out playing golf with Sam and Alexa was at Hildy's, while Charlotte was in the kitchen lining up the ingredients for lasagne. She looked up as Tyler came through the door, "Hi there," she said, "did you have a good night's sleep?"

Tyler ran his hand through his hair and yawned, "Yes, Mom, I guess so. Where's everybody."

"Dad's golfing and your sister's at Hildy's, now how about some breakfast?"

"Just coffee and some toast please. I'm not really hungry."

Charlotte put some bread in the toaster and filled a mug with some coffee, which she had just finished brewing a few minutes earlier. "Nana will be here in half an hour. She's dying to see you."

Tyler's face lit up as Charlotte passed him the coffee, "Oh, good. Is she staying for lunch?"

"Yes she is and then we were just going to relax in the garden for a while and maybe have a swim. It's still really warm out and, from what I hear, this will probably be the last good weekend before fall starts to set in, so we should take advantage of it."

Just then the toast popped up and after Charlotte buttered it and put it on a plate, she passed it to Tyler, "There you are, eat up."

Tyler picked up a piece of toast and then put it down again, "Mom, I need to talk to you before Dad gets back."

Charlotte sat down opposite him with a concerned look on her face, "What is it, Tyler?"

"You know I didn't want to come home, don't you, Mom?"

Charlotte nodded, "Yes, I know, you wanted to stay in London."

"It isn't that I don't miss you, because I do, but I really think I'm in love, Mom. When I got to Heathrow and had to say goodbye to Shelby, it was like I was leaving my heart behind. It was all I could do to keep on walking away from her and getting on the plane."

Charlotte smiled, "She must be awfully special."

"Oh, she is. You would just love her. She's just a beautiful person both inside and out."

"I'd like to see a picture of her."

"Would you really, Mom," Tyler asked: his face lighting up with enthusiasm.

"Yes, of course. Finish your breakfast and then go and bring down your photos."

Tyler started to gobble down his toast, "I have to download them onto my computer. It will only take a few moments."

"Okay, then call me when you're ready and I'll come upstairs and look at them."

Less than ten minutes later, Tyler and Charlotte were sitting side by side in front of his computer and he was scrolling through the dozens of photos he had taken on his trip through Europe. "I want to show you the one I took of her outside the Vatican, Mom, it's a fabulous picture."

Soon Charlotte found herself looking at the image of a slight young woman, with long, ash blond hair and a face reminiscent of Mia Farrow. She had on a strapless maxi dress in a pale shade of blue which matched the colour of her eyes and she was looking straight into the camera and grinning, showing perfectly straight teeth. "Oh my," Charlotte remarked, "She really is lovely."

Tyler sighed, "Isn't she though? After this next school year I want to go back to London and then we're talking about going to Egypt."

Charlotte put her arm around him, "A year is a long time, anything could happen."

"No, Mom, we're committed to each other and I may even fly over at Christmas or during the March break."

"What about money? How are you going to afford all this?"

Tyler lowered his gaze, "Well, I was hoping you and Dad would help me out. But if you can't then Shelby can come here for a week or two. Her parents are really well off and she has a trust fund her grandmother left her."

Right at that moment, the doorbell rang and Charlotte got up, "Speaking of grandmothers that must be Nana. I'll run down and answer the door. Just make sure you come down in a few minutes."

Tyler nodded, "I will, Mom, but can we talk about this again later?"

"Yes, but I think your father should be in on the conversation too."

Tyler shrugged and went back to studying the photo of Shelby. He knew his father was a tougher nut to crack.

As it turned out, Tyler wasn't able to go to London at Christmas, even though Adam had been quite amenable to the idea. He had been struggling a little with his studies, all the while wishing he was in London, and he was virtually counting the days until the holidays. Shelby was going on a Scandinavian cruise with her parents and her cousin, Polly, and wouldn't be back until the New Year. Tyler took it a lot harder than Shelby but, he had to admit, he understood why she couldn't pass up the opportunity of visiting Norway and Sweden.

Charlotte and Adam had always tried their best to make Christmas a very special time in their childrens' lives and this holiday was no exception. They decorated the house, both inside and out, and planned a number of activities besides the traditional feast which Charlotte took two days to prepare. Nancy would spend the day with them, as always, and this time Peggy would be joining them too. She had flown in from Victoria for a visit and they were excited about seeing her. Adam's mother and step-father were also invited but, as usual, they turned the invitation down. Charlotte breathed a sigh of relief. She didn't have the energy to deal with Mary.

Despite the fact Tyler was disappointed about not seeing Shelby, he seemed to have a really good time and then, just before March break he announced he was flying to London to see her. This was no surprise to Charlotte or Adam and they even agreed to finance the trip. Meanwhile Alexa wasn't too happy about the idea. She had enjoyed having her brother back home and they had spent more time together than ever before. He was particularly sympathetic about the situation with Joshua and she was anxious to learn everything she could about Shelby, "I hope you'll meet her one day, Sis," Tyler remarked as they were looking at his photos again.

"I hope so too. You are coming back, aren't you?" She asked anxiously.

"Yes, of course I'm coming back," he replied but he wouldn't look her in the eye and she was almost certain he was lying to her.

As it turned out, Alexa's fear was well founded. As March break came to end, Charlotte got a call from Tyler. "I'm staying here, Mom," he said, without any preamble.

"Oh, Tyler, you can't do that. Your father and I want you to come home. You're going to miss school. It's only three more months and then you can do whatever you like."

"I can't help it. I love Shelby and we want to be together."

Charlotte sighed, "What do her parents have to say about this?"

"They're okay with it. I'm going to be staying with them again so you know I'm in good hands. Please, Mom, I need you to support me."

Charlotte knew there was very little she could do. Tyler was beyond the age of consent but she did have one concern, "We still need to discuss the money issue, Tyler. Are you going to try and get a job? You can't expect Shelby's parents to give you free room and board."

"Shelby's uncle owns a pub and he's going to let me work there for the time being. Dr. Lewiston refuses to take any money from me but he does expect me to work hard and save enough money to pay for the trip to Egypt we're planning."

"Well, he sounds like a responsible person."

Tyler chuckled, "I told you, Mom, he's a Harley Street specialist, so he's no slouch."

"No, I guess you're right. Okay, I guess I don't have any choice but to let you stay but I'm not happy about it. Don't be surprised if you get a call from your father after I tell him tonight. He won't be as accommodating as I am."

"I know, Mom, you're a soft touch but I love you for it. I'll stay in touch all the time, I promise."

"All right, Tyler. You take good care of yourself and say hi to Shelby for me."

"Okay, Mom, love you."

"Love you too," Charlotte whispered.

Adam didn't express any surprise when he heard the news. When he had been Tyler's age, he had experienced the same wanderlust and he felt it was something every young person had to get out of their system. As for the relationship with Shelby, he assumed it was merely an infatuation and would fizzle out in time.

Charlotte was relieved Adam was not going to put any pressure on Tyler. She couldn't bear any tension within the family and was grateful life had returned to normal after the disruption that had taken place, the previous summer. She had no idea that, within a few months, her world would turn topsy-turvy again.

Chapter Eleven

Other than Tyler leaving to go back to London, by the time June came around, life had settled down and Charlotte was preparing to enjoy the summer. Adam had agreed to take some time off and they planned to take a trip to the east coast at the end of July. When Alexa discovered her father was considering renting an RV, she was thrilled and begged him to take Zoe too but he wouldn't go along with the idea. "Nana will take Zoe," he said emphatically.

"But Gypsy and Luna don't like her," she moaned.

Charlotte decided to intervene, "She'll be much better off with Nana than with us. She doesn't even like being in the car for very long, never mind being couped up for almost three weeks."

Alexa put on her sulky face, "I suppose you're right, Mom, but I'll miss her."

"You didn't miss her when you were in Victoria and what about when we went to Italy? Nana looked after her then and you didn't complain."

Alexa looked at her father and shrugged, "I can't win can I?"

Adam grinned, "Not in a debate with your mother, that's for sure."

In the weeks leading up to the start of their trip, Alexa spent most of her time hanging out with her friends while Charlotte got involved with researching the places she thought they should visit on their trip east. Working in the library gave her access to all kinds of material and, even on her days off, she could sometimes be seen in the reference area pouring over maps or reading guide books. She had always strived to put her best effort into everything she did, whether it was cooking, cleaning or bringing up the children. Nancy had often told her she should chill out and not try to be so perfect but all of her mother's advice fell on deaf ears.

Adam had been working extra-long hours as they were involved in the design of a new hotel being built on the lakefront. His issues with the project in Montreal had long been resolved and he had only been back on two occasions, both times on a flying visit and returning the same day. He didn't expect to be out of town again before they left on vacation but, when he got a call from an important client in Ottawa about a new sub-division being planned, he felt compelled to meet with him or risk losing a lucrative contract. Charlotte wasn't happy when she discovered he would be staying in Ottawa for at least two nights, "Why so long?" she asked.

"Because I need to see the site and go over the plans, you have no idea how much there is to discuss on a project like this. We're talking about a whole sub-division with houses, roads, and parks and so on. I may even need to stay longer but I can let you know how long once I've spent some time with Howard. He's pretty demanding but he's only interested in the best and he's willing to pay for it."

"Why can't Sam go instead of you?"

"Sam is busy with the hotel being planned at the lakefront. We've been working together on it but now he has to carry the load. It's easier for me to make these trips than Sam. He didn't want me to mention it to anyone but I might as well tell you. He's having hip replacement surgery in the next few months so it's hard for him to get around."

"Oh no, I didn't notice he was having any problem walking."

"That's because you haven't seen him for a while but lately he's been limping quite a bit and I know he's in a lot of pain."

Charlotte nodded, "Well then of course you must go. I'm sorry, honey, I wasn't trying to give you the third degree. I do worry about you though when you work so hard."

Adam gave her a hug, "I'm made of strong stuff. No need to worry about me."

When Adam left on the following Wednesday, Charlotte hoped he would be back by Friday. Nancy had decided to drive up to a friend's cottage in Muskoka and planned to take Alexa with her, so Charlotte thought, if Adam wasn't too tired, maybe they could enjoy a weekend away too. It had been a long time since they had gone anywhere without one, or both, of the children and she began to fantasize about a wonderful inn she had heard about in Prince Edward County. Then, on Thursday, her dream of a romantic getaway was shattered when Adam called to say he had to stay over until Saturday and possibly even Sunday as there was just too much to discuss. After Charlotte put down the phone, she was upset and not looking forward to another Friday night alone. She even thought about asking Alexa to stay home but she realized that would be selfish and she didn't want to disappoint Nancy, who was looking forward to taking her granddaughter away.

Later that evening she decided to call Jodi. She hadn't seen her for about a month, when they had accompanied each other to an in-home lingerie party. It had been a lot of fun and Charlotte had even bought a rather sexy red lace bra and matching panties which she hadn't yet worn. She sighed when she thought of Adam's reaction if she'd been able to surprise him by wearing them on the weekend. It would have been the perfect outfit to spice up their sex life. She smiled as she picked up the phone and called Jodi's number. It only rang twice before she recognized Jodi's familiar throaty voice, "Hi, this is Jodi."

"Hi it's Charlotte. How are you?"

"Oh, what a coincidence, I was just thinking about you and wondering when we could get together for dinner."

"Well, actually I'm free tomorrow but I expect you have other plans on a Friday."

"No, I don't. Rick's in Chicago until Saturday so I'm free as a bird."

"What's Rick doing in Chicago?"

"His father lives there and he's recovering from a heart operation so Rick needed to go back and see him. He was with him right after he came out of surgery three weeks ago but he wanted to make sure he was doing okay."

"What about his mother? Isn't she there too?"

"No, they've been divorced for a donkey's age. She lives just outside of Kingston."

"I see, so how about we meet up tomorrow for dinner and maybe a movie too if you're available?"

"Mmmmm not sure about a movie unless we go after dinner because I have an appointment late in the afternoon and I have no idea how long it will take."

"Okay, well let's play it by ear. Where would you like to go?"

"Let's go back to Sambucca's on Baldwin. Can you meet me at seven?"

"Perfect! Yes, I'll see you at seven. Look forward to it."

After saying goodbye, Charlotte felt a lot better. At least she had something to do to occupy her on Friday night and the idea of a movie after dinner sounded appealing. She figured she wouldn't get home until really late and that was something she wasn't used to. Somewhere deep down she felt like she was being a little naughty and she was paying Adam back for staying away. She even hoped he tried calling her and not getting an answer. Maybe that would teach him a lesson.

Charlotte had already had breakfast and was brewing a pot of coffee hoping her mother would stay for a while when she arrived, just after eight, to pick up Alexa. Hearing Nancy's car pull into the driveway, she ran to open the door, "Hi, Mom," she called out, "you're up bright and early."

"Yes, and I hope that granddaughter of mine is ready," Nancy remarked as she mounted the steps.

"Well, she's already showered and dressed but she's still packing her bag, so come in and have a coffee with me while you're waiting."

Nancy followed Charlotte into the kitchen and sat down, "I think I could manage another cup. Where's Adam, don't tell me he's still in bed?"

Charlotte started to pour the coffee into two mugs, "I told you on Wednesday, he had to go to Ottawa."

"Oh, that's right, I forgot. So, what are you planning to do today?"

"Not too much," Charlotte replied as she passed Nancy one of the mugs and put cream and sugar on the table, "although tonight I'm going to dinner with Jodi and maybe to a movie afterwards."

"Oh how lovely, how is Jodi? I haven't seen her for ages."

"She seems to be doing really well at her job and she's still dating the fellow you met at Alexa's party last year. I'm not sure how serious the relationship is but I plan to pry it out of her tonight."

Nancy nodded, "They do make an attractive couple. I've always admired Jodi's sense of style. Sometimes it makes me wish I was thirty again and I could wear all the fabulous new fashions."

Charlotte chuckled, "Mom, you always seem to keep up with the latest trends but no one expects to see you in a pair of low riders and a crop top."

Nancy started to roar with laughter just as Alexa came through the door, "Hi, Nana, what's so funny?"

"Oh nothing, sweetie, your Mom was just being silly. My, you look nice this morning," she continued, noticing Alexa's crisp white shorts and fuchsia tank top.

"Thanks, Nana, you look nice too. I like your yellow capris."

Nancy stood up and did a pirouette, "You don't think they're too young for me?" she asked grinning at Charlotte.

"No way," Alexa answered.

"Good, then I guess we can be on our way."

"What about breakfast?" Charlotte asked. "You can't drive all that way on an empty stomach."

Alexa smiled at her grandmother, "We're stopping at McDonalds and I'm having an egg McMuffin."

Charlotte rolled her eyes, "Your Nana thoroughly spoils you. You do know that don't you?"

"Yes, but I'm worth it," Alexa replied, playfully sticking out her tongue.

After her mother and Alexa left, Charlotte decided to do a little laundry and then drove to the library to do more research for their east coast trip. Not looking forward to eating lunch at home by herself, she then drove to the Don Mills Centre and ordered a tuna melt at Anthony's Grill. She didn't feel so badly when she looked around and noticed four or five other women sitting by themselves. She couldn't help wondering if they were married and if their husbands were out of town doing heaven knows what. Then, she suddenly realized where her mind was running to and she didn't want to go there again.

Later, as she soaked in the tub, she realized just how much she was looking forward to seeing Jodi. She couldn't decide on what to wear but, after sorting through her closet, she settled on a sleeveless deep rose shift with a square neck and a pair of white three-inch sandals. After applying a little more make-up than usual and piling her hair on top of her head, she surveyed herself in the mirror. The dress didn't need a necklace but it definitely needed something. She suddenly remembered the pair of drop earrings with the seed pearls Nancy had given her at Christmas and once she put them on, she was satisfied that she wouldn't feel like a country mouse compared to Jodi. It irked her in a way that she felt she had to always compete with her closest friend. She wished she had a little more self-confidence when it came to her appearance. Countless people had told her she was attractive and Adam had even called her beautiful on many occasions. She knew she looked young for her age but she wished she had more sense of style and, when it came right down to it, she was more concerned about her tendency to be rather introverted. She wasn't sure where this aspect of her character came from because her mother had always brought her up to believe in herself. She was convinced she was an excellent homemaker and a good mother to her children but longed to be more outgoing, just like Jodi.

When she arrived on Baldwin, as she was parking the car, she noticed Jodi's silver Lexus pulling into the spot behind her. They both stepped out onto the sidewalk at the same time and grinned, "How's that for timing?" Jodi called out.

Charlotte walked over and gave her a hug, "Amazing and very lucky that we managed to get two spots together."

Jodi looped her arm through Charlotte's and they headed towards the restaurant, "I love your dress," she said, "and those earrings are fab."

"Thanks, Mom gave them to me."

"She always did have good taste," Jodi remarked.

At Sambucca's, they both ordered the signature dish of apple chicken and a bottle of Chardonnay. "We're going to get drunk if we finish this bottle," Charlotte said grinning.

"Nonsense, and even if we do, you're not worrying about Adam seeing you tiddly are you?"

"No, couldn't care less," Charlotte replied rather flippantly. "He's not home. He's in Ottawa until tomorrow or maybe even Sunday."

Jodi frowned, "Is everything okay between you two?"

Charlotte nodded, "Yes, everything's fine. One of their biggest clients is planning on building a new subdivision up there and it could be worth a lot of money to the firm."

"I'm so glad, Charlotte, I was a bit concerned about you."

"Well, you needn't be so let's not talk about me. I want to hear what you've been up to. You look really good, by the way. I really like your outfit," she continued while admiring Jodi's short white jacket worn over a lime green camisole.

"Thanks, this is my favourite shade of green and it's Rick's too."

"So what's going on with you and Rick? You've been going steady for a long time. Any plans of moving in together?"

Jodi grinned, "We've talked about it but it would mean getting a place we're both comfortable with."

"What's wrong with your townhouse? It's lovely and it's right downtown. How much more could one want?"

"I know and that's the problem. I love it there and Rick likes it too but it would still be my place and I think, if we move in together, we should find somewhere that belongs to both of us."

"I guess that makes sense. It would be too easy for him to just walk out if you were in the townhouse and things weren't going well. How is his landscaping business doing?"

"It's doing really well and especially at this time of the year. Thank goodness he doesn't have to do any of the heavy work anymore. He has about six people working for him now and he's planning on hiring two more."

"I guess you can get him a few leads considering the business you're in."

Jodi laughed, "I certainly can and I already have. I sold a house two weeks ago on the Bridle Path and they've already hired Rick's company to do all of the landscaping."

"Sounds like you're on to a good thing," Charlotte remarked.

Jodi nodded, "Yes, I think he's a keeper."

After dinner they drove to the Cumberland Theatre to see a foreign film Nancy had recommended and then took a walk through Yorkville. It was another perfect evening and there were dozens of people roaming the streets and filling the patios of the numerous restaurants along the way. Finally, they doubled back and stopped in for a nightcap at the Four Seasons. Sitting by the window, Charlotte gazed out at the crowds on the sidewalk, "This has been a lovely evening, Jodi. We should get together more often."

"Yes, we should," Jodi replied. "It would be nice if the four of us went out sometime. I don't know why we haven't managed to do that yet and I think Rick and Adam would really get along."

"That seems like a great idea. Actually, I feel a little guilty. I should have invited the two of you over to the house by now. I can't believe it's been almost a year since you were at Alexa's party."

"I know, time just flies by but we'll set something up in the next couple of weeks."

Charlotte nodded, "For sure, I'll see when Adam's free and I'll call you."

A half hour later, Charlotte was on her way home and when she climbed into bed just after midnight, she was feeling very mellow. There had been no call from Adam but it didn't stop her from falling asleep almost immediately with Zoe curled up alongside her.

Chapter Twelve

On Saturday morning, Charlotte left the house at around eleven to drive over to Nancy's and check on Gypsy and Luna. Mrs. Walker had raved over her honey rhubarb muffins so she decided to drop in and take her some oatmeal raisin cookies, she had baked earlier in the week. The cats were both sleeping soundly on Nancy's bed so she made sure they had sufficient food and water and then went next door to call on the neighbour. Mrs. Walker was genuinely pleased to see her and invited her to stay for lunch. Like Nancy, she was a widow, but she had no family in Toronto and loved to have company.

After lunch, Charlotte picked up some groceries at the Summerhill market and then returned home hoping Adam would already be there. Just as she was pulling into the driveway, her cell phone rang. She stopped the car and checked the caller ID, it was Adam. "Hi, honey," he said, "what are you doing?"

"I just came back from the market and I was at Mom's checking on the cats. Where are you?"

"I'm still here. Howard and I are going to take another run out to the site and then he's invited me back to his home for dinner. I'm sorry, but I can't turn him down."

"Does that mean you won't be coming back today?"

"I'm afraid so. It will be much too late to drive home but I'll be leaving here first thing in the morning."

Charlotte was irritated, "I don't understand why you can't turn down his invitation."

"Come on, honey, please don't give me a hard time. I've been working my butt off and it's a long drive. Even if we get back from the site by five, I'm not going to feel like coming all the way back to Toronto."

Charlotte sighed, "Okay, well I guess I'll see you tomorrow then."

"Is everything else all right? Did you do anything exciting last night?"

"As a matter of fact I was out with Jodi until almost midnight," Charlotte replied rather smugly.

"Oh, good," Adam responded, "I hope you had a good time. Look, I have to run. I'll see you tomorrow at around noon. Bye, hon."

Charlotte didn't get a chance to say goodbye. She heard the dial tone and stared at the phone in her hand. He didn't even react to the fact she'd been out until midnight. Did that mean he trusted her or did it mean he didn't care?

Just before five, Charlotte's neighbour Rolf Erikson phoned to see if she and Adam would like to come over later for a drink. When she explained that Adam was out of town he told her she was still welcome to join them but, while she considered it momentarily, she really didn't feel like socializing. She wasn't hungry, but knew she needed to eat, so she made herself a cheese omelette and a fruit salad and then settled down to read the paper. It was still only six-thirty when she was through reading nearly every section, except the sports news, and she was feeling restless. She decided to pour herself a glass of wine, then took it out into the garden and sat down on one of the lawn chairs. Soon, Zoe came creeping through the grass and landed with a thump on her lap, nearly knocking the glass out of her hand. Charlotte was startled but pleased to have the companionship, "Oh, Zoe," she whispered, "I guess it's just you and me tonight."

Zoe settled down purring with delight but with one eye open watching the birds that could be seen flitting among the trees. Just the closeness of her made Charlotte more relaxed and, after she finished the wine, she closed her eyes and started to doze off. She wasn't sure how long she'd been asleep but, when the sound of the telephone ringing in the house awoke her, it was already getting dark. She jumped up, tipping Zoe onto the grass, ran through the back door, and grabbed the phone sitting on the kitchen counter, "Hello," she said breathing heavily.

"Charlotte, are you all right?"

It was Jodi. "Oh, yes. I was out in the garden and had to run indoors. I'm surprised to hear from you again so soon. Did you forget something last night?"

Jodi hesitated, "I've been debating whether to call you or not."

"Why what's wrong? Is there something I can do to help?"

"No, Charlotte, I'm fine but I need to see you."

"What tonight? I saw you last night. Now you're making me curious. Do you want to come here?"

"No, I want you to get in your car and come downtown . . . ."

Charlotte cut in, "No way, not until you tell me what this is all about."

There was a long pause and then Jodi said, "Adam's here."

Charlotte gasped, "Where? Where are you?"

"I'm with Rick in the Rooftop Lounge of the Thompson and Adam's sitting at the end of the bar."

Charlotte felt her anger rising, "I don't believe you. Why are you doing this to me again?"

"Why on earth would I be telling you to come and see for yourself? This is the last thing I would wish on my best friend."

"Well, if you're so sure it's him why don't you go and talk to him?" Charlotte snapped back.

"Because then he might take off and then you'll question whether I'm telling you the truth even though Rick is here to back me up."

Charlotte's mind was racing, "The Thompson, that's on King Street isn't it?"

"Yes, at Bathurst and hurry. He only just arrived a few minutes ago but who knows how long he'll stay."

"I'll be there," Charlotte called out at the same time as she was hanging up the receiver.

She hardly remembered racing upstairs, changing into a pair of white capris and a black tank top, checking her make up and running a comb through her hair. All the way from the house to the hotel her mind was in turmoil. This couldn't be Adam, he was in Ottawa. If it was him, was he alone? She forgot to ask Jodi that. What was she going to say to him? Could she ever trust him again? Was this the end of their marriage? She was so overwhelmed with her thoughts that, when she saw the hotel had valet parking, she quickly handed over her keys and raced through the lobby searching for an elevator. Once inside, she saw the indicator for the Rooftop Lounge and held her breath as the elevator ascended, occasionally stopping to let guests on or off. Finally she was standing at the entrance to the lounge and looking around her in a panic. Just seconds later, Jodi was embracing her and leading her to a banquette just a few steps away. Rick got up to greet her and she quickly shook his hand but her eyes were searching the room. "Where is he?" she demanded still standing.

Jodi motioned for her to sit down but Charlotte shook her head, "He's at the far end of the bar but I think you need to calm down before you race over there."

Charlotte strained to see in the subdued lighting, "Is that him with some blond woman?" she asked.

Jodi nodded and grabbed Charlotte's hand, "Please think about what you're going to say. You don't want to make a big scene."

Charlotte stared at Jodi and frowned, "And why not? My husband who is supposed to be in Ottawa is sitting in a bar in Toronto with another woman and I'm not allowed to make a scene. Watch me."

Jodi started to follow as Charlotte stalked through the lounge and headed for the couple at the far end of the bar. Rick look on helplessly as Jodi stepped up her pace but Charlotte was too quick for her. When she finally got close enough to see that, even with his back to her, it was indeed

Adam, she stopped in her tracks and Jodi finally caught up with her. She grabbed Charlotte's arm but she shook her off and took a step forward, "Adam" she whispered. The only reaction was from the attractive blond perched on the side of the barstool. She stared up at Charlotte with a puzzled look on her face. Charlotte returned the look with a scowl and repeated in a louder voice, "Adam."

The man swivelled around and Charlotte immediately stepped back, almost knocking Jodi over. Her hand flew to her mouth and she was speechless for a moment then she cried out, "Who are you?"

The man smiled and stood up, "Well, I'm certainly not Adam."

Both Charlotte and Jodi were staring with their mouths open. The man standing in front of them was almost identical in looks to Adam, same height, same features and same brown hair. Charlotte leaned forward trying to take it all in and even, in the dim light, she could see the same green eyes. Why did she instinctively know it wasn't Adam, the difference was almost imperceptible? It wasn't the clothes, even though he was wearing an outfit she knew Adam didn't possess. Then she suddenly noticed it, the small scar running from the top of his lip to the bottom of his nose. This was not her husband.

The man stood there being observed and still smiling, "Well ladies, I'm not used to all this attention but I'm rather enjoying it. How about I buy you both a drink?"

Jodi motioned to the blond, "You're friend might object."

The man turned to look at the woman, "Oh, we only just met a few minutes ago. If you will excuse me I'm going to join these ladies."

The blond shrugged and turned her back on them as he steered Jodi and Charlotte to a banquette near the windows. Both of them were too shocked to object until after they were all seated and he was motioning to the waiter. Jodi was the first to find her voice, "Who are you?" she asked.

"Julian Richards," he replied, "and who are you?" he said looking directly at Charlotte.

"I'm Jodi and this is my friend Charlotte."

Julian continued to stare at Charlotte who was staring back with her hand held at her throat. "I think the lady can speak for herself," he retorted, almost in a whisper.

Jodi shook her head, "Personally, I think you'll find she's in shock at the moment. You have an uncanny resemblance to her husband in fact, you could be his twin."

Julian glanced over at Jodi, "Funny you should say that, I got stopped by someone on the street yesterday thinking I was someone else."

At that moment, the waiter arrived to take their order but hesitated when Rick tapped him on the shoulder and said, "Excuse me for a moment, could you come back in a few minutes?" The waiter nodded and went back to the bar. "What's going on, Jodi?" Rick asked.

Julian got to his feet, "Hi, I'm Julian," he said, "I'm sorry I didn't realize these ladies were with anyone."

Rick got his first real look at Julian and slowly extended his hand, "Rick Chalmers, holy crow man, you're the spitting image of Charlotte's husband."

"So I've just been told. Why don't you join us?" Julian responded.

Rick shook his head, "No thanks, I think Jodi and I will head home."

Jodi looked up at him, "What about Charlotte, we can't leave her here?"

For the first time since they sat down, Charlotte finally reacted. She reached over and took Jodi's hand, "It's okay, I want to stay. You go with Rick and I'll talk to you tomorrow."

Jodi withdrew her hand, gathered up her purse, and stood up, "Are you absolutely sure you're going to be all right?"

"I'm absolutely sure," Charlotte answered turning back to look at Julian.

Rick said goodnight and then taking Jodi by the arm, he led her towards the elevator but she kept looking back over her shoulder. She couldn't imagine what Charlotte must be thinking.

Chapter Thirteen

Julian smiled and moved closer to Charlotte, "Maybe we can have that drink now that your friends have gone," he said.

Charlotte lowered her gaze, "I'm sorry but I can't stop staring at you. You really do look exactly like my husband."

Julian beckoned to the waiter who was circling the room and ordered two vodka martinis. "I hope you like martinis," he said, making a statement rather than asking a question.

Charlotte ignored his remark, "I really need you to tell me who you are."

Julian smiled, "I'll be happy to tell you all about myself once I get to know you better. In the meantime, tell me why you came here tonight. Were you looking for your husband?"

Just then the waiter returned with their drinks but when Charlotte attempted to pick up her glass her hand was shaking, "I'm really nervous," she admitted, leaving the glass on the table.

"I guarantee if you drink that down you won't be nervous anymore."

Charlotte tried again and managed to bring the glass up to her lips. She took a sip and made a face, "Oh, my goodness, that's so strong."

Julian chuckled, "I bet you're usually a wine drinker. Don't worry you'll get used to it."

Charlotte put the glass down and started to pick up her purse, "I think I should leave."

Julian reached over and took the purse out of her hand and laid it on the table, "You can't leave now. We've only just met."

"I need to go home. My husband might be waiting for me."

Julian smiled, "I don't believe you. A short while ago, you thought he was here. In fact, I think you expected to find him with another woman."

Charlotte reached for her purse again and tried to stand up but Julian scooted along the banquette beside her and pulled her back down, "Please don't go. At least finish your drink. It isn't often I'm fortunate enough to meet such a beautiful woman."

Charlotte glanced around and noticed several woman wearing elegant cocktail dresses and then looked down at her own simple outfit. She paused for a moment and then looked directly at Julian, "What do you want from me? I shouldn't even be here."

"I'd just like to get to know you better," Julian whispered taking her hand.

Charlotte struggled to control her emotions. Her head was telling her to run for the nearest exit but her heart was telling her something else. She picked up her glass and took another sip of the martini, "I'll stay for just a little while," she said.

Thirty minutes later, Julian had managed to discover almost everything there was to know about Charlotte and her family but she still knew nothing about him. By the time she had finished her second martini, she really didn't care. She was more relaxed than she had been for a long time and all thoughts of going home had vanished. When Julian suggested going to a nightclub, a block or two away where they had a dance floor, Charlotte was too caught up in the moment to refuse. A short time later, she found herself at the Reservoir Lounge in the arms of a stranger and she suddenly felt more alive than she had for years. Adam had never been keen on dancing and whenever they had been to a club and seen couples whirling around the floor, she had always felt envious and a little resentful. Now, she was in her element and it seemed as though Julian was too. It was obvious from the moment they took their first few steps, he knew exactly what he was doing.

Charlotte lost count of the time they stayed on the dance floor and during that time they never spoke a word. It was enough that, every now and again, Julian would stare into her eyes or she would lay her head on his shoulder and he would tighten his arm around her. Warning bells were ringing in Charlotte's head but she didn't want the night to end. Just before closing time, Julian led her back to the table to have one last drink. "I want to see you again," he said.

Charlotte shook her head, "That's not possible. I'm a married woman."

Julian smiled, "A married woman looking for a husband who she thinks is cheating on her."

"But it was you all along. He wasn't cheating on me."

"Nevertheless, you obviously don't trust him."

"I can't do this," Charlotte said reaching for her purse, "I have to go home."

"I assume you're taking a taxi, you've had too much to drink to drive."

"I'm perfectly okay," Charlotte shot back as she stood up and then sat down again rather abruptly.

Julian nodded very slowly, "I don't think you are. Let me drive you."

Charlotte gasped, "What come to my house? No, absolutely not."

"I wasn't intending to come in. Look, we'll walk outside and I'll flag down a taxi."

"What about my car?"

"You can pick it up tomorrow. I'm sure you can find some excuse for why you couldn't drive home."

Charlotte got up again, a little more steadily this time. "I really have to go."

Julian signalled for the waiter and stood up, "I'll just settle this bill and then we can leave."

Outside on the street, a few moments later, Julian was holding Charlotte's hand and for some reason she didn't attempt to pull away. They noticed a taxi parked near the hotel just over a short block away and started to walk towards it, "I'll be here tomorrow," Julian said. "Why don't you meet me for lunch and then you can pick up your car."

Charlotte shook her head, "No, I can't see you again. I just need to go home now."

Julian squeezed Charlotte's hand and then swung her around so that she was facing him. "Are you sure that's what you want?"

Charlotte nodded but, as she did so, Julian leaned forward and kissed her on the lips and Charlotte could no longer resist him. "What time and where?" she whispered.

"There's a great restaurant called Brassaii on King Street. Meet me there for brunch at noon. I'm not sure of the exact address but it's just west of Spadina."

"I'll find it," Charlotte replied.

When Charlotte arrived home, she was greeted by Zoe meowing for her favourite treats, which were already long overdue. Charlotte picked her up and cuddled her trying to bring back a sense of normalcy but her head was still spinning from her encounter with Julian. Later, in the bedroom, she peeled off her clothes and, without even bothering to remove her make-up, she crawled under the covers not wanting to waste a moment thinking back over the time she had spent with him. Who was this man who could have easily passed for her husband? Was that why she was so attracted to him? Was it really possible they weren't related in some way? Maybe a distant cousin who Adam had never met? She hadn't learned a single thing about him, she had been so caught up in the moment and maybe a little drunk, but she was determined to find out. Her heart skipped a beat when she thought about seeing him again within a few hours and then she suddenly remembered Adam. He said he would be arriving home at noon. What excuse could she give for not being there? As she pondered this dilemma, she began to feel drowsy and then promptly fell asleep only to wake up as dawn broke and begin pondering all over again.

Chapter Fourteen

Charlotte arrived at the Brassaii at noon. She had left a note for Adam telling him she'd had a call about a problem with one of Nancy's cats. She was going over to the house to take care of it and hoped to be back by mid-afternoon. As she wrote the words, she wondered how the lie came so easily to her. It wasn't in her nature to be deceptive and she felt guilty but, at the same time, she also sensed an element of excitement and even danger. What on earth was she doing and how would she explain the way she was dressed for a casual run over to her mother's house? Temperatures were above normal again and after searching through her closet, she came upon a dress she hadn't worn for a number of years. It was white with tiny pink flowers, a flowing knee length skirt, capped sleeves and a rather low scooped neck. After she put it on with her white, four-inch heel sandals and pink crystal earrings, she surveyed herself in the mirror and then did a pirouette. With her hair lightly curled and the make-up she had applied so carefully, she thought she looked rather attractive and she knew all her efforts were for Julian.

The moment she walked through the doors of the restaurant, she saw him. He was seated at a table near a window but immediately got up and came towards her.

She gasped when she saw him, the likeness to Adam was so astounding, but then she noticed his clothes. He was wearing a light-weight beige suit with the palest blue shirt open at the neck and she could tell, in the clear light of day, his outfit was expensive. Adam had always dressed well but he had always been conservative and wasn't inclined to follow current trends. Suddenly, her thoughts were cut off as Julian reached for her hand and looked straight into her eyes, "I wasn't sure you would come," he said.

"I wasn't sure I would either," Charlotte lied.

He led her back to the table, motioned to the waiter, ordered a bottle of Chardonnay and then smiled at her. "Well, this is really nice and you look absolutely stunning. I'm going to be the envy of every man in this room."

Charlotte smiled, "Thank you but I think that's a little bit of an exaggeration."

"Where did you tell your husband you were going looking so lovely?"

Charlotte hesitated rather surprised at such a direct question, "He's not home yet. He's on his way back from Ottawa."

"I see," Julian remarked nodding very slowly.

Just at that moment the waiter appeared with the wine and, after pouring two glasses, asked if they were ready to order. Julian requested a few more moments while they looked at the menu and after they both ended up ordering an egg dish, benedict for Julian and quiche for Charlotte, Julian said. "Drink up, the service is a bit slow here but the food is good."

Charlotte picked up her glass, "Maybe this would be a good time for you to tell me all about yourself. I got the feeling you were avoiding the subject last night."

Julian grinned, "Well, don't expect some epic story about how I grew up to be famous or anything like that. My life has been pretty ordinary really. Anyway, I guess I'll start at the beginning seeing that you're so interested. My mother came to Canada from Scotland when she was nineteen. She met my father soon after she arrived and they were married within a year. They settled in Laval, just outside of Montreal and that's where I was born and raised. When I was eight years old, my father left and I haven't seen him since. He could be dead for all I know and for all I care. My mother was a schoolteacher and my father, when he felt like working, was a carpenter. I don't have any brothers or sisters but it was still hard for my mother to take care of me. I was pretty rebellious when I was young but I realized when I got into my teens, I was just rebelling against my father and he wasn't even around. I've always regretted the times I was disrespectful to my mother and I've tried to make it up to her."

"Why did your father leave?"

"He left because he was selfish and didn't want to be responsible for a wife and child anymore. He had a violent temper and, although he never hit my mother, he was happy when I gave him a reason to take off his belt and use it on me."

"Oh, that's awful, I am so sorry. Where is your mother now?"

Charlotte watched as she saw Julian's eyes tear up, "She's in a long term care home in Montreal. She has Alzheimer's."

"Oh, how terrible for you," Charlotte said automatically reaching for Julian's hand.

Julian put his other hand on top of hers and then shook his head as if to shake away the memories and continued, "I went to Concordia University and majored in photography. Taking photos had become a passion of mine after Mom gave me a camera for my fourteenth birthday. Now I still live in Montreal and work for the Gazette. It's the only English language newspaper there."

"Surely you must be able to speak French?"

"Yes, fluently. My father was third generation French Canadian so I was brought up speaking both French and English."

"Have you ever been married? Do you have any children?"

Julian laughed, "My, you really do want to know everything, don't you? No, I've never been married."

Charlotte looked thoughtful, "Is there a possibility you could have been adopted or anything like that?"

Julian frowned, "No, of course not, why would you ask?"

"Because you look exactly like Adam; everything about you is identical except for this," and she gently reached over and touched the scar above his lip.

Julian immediately grabbed her hand, "Don't," he said abruptly.

Charlotte pulled away, "I'm sorry, I didn't mean to do that."

Just as she stopped speaking she heard the sound of a telephone and watched as Julian reached inside his jacket and retrieved a cell phone. He glanced down at it and then over at her, "Excuse me," he said, "but I need to answer this" And, with that, he got up from the table and walked towards the entrance to the restaurant.

Charlotte watched him go and wondered who was calling him. It was Sunday, so it couldn't have been anything to do with work. What if it was some woman? Why did she suddenly feel jealous? She toyed with her wine and looked around at the other tables. What if someone saw her here? How would she explain being with Julian? All kinds of ideas began to form in her head. Maybe she could pretend he was Adam's brother or perhaps a cousin. The more she thought about it, the more suspicious she became that there had to be some connection but what could it be? She was interrupted by the waiter bringing their lunch and then Julian suddenly appeared and sat down with a sigh, "Sorry, that was the paper. I was supposed to go back to Montreal on Tuesday but now they need me to stay in Toronto for the rest of the week to cover a news conference that's scheduled."

"You sound disappointed. Did you want to go back?"

"I did up until last night. Now, I couldn't be happier." He reached across the table and took Charlotte's hand. "I want to spend more time with you before I leave."

Charlotte withdrew her hand and picked up her fork, "Your lunch is getting cold," she remarked while secretly relieved at this new turn of events.

Julian sighed again and took another sip of wine, "You can ignore me until you've finished eating that rather appetizing looking quiche and then we'll have to have a serious conversation."

Charlotte looked across at him and grinned, "Eat your eggs and then maybe we'll talk."

Less than ten minutes later they were both enjoying a cup of Brassaii's delicious coffee and Charlotte could no longer avoid the inevitable. She had never felt so torn before. Every ounce of logic told her to stop this situation from going any further but her heart was telling her something else so, when Julian talked about seeing her again, she heard herself saying, "I'm free tomorrow, all day."

It was almost three o'clock when Julian escorted Charlotte back to the hotel to pick up her car. As they said their goodbyes, he kissed her a little more passionately than the day before and she drove away feeling exhilarated, desirable and not in the least bit guilty.

Chapter Fifteen

Charlotte was just leaving the downtown area when she heard her cell phone ringing on the seat beside her. She glanced down and saw it was Jodi calling but she didn't want to stop and she hadn't decided what she wanted to say to her. Then, as she turned onto Highland, she got another call and saw it was Jodi again so she stopped the car a block from the house and picked up the phone, "Hi Jodi," she said, "how are you?"

"Charlotte, where are you? I called you a few minutes ago and you didn't answer," Jodi responded rather abruptly.

"That's because I was driving and didn't want to stop. I'm just on my way home from Mom's. I was there checking on Gypsy and Luna."

"What happened last night after we left you? I've been dying to know. I meant to call you earlier but I was late getting up and then Rick and I went out for brunch."

"Nothing happened after you left."

There was a pause, "What do you mean nothing happened? Who was that guy? What did you find out about him?"

Charlotte sighed, "He was just someone who looked just like Adam but there's no connection. I guess everybody has a double somewhere."

"Come on Charlotte, that guy could be his twin. I'm not buying it. Where was he from? What does he do for a living? You must have asked him a lot of questions."

"Actually I didn't," Charlotte lied. "All I know is, he comes from Montreal and he works for a newspaper. He's in Toronto on an assignment."

"That's it? That's all you know about him? What else did you two talk about?"

Charlotte hesitated for a moment, "Look Jodi, I have to get home. I expect Adam is there by now and he's probably wondering where I am. We can talk about this some other time."

"You're stalling Charlotte, there's more to this isn't there?"

Charlotte began to feel the pressure and snapped back, "I have to go, I'll talk to you later," and she rang off.

Moments later she was walking through her front door. She knew Adam had arrived because his car was in the driveway so, as she made her way down the hall, she tried to put a smile on her face and called out, "Adam where are you?" There wasn't any answer so she checked the living room and family room and then decided to see if he was in the garden. When she noticed him lounging beside the pool with Zoe on the grass beside him she suddenly realized it gave her the perfect opportunity to run upstairs and change her clothes. It would be a lot simpler than having to make up some story about why she was all dolled up in a dress and heels. She could have said she was out having lunch with Jodi but she couldn't be certain Jodi hadn't tried to call her at home. She took two stairs at a time up to the bedroom, stripped off her dress and shoes and changed into a pair of white shorts and a pink tee. Then she ran into the bathroom and took off most of her make-up and realized she was still wearing the crystal earrings. She almost ripped them off of her ears just as she heard footsteps downstairs and Adam's voice calling out, "Charlotte, honey, is that you?"

She flushed the toilet for effect and then walked through the bedroom out onto the hallway. "Hi, hon," she called back, "yes it's me," and slowly she descended the stairs.

Adam looked up at her and smiled. "Well you look nice and fresh even though it's bloody hot out there. Where were you?"

Charlotte smiled back as she reached the bottom step, "Needed to go to the bathroom so badly, I almost didn't make it home."

Adam reached out for her and took her into his arms then kissed her on the cheek, "I didn't mean just now. Where did you go to? I've been home for a couple of hours. I was going to call you but I thought you'd show up at any moment."

Charlotte slipped out of his embrace, "I was at Mom's checking on the cats and then Mrs. Walker showed up and invited me to lunch. I just lost track of time. I'm sorry, Adam."

"No problem," he responded taking her hand, "you're here now. Why don't I open a bottle of wine and we can sit out by the pool for a while."

Charlotte nodded and walked with him into the kitchen, "I really should think about preparing dinner," she said.

Adam released her hand and pulled a bottle of Riesling from the wine rack, "Let's just order in," he suggested, it's too hot to cook. I wouldn't mind Chinese tonight if that's okay with you."

"That's fine with me," Charlotte answered, "I'll just go back upstairs and put on my bathing suit. I feel like having a swim."

"Good idea," Adam remarked as she walked out of the door.

The rest of the day was like any other Sunday except that Charlotte was terrified each time she heard the ringing of her cell phone. She had given Julian her number but he had promised he wouldn't call until Monday morning. The first call she got was from Jodi but she didn't answer it and when Adam questioned her she said she just didn't feel like talking to her right then. Later, she got a call from the library apologizing for the short notice but asking if she could come in on Monday instead of Tuesday as originally scheduled. When she responded she was sorry but she wasn't available on Monday, Adam wanted to know why. She could hardly believe how easily the lie came to her when she claimed she had a dental appointment and quickly tried to steer the conversation in another direction. She feigned interest in the work Adam was doing with Howard, creating a whole new sub-division just outside of Ottawa, and wanted to know if he would be going back in the near future. When he told her there was a possibility he would have to meet with Howard again on Thursday and hoped she wouldn't be too upset about him being out of town again, she felt a sense of relief. She immediately thought of Julian but pretended to be mildly disappointed, "Oh, that's too bad. It gets a little lonely around here without you and the kids. I'll be glad when Alexa gets back."

Just before eleven, after watching the latest news on CNN, Charlotte announced she was tired and going up to bed. Adam stretched out on the sofa, "Okay, hon, you go on up and I'll be along in a few minutes. I just want to catch the baseball scores on CTV."

Charlotte crawled into bed hoping against hope Adam wasn't in an amorous mood when he finally came upstairs. She needn't have worried because he fell asleep on the sofa and didn't get to bed until almost two, when she was sound asleep and dreaming of someone else.

Chapter Sixteen

On Monday morning, Charlotte was up at the crack of dawn, preparing his breakfast, when Adam made it downstairs at just after seven. He was in his usual business attire, dark suit, crisp white shirt and muted tie, clean shaven and not a hair out of place. Charlotte couldn't help comparing him to Julian, who had the same handsome features but a distinctly different style. She had always been proud of Adam and the way he presented himself to others but when she thought about Julian with his hair falling forward over his forehead and curling slightly over his collar and his trendy clothes, she was aware there was something clearly sensual about him. Adam interrupted her thoughts as he sat down at the table and took a sip of his coffee, "Sorry about last night, hon. I didn't realize how tired I was. It was a bit of a shock when I woke up on the sofa."

"It's all right, I was tired too. I fell asleep as soon as my head touched the pillow," Charlotte responded as she buttered two pieces of toast.

"I'll try and be home early. Don't make dinner. We'll go out somewhere, maybe somewhere on King Street."

Charlotte stopped what she was doing for a brief moment when her hand started to shake, "Ummm, let's wait until later to decide where to go." Again, the lie came so effortlessly,

"Mom told me there was a really nice new restaurant near here."

"Okay, I'm easy. Find out the name and we'll give it a try."

Charlotte excused herself claiming she was in the middle of doing laundry and, twenty minutes later, Adam called out that he was leaving and she heard the front door close. She immediately raced up from the laundry room and, peeking through the front window, watched his car drive away. It was still not even eight o'clock and she was already wondering when Julian would call her.

Just after ten, her cell phone rang and she pulled it from the pocket of her shorts. She didn't recognize the number and answered with almost a whisper, "Hello?"

The voice at the other end was unmistakable, "How is my beautiful lady this morning?"

Charlotte's heart skipped a beat, "Julian, I was wondering if you would call."

"Did you doubt it for a moment? You said you were free today, when can I see you?"

"How about this afternoon, but I have to be home in time for dinner?"

"Ah, I gather hubby is back but that's okay, I can meet you at around two. What would you like to do?"

"I'm not sure but perhaps we could go for a drive. It would be a shame to spend the time indoors."

"Mmmmm . . . depends what one is doing indoors," Julian replied suggestively.

Charlotte pretended to ignore the remark, "We might as well just take my car. I'll pick you up outside your hotel at two and we can drive to the Scarborough Bluffs. Have you ever been there?"

"No I haven't but I've heard about it. Bring a blanket and a couple of glasses and I'll bring some wine."

After they said goodbye Charlotte ran upstairs to try and figure out what to wear. After sorting through her closet, she realized she really needed to buy some new clothes and vowed to make a trip to the mall before the week was out. She eventually decided on a lavender calf-length skirt Nancy had given her, a plain white tank top and a pair of white sandals with wedge heels. She quickly slipped the outfit on, added a white bead necklace and then stood back to survey herself in the mirror. Satisfied that she would be dressed appropriately for an afternoon drive, she took the outfit off again, put on her shorts and tee and went back to the kitchen to retrieve all of the ingredients she needed for making a chocolate peanut butter pie. As she began to crush the Oreo cookies for the crust, she glanced up at the clock. It was still only just after eleven and she had about two and a half hours to kill before she left the house. The minutes seem to crawl by but by the time she finally finished with the pie and it was already in the freezer, it was almost noon. She decided to make herself a sandwich and take it out to the garden to relax for a while but, just as she was about to go out of the back door, she heard her cell phone. Running back to the kitchen, plate still in hand, she glanced at the phone and saw it was Jodi. She was the last person Charlotte wanted to speak to right then. There was no way she could tell Jodi what was really going on. Letting the phone continue to ring, she retraced her steps and exited the door to the garden.

Settling down in a lounge chair near the pool she looked around her at the trees bordering the huge lawn and then back up at the house. Suddenly, it began to dawn on her that she could lose everything. She loved Adam and the home he had made for her and the children. She could be jeopardizing all of the things she treasured the most by seeing Julian. Then she began to rationalize that she hadn't really done anything wrong. All they'd ever done was talk, except for a small goodbye kiss. Then why was she so concerned about how she looked? Just then Zoe appeared at her feet and she picked off a piece of prosciutto and placed it on the grass under her nose. She sniffed at it once and then walked away. "Fussy little miss, aren't you." Charlotte remarked shaking her head.

She continued to consider whether what she was doing was foolish and even thought about not showing up at the hotel but the attraction was too strong. Just before one-fifteen she stepped out of the bathtub, dried herself off and slipped into the outfit she had picked out earlier. She had actually deliberated about wearing the red lace bra and panties she bought at the lingerie party but when she realized what she was really thinking, she quickly changed her mind. It took her almost ten minutes to get her hair looking just right and she had little time left to put on her make-up but at exactly twenty minutes to two she was backing out of her driveway onto Highland.

Julian was waiting outside the hotel when she arrived, even though she was a few minutes early. She couldn't help noticing how incredibly sexy he looked in a pair of tailored khaki chinos and a black tee that emphasized his broad shoulders and muscular arms. She hadn't seen him without a jacket before and it was obvious he worked out. Once again, she was comparing him to Adam who still had a good physique but had gained ten pounds in the past few years, mostly around his mid-section.

Julian jumped into the passenger seat, "Bonjour beautiful lady," he said reaching across to give her a peck on the cheek. "Drive on to the bluffs!"

Charlotte smiled, "Not until you fasten your seat belt."

Charlotte had been to Scarborough Bluffs on a number of occasions but sharing the experience with Julian was special. It was as though she was seeing the great rock formations for the first time and the view of the lake with dozens of sail boats had her dreaming of far off places. Later they visited Bluffer's Park beach and stretched out on the sand on a blanket discreetly sipping on the Chardonnay that Julian had brought with him. There were a number of other people on the beach and several swimming just off shore but it seemed as though they only had eyes for each other.

"What are you thinking about?" Julian asked gently stroking Charlotte's arm.

"I just can't believe I'm here with you," she replied. "Never in my wildest dreams did I ever imagine deceiving Adam."

"But apparently you thought he was deceiving you. The night we met, was that the first time you thought he might be with someone else?"

Charlotte shook her head, "No, actually it wasn't. Over a year ago, when Adam was supposed to be in Montreal, Jodi's brother was positive he saw him with a woman in New York at the St. Regis."

Julian suddenly looked shocked, "That's where I always stay when I'm there, so I guess that must have been me too."

"My mother talked me out of saying anything to Adam because she was sure it was a case of mistaken identity but when it happened again, I confronted him."

"When was the second time?"

"Jodi was at the theatre with Rick and she was sure she saw Adam, this time with a blond woman."

"Which theatre was this?"

"The Princess of Wales, here in Toronto."

Julian gasped, "Oh that's right, I was there. What happened when you confronted Adam?"

"He vehemently denied it and we had an awful row. Then he spoke to Eleanor, she's the wife of his business partner, and she made him understand why I reacted the way I did. I've known Jodi since high school and she's my best friend so she had no reason to lie to me. After that he apologized for the way he snapped at me and I decided to try and forget about it."

"So what happened on Saturday?"

"Well, Adam was supposed to be in Ottawa and I got a call from Jodi telling me she was at the Thompson and Adam was sitting at the end of the bar with a woman. She insisted I get in my car and see for myself. You know the rest."

"I can't believe I really look that much like your husband."

Charlotte reached up and brushed Julian's hair away from his forehead, "That's what's so uncanny. You look exactly like him except, I can see now, you're a little more muscular and then there's the scar."

Julian rubbed his hand across his mouth but Charlotte grasped his fingers and pulled his hand away, "You seem to be very self-conscious about it. How did you get it?"

Julian shook his head, "I'd really rather not talk about it if you don't mind," he said in a gentle voice.

Charlotte slowly nodded, "All right but I'd like to ask you something. Is there any possibility that you might be related to Adam? Did your mother or father have brothers or sisters? Maybe you're cousins."

"My father didn't have any siblings and my mother had a sister but she never had any children."

"I just can't help feeling there's a connection somewhere."

Julian laughed, "Maybe my mother had a secret son but even if I asked her she wouldn't be able to tell me."

"I'm sorry about your mom, I really am."

Julian jumped up, "Me too, but let's not think about sad things. I challenge you to a race along the beach."

Charlotte looked up at him and grinned, "You're kidding, right?"

"No, I'm not kidding," he replied pulling her to her feet. "I'll race you to that tree and the loser gets to buy dinner".

Charlotte pulled him around to face her, "I told you, I have to be home for dinner today."

Julian sighed, "That's right, I forgot." Then he raced off along the sand while Charlotte watched and wondered what she was going to do.

On the drive back, Julian was quiet while Charlotte's mind was in a whirlwind. Not only was she curious as to what he was thinking but his hand was resting on her bare thigh where her skirt has crept up over her knees. When she had to stop rather suddenly at a crossing and his hand slid even further up her thigh, she began to feel a sensation between her legs and shifted awkwardly in her seat. Julian looked over at her, "Is something bothering you?"

Charlotte gave a deep sigh, "I think you know what's bothering me."

"Is it this?" he asked as his fingers crept a little higher.

She let out a gasp and reached down to stop him from going any further, "Please not here," she begged.

"Where then?" he asked as she began to drive off again. "You have to know by now that I really want you."

Charlotte hesitated and then shook her head, "I can't do this, Julian. I thought I could but I can't. I love Adam and I've never looked at another man in all the years we've been together."

"Are you saying you don't want to sleep with me?"

"I'm saying I can't see you again after today. I'll drop you off at the hotel and then I'm going straight home to my husband."

Julian slowly nodded and then to Charlotte's surprise said, "If that's what you really want I'm not going to pressure you."

She turned to look at him but he was staring straight ahead, "Do you really mean that?"

"Of course I mean it but if you change your mind within the next couple of days, you know where to reach me."

Neither one of them spoke during the rest of the drive back to the hotel but, when Charlotte stopped the car to let Julian out, he reached over and pulled her towards him. She didn't resist as he kissed her on the lips and then said, "Ciao, pretty lady," and then he was gone.

All the way back to the house Charlotte wavered between two emotions, regret and relief. She regretted ending the brief affair because the attraction to Julian was so strong but relieved she had never taken it further and could face Adam with a clear conscience. He would never need to know she had been seeing Julian and, in a few days, she was sure she could put it all behind her but it didn't quite turn out that way.

Chapter Seventeen

That evening, Adam took Charlotte to dinner at the new restaurant Nancy had mentioned and most of the conversation centred on Adam's work and the children. Occasionally, Charlotte felt her mind drifting to thoughts of Julian but she quickly pulled herself back and concentrated on what Adam was saying. It was only when they later crawled into bed and he pulled her into his arms that she felt herself tense up, "I'm awfully tired, hon. I think I might be coming down with something."

Adam rolled onto his back, "You seemed fine before."

"I know. I'm sorry. My stomach feels a bit upset. Do you mind if we just go to sleep."

Adam reached over and patted her shoulder then turned his back on her, "No problem. Hope you feel better in the morning."

Charlotte stared at the ceiling for a few minutes and then closed her eyes. Suddenly all her thoughts were of Julian.

On Tuesday, Charlotte worked at the library all day and arrived home at five in time to prepare dinner. Adam had already called to say he would be home by six and it seemed as though life was already returning to normal. Then, thirty minutes before Adam was due to walk through the front door, the doorbell rang. Charlotte had no idea who it could be and answered with a little trepidation. Her heart skipped a beat when she was confronted by a delivery man carrying a very large bouquet of red roses. In a daze, she signed the delivery slip and then quietly closed the door and walked back to the kitchen. Gently, she unwrapped the cellophane and removed a small white card from one of the stems. It simply said, "*I miss you already.*"

She looked up at the clock in a panic. Adam would be home soon and she had no idea how she would explain the roses. Quickly she tore up the card, threw it into the trash can and was looking for a vase when, a moment later, she heard the front door open and Adam called out, "Hi, hon, I'm home."

Holding her breath, she hesitated and then called back, "I'm in the kitchen."

The sight of two dozen roses scattered on the kitchen counter stopped Adam in his tracks as he entered through the kitchen door, "Whoa, what's all this?" he asked.

Charlotte shrugged her shoulders, "I have no idea," she lied. "They just arrived and I don't know who they're from."

Adam walked over and picked up one of the roses, "Wasn't there a card?"

Charlotte shook her head, "No, nothing."

"Well, were they for you? Do you have a copy of the delivery slip?"

"Yes they were for me and I don't have any slip."

"And you don't have any idea who they're from?"

Charlotte grinned, "I think you sent them."

Adam shook his head, "I assure you, I didn't. I can only assume you have a secret admirer."

"Well if I do, I don't know who it is."

Adam started to walk away, "Well I guess you'd better put them in some water. I'm going up to change."

Charlotte stared at his back as he left the kitchen. Her hands began to shake as she put the roses, one by one, in the vase and stooped over to take in the scent. "Oh, Julian," she thought, "why did you do this?"

There was no further talk about the roses even though they sat predominantly in the family room near the entertainment centre and were in Adam's line of sight as he watched television later that evening. Charlotte tried to keep busy doing the odd chore around the house and was tempted, on two or three occasions, to call Julian to tell him not to contact her again but she never made the call.

On Wednesday, Adam left for the office as usual, and Charlotte decided to continue her research for their planned trip east and then check on Gypsy and Luna again. All day, she was on edge wondering if there would be any more surprise deliveries she wouldn't be able to explain or if Julian would try and contact her in some other way but, by late that night, she had not heard from him.

The next morning, as planned, Adam left to go to Ottawa. She expected him back on Saturday and she had two whole days to herself. She was supposed to be at the library but couldn't face it and, for the first time that she could remember, she called in sick. She had always enjoyed being around books and she liked dealing with people. She had even thought about applying for a full time position but today her mind was miles away from discussing who was on the best seller list or where to locate the history of the ancient world. She had asked Julian not to contact her but all day, whenever the phone rang or there was a knock on the door, her heart beat a little faster. Not expecting her to be home on a work day, Nancy had called to leave her a message and was surprised when Charlotte picked up the phone. They were having such a great time and were taking the ferry to Vancouver for a couple of days to stay with Peggy's daughter and would be out of touch until Sunday. Then there were the usual amount of telemarketing calls where, in total frustration, Charlotte would listen to the typical few seconds of silence but, before the robotic voice came on, she would hang up the phone. When there was someone at the door, she prayed it was more roses, but it was UPS delivering the coffee she had ordered for her Keurig coffee maker.

By mid-afternoon, desperate to hear Julian's voice again, she placed a call to the hotel and asked to be put through to his room. It seemed to take forever before she heard the ringing tone and she held her breath. Then, suddenly, the operator came back on and advised her Mr. Richards was not in his room and asked if she wished to leave a message. Flustered, she quickly rang off and sank down onto the nearest chair. She knew she was playing a dangerous game but she couldn't help herself and, a few minutes later, she was rummaging in a drawer for a notepad.

Traffic was already starting to build up as rush hour began and Charlotte grew more and more impatient as she headed downtown towards the hotel. Not wanting to park, she begged one of the valets to watch her car while she ran into the lobby. When he shook his head, she slipped him a ten dollar bill and his demeanour changed. Smiling, he told her she had five minutes and she was off running through the front doors and up to the reception desk, all the while looking around her hoping Julian wouldn't see her dressed only in a pair of shorts and a tank top with her hair in a pony tail. Her note addressed to Mr. Julian Richards was accepted by the reservations clerk who assured her it would be delivered to him as soon as possible. At that point, she almost snatched it back from the woman, who was already eyeing her with a little suspicion, but then without responding she looked nervously around her again and ran back to retrieve her car and race back home. All the way there, she was so tense, she cut off another driver and was oblivious to his profanity as he yelled insults at her. She couldn't help wishing she could turn back the clock and make it all go away but it was too late. Julian would get her note and he would either ignore it or he would get in touch with her. Waiting would be unbearable.

The phone was ringing as Charlotte walked through the front door of her house. Dropping her keys onto the hall table, she raced into the kitchen and, with a shaking hand, she picked up the phone. It was Adam. "Hi, hon," he said, "I wasn't sure if you'd be home from work yet. I was going to leave a message."

"I just got here. Why are you calling?" she asked rather abruptly.

"Whoa, sorry if I disturbed you," he shot back sarcastically.

Charlotte sighed, "I'm sorry, I was just in a rush when I heard the phone. How was the drive up?"

"Oh, pretty boring, as usual, but it gave me more time to think about the project and prepare for anything Howard throws at me. I just wanted you to know I'm not staying at the hotel. Howard's invited me to stay at his house. I can give you the number in case you need to get in touch with me."

Charlotte took down the number and they chatted for a few more minutes but she couldn't wait to get him off the line. What if Julian was trying to call her and the line was busy? But, two hours later, there had been no more calls and her mind was in turmoil again. Maybe he didn't get the note yet. Maybe he got it but decided not to contact her. Maybe he got it but was busy and would call her later or maybe, and the most alarming thought, he would show up on her doorstep. At seven o'clock, after not having eaten since eleven that day, she felt the beginnings of a headache coming on and knew she needed to put something in her stomach. She was in the kitchen when Zoe wandered in crying pitifully because her bowl was empty and Charlotte realized just how obsessed she'd been thinking about Julian. She had almost forgotten about her precious pet. She quickly filled Zoe's bowl then tried to decide what to get for herself but, at that moment, the phone on the counter right beside her rang. It startled her and her heart began to race as she tentatively picked it up and said, "Hello."

There was no mistaking the voice on the other end of the line. "Charlotte, it's Julian, I was pleasantly surprised to get your note. How are you?" he asked in almost a whisper.

Charlotte's hand flew to her throat and she almost tripped over her words as she answered, "Oh, Julian, I'm so happy you called. I had to talk to you or see you again before you went back to Montreal."

"Why didn't you just telephone me?"

"I did but you weren't in your room and I didn't want to leave a message. Then I thought about it again and decided to leave you a note instead."

"So you drove all the way to the hotel?"

"Well, I was downtown so it was easy to just drop in," she lied. "I hope you're not annoyed with me."

"On the contrary, I've been thinking about you a lot but you asked me not to contact you and I had to respect your wishes."

"But it's not what I want any more. I've been thinking about you too, in fact I haven't stopped thinking about you." There was silence and then Charlotte asked, "Julian, are you still there?"

"Yes. Where's your husband. Is he out of town again?" he asked abruptly.

Charlotte hesitated. She was beginning to feel a sense of desperation. "Please, Julian, I don't want to talk about Adam. I just want to see you."

Julian paused and then replied, "Then come to my hotel room tonight."

Charlotte grasped the edge of the counter for support as she began to feel weak at the knees, "I'll be there," she whispered, "I just need some time to change."

"I'm in Room 582, I'll be waiting," Julian whispered back and then hung up the phone.

Chapter Eighteen

Less than an hour later, Charlotte was knocking on the door of Room 582. After Julian's call, she had frantically run upstairs, showered, and then pulled half her clothes out of her closet searching for something to wear. It didn't take long to find the little black dress with the cap sleeves and scoop neck she had bought on a whim a year ago but had never worn. She threw it onto the bed and then opened the drawer where she knew she would find the red bra and panties. Standing naked, in front of the mirror, she held them up in front of her. It took her just seconds to make a decision. Hurriedly she put them on, glanced in the mirror again and then pulled the dress over her head. Ten minutes later, she had straightened her hair so that it fell like a golden curtain around her shoulders, put on her make-up and a pair of silver earrings and then, slipping into black four-inch sandals, was running out the front door.

All the way to the hotel, she experienced an emotion she had never felt before. When she first met Adam, before every date, she was always excited but this was different. She was exhilarated and her heart was racing and she knew what she was doing was dangerous. What was it about Julian, who looked so much like Adam that made her feel this way? Was that what this was really all about? Was she intrigued by the possibility there was some connection and some deep dark secret lurking in the past? Would this be the last time she would see Julian?

She held her breath waiting for him to answer the door and then suddenly he was standing there reaching for her hand and pulling her inside. A moment later, she was in his arms and he was kissing her with such passion, she felt completely helpless and when he finally pulled away and drew her towards the bed she knew there was no turning back.

Laying her down gently, he slowly turned her over and while kissing the back of her neck, unzipped her dress and pulled it down off one shoulder so that most of her back was exposed. Then he proceeded to place feather like kisses all over her back until she could no longer bear it. She rolled over, slid off the bed, kicked off her shoes, and dropped her dress onto the floor. Julian wasted no time; he was on his feet and gathering her into his arms again. "You are beautiful," he murmured. "You must know how much I want to make love to you."

Charlotte could already feel that he was aroused. "That's why I'm here," she whispered.

In the next two hours, they made love three times. It was an experience Charlotte had never encountered before and she felt almost immoral, but very sensual and absolutely exhausted. It didn't take a genius to realize Julian was skilled in the art of making love to a woman and she had reacted in ways that both excited and frightened her at the same time. Charlotte couldn't help wondering just how many women he had been with. She was on the verge of falling asleep when Julian patted her playfully on her rear end and said, "Come on sleepy head, I'm hungry. If you'd like to wash up, there's a robe in the bathroom you can wear and while you're doing that, I'll order room service."

Charlotte remembered she hadn't eaten for almost twelve hours, "Okay, I just want to hang these up," she said slipping off the bed and gathering up her clothes as she headed for the bathroom.

When she came back, five minutes later, Julian was sitting in one of the wing chairs beside a small round table, wearing a short tartan robe and a pair of matching mules. Charlotte smiled, "Nice outfit," she commented.

"Thanks," Julian replied grinning. "Come and sit down, the food should be here in a few minutes and I've ordered a bottle of Chardonnay."

"It's awfully late to be eating but I haven't had anything since eleven this morning."

"Me neither. I was going to take you to dinner but when I opened the door and saw you, all thoughts of food went out the window."

Charlotte sat down and reached for his hand, "Eating was the last thing on my mind when I was driving down here."

Julian laughed, "I gathered that when I saw that sexy red outfit you had on. I didn't think you normally dressed that way."

Charlotte shook her head, "You were pretty sure of yourself weren't you?"

"Look, Charlotte, there was no denying the fact there was chemistry between us. I knew it was only a matter of time before we'd be sleeping together."

"Even though I told you never to contact me again?"

Julian squeezed her hand, "I knew you'd come around."

"You did? What gave you that idea?"

Julian smiled, "Underneath all that conventional wife and mother exterior, I could tell there was a tigress waiting to emerge."

Charlotte blushed, "You certainly have a way with words. No wonder women are attracted to you."

"Contrary to what you may think, there haven't been that many women in my life."

"Oh? There are two I can think of. One was a brunette in New York and another was a blond at the theatre here in Toronto, never mind that other blond you were in the process of picking up in the bar the other night."

Julian started to laugh, "I think I detect a little bit of jealousy. They were all just passing acquaintances; dalliances if you prefer. They didn't mean a hoot to me."

"What about me? Am I in the same category?"

Julian took both of her hands in his and looked straight into her eyes, "You my lovely Charlotte are special and I'd like to spend a lot more time with you. I can postpone my flight back to Montreal and leave on Sunday instead. We can have all day tomorrow and most of the weekend together."

Charlotte shook her head, "Adam is coming back on Saturday. I have to be there when he arrives."

"Okay, but we still have tomorrow. Stay with me tonight."

"No, I need to go home. Adam might call me and I have to make sure Zoe is all right."

"Surely you have your cell phone with you. If your husband calls you can still answer and I'm pretty sure your cat can be alone for a night."

Charlotte pulled her hands away and sighed, "I left my cell phone in the car and, in any case, how could you possibly expect me to speak to him here? As for Zoe, yes she would be fine but I still worry about her."

Julian got up and threw his hands in the air, "Okay, have it your way. We'll eat and then you can leave and I'll go back to Montreal tomorrow as planned."

Charlotte jumped to her feet and put her arms around him, "Please don't be angry and don't leave," she begged, "I'll stay tonight but I need to go home in the morning to change and check on Zoe and then I'll come back."

Julian pushed her away and shrugged his shoulders, "Suit yourself, I don't want to force you to do anything you're not comfortable with."

At first, Charlotte wasn't sure how to react. She knew Julian was manipulating her but, a moment later, she found herself trying to reassure him she really wanted to stay. Before he had time to respond, there was a knock on the door and room service arrived with their order. Charlotte felt awkward standing there in her robe while waiting for Julian to sign the tab. Why did she suddenly feel like a scarlet woman?

Later, after feasting on Lobster Panini, crème brulee and drinking almost a whole bottle of wine, Charlotte was so tired she could hardly keep her eyes open. "I've got nothing to wear in bed," she complained.

Julian chuckled, "You don't need anything I'll keep you warm."

"No, I really need something. I've never liked to sleep in the nude. Perhaps you have a tee shirt I can borrow."

"Coming right up," Julian replied bouncing up from the chair and reaching up to a shelf in the closet.

Charlotte excused herself while she locked herself in the bathroom. She had no intention of allowing Julian to walk in on her and she took her time combing through her hair and removing her make-up. It was only after she looked in the mirror, she realized she had automatically cleansed her face without thinking about the consequences. Now she was left with a bare face and hadn't brought any make-up with her, except for her lipstick. She would have to drive home in the morning looking just like the image in the mirror. It took her a few minutes to convince herself she actually looked pretty good considering it was midnight and she was exhausted. Finally, she slipped on the pale blue tee shirt, opened the bathroom door and breathed a sigh of relief when she saw Julian had turned off all the lights, except for a small lamp near the bed. He looked up from the chair where he had been sitting with his eyes closed, "Ah there you are. Why don't you hop into bed and I'll be right back."

Charlotte woke up the next morning wondering where on earth she was and then, suddenly remembering, sat up with a start. She must have fallen asleep while Julian was in the bathroom and now here he was lying on his back beside her and breathing very gently. She stared at him, taking in every angle and feature and although the resemblance to Adam was remarkable, there were subtle differences like the width of his jaw and the almost undetectable bump on the bridge of his nose. The only obvious difference was the scar which appeared to be a sensitive subject. How did he get it, she wondered? If it had been in a fight or an accident, then surely it was nothing to be ashamed of. Maybe he had been abused by his father. He did say his father left when he was eight and he didn't care whether he was dead or alive. That had to be it and that's why he didn't want to talk about it. The thoughts were still churning in Charlotte's head when Julian opened his eyes and looked up at her. "Good morning, pretty lady," he said.

Charlotte was suddenly aware she had no make-up on and probably looked a fright in the bright sunlight streaming through a chink in the curtains directly onto the bed. "Good morning," she whispered as she started to clamber out of the bed but Julian caught her by the arm.

"Oh, no you don't," he said pulling her back, "early morning's my favourite time of the day."

Charlotte immediately caught his meaning and struggled to get out of his grasp, "I have to go to the bathroom," she pleaded.

Julian slowly shook his head as he released her arm, "Okay, I'll let you go but I'll be right here waiting for you."

She scurried to the bathroom, relieved herself and then searched through the toiletries, lined up behind the sink, for some toothpaste. Finding a tube of Crest, she squeezed some onto her finger, rubbed it over her teeth, splashed cold water on her face and ran her fingers through her hair. Then, she gingerly opened the door and walked back towards the bed where Julian was sitting leaning against the headboard naked from the waist up, his lower half covered by a sheet and looking extremely sexy. "Ah, the wench returns," he said grinning.

Charlotte smiled and crawled back onto the bed, "Were you waiting long, sir?" she asked coyly.

"Too long," he answered and grabbed her roughly, pulling her on top of him. "Take that bloody thing off," he continued as he stripped the tee shirt from her body.

She was sitting astride him, completely naked in broad daylight and felt more desirable than ever before. "Make love to me," she whispered.

"My pleasure ma'am," he replied ramming himself inside her.

Chapter Nineteen

Two hours later, Charlotte was on her way home. She had checked her cell phone and noticed two messages from Adam wondering where she was. She decided to wait until she reached the house before calling him back. When she walked through the front door, Zoe was nowhere to be seen and both her food and water bowls were empty. She wandered through the house looking for her and finally found her fast asleep on Tyler's bed. Rather than wake her, she left her there and went back to the kitchen to refill her bowls and call Adam. As she went to pick up the phone on the counter, she saw there was another message and as she listened to Adam's voice, it was obvious he was concerned that he hadn't been able to reach her. When she called him back, the lies came easily. She claimed to have left her cell phone in the car, which was actually the truth, and had spent the night at her mother's house because Gypsy was sick and she didn't want to leave her. "What about Mrs. Walker?" Adam asked, "I thought she was supposed to be cat sitting."

"She is," Charlotte shot back, "but I couldn't expect her to stay overnight. I just came home to change and I'm going back there. I may stay over again so don't worry about me. I'll see you tomorrow anyway."

"Maybe you should take the darn cat to the vet if she's that sick," Adam suggested.

Charlotte was annoyed when Adam sounded so insensitive, "I just may do that," she said abruptly. "Anyway, I have to get going. What time will you be home?"

"Some time in the afternoon depending on the traffic."

"Okay, I'll see you then. Bye."

"Bye, Charlotte," Adam answered and immediately hung up.

Despite how easily she had managed to lie to her husband, Charlotte felt some degree of guilt but minutes later she was justifying the deception by telling herself it would all be over by the next day. Then it really hit her, is that what she really wanted? What was going to happen after tomorrow? Would she ever see Julian again? How could she just go back to being plain old Charlotte with her mundane life? How was it possible, after just a few days, that Julian could make her feel so special? She couldn't let him walk away; she had to see him again no matter what the consequences.

After changing into a pair of white capris and a lime green tank top, she stuffed a short cotton nightgown, some toiletries and her make-up into a bag and drove back to the hotel. Julian answered her knock by sweeping her into his arms and kissing her passionately before she even had a chance to speak. "I missed you," he said. "What took you so long?"

Charlotte giggled as she released herself and walked into the room, "I've been gone for just over an hour. I raced home, took care of Zoe, changed my clothes and drove straight back." She turned to look at him, noticing his tailored jeans and the black tee that emphasized the muscles in his arms. "What have you been doing while I've been gone?"

"I've just been reading the paper, watching CNN and waiting for you. I thought we might go out for brunch and then go for a drive."

Charlotte crossed over to him and took both of his hands in hers, "That sounds like a lovely idea. How about we head towards the falls? I haven't been there for years and it's such a gorgeous day."

Julian pulled her closer, "Never mind the falls, you're the one who's gorgeous. Maybe we should just stay here."

Charlotte shook her head, "Uh, uh, I'm starving and we'll have all night."

"So you really are going to stay until tomorrow? What about your husband?"

"I've already spoken to him."

Julian tipped her chin up and looked directly into her eyes, "What did you tell him?"

Charlotte turned her head and pushed him away, "Don't do this, Julian. Let's just enjoy the time we have together. No more questions, please."

Julian nodded very slowly, "All right, let me just find my room key and then we can leave."

Later, standing above Niagara Falls and holding Julian's hand, Charlotte wanted to savour every moment. The last time she stood in almost the same spot, she had been with Adam and the children. She remembered how much joy it had given her to watch Alexa's and Tyler's excitement, but this was different. Despite the thunder of the water and the babble from the hundreds of tourists surrounding them, she felt at peace. She looked up at Julian then leaned close to him and whispered, "I'm so happy being here with you."

He released her hand, put his arm around her and kissed her on the top of her head, "I'm happy I stayed."

On the way back to the city, they stopped at Turtle Jack's and dined on Atlantic salmon with mango salsa and drank a whole bottle of Chardonnay. Inevitably, the talk turned to Julian's leaving the next day. "When will you be coming back again?" Charlotte asked.

Julian sighed, "I won't know my next assignment until I get into the office on Monday. I called the paper early this morning and they still didn't have my schedule"

Charlotte reached across the table and took his hand, "Tell me the truth, Julian, do you have any intention of seeing me again after you leave tomorrow?"

"Of course I want to see you again. How could you ever doubt that?" He answered squeezing her hand. "Maybe I'll be back in Toronto in a couple of weeks or maybe you could even come to Montreal. Do you think that would be possible?"

Charlotte hesitated, "I'm not sure. Jodi and I went away for the weekend a couple of times, once to a spa and another time to a cottage belonging to one of her cousins. It would mean she would have to lie for me and I don't know if I can ask her to do that."

"Would your husband be likely to check up on you?"

"No, of course not. I've never given him a reason not to trust me."

Just at that moment Charlotte heard the sound of chimes and Julian pulled a cell phone from the back pocket of his jeans. He glanced at it and said, "I have to take this, it's the home where my mother's being taken care of," then he stood up and walked away from the table towards the exit.

Charlotte watched him go hoping it wasn't bad news but, at the same time, wondering why he chose not to answer the call in front of her. Maybe it had nothing to do with his mother. Maybe it was somebody else. When he arrived back, it was pretty obvious something was wrong. He looked grim and sat down with a sigh. "What is it?" Charlotte asked reaching for his hand.

"They've taken my mother to the hospital. They think she's had a heart attack. I need to get a flight out tonight."

Charlotte immediately got to her feet, "Of course, let's just settle the bill and then we can drive straight back to the hotel and you can check out."

Julian nodded and beckoned to the waiter, "Okay, why don't you go and bring the car around and I'll be out in a few minutes."

The ride back into Toronto was brief but tense. Charlotte was feeling conflicted. The last thing she wanted was for Julian to leave but, on the other hand, she felt compelled to be supportive. It was evident from the way Julian talked about his mother that he cared about her a great deal and she could sense the anxiety building up in him as he called the airlines and waited to hear if he could get on a flight that evening. He breathed a sigh of relief when he got off the phone and announced there were a number of flights available and several vacant seats.

"When we get to the hotel, I'll wait for you while you pack up and check out and then I'll drive you to the ferry."

"Believe me, I didn't want today to end like this. I thought we would at least spend one more night together."

"There'll be other nights," Charlotte whispered, "I'm not sure when or how, but if you can't come to me, I'll come to you."

Less than an hour later, Charlotte was watching Julian as he packed his suitcase and gathered together all of his camera equipment. He was just about ready when he suddenly stopped and said, "I'd like to take a photo of you. Will you let me?"

Charlotte smiled, "I have a better idea, you must have time lapse. Let's have a photo of the two of us together."

Julian grinned back, "I think I can manage that," he said and then quickly set up the camera, took three giant strides towards her, and put his arm around her shoulders. "Now, say cheese," he said.

"I want a copy," Charlotte said after they were finished.

Julian nodded, "Okay, how about if I email it to you?"

Charlotte paused, "I'm not sure that's a good idea. Why don't you print it out and mail it to me at the library? That way there's no chance of anybody else seeing it."

She wrote down the address, stuffed it into his jacket pocket, and followed him as he exited the room. He seemed a bit distracted but she thought it was only natural. He must be worrying about his mother. While he was checking out, she drove the car to the front of the hotel and got out to help him put his luggage in the trunk. She was just getting back into the driver's seat when she heard somebody calling her, "Charlotte, yoo-hoo!" She didn't even look to see who it was; she just jumped inside, yelled at Julian to get in and tore off along King Street. "Who was it?" Julian asked.

"I'm not sure but it sounded like my neighbour, Annette. If it was, and she saw you, then she would have thought you were Adam."

Julian could see she was shaking, "Don't worry, we'll meet somewhere else next time."

It only took a few minutes to reach the dock where the ferry would take Julian to the island airport and it was already growing dark. "I'll help you get your luggage," Charlotte said as she stopped the car.

Once they had unloaded the trunk, Julian pulled her into his arms, "You can't leave the car here. We'll have to say goodbye now."

Charlotte reached up and held his face in her hands, "I'm going to miss you," she whispered, "but I'll be thinking about you all the time and praying that your mother is all right."

Julian took her hands away and held them against his chest, "I'm so sorry to leave you like this. I'll call you on your cell phone and let you know how my mom is."

"I'll be waiting to hear from you. Please don't forget to call."

Julian smiled, "I could never forget you, Charlotte. Now, give me a kiss and go on home."

Chapter Twenty

As Charlotte pulled into her driveway, she heard her cell phone ringing. Hoping it was Julian calling before he boarded the plane, she quickly answered without checking to see who it was, "Hi," she said in a breathy voice.

It was Adam. "Well hello there, you sound kind of sexy," he said. "Where are you?"

Charlotte tried to keep the disappointment out of her voice, "Oh, I was just getting back from Mom's."

"I see, so I gather Gypsy's better and you decided not to stay over."

"Yes she is and I prefer to sleep in my own bed. How are things going there? Will you still be home tomorrow?"

"Yes, I should be there by noon. I'll be leaving here early and only stopping for a quick bite on the way. Will you be home when I arrive?

Charlotte paused, "I'm not sure. If I'm not here, I'll just be out shopping and I won't be long."

"Good, because I was hoping we could spend a lazy afternoon by the pool and then go out to dinner later."

"That sounds nice, "Charlotte responded trying to sound enthusiastic.

"Okay. By the way, have you heard from Alexa?"

"Mom called and said they were taking the ferry to Vancouver and would be staying with Peggy's daughter until Sunday. You may remember her, she came for a visit once and we had dinner at Mom's place. It was a number of years ago. Her name's Lesley and she's rather plump with short reddish hair."

"I do remember her and if I recall she was quite amusing. I bet Alexa's having a good time. Any idea when she'll be home?"

"I expect they'll be back at the end of next week but I'll know more when Mom calls me on Sunday."

"I guess we have to get used to her being away from home. One of these days she'll be leaving for good."

"Oh goodness, she won't be leaving yet."

"I know, but look at Tyler; we didn't think he'd go off on his own and here he is living thousands of miles away."

Charlotte began to feel uncomfortable both emotionally and physically, "Look, hon, I'm still sitting in the car and the engine's turned off so it's getting pretty hot in here. We can finish this conversation tomorrow."

"Oh, sorry, I didn't realize. I'll see you tomorrow. Love you, hon."

"Love you too," Charlotte responded half-heartedly and slowly put the phone down. Despite the heat, she sat there for a few moments with her hands gripping the steering wheel and stared at the house. In the space of one short hour, the excitement of the last twenty-four, when she had been made to feel like a desirable and attractive woman, had been wiped out. Now she was back to being a wife and mother discussing her children with her husband. What was wrong with her? Adam was a wonderful provider and she couldn't be more proud of Alexa and Tyler but her life was so predictable. She almost wished she'd never met Julian. He had breathed new life into her and she had treasured every moment spent with him. The thought of giving him up now was unimaginable. Pulling herself together, she picked up her cell phone and rang his number but it went to voice mail. She figured he must be on the plane and didn't leave a message. She wondered if he was thinking about her and when she would hear from him again. If he went straight to the hospital to see his mother he might be home in time to call her later tonight. With that thought in mind, she got out of the car prepared to spend the rest of the evening waiting to hear his voice.

At midnight, after attempting to read and watch television, Charlotte crawled into bed and lay there, for what seemed like hours, wide awake. With no word from Julian, her mind raced through every possibility. Was he keeping vigil by his mother's bedside? Had she actually died before he even got to the hospital? Or, had he completely forgotten about her already? Maybe she was just another woman he'd managed to lure into his bed. Maybe all the compliments were just lies. Finally, she fell asleep and was surprised to wake up and see the sun streaming through the windows. For a moment, she was lost in a fog and then it all came back and it felt like a dark cloud descending in her mind. Why hadn't Julian called her?

Zoe was sleeping at the foot of the bed so she gently slid out from under the covers and tiptoed to the bathroom. Looking in the mirror and noticing the dark circles under her eyes, she suddenly heard a noise. It was her cell phone which was lying on the bedside table and Zoe was already sitting up with ears erect. She raced to answer it, nearly tripping over her nightgown, and said, "Hello," almost in a whisper.

It was Julian, "Charlotte, I hope I didn't wake you."

Charlotte's hand flew to her throat, "Julian, oh I'm so glad you called me. I've been awake half the night thinking about you."

Julian's voice dropped to the point where she could hardly hear him, "Mom died at two this morning."

Charlotte gasped, "Oh, Julian, I'm so sorry. Were you with her?"

"Yes, I was holding her hand and she went peacefully. Now I'm going to try and remember her the way she was before she got that bloody disease. I know I haven't talked much about her but she was a great mother and I'm going to miss her. Thankfully she's in a better place now."

"I wish I was there with you. Have you spoken to any of your family?"

"Just my mom's sister, my Aunt Beth. She's driving in from Kingston today. I haven't made any arrangements yet but I'm meeting with the funeral director in an hour. We're just going to have a private service in the chapel and then the burial will be at Mount Royal tomorrow."

"Don't you have any other relatives?"

"No, I'm afraid not but I expect two or three of my colleagues from the paper will be there and my closest friend, Raj, will come with his wife."

"I've never heard you mention Raj before."

"Well, we don't see each other very often lately. He got married four or five years ago and last year they had twin girls so he's pretty busy playing daddy these days."

"Will you call me after you come back from the cemetery?"

"Yes, but I'm not sure where we'll be yet. I expect we'll all end up at some restaurant but I'll call as soon as I get the chance."

"Please don't forget, Julian. I'll be thinking about you all the time until I hear from you."

"What about your husband? Won't he be home today? How are you going to answer the phone?"

Charlotte hesitated, "Don't worry, it will be all right. Just call me, no matter what."

"Okay, I'd better go. I have a lot to take care of."

"Again, I am so sorry. I'll talk to you soon. Bye, Julian."

Minutes after saying goodbye, the phone rang again. Thinking he had forgotten something, she snatched it up from the counter but it was Tyler. For a second she was disappointed and then immediately felt guilty. This was her son calling all the way from London, "Hi, Mom, it's me. How are you doing?"

Charlotte couldn't help smiling, "Tyler, how lovely to hear from you. I'm just fine, honey. How come you're up so early?"

Tyler chuckled, "Mom, it's early afternoon here. You forgot the time difference."

"Oh, that's right. Is everything all right? How's Shelby?"

"Everything's really cool. I love it here, Mom. The job at the pub is a lot of fun and I've saved quite a bit already. The pay isn't great but I get a lot of tips. Shelby's not here right now otherwise I'd let you talk to her. We think we'll be going to Egypt sooner that we first planned and we're getting pretty excited."

"That sounds wonderful. Let me know exactly when you're leaving."

"Why, Mom? So you can worry yourself sick about me?"

Charlotte sighed, "I always worry about you, honey. I really miss you and I wish you'd come home."

"I know but I like it here. Why don't you come for a visit? I'd love for you to meet Shelby's parents."

"Well, your Dad's pretty busy right now and we were already planning a trip out east."

"Where is Dad? Can I speak to him?"

"Sorry, Tyler, but he's been in Ottawa for a few days and he's probably on his way back right now."

"What about, Sis, is she there?"

"No, she's with Nana in Vancouver visiting Aunt Peggy's sister."

"Oh well, I guess I'll catch them next time. How are you doing, Mom?"

"I'm fine but feeling a bit lonely. It's been pretty quiet around here with everybody gone."

"Yes but Dad should be home soon. Look, Mom, I'd better go because I'm using the phone in Dr. Lewiston's office and I don't want to take advantage. I just wanted to make sure you were all right."

"That's really thoughtful of you. I'm proud of you, Tyler."

"Thanks, Mom. I'll talk to you again soon and I'll let you know as soon as we know when we're leaving for Egypt."

"Okay, honey. I love you."

"Love you too. Say hi to Dad for me. Bye, bye."

Charlotte put the phone down and sank down onto the edge of the bed. She suddenly felt lonelier than ever and the thought of Adam arriving home later didn't make her feel any better. Talking to Tyler had reminded her she was supposed to be planning for their trip out east but now she dreaded the very idea of spending two weeks away from home and the possibility of missing a chance to see Julian. Slowly she gathered herself together, took a thirty minute soak in the tub, and dressed to go shopping at the market. On the drive there, she decided she didn't want to be at the house when Adam arrived so, to kill time, she took a detour to Nancy's house to check on the cats. Mrs. Walker happened to be watering the plants in the back yard when she got there so she spent some time chatting with her and then drove to the Beaches and sat on a bench facing the lake. It reminded her of being with Julian at Bluffer's Park and she smiled at the memory. Soon her stomach began to growl and she realized she hadn't eaten so she walked along Queen Street and came across the Green Eggplant where she ordered an asparagus and goat cheese omelet. When the waitress served her coffee, she glanced at her watch and saw it was already past noon and the thought of Adam's arrival dominated her thoughts. How was she going to face him knowing she had slept with another man? Not only had she slept with Julian, she had taken pleasure in every moment, delighted in every touch, every caress. He had made her feel beautiful.

She sat there for a long time, not wanting to face the idea of going home but she knew it was inevitable. She took her time driving back to Rosedale, stopping at the gas station and the car wash on the way. Then she drove to the market and spent another half hour picking through the produce for the freshest fruit and vegetables and squeezing nearly every loaf of bread on display. She eventually faced the fact that she couldn't delay any longer and soon found herself turning the corner onto Highland. She held her breath as she approached the house and felt her hands start to shake when she saw Adam's Tesla in the driveway. She knew she couldn't delay seeing Adam any longer and attempted to put a smile on her face when she came through the front door, "Hi, I'm home," she called out.

"In the kitchen, hon," Adam replied then stopped what he was doing and rushed forward when he saw her carrying two bags full of groceries. "Here let me take those. Why didn't you come and get me, I could have helped you bring them in from the car?"

Charlotte passed the bags to him, "Thanks. I got carried away with all the fresh fruit and I know how much you like peaches, so I bought about a dozen of them."

"That's my girl, always thinking of others," Adam remarked as he began to unload the bags onto the kitchen table.

"What were you doing when I came in?"

"I was just making a sandwich. I decided not to stop to eat on the way home. Would you like something?"

"No thanks, I already had lunch. You go ahead and I'll put this stuff away."

"Okay but how about having a coffee with me, we haven't had a chance to talk for a while?"

Charlotte shook her head, "No, I think I'll just finish up here and then I need to go and take a bath."

Adam frowned "Isn't it a strange time to be taking a bath?"

"Well, normally I'd agree but I've been out for most of the morning and it's unbearably hot out. I just need to freshen up."

"What about taking a swim? I thought we were going to spend the afternoon out by the pool?"

"It's not the same; you know how I like to soak. You have your lunch and I'll see you out at the pool later."

Adam shrugged and went back to making his sandwich while Charlotte continued to put away the groceries. She felt like a robot just going through the motions and she was anxious to get out of the kitchen but almost fifteen minutes passed before she found herself slipping into a warm bath and feeling most of the tension drain from her body. She wished she could relax her mind in the same way but the questions kept coming. How had she managed to act as though everything was normal? Why didn't Adam even give her a hug after not seeing her for two days? Is this what her life was going to be like from now on? Tyler was already out of the picture and soon, Alexa would be gone too. That would leave her with nobody to care for except Adam. Did he really appreciate her or did he just take her for granted? What would happen if she just left? Would she end up with Julian? She knew she was being irrational, she had only just met him but he had awakened something in her she never knew existed. She suddenly had a craving for life and had visions of running off and travelling the world. Why should her son be able to visit all the wonderful places she had only ever dreamed about? She had always imagined that, after Adam retired, they would

spend at least three months in Florida every year and the rest
of the time take trips to far off places. By then she would be in
her sixties, maybe even older, and in the meantime, what did
she have to look forward to?

She continued to wrestle with her thoughts until she
suddenly felt exhausted and her eyes began to close. As her
body relaxed even more, she felt herself slipping lower into the
water and she shot upright wondering why she was so tired.
She couldn't allow herself to fall asleep so, reluctantly, she
climbed out of the tub, dried herself off, and put on a pair of
shorts and a tube top before going downstairs.

Looking out of the back door she could see Adam
reclining on a lawn chair in his bathing trunks with Zoe on
the grass beside him. She didn't know how she was going to
get through the rest of the day but she knew she had to.

Later that night when Adam crawled into bed, she was
already half asleep. She couldn't bear the idea of him touching
her so she had feigned a headache and gone upstairs at nine
o'clock. The afternoon and evening had actually gone quite
well because the Eriksons' had dropped in and then invited
them back to their place for a barbecue. When Charlotte first
opened the door to Annette she was terrified she'd mention
seeing her near the hotel and when Annette did bring it up, it
was obvious she hadn't noticed Julian so Charlotte pretended
she'd been shopping along King Street and hadn't heard her
calling.

Chapter Twenty-One

On Sunday, Charlotte made Adam's favourite weekend breakfast and then announced she was going to Nancy's to check on the cats. He asked her to wait so that he could come with her but she managed to discourage him by claiming she was also going shopping downtown. She was well aware he hated shopping and would probably be grateful to just relax at home. "When do you expect to be back?" he asked.

"I'm not sure. I may even have lunch out somewhere if it starts getting late."

"Beats me why you'd go shopping on a Sunday. Why didn't you go during the week?"

Charlotte sighed, "Because I had other things to do and it's a lot easier on Sunday. There are a lot fewer people in the stores, especially in this warm weather."

"What are you shopping for anyway?"

Charlotte started to head for the kitchen door, "Boy, you're asking a lot of questions."

Adam chuckled, "Are you sure you're not running off to meet some man?"

Charlotte pretended she didn't hear and ran up the stairs to get ready. Her heart was pounding even though she knew Adam was only joking. She couldn't wait to leave the house in case Julian called on her cell phone. Half an hour later, she was at Nancy's watering the plants and making sure Gypsy and Luna had food and water. It was obvious Mrs. Walker was taking good care of them, so she took a little time to play with them and then went to sit in the garden for a while. She kept glancing at her cell phone but knew it was much too early for Julian to call. He was probably at the cemetery and wouldn't get in touch with her until early afternoon. She decided to go shopping after all even though, at first, it had just been an excuse.

Charlotte had never been like Jodi, always into the latest fashions and well put together but as she wandered through the shopping mall she began to realize that she really needed to update her wardrobe. She saw a wonderful lavender dress in a store window that looked so feminine, she couldn't resist trying it on. It looked so perfect on her, even another shopper stopped and commented on how lovely she looked. After that, there was no stopping her and when she finally exited the store, almost an hour later, she had purchased the dress, two blouses, a skirt, a pair of capris and a pale grey wool jacket. Still not completely satisfied, she stopped in at Victoria Secret and, thinking of Julian's reaction, walked out with a black lace panty set, a leopard print push-up bra and three sets of fancy panties in various colours. Shoes were next on her list but she was getting a little tired and decided to stop for lunch at Milestones, just a block away. Even though it was just after twelve o'clock and there were quite a few tourists in the downtown area, she managed to get a table on the patio, three floors above street level. She ordered a glass of Zinfandel and a seafood salad and placed her cell phone on the table beside her. Then just as the waiter was serving the wine, the phone rang. The moment she recognized the Montreal area code displayed on the screen, she snatched it up and said, "Julian, is that you?"

"Yes, it's me. Is it okay to talk?"

"Yes, I'm in a restaurant all by myself just about to have lunch. I've been waiting for your call. How was the service and how are you feeling?"

"Everything went smoothly and now we're just about to have lunch too. My Aunt Beth will be in town until Tuesday.

I thought she'd stay with me but she already booked into a hotel. I'm going to have to spend some time with her."

"It must be comforting to have her there with you. I've been thinking about you so much."

"I've been thinking about you too, Charlotte. I'm really sorry we couldn't spend Friday night together."

"Oh, don't be silly, you needed to be with your mother. I'm just terribly sad that she didn't make it, Julian."

"I know. My aunt and I are going to sort through her belongings tomorrow. There are just two or three boxes of stuff, mostly papers and photos. Then, after that, I'll have some legal issues to take care of. I already had Mom's power of attorney and a copy of her will so I'll probably clear everything up pretty quickly."

"Do you know when you'll be able to get back to work?"

"Not until my aunt leaves. I'll check into the office tomorrow and see what they have scheduled for me."

"I hope they send you back to Toronto."

Julian chuckled, "Not much chance of that but if they do, you'll be the first to know. Anyway, what have you been doing since I left."

"Well, I've been doing a little shopping this morning," Charlotte replied lowering her voice. "I bought some really sexy lingerie I can't wait to show you."

"Really, sexier than that little red number you had on?"

"Mmmmm could be, how about leopard skin?"

"Wow, I think I'm bringing out the wanton woman in you"

"I think so too and it's about time someone did," Charlotte responded rather seriously.

There was a pause and she could hear muffled voices on the other end of the line then Julian came back on, "My aunt just found me. Apparently lunch is already being served so I had better go."

"Where are you?"

"We're at Bonaparte's in Old Montreal. I'd love to bring you here sometime."

"I'd love to be there with you but I guess I'll have to wait. Please call me after your aunt leaves."

"I will, Charlotte. Take care of yourself."

"You too, Julian, bye."

As soon as she put the phone down, her lunch arrived and she was content to just sit, eat, and sip on the wine while she looked down at the scene below and thought about Julian.

When she finally returned home at around three, she felt more content. Just the fact that Julian had called her convinced her, at least for the time being, that he really was thinking about her and they had made a real connection. She even felt more at ease around Adam although she wasn't sure why and suggested they go out to dinner and then to a movie. Adam was all for it and for the rest of the afternoon, while Charlotte did a little gardening; he relaxed in the family room watching a tennis match with Zoe sprawled out beside him.

Later, Charlotte was changing her clothes and feeling rather pleased with herself for having smuggled most of her shopping into the house before Adam saw it, when suddenly her cell phone rang. It was Jodi wanting to know if she was free to meet her for a drink. As Rick was out of town, she was at loose ends. She was also anxious to learn more about the stranger in the bar. She suspected Charlotte was holding back and determined to get some answers but was disappointed to learn Charlotte was tied up for the evening. Adam happened to come into the bedroom and, after hearing part of the conversation, suggested Jodi join them for dinner. Hesitating for a moment, Charlotte suddenly realized it would be an ideal situation. She could see Jodi and have no fear of being asked any questions.

At seven o'clock, Adam and Charlotte met Jodi at Auberge du Pommier, an upscale restaurant in North York. When Adam had announced where they were going and Charlotte was sure Jodi would arrive looking like a million dollars, she decided to wear her new lavender dress. Adam whistled when she finally came downstairs with her hair swept back from her face and wearing a pair of four-inch white sandals. "Wow, when did you get that?" he asked.

Charlotte smiled, "I bought it today. Do you really like it?"

"Yes. What is it the Brits say? Ah, yes, you look smashing."

Charlotte whirled around and then slipping her arm through his said, "Come on, Jodi will be waiting"

She was relieved she had chosen to wear the dress when she saw Jodi walk through the door of the restaurant. She had on a simple black sheath but it fit her body like a second skin and had a dangerously low scooped neck which attracted a lot of attention from some of the male patrons, including Adam. He rose from the table as she approached and gave her a hug. Obviously any animosity he felt towards her, for allowing Charlotte to think he'd been cheating, had been forgotten.

The evening was going really well with excellent food and good conversation until Charlotte announced she was going to the ladies room and Jodi elected to follow her. It was here that she was able to confront Charlotte and ask if she had seen Julian again. When Charlotte responded that they had already discussed the issue and nothing was going on, Jodi refused to believe her. Eventually, Charlotte broke down and admitted she had seen Julian more than once but she needed to get back to the table and promised to meet with Jodi on Tuesday to talk some more. After that, Adam noticed a change in the atmosphere and asked what was going on. Jodi was quick to make an excuse telling Adam she was having a little problem with Rick and had sounded off to Charlotte. She apologized for spoiling the evening. Adam was his usual gracious self and offered to help if he could but Jodi just waved him off and said it was something she was sure she could handle.

After dinner, they walked Jodi to her car and watched her drive off. "What was that all about with Rick?" Adam asked.

"She'd rather I didn't talk about it," Charlotte responded.

"Well, I hope it's nothing serious. They've been together a long time."

Charlotte decided to change the subject, "Let's find the car and go home. I expect Mom to call me tonight. It's about six o'clock there now so she'll probably be calling soon."

"When are you expecting them back?"

"I'm not sure and that's what I want to find out."

On the way home, Adam asked how Charlotte was getting on with researching their trip east. It was a bit of shock for her to realize she hadn't even thought about the vacation for a few days and now he'd brought it up, she really didn't want to go. She paused before answering him, "I'm not sure we should go now."

"Why on earth not? I thought you were excited about it. What changed your mind?"

"Well, Alexa's been away a lot and I think she should spend some time here with her friends. Before you know it, she'll be back in school and not had a chance to interact with them at all."

"Okay, but what about you? Don't you think you deserve a holiday?"

Charlotte sighed, "I would like a change of scenery but I'd be happy with a long weekend away somewhere. Maybe I'll ask Jodi if she's free and we can take off for a few days," she continued as an idea began to take seed in her mind.

Adam stared straight ahead as they continued to drive south, "So I guess I don't get a vacation this year?"

Charlotte reached over and touched his arm, "Maybe we'll go somewhere later in the fall. Mom can come to our place and look after Alexa."

"Our daughter isn't going to be too happy if you cancel the trip."

"Alexa will have to accept it. She's already had a really great time at Peggy's. Enough is enough."

Adam glanced over at her, "Is everything okay? It sounds like something else is going on."

Charlotte shook her head, "Nothing's going on. Let's drop it please, Adam."

The rest of the journey, neither one of them spoke and when they got home Charlotte announced she was going to soak in the bath and take her phone with her in case Nancy called.

Minutes after Charlotte stepped out of the bathtub, while applying moisturizer to her legs, she heard her cell phone ringing. She didn't recognize the number but was sure it was Nancy and wasn't surprised when she heard her mother's voice. They had just returned to Peggy's place in Victoria and were planning on having a late supper. They only chatted for a few moments and then Alexa came on the line and spent the next ten minutes telling Charlotte all about their visit with Peggy's daughter and all the sights she had seen in Vancouver. "It was so fabulous, Mom," she said as she began to wind down. "Now, I can't wait to go to the east coast and see what it's like there."

Charlotte paused and decided not to tell her she had changed her mind about the vacation, at least, not until she returned back home. "What day are you planning to leave there?" she asked.

"Nana said we would be leaving on Friday and we should be home late in the afternoon."

"You had better put Nana back on the line so that she can give me the flight number and then I can pick you up at the airport."

"Okay, Mom, I'll get her. Bye, bye, I'll see you soon."

After Charlotte spoke to Nancy again, she put on her nightgown and a robe, went downstairs to tell Adam the latest news, and then announced she was going right back upstairs to bed. Adam looked a little surprised, "Wouldn't you like a nightcap?"

Charlotte shook her head, "No, I'm tired. You go ahead and I'll see you in the morning."

Adam stared at her as she walked out of the room and then called out, "Goodnight and sleep well."

Chapter Twenty-Two

On Tuesday, Charlotte met Jodi at the bar in the Hazelton Hotel. Adam didn't quite understand why she wanted a night out with Jodi when they had just had dinner together but assumed Jodi wanted a private meeting to talk about her relationship with Rick. It was the perfect excuse and Charlotte felt a sense of relief as she left the house and drove to Yorkville. Jodi was already there when she arrived sipping on a glass of Riesling. As always, on a work day, she looked very professional in a cream linen suit and apricot silk blouse. She glanced up as Charlotte approached the table and noticed she was wearing a new skirt and a top which was a little more revealing than her usual style. "Well hello there." she said motioning to the seat across from her. "That's a sexy outfit and now I'm really beginning to wonder what you are up to."

Charlotte glanced around for the waiter, "Let me get something to drink and then we can talk."

Jodi waited patiently until Charlotte's wine was served and then she leaned forward and whispered, "Okay, now spill the beans. What's going on with you and Julian?"

Charlotte sighed and then, expecting Jodi to react with shock, said, "I slept with him."

She wasn't disappointed when Jodi's mouth fell open and she almost dropped her glass, "Tell me you're making this up?"

Charlotte shook her head, "I'm not and now I don't know what to do. I can't forget about him, Jodi."

"But isn't that like sleeping with Adam? This is really weird."

"He's nothing like Adam. Yes, he looks like him in fact he could be his twin but that's where the resemblance ends. He makes me feel so special. I just want to be with him all the time."

"Where is he now?"

"He's back in Montreal. He had to leave rather suddenly because his mother died. He's taking care of her affairs right now."

"Are you sure that's why he left?"

Charlotte frowned, "What do you mean? Are you suggesting he used that as an excuse to just take off?"

"Well, how can you be sure? How do you know he isn't married, although I guess that doesn't matter much because you are?"

"I know he was telling me the truth. I was there when he got the call about his mother. As for his being married, I can't be sure."

"Oh, Charlotte, think about what you're doing. How do you expect this affair to end? You could lose your family over this. You've been with Adam for over twenty years and he's been a good husband. Think about what this would do to him, never mind Tyler and Alexa."

"I know, but I can't help my feelings and that's why I need to ask you a favour"

Jodi looked apprehensive. "What is it?"

"I told Julian I'd meet him in Montreal or anywhere else as long as it wasn't here. We nearly got caught by my neighbour, Annette, the other day. I had to pretend I didn't hear her calling and we took off in the car. I can't risk that happening again. I need to make up an excuse to go away for a weekend. If I told Adam I needed a break and I was going away with you, he wouldn't question it. It's not as though we've never done it before."

"When we did it before, Charlotte, you didn't have to lie." Jodi said solemnly. "Now, not only are you lying but you're asking me to as well. Honestly, I don't think I can do that."

Charlotte reached across the table and grasped Jodi's hand. "Please, Jodi, you're my best friend. I have to see him and I don't know what else to do."

Jodi pulled her hand away and shook her head, "Sorry, but I can't do this. If Adam was a rotten husband you might have an excuse but even then, I'd tell you to leave him but not to have an affair. If you insist on going through with this, tell him whatever you like but if he ever questions me about us being away together, I won't lie for you."

"You don't understand," Charlotte protested. "Adam's never made me feel the way Julian does. I can't just forget about him."

"I do understand, more than you know. I never told you this, but when I was married, I had an affair with my boss. Gerry couldn't make me feel the way Ross did but I knew if I was going to stay married, I had to end the affair. We went on seeing each other for six months. Twice, we went out of town for the weekend and Gerry never suspected."

"Why didn't you ever tell me? Is that why you and Gerry divorced?"

"I didn't tell you because I knew you wouldn't approve and I already told you, Gerry never suspected I had an affair. We just grew apart because we were more involved with our careers than our relationship."

"You said you went on seeing this Ross for six months. I've only just met Julian, I need more time with him."

"That's the whole point. The longer you let this go on, the harder it will be to break away. When I walked away from Ross, it was one of the hardest things I'd ever done. I even changed my job so I wouldn't see him every day."

Charlotte could feel the tears start to well up, "I can't let go yet. I just can't."

Jodi paused not sure what else she could do to convince Charlotte she was heading for disaster. "What do you really know about Julian?" she asked.

Charlotte tried to remember what Julian had told her about himself including the fact he'd never been married. Then when she'd finished, she said, "That's all I know. Why are you asking me all these questions?"

"Because I can't believe there isn't some connection between him and Adam. They look too much alike not to belong to the same family. How old is Julian?"

"He's the same age as Adam, forty-five. Adam's birthday is on June 12[h] so he's a Gemini but Julian told me his sign was Cancer so he had to have been born at least two weeks later."

Jodi looked thoughtful, "Mmmm, so I guess that blows the twins theory out the window."

Charlotte beckoned the waiter to bring them the bill and then turned back to Jodi, "I wish you would stop analyzing. In fact, I'd like to just drop the subject and talk about something else. Let's pay for the wine and then go and get something to eat."

Less than ten minutes later they were seated comfortably on the patio at Hemingways, watching the constant parade of people on Cumberland Avenue. "I love this place in the summer," Jodi remarked.

Charlotte nodded, "Me too, now tell me what's going on in your life."

By the time Friday arrived and Charlotte hadn't heard from Julian she was beginning to feel down again. The fact that Alexa and her mother were arriving later only made her more anxious. She had successfully managed to maintain her image of being a good wife even to the point where she had endured Adam's advances the night before but she couldn't keep up the façade much longer. Her mother was very astute when it came to gauging her moods and it would take all her effort to put on a cheerful demeanor.

At seven o'clock in the evening, Adam and Charlotte drove to Pearson airport and, while Adam waited patiently in the arrivals lounge reading a magazine, Charlotte anxiously paced up and down. When Nancy and Alexa finally walked out through the double doors dragging their suitcases behind them, they were all smiles and she was genuinely happy to see them. There were hugs all round and on the drive downtown Alexa couldn't stop babbling on about the flight and the fact that Nana had been flirting with the man sitting beside her and they had even exchanged phone numbers. Adam shook his head and said, "Okay, Alexa, now you've tattled on your grandmother tell us about your trip."

They tried to persuade Nancy to come home with them for a while but she was anxious to get home to Gypsy and Luna, so they dropped her off and arrived back at the house a little after eight-thirty. Alexa dropped the backpack she was carrying as soon as she came through the door and immediately ran around looking for Zoe. She found her curled up on a chair in the family room and scooped her up in her arms murmuring, "Zoe, my baby, did you miss me?"

Adam walked in and put his arm around her, "We all missed you, honey."

"Really, Dad? Mom hardly said a word on the way home. Did you two have an argument or something?"

"No, of course not, your mother's probably tired, that's all. Now put Zoe down and we'll go and rustle up something to eat."

Chapter Twenty-Three

Early on Saturday morning Adam went to his office and, two hours later, Alexa left the house to visit her friend Hildy. She was still excited about her trip and wanted to tell anybody who would listen, all about it. Charlotte had been waiting for everyone to leave because she couldn't wait any longer; she had to talk to Julian. She took her cell phone out to the garden, sat down at the patio table and dialed his number. It rang several times and she was just about to hang up when he finally answered. "Charlotte, how are you," he answered rather abruptly.

"Oh, you knew it was me," she responded.

"Yes, of course, I recognized the number."

There was an awkward silence then Charlotte continued, "I was just wondering how you were. I thought I would have heard from you by now."

"Well, as you can imagine I've been a little busy and that's why I haven't called. My aunt was supposed to leave on Tuesday but she decided to stay until yesterday."

"I see. Did you manage to sort out your mothers things?"

Charlotte detected a distinct coldness in Julian's voice when he replied, "I certainly did. Look, Charlotte, you caught me at a bad time. Let me call you back later."

Charlotte hesitated, "That might be a bit difficult, Adam will be here and probably Alexa as well. She came back from Victoria yesterday."

"Well you call me then. I expect to be home this evening."

"Okay, I'll do that. I'd really like to talk to you some more."

"All right, bye for now."

"Bye, Julian," Charlotte whispered.

She gently laid the phone down on the table and stared at the trees which were swaying gently in the wind. She felt something wasn't right. Had Julian's attitude changed towards her? Would he really be there when she called him later? The seeds of doubt started to race through her mind and with it came the inevitable sense of rejection. She sat there for the longest time until Zoe startled her by jumping onto her lap. She picked her up and went back into the house determined to get on with her day and not think about Julian.

At lunch time, Alexa bounced in announcing she was starving and, while she was making herself a grilled cheese sandwich, Adam called to say he wouldn't be home until after four. Charlotte decided this would be a good time to tell Alexa she had decided to cancel their trip east. She sat down opposite her at the kitchen table and asked, "Did you have a good time with Hildy this morning?"

Alexa nodded, "Yes, I'm going back there after lunch. Her mom's taking us to the Beaches."

"You must miss your friends when you're away, honey."

"Uh, uh, not really. I had so much fun at Aunt Peggy's and I loved it in Vancouver. I can't wait for our trip to the east coast."

"That's what I wanted to talk to you about. I know you're going to be disappointed, but I'm cancelling the trip."

Alexa dropped what was left of her sandwich onto the plate and looked at her mother with disbelief, "You're not serious, Mom? Why can't we go now?"

"It isn't a question of not being able to go," Charlotte answered gently. "I just feel you need to spend more time here before you go back to school."

"Was this your idea or Dad's?" Alexa shot back angrily.

"It was my idea, so don't be angry at your father. You've been away a lot this summer and had very little time for your friends."

"What about you and Dad, you haven't been away at all. What's really going on, Mom? Have you and Dad had a fight?"

Charlotte reached over and took Alexa's hand, "Oh no, not at all. Your dad's been really busy and I think he might be relieved that he doesn't have to take time off. As for me, well I might take off for a weekend with Jodi."

"Where will you go?"

"I'm not sure yet, we still have to talk about it."

Alexa sighed and got up from the table, "Okay, well I'm just going to run up and get my bathing suit and then I'll be gone."

"Have a lovely time, Alexa," Charlotte called after her as she ran out the door. She sat there a few minutes longer staring at the half-eaten sandwich left on the plate and realized what she had just done. She had deceived her daughter. She had taken the first step towards achieving what she wanted most; a rendezvous with Julian.

Later, during the evening, when Adam and Alexa were in the family room watching a sci-fi movie on television, Charlotte went upstairs to the bedroom, quietly closed the door and sat on the edge of the bed. With some trepidation, she dialed Julian's number and was surprised when he picked up on the first ring. She could hear some loud music in the background but there was no mistaking Julian's voice, "Hi, Charlotte. I figured you'd call around this time."

"Where are you?" she asked.

"I'm at a club having a drink with an old friend."

"I wish I was there with you. I've missed you so much."

"I know. I've missed you too. This week has been a lot harder than I ever expected. If you had been here it might have been a lot easier and I'm sorry if I was a bit short with you earlier."

"It's all right. I think about you all the time, Julian, especially at night."

Julian chuckled, "You mean when you're in bed?"

"Yes, especially when I'm in bed. I can't wait to feel you beside me again."

Julian chuckled again, "Soon we'll be having phone sex. My buddy here is already looking at me with an odd expression on his face."

It was Charlotte's turn to smile, "Now you're turning me on. When can I see you again? Will you be coming back to Toronto?"

"No, and in any case, we agreed it was too dangerous there. I have no assignments outside of Montreal for the next three weeks."

"I can come there," Charlotte announced without hesitation.

"How are you going to manage that?"

"I'm going to tell Adam I'm taking a few days away with Jodi."

"What about Jodi? Will she go along with it?"

"She told me she wouldn't lie for me even if Adam questioned her but that isn't likely to happen. He hardly ever speaks to her and he trusts me."

"Why don't you set something up for next weekend then? We'll have a great time. I'll show you around Montreal and I promise to satisfy all those carnal desires of yours."

"Oh, Julian, I can't wait. I'll tell Adam tomorrow and make sure he's around for Alexa next weekend."

"Try and make it for more than a couple of days otherwise before we know it, you'll be heading back home again."

"I will, Julian. By the way, did you mail out the photo?"

"Yes, I slipped it into the postbox this afternoon so you should get it by Tuesday. Speaking of photos, I'd like to see one of the rest of your family."

Charlotte paused, "Is it the rest of my family you really want to see or is it just Adam?"

"Don't get paranoid on me, Charlotte," Julian snapped back.

"I'm sorry, I didn't mean it. I'll bring one with me."

"Okay, call me when you've made arrangements."

"I will. I'll tell Adam tomorrow and then I'll book a flight with Porter. I'll probably call you on Monday."

"Good. Well, I'd better go. Au revoir, cherie."

"Au revoir," Charlotte responded and then rested the phone in her lap with a sigh. She was actually going to Montreal. He really wanted to see her. Slowly she lay down on the bed and stared up imagining Julian's face leaning over her. When she began to feel aroused, it startled her and she jumped up quickly, ran to the bathroom and splashed cold water on her face. By the time she had composed herself and gone back downstairs, the movie was almost over and Alexa had fallen asleep with her head on Adam's shoulder. Charlotte watched them silently from the doorway and was suddenly consumed with guilt. She knew what she was doing was wrong but Julian was like a magnet and she couldn't resist him.

Chapter Twenty-Four

Charlotte waited until Monday before approaching Adam about taking a few days away. She wanted to give Alexa time to settle into a routine and be sure she was spending most of her days with her friends. Right after dinner, Alexa left to go to a movie with Hildy and Charlotte was alone with Adam. He was in a mellow mood, having had two glasses of wine to accompany the homemade lasagne they had all enjoyed, when Charlotte suggested they go out into the garden while the weather was still warm. They settled down beside the pool and were quiet for a few moments as they watched Zoe stalking some unseen creature in the grass and then Charlotte said, "I was talking to Jodi earlier."

Adam nodded, "What does she have to say for herself these days?"

"She wants me to go away with her for a few days. We haven't been away together for a long time and we'd both like a break."

"Where were you thinking of going?"

"Well, Rick's cousin has a cottage in Muskoka so we'll probably go there."

Adam frowned, "Is Rick going too?"

Charlotte shook her head, "No, of course not. Just the two of us would be going."

"When were you planning to go?" Adam asked sounding a little miffed.

"This weekend," Charlotte replied not daring to look at him.

Adam sat up abruptly, "Isn't this all a bit sudden. First of all, Alexa just got back and then you decide to cancel our family trip east. Can't you both wait a couple of weeks?"

Charlotte realized she was digging herself deeper and deeper into a hole but she had no thoughts of turning back, "No, it's not convenient for Jodi. She needs to go away now because she has some house closures coming up later."

"Hmmm, I think she could have given you a lot more notice and I wouldn't have minded more notice too. I've got a lot of work on my plate right now with this Ottawa project and I don't have time to babysit."

Charlotte completely forgot the stream of lies that had just come out of her mouth. She was too annoyed at Adam's attitude and immediately shot back, "Oh, so you don't have time to spend a few extra hours with your daughter. You don't even have to cook, I'll leave you enough food for a few days and you can eat out if you prefer. You expect me to be here when you take off all the time but I'm not allowed to take any time for myself. Well screw you, Adam." With that she got up and strode into the house while Adam gazed after her with a shocked look on his face.

Ten minutes later, he went searching for her and found her in the family room watching a cooking show on television. She didn't look up and he hesitated for a minute before saying, "I'm sorry, Charlotte, I didn't mean to upset you. I'll do some work from home if I have to. Just let me know when you'll be leaving and for how long."

Charlotte continued to watch the television screen, "I have to talk to Jodi again but, don't worry; I'll let you know as soon as I do."

Adam was a little confused about Charlotte's reaction but decided to leave well enough alone and, after picking up the latest copy of Sports Illustrated from the coffee table, he retreated to the garden.

Charlotte waited until she thought he had settled down and then, just to be sure, she made her way to the back of the house and peered through the window. Satisfied that he was not likely to come back in for some time, she went into the kitchen and called Jodi. The phone rang four times before a breathless Jodi picked up.

Charlotte was relieved she had managed to get hold of her, "Jodi, it's me. I've only got a minute or two in case Adam comes in. I told him we were going away together this weekend. If he walks in now, it will have to look like I'm making arrangements with you."

Jodi cut in, "Wait a minute, I told you I didn't want to go along with this."

"No, you told me you wouldn't lie for me. I'm not asking you to lie I'm just asking you to listen so that he thinks I'm making arrangements."

"And you don't put that in the same category as lying?"

Charlotte paused, "I'm sorry, Jodi. Look, he's not likely to come in. Please do me one favour. Don't call here in the next week or two in case he picks up."

"No likelihood of that. I usually call you on your cell. I can't believe you're actually going through with this, where are you going and when?"

"Montreal, this weekend, and I can hardly wait. Julian really wants to see me, Jodi."

"What's Adam saying about you taking off for a few days?"

"Well, at first he seemed a bit annoyed claiming he was too busy to babysit Alexa but he just apologized so now I'm all set to go. I just have to call Julian back and then book my flight."

"Did you tell Adam you were going to Montreal?"

"No, I said we were going to a cottage in Muskoka."

"So according to Adam, one of us would have to be driving. It can't be me because I would have to pick you up and I refuse to be any part of this. If you're actually flying, you'll have to drive away and leave your car somewhere else."

"Oh my goodness, I never even thought of that. Where on earth can I leave it?'

"Not at my place that's for sure."

Suddenly, Charlotte heard footsteps and realized Adam was coming towards the kitchen. "Okay, that's all settled then," she said. "I'll talk to you on Thursday to see what time I'm supposed to pick you up."

Jodi was astute enough to know Adam must be within listening range and responded, "I hope you know what you're doing, Charlotte." Then she was gone.

Charlotte put down her phone and turned as Adam came through the door, "Who was that?" he asked.

"Jodi. We're leaving on Friday morning and we'll be gone until Tuesday."

"Is she going to be driving?"

"No, I'm driving. I'll be picking her up right after breakfast."

"Then you'd better take the car in and get it checked out. You probably need an oil change and you need to put some air in your tires."

Charlotte sighed, "I know, I'll do that on Wednesday, I'm too busy tomorrow because I have to work. I don't think I'll go in on Thursday unless they really need me because I want to prepare some meals for you and Alexa."

"That's not really necessary. I'm quite capable of cooking dinner. It may only be hot dogs or spaghetti and, like you said, we can always go out to eat."

"It's no trouble. I'll make a chicken casserole, it will last for a couple of days and I'll make more lasagne. There'll be plenty of ham and pastrami for sandwiches so you won't have to worry about lunches."

Adam walked over to where Charlotte was standing and put his arm around her. "Thanks honey, I forget how hard you work to take care of us and I'm sorry again for the way I reacted earlier."

Charlotte couldn't look him in the eye so she reached up, put both of her arms around him and looked over his shoulder, "It's okay, I've already forgotten about it."

Adam released her and stepped back, "How about we go to the Dairy Queen and have one of those humungous banana splits?" he said enthusiastically.

Charlotte smiled, "I think I've had enough to eat but why don't you go?"

Adam looked disappointed, "That wouldn't be any fun. I thought we could sit on that bench overlooking the parkway like we used to."

Charlotte reached out and touched his arm, "Not tonight, honey. You go and bring back a tub of their Midnight Truffle ice cream. That's Alexa's favourite."

Adam turned and started to walk out the door, "All right, I won't be long. Maybe we can go for a walk later."

"Maybe," Charlotte called after him then, as soon as she heard the front door close, she picked up her cell phone again.

Julian answered after the first ring, "Hi, pretty lady," he said.

Charlotte's hand shook at the sound of his voice, "Julian, everything's settled. I'm coming on Friday. I haven't booked my flight yet but I'm planning on leaving here at around nine. Will you be able to pick me up?"

"Of course I'll pick you up, just let me know what time you'll be arriving. Did you talk to Jodi about this?"

Charlotte hesitated, "Yes, I did. She still refuses to lie for me and I can't really blame her but I warned her not to call the house while I'm gone."

"How long can you stay? I hope it's a few days."

"I told Adam I'd be back on Tuesday but I didn't say what time. We can have almost four whole days together."

"And four whole nights," Julian responded chuckling.

Charlotte giggled, "I can't wait. I'm so excited. I've only been to Montreal once before and that was only for a day. I want to see everything, Julian."

"Don't worry, I'll be your personal tour guide and take you to some great places to eat. I guarantee you'll love it."

"I know I will, especially being with you. I can't stop thinking about us being together and I even dreamt about you last night."

Julian chuckled again, "I hope it was an erotic dream."

"It was," Charlotte responded with a sigh, "but not as good as the real thing."

"Well, we don't have to spend all our time sightseeing," Julian said suggestively.

"As long as I'm with you, I don't mind what we do. Oh, Julian, only a few more days and I'll be there."

"Where are you now?" asked Julian changing the subject.

"I'm at home."

"Where's the rest of the family?"

"Alexa's at a movie and Adam's gone to pick up some ice cream. I'd better not be on the phone too long in case he comes back."

"Okay, pretty lady; call me when you get your arrival time."

They said their goodbyes and Charlotte waited in the family room for Adam to return. She knew she should feel tremendous guilt but all she could think about was seeing Julian.

On Tuesday, at the library, she received the photograph Julian had taken and she couldn't stop staring at it. One of her co-workers happened to peek over her shoulder to see what she was looking at and exclaimed, "Oh my, you're husband's a handsome devil." Charlotte just smiled and tucked it away in her purse. Later, in the afternoon, she booked the nine-thirty-five flight on Porter Airlines and thanked heaven she had her own credit card. When she had started working at the library, Adam had told her she could keep all of her earnings and she had amassed a tidy little sum in her account. Adam covered all of the household expenses, picked up the check if they went out to eat and paid for their vacations. In fact, Adam provided her and the children with everything except her clothes and any entertaining she indulged in with Nancy or her friends. He never questioned what she spent although he did joke once about the small fortune she must be hiding considering she hardly ever bought anything for herself. She wondered how she would manage if he wasn't there and then quickly shrugged off the thought.

After dinner that evening, she shut herself in the bathroom and called Julian to give him her flight number and arrival time. He seemed a little distant but when she asked him if anything was wrong, he claimed he was tired after a rather boring day covering the city postal worker's strike. He then said he had to run because he was having a drink with his boss but before he rang off he reminded her to be sure and bring the photograph of Adam. By the time Charlotte put the phone down, she was feeling anxious, not only was she convinced Julian was lying about just being tired but also because he had originally asked for a photo of her family. She remembered him getting annoyed when she had suggested he really wanted to see one of Adam and yet, this time, he specifically referred to him. Unable to face the rest of the evening attempting to act as though nothing was bothering her, she feigned having a headache and announced she was going to lie down. At about ten o'clock, she heard the door to the bedroom open and then, after a moment while she remained perfectly still with her eyes closed, Adam whispered to Alexa, "I think Mom's asleep, we'd better not disturb her."

Two hours later, after Adam had already climbed in beside her and immediately rolled onto his side with his back to her, she was still awake. She didn't know how she was going to get through the next two days.

Chapter Twenty-Five

On Wednesday morning, after a sleepless night, Charlotte took her cornflakes and coffee out into the garden. Zoe followed her out and then lay down beside her chair and stretched as only cats can. Charlotte, looked down at her and murmured, "Oh, Zoe, you don't know how lucky you are. All you have to do is eat and sleep."

She heard a noise behind her and Adam's voice, "You forgot poop!"

She glanced around and couldn't help smiling, "I did, didn't I?" Why are you up so early?"

"Oh, I have lots to do today but never mind about me. Why are you up so early and what's bothering you?"

Charlotte suddenly felt defensive, "Nothing's bothering me, why?"

"You were telling Zoe how lucky she was. It sounds like you're discontent for some reason."

Charlotte reached down and stroked Zoe's head, "I guess I was feeling a little miserable because I didn't sleep well."

"I know that, you woke me up a couple of times tossing and turning. Are you sure there isn't something bothering you."

Charlotte stood up, "I'm absolutely sure. Now, how about I make you some scrambled eggs and bacon before you go to work?"

Adam declined breakfast and left Charlotte in the laundry room loading the washer. She was glad, in a way that he had left her alone. She really needed time to think and for the next hour she went about her chores mulling over her last conversation with Julian for the umpteenth time. Alexa finally broke the spell when she arrived in the kitchen in an upbeat mood and excited about the day ahead. She was wearing a mini skirt Adam wouldn't have approved of but Charlotte was not in the mood to get into an argument. "Where are you going today?" she asked.

Alexa searched in the freezer for her favourite Eggo blueberry waffles, "I'm going with Hildy and Jen to the Exhibition."

"Oh, I forgot it was on. Who's Jen? I don't think I've heard you mention her before?"

"She just moved in next door to Hildy. She's really neat, Mom, and she's got her own car."

"Surely you're not driving to the Ex? Parking would cost you a fortune and you can easily get there by TTC."

Alexa popped her waffles into the toaster, "No, her mother's driving us to the streetcar stop. I'm so excited and I can't wait to go on the rides."

"Do you have enough money?"

"Yes, Dad gave me some last night when you were in bed. What was wrong with you, Mom?"

"I told you, I had a headache."

Alexa was about to respond when the landline on the counter rang. It was Nancy. "Hi, Mom, you're up early," Charlotte said trying to sound cheerful.

"I'm always up early. Wait until you get to my age and you won't be able to sleep in past six o'clock."

Charlotte decided not to tell her she'd been awake half the night and up just after five. "What are you up to today, Mom?"

"Well, I thought we could have lunch if you're not busy. We could drive to the Distillery district. I hear they have a really nice restaurant there called Archeo's and they have a patio."

"That sounds nice. Yes, I'd love to have lunch. Do you want me to pick you up?"

"Yes, that would be good. Pick me up at one and by the time we get there most of the lunch crowd will be gone."

Alexa was waving frantically at Charlotte, "I think Alexa wants to speak to you, Mom."

"Oh, she's there? I'd love to speak to her, put her on."

"Okay, I'll see you at one," Charlotte responded as she handed Alexa the phone and left the kitchen.

Charlotte picked Nancy up and drove to Trinity Street where they managed to get a table on the patio. They both ordered Caesar salads and a glass of Chardonnay and Nancy spent most of the time talking about Peggy and her family. It was only when they were finished and enjoying a cup of coffee that Nancy said, "So, what's all this I hear about you not going out east now?"

"Who told you that?" Charlotte asked defensively.

"Alexa told me and she was pretty upset about it. She seems to think you had a fight with her dad and that's why you cancelled."

"That's ridiculous, Adam and I haven't had a fight and I wish she wouldn't go telling tales like that."

Nancy raised an eyebrow, "Then what's the real reason for not going? You were up to your neck doing research on all the places you were planning on visiting and then suddenly it's all off."

"It wasn't all of a sudden, Mom. While you were away, I realized Alexa had spent too little time at home with her friends over the summer."

Nancy paused before responding, "I suppose there's some truth in that but what about you and Adam, don't you think you deserve a vacation?"

Charlotte sighed, "Oh, I've already been all over this with Adam. He's okay with it and as for me; well I'm taking off for a few days with Jodi."

Nancy was about to take a sip of coffee but changed her mind and placed the cup back in the saucer, "Really? When is this happening?"

"We're leaving on Friday and you needn't worry about Alexa, Adam plans to work from home."

"I wasn't worrying at all. Where are you going and when will you be back?"

"Rick's cousin has a cottage in Muskoka so we're going there. We'll be back on Tuesday."

Nancy looked thoughtful, "I see. It's all a bit sudden isn't it? Where in Muskoka is this cottage exactly?"

Charlotte looked exasperated, "I have no idea, mother, why all the questions?"

"Now I know something's up. You never call me mother unless you're annoyed or trying to hide something."

"What could I possibly be hiding? Jodi and I just want to get away from the city, that's all."

"Is Rick going to be at the cottage and what about his cousin? Is he going to be there too?"

Charlotte threw her hands in the air, "I can't believe you just asked me that. First of all, Rick isn't going and neither is his cousin who, incidentally, happens to be female."

Nancy shrugged, "Okay I guess you've convinced me."

"Well, thank goodness for that, now how about another glass of wine?"

"We already have coffee, dear."

Charlotte beckoned to the waiter, "So, live a little, Mom. It's a lovely afternoon and we can just relax and enjoy it."

Nancy sat back in her chair and realized she wasn't convinced at all. Charlotte was up to something.

Chapter Twenty-Six

Late on Thursday morning, Charlotte decided to go on another shopping spree to buy more clothes for her trip. She then spent the whole afternoon at the Elmwood Spa where she enjoyed a Swedish massage and treated herself to a manicure and pedicure. All the time she was there, she was hoping Julian would call. She hadn't spoken to him since their last brief conversation on Tuesday and was beginning to get a little anxious again. By five o'clock, she made up her mind to call him later but she was just turning onto Highland, when her cell phone rang. She quickly pulled over to the side of the road, well out of view of the house, and picked up the phone. It was Julian and, before she had the chance to say hello, he greeted her with "Bon jour, how's my pretty lady today?"

Charlotte smiled, "Hi! I'm wonderful now I've heard from you. Where are you?"

"I'm just finishing up work, how about you?"

"Well, I've just come from being absolutely pampered. I've been at the spa most of the afternoon."

"Ah, a lady of leisure, I hope this is all for my benefit."

Charlotte chuckled, "As a matter of fact, it is."

"Well it won't be long now. I'll be there to pick you up at the airport. I have all sorts of things planned for the weekend."

"What sort of things?" Charlotte asked suggestively.

"You'll just have to wait and see, woman."

Charlotte paused and then asked, "Will I be staying at your place?"

"Yes, but don't expect anything fancy like the palace you live in."

"I'd hardly call it a palace." Charlotte responded feeling a little uncomfortable.

"Whatever," Julian remarked rather abruptly. "Listen, I only have a minute, I just wanted to touch base but I have to go now. I'm off to have a beer with a couple of the guys."

Charlotte was surprised at the sudden change of tone in the conversation, "Oh, all right. I'll see you tomorrow."

"Okay, have a good flight. Bye, Charlotte," and then he was gone.

Charlotte stared at the phone in her hand and wondered what had just happened. Was it her imagination or did she sense Julian resented the fact that she lived in a nice house. There was so much she didn't know about him but maybe this weekend she would learn a lot more. Just then somebody knocked on the car window and she looked across to see Alexa staring through the glass and grinning like a Cheshire cat. She wound down the window, "Hi, honey, I thought you were in the house."

"What are you doing, Mom, talking to your secret lover?"

Charlotte kept her composure, "No, Jodi just called and like a good citizen I pulled over to answer the phone."

Alexa opened the door and jumped into the passenger seat, "Okay, I believe you but thousands wouldn't."

Charlotte frowned, "Can't you walk the rest of the way home?"

Alexa shook her head and held up a rolled up towel, "Not if I can help it. Hildy and I were at Jen's all day swimming in her pool. It's not as nice as ours, Mom, but they have a diving board and her dad was teaching us how to dive."

Charlotte pulled out onto the road, "Well, I'm glad you're spending time with your friends. Just make sure while I'm away to let your dad know where you are at all times."

"When will you be back, Mom?"

"Not until Tuesday. I've left all kinds of food in the freezer so you don't have to worry about starving to death."

"I still think it sucks that we aren't going out east."

"Maybe next year, we'll see."

Alexa sighed, "That's eons away. Anything could happen by then."

Charlotte nodded as her thoughts flew back to Julian and she wondered if he would still be in her life a year later.

Early on Friday morning, when Adam left for the office, he patted Charlotte playfully on her rear, kissed her goodbye and promised to be home by five to be with Alexa. After that, Charlotte was in a panic as she finished packing and got ready to leave for the airport. She was hoping Alexa wouldn't come down for breakfast before she left. She didn't think she could answer any more questions and Alexa would be sure to ask why she was taking such a large suitcase just to go to a cottage. Luck was with her and, just before she walked out of the house, she scribbled Alexa a brief note and left it on the kitchen table.

She had decided to leave her car in the parking lot, just a minute's walk from the ferry which would take her to the island airport. On the drive down she felt a tremendous sense of relief. For the next few days, except when she spoke to her family by phone, there would be no more lying. With Julian, she would be able to relax and throw caution to the winds. She wondered what he had planned for her.

The flight left on time and by eleven o'clock she entered the arrivals lounge at Pierre Elliott Trudeau airport, dragging her suitcase behind her and searching the crowd for Julian. She paused for a few seconds before recognizing the face she was so familiar with and she almost called out Adam's name but suddenly caught herself and stood there smiling as Julian approached her and took her in his arms, "Welcome to Montreal," he said and kissed her passionately. Charlotte was completely unaware a crowd of people were watching with smiles on their faces.

They walked out of the terminal and Julian left her while he went to get his car from airport parking. For a few minutes she felt very much alone, almost as though she had been abandoned in a strange place and then suddenly she heard the sound of a horn beeping and a bright red BMW convertible drew up alongside the curb. Julian jumped out and hauled her suitcase into the trunk as she settled into the passenger seat. When they drove away the light breeze blew Charlotte's hair across her face, "This is a fabulous car," she remarked. "You're full of surprises."

Julian glanced over at her and grinned, "I know. I always wanted a BMW and I eventually saved up enough to buy one. It's the one luxury I own. Like I told you, don't expect my home to be very elegant. It's just a place I hang my hat."

Charlotte put her hand on his knee, "As long as I'm with you I don't care where I am," she replied.

The remark came back to haunt her when she walked into Julian's one bedroom flat on Avenue Claremont. Her house on Highland really was a palace in comparison. Throughout, there were hardwood floors devoid of any carpeting and the living room was filled with mismatched furniture. Julian didn't say a word as he led her to the bedroom. Once inside, he suggested she hang her clothes in the closet, which was only half full, and put her other things in the dresser drawer he had emptied for her. After he walked out of the room, she looked around in dismay at the double bed covered in a thin red cotton cover and wondered how on earth she would be able to sleep in it after being used to her king sized bed at home. She walked over to the window and pulled aside the matching red cotton drapes and immediately closed them again. The window was situated just a few yards across from a neighboring building and she was able to see directly into an apartment opposite where a rather obese man was reclining in an armchair completely naked. She wasn't sure whether to laugh or cry. Once she had finished unpacking her clothes, she gathered up her toiletries and walked back towards the living room. She noticed a door adjacent to the bedroom and gingerly pushed it open. The bathroom was even more depressing with dark brown walls, cream fittings and a plain beige shower curtain. Charlotte placed the toiletry bag unopened on the ledge behind the sink and left the bathroom, closing the door behind her. It was very quiet in the flat and after checking in the kitchen, which surprised her with its contemporary stainless steel appliances, still unable to see Julian, she walked back into the living room. It was then that she saw the open French doors leading out to a small balcony and where she found Julian. He looked up when he heard her footstep, "Ah, there you are. Are you all settled?"

Charlotte nodded, "Yes, but I need to find some space in the bathroom for my things."

"Oh, I forgot about that, I'll take care of that later but right now why don't you just sit down right here," he responded, indicating one of two rattan chairs fitted with bright green cushions. "I make a mean bloody Caesar and after that we can go to lunch."

Charlotte walked across the wood decking and peered over the railing where, between some buildings, she could see some green space. "Is that a park over there?" she asked.

Julian came over to stand beside her, "Yes, but they call it Prince Albert's Playground, don't ask me why."

Charlotte turned and wound her arms around his neck, "I'm so happy I'm here with you," she murmured, even though she was feeling somewhat ill at ease in her surroundings.

Julian pulled her closer and kissed her gently on the lips, "I'm glad you could make it," he whispered and then broke away. "Now sit, woman, and I'll go get that drink."

Charlotte grinned and sat down but she was still feeling unsettled. Was it her imagination, or was she always the first to express how she felt? There was no question in her mind she was falling in love with Julian but did he feel the same way? She was determined to find out by the time she returned home.

Chapter Twenty-Seven

When Julian took Charlotte back to the airport on Tuesday, she still wasn't sure how he really felt about her. He had certainly lived up to his promise to show her around Montreal and they had even driven to Quebec City on Sunday where she was reminded of the vacation she had spent in Europe with her family. They had eaten in some wonderful restaurants and she took great delight in sampling the traditional foods, like Poutine and Sugar Pie, while nights were spent making passionate love in the narrow bed in Julian's dreary little flat.

It was on Sunday night when they got into a deep conversation that Charlotte began to feel uneasy. They had just returned from their day trip and were both very tired when Julian suggested ordering in Chinese food rather than going out to dinner. Charlotte immediately offered to cook a meal and was taken aback when he threw open all of the cupboard doors and the refrigerator to reveal they were virtually empty, "What do you propose to make?" he asked rather abruptly.

Charlotte walked over and slowly began closing the doors while he stood there watching her. She then slowly turned to him and said, "We could go and buy some groceries. I thought I saw a supermarket close by."

Julian shook his head, "No, let's not get all domesticated, Charlotte."

She walked over and took both of his hands, "It's just one meal and I love to cook. Please let me do this for you."

Julian pulled away from her, "No, I'll only be gone a few minutes. If you don't like Chinese, I'll get something else."

Charlotte sighed, "All right if that's what you really want. Chinese is fine."

After he left, she walked around the flat aimlessly, once again noticing how depressing it was and suddenly realizing there were no photographs anywhere. Julian was becoming even more of a mystery.

When he returned fifteen minutes later with two paper sacks filled with fried rice, curried chicken, chow mein and some foods Charlotte didn't recognize, they sat down at the small rattan table on the balcony and ate in almost relative silence. Julian opened a bottle of Sauvignon and Charlotte had already finished two glasses by the time they finished eating. She leaned back in her chair and said, "Thank you. That was really good."

"Better than something you would have cooked?" Julian asked raising an eyebrow.

Charlotte frowned, "What's wrong, Julian? It wasn't a big deal, I just like cooking and I thought you'd enjoy a home cooked meal."

"The last person who made a home cooked meal for me was my mother. Let's just leave it at that."

Charlotte reached over and laid a hand on his arm, "I'm sorry. You really must miss her."

Julian stood up and started to clear away the left overs, "I'll just clean up out here while you relax and have more wine."

Charlotte's instinct was to help but she stayed where she was and watched him as he carried the leftover food inside. She knew mentioning his mother had upset him but it had opened the door to more conversation and, when he came back outside with another bottle of wine, she said, "I know you don't want to talk about your mother but sometimes it helps. It isn't good to grieve all alone."

Julian looked grim, "I prefer it that way. Can't you let it alone?"

Charlotte shook her head, "No, it doesn't make any sense. Tell me, why aren't there any photographs of her. In fact, why don't you have photographs of anybody in the flat?"

"I don't need a photograph of my mother, I can see her in here," Julian replied angrily pointing to his head.

Charlotte lowered her voice, "I know, but it's just a little unusual, that's all."

Julian shrugged, "Guess I'm just an unusual type of guy," he remarked, "which reminds me. Where's the photo I asked you to bring of your family?"

Charlotte paused, then got up and went inside to find her purse, returning with a small plastic folder. She handed it to Julian and watched as he opened the folder and sat studying the two photos inside. It seemed like an eternity before he spoke, "Where were these taken?" he asked.

"The one of me with Alexa and our cat Zoe was taken in the garden last summer and the other one with Adam and Tyler was taken in our family room at Christmas."

"Your daughter is very pretty. She looks a lot like you."

Charlotte frowned, "Is that all you have to say? What about Adam, he looks like he could be your twin, doesn't he?"

Julian nodded very slowly without looking up, "Yes, he does."

Charlotte waited expecting more but Julian handed back the folder and said, "You have a very nice home, it probably cost a fortune. Your husband must be a very successful man."

Once again, Charlotte detected resentment in Julian's remark and wasn't sure how to respond. She hesitated and then, looking down at the photo of Adam, said, "Yes, he is, but he worked very hard to get where he is."

"I guess he had a good education too? Did his family have money?"

Charlotte was surprised at the direction the conversation was going, "Why all the sudden interest in my husband?" she asked.

"Forget it," Julian snapped as he rose from his chair.

Charlotte jumped up and grasped his arm, "No, I won't forget it. Why are you behaving this way? So, I live in a nice house but that's not what makes me happy. You live in this place because you choose to but I'm sure you could afford better. You seem to have a good job and you don't have any family to take care of."

Julian pushed her hand away and slumped back down onto his chair, "I had my mother to take care of," he whispered, bowing his head.

Charlotte dropped to her knees in front of him and tilted his chin up so that she could look into his eyes, "I'm so sorry, Julian, I wasn't thinking. It must have been very difficult but didn't your mother have any medical insurance?"

Julian shook his head and then in a low voice answered, "No. When she first started showing serious symptoms of her illness, almost nine years ago, I had someone living in her home with her full time. Three years later, she had to be moved to a facility specializing in Alzheimer's and I made sure she got the best treatment. I sold her house but real estate was at an all-time low and the proceeds soon got eaten up. I'd actually been saving up to buy a condo of my own but that dream soon flew out the window."

"Oh, my goodness, it must have been very expensive."

Julian nodded, "It was, but I don't regret any of it. I always thought she was a great mom but after she died, I found out she was the best mother in the world."

"What do you mean? Did you find out something about her, like some sort of secret?"

Julian stood up and Charlotte was forced to jump up too, "I don't want to talk about this anymore."

"But maybe it would help to talk about it," Charlotte protested.

Julian grasped her around the waist and, out of the blue, said, "Would you leave your husband if I asked you to?"

Charlotte gasped, "Where did that come from? You can't really mean that."

Julian grinned, "I didn't ask you to leave. I was just wondering if you would."

Charlotte pulled away, "I think you're just playing with my head. I can't possibly tell you what I would do right now. I do know I love being with you and when I'm not, I'm pretty miserable but leaving my family would be a big step. It's not just Adam I would be leaving. It would be Alexa and Tyler too."

"And the big comfortable house, don't forget that," Julian remarked.

"Please don't talk like that, Julian. You're not being fair."

"Life isn't fair," he shot back as he released his hold on her and walked away.

Charlotte went over the conversation on the flight back to Toronto and then tried to push it out of her mind. She thought about their last few moments together before going through the gate to board the plane. Julian had been especially attentive and kept telling her how much he'd enjoyed being with her. He promised to call the next day and, when they heard the boarding call, he kissed her with such passion; it was hard for her to break away.

Chapter Twenty-Eight

Charlotte arrived home, late in the afternoon to find Adam was already there warming up a casserole for dinner. She had called him twice while she was away and had been forced to make up lies about the cottage where she was supposed to be staying with Jodi. She hoped he wouldn't ask for more details because she wasn't sure she could keep up the charade.

She almost got caught with her large suitcase, which would have prompted more questions, but she managed to carry it upstairs and hurriedly empty it before heading down to the kitchen. Adam was surprised when she walked through the door, "Oh, hi honey I didn't hear you come in," he said walking forward and folding her into his arms.

Charlotte pulled away, "I guess that's because you were too busy cooking," she responded grinning.

"I'd hardly call it cooking. I just stuck the casserole in the oven."

Charlotte looked around, "Where's Alexa?"

Adam got busy putting plates on the table, "She's in the garden with Hildy. I told her Hildy could stay for dinner"

Just at that moment, Zoe wandered in. Charlotte picked her up and nuzzled her nose into the fur on the back of her neck, "I think I'll go out and say hello," she said.

She was starting to walk away when Adam called out, "Okay, but don't be too long, everything should be ready in about fifteen minutes then you can tell us all about your trip."

As it turned out, Alexa dominated the conversation at dinner and showed little interest in Charlotte's responses to Adam's questions about her weekend. She kept her account of the days spent with Jodi to a bare minimum, claiming they did very little but swim, sunbathe, eat and sleep. Meanwhile Alexa babbled on about going to Wonderland with Hildy and Jen and going on all the rides. She couldn't wait to go again and she'd heard a rumour they were going to build a new roller coaster which would be the biggest one in Canada. "You should come with us one day, Mom. Jen's mom took us and she was so much fun. I think you two would really get along."

Charlotte nodded, "Maybe next summer, honey," she answered half-heartedly.

Adam reached over and took Charlotte's hand, "You look tired, why don't you go and lie down and I'll clear up here."

Charlotte got up, "I think I will. I am feeling a little weary." She started to walk out of the kitchen and then turned back and put her hand on Hildy's shoulder, "Come for dinner again soon, Hildy."

Hildy responded, "Thank you Mrs. Hamilton, I'd like that," as Charlotte continued to walk away.

Alexa looked at her father, "Mom's acting a bit funny. Why is she so tired when she's been away doing nothing all weekend?"

Adam sighed, "It's about a three hour drive back from the cottage and you know how your mother hates driving on the highway. When she gets anxious, it takes a lot out of her."

"Then why didn't she let Jodi drive?"

"Who knows, maybe Jodi did drive even though they took Mom's car. Anyway enough questions. Now help me clear the table and then you and Hildy can go over to Jen's like you planned."

Both Alexa and Hildy jumped up and, after piling all the dishes in the sink, quickly took their leave. As Adam heard them racing out the front door, he called out, "Make sure you're home by eleven and not a minute later."

From the bedroom upstairs, Charlotte heard the girls as they ran down the hall but her thoughts were back with Julian. She rolled over onto her side in a fetal position and closed her eyes. She was already wishing it was tomorrow and she could hear the sound of his voice.

The next morning, seemed like any other weekday morning. Adam had gone off to work and Alexa was still in bed. Charlotte had stayed in her bedroom the night before until just after eight and then joined Adam in the family room to watch a movie on television but her mind had been elsewhere. Later, Adam had attempted to make love to her but she claimed she was still very tired and was grateful when he just kissed her gently and told her to get some sleep. Now, she had the whole day to catch up on some chores and wait for Julian to call. She just hoped Alexa had plans with her friends because she didn't feel up to keeping her entertained.

It was just after nine, when she heard the telephone ring in the kitchen. She knew it couldn't be Julian because he only ever called on her cell phone and she hoped it wasn't her mother because Nancy was the one person she had never been able to deceive, even over the most trivial things. She picked up the receiver after four rings and, before she could even speak, heard her mother's voice, "Charlotte, oh you are there, I thought you weren't going to pick up."

Charlotte attempted to sound cheerful, "Hi, Mom, how are you?"

"I'm just fine, dear. How was your trip?"

"It was nice; very relaxing."

Nancy waited expecting to hear more, "Well, what did you and Jodi get up to? Did you find any good restaurants up there?"

"We just spent most of the time hanging around the cottage. We went swimming in the lake a couple of times and we ate all our meals in."

"Hmmm, I thought you would have had enough of cooking at home. Why didn't you go out to eat?"

Charlotte was beginning to feel uncomfortable, "We just didn't feel like it," she said rather irritably.

Nancy paused, "I see. Well, how about going out to lunch with me?"

That was the last thing Charlotte wanted to do so she was forced to tell another lie, "Sorry, Mom, I'm busy this morning catching up on some chores and I have a lot of errands to run this afternoon."

"What about tomorrow then?"

"It's Thursday, I work at the library on Thursday's, remember?"

"Oh, that's right, I forgot. I guess it will have to wait until next week then. I'm leaving on Friday to visit your cousin Lacey for the weekend."

"Lacey? When did she call you? I haven't spoken to her in ages."

"I know. I was surprised when I heard from her on Saturday. She's still living in Picton with Geoff. Her son moved out in March and he's getting married next year. I expect we'll be invited to the wedding."

Charlotte was relieved the focus was no longer on her trip, "I should have called her but we seem to have lost touch after Dave died. I remember the time we spent at her place a few years ago. The kids loved the beaches and Adam and I enjoyed visiting the wineries. I'm glad she found someone else to spend her life with. I'd like to meet Geoff one of these days."

"Lacey called him to the phone before she rang off and he sounded really charming"

"I'm sure you're going to have a great time, Mom. Do you want me to come and check on Gypsy and Luna?"

"That would be lovely, dear. Mrs. Walker will be coming in on a regular basis as usual but I feel a lot better when you look in on them too."

"No problem. I'm happy to do it. You go and enjoy yourself and say hi to Lacey for me and tell her I'll be in touch."

"All right, dear, give Adam and Alexa my love and I'll see you next week"

When Charlotte hung up the phone, she felt like a weight had lifted off her shoulders. There would be no lunch with her mother and no need to talk about her trip. She hoped, by the time she saw Nancy again, she would have forgotten all about it.

Alexa arrived downstairs, just after ten, wearing a pair of brief shorts and a tank top, revealing her bathing suit underneath. "Are you going swimming again?" Charlotte asked.

"Yes, Jen's mom said we could spend the day there and her dad will be home later to teach us some more dives"

"I hope he knows what he's doing, diving into a pool can be very dangerous."

"He does, Mom. He used to be captain of the swim team when he was at U of T."

"All right as long as you're careful but before you go, you need to eat breakfast. Sit down and I'll make you something."

"No, Mom," Alexa whined, "I'm meeting Hildy at McDonalds. We'll get something to eat there."

"That's not very healthy, Alexa."

"I know but it's only once in a while. Pleeeeease Mom, can I go?"

Charlotte grinned, "Okay, you can go and make sure you girls have a good time. Remember, it won't be long now and you'll be back in school so make the most of it."

Alexa groaned, "Ugh, don't remind me. It's not fair, Tyler, gets to skip school and go off to England and then he gets to go to Egypt."

"Your brother's a little older than you and it will be a while before he's saved up enough money to go to Egypt."

"He's still lucky he doesn't have to sit in some stuffy old classroom listening to a bunch of old teachers rambling on about stuff we're never going to need to know anyway."

Charlotte laughed, "Oh my, nothing's changed. You sound exactly like me when I used to moan to Nana about school. That reminds me, Nana's going away to visit my cousin Lacey for the weekend and she sent her love."

"You mean cousin Lacey where we went once where all those great beaches were?" Alexa asked, her voice rising with excitement.

"Yes, that's the place. Her son's getting married next year so we may be lucky and get invited to the wedding."

"But why can't I go with Nana now. Can you phone and ask her?"

"No, I can't. She's already taken you away twice this year and that's quite enough."

Alexa started to sulk, "I bet she'd take me if you asked."

"No she won't," Charlotte answered emphatically, "and I forbid you to ask her yourself."

Alexa stamped her foot and headed for the door, "Okay, I won't call but I still think it sucks."

Charlotte rolled her eyes but stopped herself from saying another word.

At three o'clock, Jodi called and quizzed her about her weekend with Julian. She wanted to know every detail, where they went, what they ate, how great he was in bed. At first, Charlotte was reluctant to tell her anything but eventually she got carried away and it was a relief being able to talk to someone and express how she really felt. It was obvious Jodi didn't approve and still had no intention of covering up for her but she was prepared to listen and try to help Charlotte sort out her emotions, "I'm here for you if you want to talk," she said.

"Thank you, you're a good friend," Charlotte said. "How about we get together for dinner one night next week?"

"I'd like that. I'll just check my schedule and call you on the weekend."

They said their goodbyes and Charlotte put down the phone then glanced up at the clock. She was beginning to get anxious again. When would Julian call? She hoped it was before Adam got home.

At just after five, Alexa called to ask if she could stay at Jen's for dinner and Charlotte reluctantly gave her permission. That would mean eating alone with Adam and spending the evening with him without any distraction. What would she do if he tried to make love to her again? She couldn't continue to refuse him without him becoming suspicious.

Right at six o'clock, her cell phone rang and she recognized Julian's home number. She raced from the kitchen upstairs to the bathroom, locked the door in case Adam arrived home, and was breathing heavily when she answered on the fifth ring. "Hi, Julian, I'm so glad you didn't hang up."

"Hi, pretty lady, what were you doing? You sound out of breath?"

"I just ran upstairs to the bathroom. Adam might be home any minute and I didn't want him to catch me talking to you."

"Well, I would have called earlier but I've been out on assignment all day. There was a major fire in Lachine. Ten families were forced from their homes and one firefighter was seriously injured."

"Oh, my goodness, are you all right?"

"Of course I'm all right, just a bit tired lugging my equipment around for so long. I was just going to pick up a pizza and then go home and relax but I had to talk to my love first. Do you miss me?"

"Yes, I miss you all the time. The family, including my mom have been asking me about the weekend and it's been really hard telling them so many lies."

"But it was worth it, right?"

"Totally, every single minute and I wish I was there with you right now."

There was silence for a moment and then Julian said "I may actually have a surprise for you."

Charlotte put her hand to her chest, "What is it? What kind of surprise? When will I get it?"

"Ah, that would be telling but probably on Monday."

"You're sending me something aren't you? Can't you give me a hint?"

"Absolutely not," Julian teased. "You'll just have to wait and see."

Just then, Charlotte heard the front door slam shut and knew Adam had to be home. She lowered her voice and said, "Adam just came in, I'm going to have to ring off in a minute or he'll come looking for me."

"Maybe he'll think you're out somewhere."

"No, he knows I wouldn't go out and leave the oven turned on and he'll probably be coming upstairs to change."

"All right, I'll call on Friday at about five. I'll be finishing work early unless there's some big news story."

"Okay, I love you," Charlotte whispered and then, realizing what she had just said, held her breath.

"Bye, pretty lady," Julian answered.

Charlotte sat down on the edge of the bathtub and held the phone between her knees. Why had she told him she loved him? Why didn't he say he loved her too? Suddenly she heard Adam call out, "Charlotte, are you up here?" She stood up and quickly hid the cell phone inside the bathroom cabinet, to be retrieved later. Then there was a gentle knock on the door, "Charlotte, are you in there?"

"Yes, Adam, I'll be out in a minute," she answered.

She flushed the toilet, washed her hands and opened the door. Adam was standing near the bed, in his boxers, pulling a tee shirt over his head.

"Hi, honey," he said, "how was your day?"

Charlotte picked up a pair of shorts, which were lying on the bed, and handed them to him, "It was good, I got a lot done and I talked to Mom. She's going to visit Lacey on the weekend."

"Ah, your cousin Lacey in Picton, I remember that vacation. How's she doing?"

Charlotte recounted what Nancy had told her while, in the back of her mind, she was thinking about Julian and wondering what his surprise would be.

Chapter Twenty-Nine

By the time Monday arrived, Charlotte was more anxious than ever. She hadn't heard from Julian again and it had taken all of her will power not to call him. This was the day he was supposed to have a surprise for her and as she watched the hours tick by, expecting a knock on the door and a package of some kind, her hopes began to fade. She had been wondering how she would explain it to Alexa if a package did arrive, but there would be no need. Alex was spending the day at the Beaches with Hildy and two other friends she had never met. When she thought about it later, she realized she hadn't even asked who the friends were and she felt a little guilty. She had been so obsessed with thinking about Julian, she was losing touch with what was going on in her daughter's life.

At four o'clock when she was almost ready to give up, her cell phone rang. She had been carrying it with her, and immediately snatched it from her pocket and saw it was Julian. "Hi, I was wondering when you'd call," she said trying to sound upbeat. "It seems like such a long time since I heard from you and I've been all day waiting for my surprise."

She heard Julian chuckle, "Aha, I thought you might be waiting but I said it would probably be on Monday, I didn't actually promise."

Charlotte couldn't hide her disappointment, "So it won't be today?"

Julian chuckled again, "I'm just teasing you. Your surprise will be arriving any minute. If you go to the window you may see it coming."

Charlotte started to walk towards the living room where the windows overlooked Highland, "Now I'm getting really excited. Whatever is it?"

"You'll see. I'm hanging up now and I'll talk to you later."

Charlotte tightened her grip on the phone, "No, don't go Julian, please."

"Have to, my love," he answered and then rang off.

Charlotte stood by the window gazing out for a moment but couldn't contain her impatience. She raced to the front door and stood on the step glancing from left to right and then back again. Then she saw it, a bright red BMW parked across the street, about six houses down, and her heart leapt into her chest. She took off running towards the car and as she got closer she saw the Quebec license plate and knew it was Julian. Suddenly she became conscious of the clothes she was wearing, the faded denim shorts and the pale pink t-shirt, that had seen better days and the fact she wore no make-up and her hair was in a pony-tail, but she couldn't turn back. She caught a glimpse of Julian grinning through the windshield as she approached and, seconds later, she jumped into the passenger seat beside him and he was gathering her into his arms. "How do you like you're surprise?" he whispered.

"I love it," she answered, "but what are you doing here? I thought we agreed we shouldn't be seen here?"

Julian looked around, "I don't think anyone can see us unless you've got some nosey neighbours peeking through the windows."

"But how long are you in town for and why didn't you let me know you were coming?"

"That would have spoiled the surprise now, wouldn't it? Anyway, I'm here until Thursday morning and I'm staying at the Thompson again so, if you can manage to get away, we can spend some time together."

"I don't know how I can make an excuse for tonight but I'll find some reason to be out of the house tomorrow and Wednesday. I guess you're working during the day?"

"Yes, I will be but I'll be through by six and we can meet for dinner and spend the evenings together. Too bad you won't be able to stay all night."

Charlotte stroked Julian's cheek, "I'm going to have to be very careful in case someone sees us together; in fact it might be a good idea if we ordered room service."

"Hmmm sounds like a good idea, that way we can spend more time in bed."

Charlotte wagged her finger at him, "You are very bad but too sexy to refuse." She looked down at the clothes she was wearing, "I feel such a mess, I don't know why you'd want to make love to me."

Julian tipped up her chin, "Because you're great in the sack and you still look gorgeous even without all the war paint and the fancy clothes."

She slapped him on the thigh, "You are such a liar but I'm flattered anyway."

Just then, one of her neighbours walked by on the other side of the street with his dog and seeing Charlotte, with someone he thought was Adam, raised his hand in greeting and called out, "Nice car."

Charlotte waived back half-heartedly and then turned to Julian, "You have to get away from here and promise me you won't come back to the neighbourhood."

"Don't worry I won't as long as you meet me as planned. Come to the hotel tomorrow at six. I'll be waiting for you."

Charlotte started to open the door then turned back and kissed him on the cheek, "I'll be there; you can count on it. Now go before someone else sees you."

Julian patted her on the rear and started up the car as she slammed the door and began to run back across the street. When she reached the house she looked back and saw him turning the corner onto Roxborough. Now all she had to do was come up with some excuse to be out of the house for the next two evenings and it wouldn't be easy but nothing was going to stop her from seeing Julian.

As soon as she got back inside, she ran upstairs and called Jodi, breathing a sigh of relief when she answered on the third ring, "Hi, Jodi," she said trying to sound casual, "It's Charlotte. I hope this isn't a bad time."

"Charlotte? No this is the perfect time. I have another twenty minutes before my next showing. By the way," she continued, "I meant to call you yesterday about getting together for dinner but Rick and I were visiting some friends of his in Kitchener."

Charlotte cut in, "It's okay, but I can't make it this week. I need to ask you a favour."

"What is it?" Jodi asked sounding apprehensive.

"I just don't want you to call the house for the next couple of days."

"Why, what's going on? I already told you, I usually call you on your cell anyway so I don't see how there could be a problem."

Charlotte lowered her voice, "Julian's here until Thursday."

Jodi sighed, "I suppose that means you'll be seeing him over the next two days?"

"Yes. He's here on an assignment but free in the evenings."

"And I suppose dinner with me is your alibi for one of those evenings?" Jodi asked abruptly.

Charlotte detected the disapproval in Jodi's voice, "I thought you weren't going to judge me."

"How can I not? You're getting yourself in deeper and deeper and have you ever considered how this is all going to end up? Frankly, I can't understand how you can sleep with someone who looks almost identical to Adam. It's all a little creepy and bound to end in disaster."

"Well, he may look like Adam but other than that, he's completely different," Charlotte shot back defensively.

"How is he so different, Charlotte?"

"He's exciting and very sexy and he makes me laugh."

"It's the underhanded affair and having to come up with excuses and lies and being afraid you might get caught that's exciting. As for making you laugh, well I always thought Adam had a good sense of humour and when it comes to sex, you always told me you were satisfied with your sex life."

"That's only because I didn't know any different, Jodi. I feel like such a babe-in-the-woods."

"Oh, Charlotte, sex isn't everything. Adam's a good man and you're going to lose him if you don't stop seeing Julian. Think how it would affect Alexa and Tyler as well."

Just then Charlotte heard the front door opening, "Someone just came in," she whispered, "I'm going to have to go. I'll call you later in the week."

"Okay, but think about what I've said. I don't want to see anyone get hurt."

Charlotte heard Alexa call out, "Mom, are you home?"

"I have to go, bye Jodi," and she put the phone down and raced to the top of the stairs.

Alexa looked up, "Oh, there you are. I thought I heard someone talking. Were you on the phone?"

Charlotte nodded, "It was just some telemarketer, honey. I'll be right down and you can tell me about your day."

Later after dinner, while Charlotte was clearing away the dishes she told Adam about the retirement party she had been invited to attend at the library the next night. "I'm sorry I didn't tell you earlier," she said, "but I completely forgot about it. I won't be home after work so you and Alexa will have to fend for yourselves."

Adam was still savouring his second glass of Sauvignon, "Who's retiring?" he asked.

Charlotte had her back to him as she replied, "Mmmmm . . . . Carol Levison. She's been there for thirty five years."

"So, where's the party, inside the library?"

"Yes, and before I forget, I'll be out with Jodi for dinner on Wednesday too."

Adam got up and walked over to Charlotte, slipping his hands around her waist, "I'm beginning to feel neglected," he said softly.

Charlotte released herself from his grasp and turned around, "Don't be silly. I'd change the date with Jodi if I could but she's busy the rest of the week."

Adam shrugged, "No problem, except I'll be out myself on Wednesday. Howard's coming into town and we're having dinner together."

"What about Alexa?"

"What about her? She's old enough to take care of herself."

"I suppose you're right," Charlotte responded as she picked up Adam's empty glass from the table then, she hesitated for a moment as a thought occurred to her, "Where will Howard be staying?" she asked.

"I think Diane booked him a room at the Marriott, why?"

"Oh, just curious," Charlotte replied breathing a sigh of relief.

Chapter Thirty

On Tuesday morning, as soon as Adam had left for work and Alexa was still asleep, Charlotte quickly gathered together the clothes she would need for the evening. They wouldn't be going out to dinner so she packed a simple cotton dress with a halter top, she had bought on a whim, a pair of strappy sandals and a set of her new lacy underwear. The idea of spending the next eight hours at the library before she saw Julian again seemed daunting but somehow she had to get through it.

At just before six o'clock, she was in the lobby of the Thompson and calling Julian on her cell phone but there was no answer. She looked around, not sure what to do, and then decided to sit down and wait a few minutes before trying again. She was just starting to call for the second time when she felt a hand on her bare shoulder. She looked behind her and there he was grinning down at her and her heart melted. He was wearing jeans along with a lightweight tan jacket and looked incredible. "Hi," she said, "I'm glad you showed up."

He came around and sat beside her, "Did you doubt me for a minute? I was through at five so I unloaded all my camera equipment and came back down for a drink. I had a feeling I might find you here."

Charlotte looked around nervously, "Let's go up to your room, someone might see us together."

Julian took her hand, "Maybe they'll just think I'm Adam?"

"No, you'll never pull it off. Up close, they'll know you're not him. Let's go upstairs, Julian," she begged, starting to get up.

Julian nodded, "Okay, how can I refuse when you look so ravishing. I love the outfit."

"Do you really? I just bought it."

"It's fabulous and so are you. Now come on, woman, let's go to my room and then order some dinner. I'm starting to get peckish."

Charlotte followed him into the elevator, still scanning the faces of the people coming and going through the lobby, and it was only when they were inside his room that she finally relaxed.

They ordered chicken fingers and fries and while they waited, Julian opened a bottle of Riesling. They lounged on the bed taking occasional sips in between passionate kisses until suddenly Julian sat up, startling Charlotte, and said, "If we don't stop doing this, I'm going to be tearing your clothes off. I wish we hadn't ordered our food yet."

"We could cancel it," Charlotte said suggestively.

"No, it's too late for that. I think I'll go and take a cold shower. If the food arrives, ask them to charge it to the room and give them this," he said taking a five dollar bill from his wallet.

"I wouldn't mind taking a shower too," she said getting up and putting her arms around him.

"Uh, uh, my love, someone needs to answer the door."

"Oh, all right," Charlotte said making a face, "don't be long though."

Julian gently pushed her back onto the bed, "I won't, I promise. Why don't you watch the news while you're waiting?"

After they had eaten and finished the wine, Julian produced a small bottle of Frangelico and two shot glasses. "I've never tasted that," Charlotte remarked.

"You'll like it, it has a hazelnut flavour," Julian responded as he filled the two glasses.

"Are you trying to get me drunk?"

"Of course, but not too drunk to experience what I'm going to do to you."

"I can hardly wait," Charlotte replied as she let the liqueur slide down her throat and emptied the glass.

"Hey, steady on," Julian said reaching out and grasping her arm.

"Why?" Charlotte asked as he refilled her glass and with one hand reached back and untied the bow at the back of her neck. Julian smiled as the top of Charlotte's dress fell, exposing her bare breasts, and she sidled towards him and rubbed herself against his chest. He took the glass from her, laid it on the bedside table, then gently eased her dress past her waist and over her hips until it fell in a puddle at her feet. She was now completely naked except for a white lace thong and her sandals. He sat her on the edge of the bed and then slowly began to take off his own clothes, first the tee-shirt and then his jeans so that he was soon standing in a pair of black briefs that could hardly contain his obvious erection. Charlotte breathed in the masculine scent of him and then reached out and touched him. "I want you," she whispered.

Julian didn't answer; he just pushed her back so that she was lying with her legs hanging over the side of the bed, He then slipped the thong over her thighs and pulled the sandals from her feet. When he opened her legs and lowered his head, she shuddered in anticipation and gave herself up completely to him. This was just the beginning of a night she would remember for a long time.

Exhausted, they had both fallen asleep and panic set in when Charlotte woke up, with a start, and realized it was almost four o'clock. Not wanting to disturb Julian, she slipped out of bed, gathered up her clothes and ran into the bathroom to get dressed. She was just running a comb through her hair when there was a gentle knock on the door. "I'll be right out," she said.

Julian was sitting on the edge of the bed, completely naked, when she came out. "Please don't leave," he said.

She walked over to him and bent down and kissed the top of his head, "I have to. It's almost morning and I need to get home but I'll see you tonight."

Julian stood up and gathered her in his arms but she pulled away, "Please don't do this. I really have to go."

Julian released her and sat back down, "So go," he said rather abruptly.

Charlotte turned to leave, took a few steps, and then turned back to look at him, "I said I'd be back. I'll be here at six." Julian merely shrugged and she opened the door, slipped out into the hallway, and closed it gently behind her.

The experience of walking through an almost deserted lobby, at that hour of the night, attracted some attention from hotel staff. She was sure they thought she was some kind of escort and scurried along trying to avoid their eyes. She couldn't wait to get into her car so she could think up a story to tell Adam.

Zoe greeted her at the door, when she crept into the house, and she had to pick her up to stop her pitiful crying, "What's wrong?" she whispered as she carried her into the kitchen. "Did you miss me?" She quickly fished in the cupboard for some of her favourite salmon treats, scattered them on the floor and then left her there to climb the stairs to the bedroom. Adam was fast asleep and she breathed a sigh of relief as she quickly changed into her nightgown before slipping under the covers. She closed her eyes but sleep was elusive, her thoughts were all about Julian and it seemed like only minutes had passed when the alarm signalled it was already seven o'clock and time to start a new day. She jumped out of bed, threw on a robe and headed downstairs to prepare breakfast while leaving Adam to shower and get ready for work. She was scrambling some eggs when he arrived in the kitchen, dressed for the office and carrying the morning paper which he'd retrieved from the front step, "Good morning, honey," he said cheerfully.

"Hi," she answered with her back to him, "would you like some jam on your toast?"

Adam was lowering himself onto his chair, "What?" he asked as he scanned the headlines.

"Never mind," Charlotte responded bringing a pot of raspberry jam to the table.

She was turning to walk back to the counter when Adam grasped her arm, "What time did you come home last night? I waited up until just after twelve."

Charlotte shook him off and continued to walk away, "I'm not sure, maybe around two."

"What an earth were you doing until two in the morning with a bunch of old fuddy-duddies?"

"Excuse me," Charlotte answered indignantly, "they are not fuddy-duddies. It was actually a very nice party. I just had a little too much to drink and didn't want to drive home so Carol suggested we go to this little all-night coffee shop and sober up."

"Good thinking," Adam said opening up the paper. "I'm glad you enjoyed yourself."

Charlotte was relieved and annoyed at the same time. Relieved that Adam hadn't given her the third degree and annoyed that he appeared to have little interest in how she had spent her evening. "I'm going out again tonight, I hope you remembered," she said.

"Uh, uh, I remembered," Adam responded. "Don't forget I'll be out with Howard."

"Oh, that's right. I'll try not to be too late although I expect Alexa has plans with her friends."

"Yes she does. She's going to a movie with Hildy."

Charlotte filled a bowl with cornflakes, poured herself a cup of coffee and said, "I'm taking this out to the garden. Have a good day at work."

Adam continued to read the paper, "Okay, hon," he muttered. "You have a good day too."

Charlotte was still sitting in the garden at eight o'clock when she heard the telephone. She knew it was the land line in the kitchen and realized Nancy would be back from her trip and was probably calling her. She really didn't want to speak to her mother at that moment so she decided not to answer and let it ring. She just hoped it wouldn't wake up Alexa.

By ten o'clock, Alexa had arrived downstairs, eaten breakfast and was sunbathing by the pool. Charlotte was busy in the kitchen, rolling out pastry for a pecan pie, when the phone rang again only it wasn't Nancy, it was Tyler. Immediately, he began to ramble on about what a great place London was and what great people the Lewistons' were, especially Shelby. He was obviously in love with this girl and Charlotte was happy for him but she missed him a lot and wished he would come home, "When are you going to Egypt?" she asked hoping he'd changed his mind.

"Probably in January. We should have enough saved by then."

"I guess that means you won't be home for Christmas this year?" Charlotte asked hopefully.

"No, I guess not. Sorry, Mom, but I won't be able to afford it."

"Your dad will be disappointed, so will Alexa."

"Is, Sis, there? I'd like to talk to her."

"Yes, she's out back but I'll go get her. You take good care, Tyler. I love you."

"Love you too, Mom."

After Tyler's call, Charlotte started to think about how much her family really meant to her but she had already lost her son to the temptation of far off places and soon it would be Alexa's turn to leave the nest. As for Adam, there was no question she loved him but her marriage lacked passion and once again her thoughts turned to Julian. Only a few more hours and she would be with him but she couldn't afford to fall asleep in his arms again. She was supposed to be out with Jodi and if she came home late this time, it would definitely raise some suspicion.

Alexa had just put the phone down when it rang again and when she picked it up and Charlotte heard her say, "Hi, Nana, how are you?" she knew there was no way she could avoid talking to her mother now. Nancy was full of news about her weekend away and wanted to meet Charlotte for lunch but she put her off until Friday, claiming she already had plans for the day and would be at the library on Thursday. "We'll have a nice talk when I see you, Mom," she said.

Alexa went back to her sunbathing while Charlotte decided to drive to the market and pick up some fresh vegetables. On the way back, she heard her cell phone ring and pulled over to the curb to answer it. She was surprised and a little apprehensive when she heard Julian's voice especially when all he said was, "Good morning."

"Julian, I didn't expect to hear from you."

"There's been a change in plans," he said, "I'm going to be at the Hilton in Thornhill late this afternoon. I'll be leaving my car downtown so I'd like you to drive up and meet me there instead."

Charlotte paused for a moment, "I see, did you want us to drive back to your hotel after I pick you up."

"No, someone recommended this restaurant called Fraticelli's in Richmond Hill and I thought it would be a great place for dinner. I'm pretty sure we're not going to run into anyone there."

Charlotte had envisioned spending the evening in Julian's hotel room again and was a little disappointed. "It sounds nice," she said, in a low voice.

"Is something wrong?" Julian shot back abruptly.

Obviously he had detected she wasn't exactly happy with the change in plans. "No, nothing's wrong. I can't wait to see you," trying to show some enthusiasm.

"Good, then that's settled. Don't get too gussied up because I'll still be in my work clothes."

"Oh, okay," Charlotte replied already mulling over what she was going to wear.

Chapter Thirty-One

Dinner at Fraticelli's was more enjoyable than Charlotte had imagined. There was a party of eight from Montreal celebrating an engagement and when Julian walked over to the table and congratulated the couple in French, they asked him to join them. They dined on veal piccata, chicken carbonara, and some wonderful pasta and as the wine continued to flow and the party got rowdier Charlotte began to relax. She even kept her composure when someone, noticing her wedding ring, assumed she and Julian were married and asked them if they had any children. Julian immediately responded with a wink, "Not yet but we're working on it."

It was already after nine when they left the restaurant and Charlotte was concerned she'd had a little too much to drink. By the time they reached half-way, she was so nervous Julian suggested he should drive but after he climbed into the driver's seat, he pulled off of the main road and turned onto a side street and parked the car. "What are you doing?" Charlotte asked nervously looking around her to see if anyone was walking by.

"I've been wanting to kiss you all night," Julian said reaching over and pulling her into his arms.

Charlotte tried to push him away, "Not here. Let's go back to the hotel."

Julian shook his head, "No, it's going to be late by the time we get there and, unless you plan to stay over, there's no point in you even coming up to the room."

Charlotte placed her hand on his shoulder, "I could stay until at least midnight. I'll think of some excuse to be out with Jodi that late."

"Yes, and I'll be watching the clock to make sure you don't get into trouble when you get home to hubby," Julian shot back sarcastically. "What's the matter, haven't you ever made out in a car before?" With that, he pushed her back so her head hit the passenger door window and he reached up under her skirt and tugged at her underpants.

Charlotte was shocked and struggled to keep him from going any further but at the same time she was excited and aroused. "Stop it, Julian. Someone might see us," she cried out.

Julian withdrew his hand and then, pulling her back towards him, murmured in her ear, "Why don't you climb in the back with me. It's dark; nobody's going to see us."

Later that evening, after she had dropped Julian off at the hotel and was on her way home, Charlotte relived every moment of the frantic lovemaking session she had shared with him. The danger of being caught half-naked having sex in the back of a car only made it more exhilarating and it was an experience she would always remember. The memory would have to sustain her during the time she was away from Julian. She had no idea when she would see him again. How many more lies could she tell? How many more excuses could she make up?

Adam was still out when she arrived home and Alexa was watching a game show on television, "Hi, Mom, how was your night out with Jodi," she asked.

"It was nice. How about you, what movie did you go to?"

"Oh, some dumb sci-fi thing Hildy wanted to see," Alexa replied not taking her eyes off the screen.

Charlotte started to walk away, "Well, don't stay up too late. I'm tired, so I'm off to bed.

On Thursday morning, Charlotte awoke before the sun came up. She had feigned sleep when Adam came in the night before and was determined to avoid seeing him before she left for the library. She quickly showered in the bathroom down the hall and got dressed in Tyler's room so that she wouldn't wake him. Feeling a little guilty about not making his breakfast, she left a note on the kitchen table telling him she had an early meeting and he'd have to fend for himself. As she drove away from the house, heading to the Rosedale Café, where she would have to be content with something other than her usual cornflakes, she realized Adam would probably be perfectly happy settling for an Egg McMuffin. She had always tried to discourage him from eating fast food but, every now and again when the children were younger, he would sneak out and take them to MacDonalds. She smiled now when she remembered those times. Why had everything changed?

The hours at the library seemed to drag by. She had always loved working with books and was an avid reader but she could hardly wait for the day to end. She couldn't get Julian out of her mind and was determined to try and reach him later even if it meant leaving the house to go on some false errand. She was still dreaming up an excuse, as she turned onto Highland, when her cell phone rang. She pulled over and snatched it up from the seat beside her, "Hello," she said hopefully not recognizing the number displayed.

"Hi, my lovely," Julian replied. "Where are you?"

"Oh, Julian, I'm so happy you called. I'm just coming home from the library. Are you in Montreal now?"

"Yes, but not for long; I got another assignment but this time it's up near James Bay and we'll be gone for nearly two weeks. The area's pretty remote and I'm not sure when I'll be able to contact you."

Charlotte's heart sank, "When are you leaving and what's the assignment?"

"We're leaving first thing in the morning. We're doing a story on the Taykwa Tagamou Nation and don't tell me you've never heard of them because I've never heard of them either. I'll probably be bored to tears after a few days and I'm going to miss you but I'll try and keep in touch."

"I'm going to miss you too, more than you know."

"Did you get the third degree from hubby when you got home last night?" Julian asked abruptly changing the subject.

Charlotte felt uncomfortable whenever Julian mentioned Adam and paused before answering, "No, he came home after I was asleep. He was out with a client of his."

"Male or female?" Julian asked with a chuckle.

"Male of course," Charlotte responded defensively. "He's working on building a sub-division in Ottawa. It was just a business meeting."

"Okay, okay, if you say so, sweetheart."

Charlotte felt the hairs on the back of her neck go up, "Please don't be like that, Julian, especially now when I may not be able to talk to you for a while."

"Now you're being much too sensitive, Charlotte. Look, I'm sorry but I have to go. I have a lot to do before we leave. We have a late meeting at the paper and then I have to pack. I promise I'll do my best to stay in touch but, depending on where we are, it may be difficult."

"I'll be thinking of you every minute. Please take care of yourself."

Charlotte heard someone in the background calling Julian's name and a moment later he was gone. She whispered good-bye, put the phone down and then buried her head in her hands. How would she get through the next two weeks?

Chapter Thirty-Two

Ten days later, Charlotte still hadn't heard from Julian and had no idea what to do. Alexa had just returned to school after the summer break and the prospect of cooler weather and the inevitable Canadian winter did little to keep her spirits up. She had seen her mother twice since her return from Picton, once for lunch after her last conversation with Julian and a week later when Nancy showed up at the house unexpectedly. On both occasions, Nancy noticed the change in Charlotte and was determined to get to the bottom of it. "I know you told me you were fine last week," she said, "but I don't believe you. I've been worrying about you for days so you need to tell me what's going on."

Charlotte shook her head, "I'm just tired, that's all. There's no need for you to be concerned."

Nancy was persistent, "That's not good enough. You're not your usual self, dear. Maybe you should see the doctor. You could be coming down with something."

"It's probably the start of menopause. It's nothing to be concerned about," Charlotte responded.

Nancy frowned, "You're a bit young for that. Have you had any symptoms?"

Charlotte sighed, "Not really. I've always been irregular so I'm not really sure."

"Well, I suggest you go and find out. Promise me you'll make an appointment."

Charlotte knew there was no way she would satisfy her mother until she promised to do what she wanted, "Okay, I'll make an appointment tomorrow. Now stop worrying about me."

That evening, after having cleared away the dinner dishes, she announced she was going to pick up some wine at the liquor store. "I'll go," Adam said, "I need to put some gas in the car and I don't want to leave it until tomorrow."

Charlotte paused for a moment, "I'll leave my car here and take yours. I can take it to the gas station for you. You must be tired after a long day so why don't you just relax and watch some TV."

"It sounds tempting," Adam replied. "Are you sure you don't mind?"

"No, of course I don't mind. Where are your keys?"

At that moment Alexa came bounding back into the kitchen with Zoe in her arms, "Where are you going, Mom?" she asked, noticing Charlotte with her purse strung over her shoulder.

"Just on a couple of errands," Charlotte answered, praying Alexa wouldn't ask to come along.

"Can you drop me off at Hildy's house? I just have to run upstairs and change my top?"

Charlotte nodded, "I'll go wait in the car. We're taking Dad's."

Zoe let out a distinctly indignant meow when Alexa dropped her abruptly onto the floor and then raced out the door.

After Charlotte deposited Alexa at the front gate of Hildy's house, she drove into the lot of the LCBO store just south of Summerhill Station and parked. She hesitated for a while before summoning up enough courage to call Julian. Would he be angry with her for calling him? Maybe he was busy and then again maybe she wouldn't be able to reach him. Finally she tapped in his number and held her breath as she listened to the ringing tone. She longed to hear his voice, while afraid what his reaction might be, but the ringing continued until she had to accept the fact he wasn't going to answer. She set the phone down on her lap and exhaled. Where was he? Why couldn't she even leave a message? Should she try again later? That would mean leaving the house again or locking herself in the bathroom. She decided to wait until morning when she would be alone.

Two days later, in desperation, Charlotte telephoned the Gazette and asked to speak to Julian Richards. She was put through to an individual with a heavy French accent who advised her Julian was out of the office on vacation. When Charlotte insisted on the need to contact him, she got the third degree and after a few minutes she angrily slammed the phone down. Why had he lied to her? Where was he? Who was he with? Why hadn't he called her?

For the rest of the day she went on a cleaning spree in order to work off some of her pent up energy but it didn't really help. The thought of having dinner with her family that night was just too much and she just couldn't face it. She had to get away. Hoping Jodi might be available, she called her only to discover she was out of town all week. She was wondering what to do next when there was a knock on the door and her mind went into overdrive. Was it Julian; had he come back to surprise her again? But it wasn't Julian, it was Nancy.

"What are you doing here, Mom," she asked. "This is the second time you've shown up without calling first."

"Well, that's a nice greeting, I must say," Nancy responded bustling past Charlotte and heading for the kitchen. "We need to talk so how about some coffee?"

Charlotte reluctantly followed her mother into the kitchen and stood with arms akimbo frowning, "What's so important we have to talk about it?"

Nancy ignored her while she filled the coffee maker with water and fished for some K-cups in the cupboard. "Just sit down and wait until the coffee's ready."

Charlotte pulled out a chair and sat staring at her mother's back, "Why don't you make yourself at home," she said with sarcasm.

Nancy pretended she hadn't heard and continued to prepare the coffee while Charlotte sat in silence. Eventually, Nancy brought two mugs to the table along with cream and sugar and then returned to raid the cookie jar for some shortbread. When she finally settled opposite Charlotte, she said, "Well what do you have to say for yourself?"

Charlotte shrugged, "What do you want me to say?"

"Have you made an appointment yet?"

"No, I haven't. I got my period yesterday and I don't want to see the doctor right now."

"You can still make an appointment for a week or so from now. You promised me, Charlotte."

"I know I promised but I've been busy."

"You're not too busy to pick up the phone. You need to look after yourself. You won't be any use to your family if you get taken ill."

"I'm not much use to them now," Charlotte murmured looking down at the table.

Nancy reached across the table, "What do you mean? You're a wonderful wife and mother."

Charlotte raised her head and Nancy was shocked when she saw tears in her eyes. She got up immediately and came around the table to sit beside her, "Talk to me, honey. Tell me what's bothering you."

Charlotte looked into her mother's eyes and then buried her head on her shoulder and started to sob. Nancy held her close and stroked her head until the crying subsided, "I've done a terrible thing, Mom," she said.

"What could you possibly have done to make you this upset?"

Charlotte pulled away and started to shake her head vehemently, "You're going to think I'm awful."

Nancy reached out and grasped her hand, "I'm your mother. No matter what you've done, I'll always think of you as my precious daughter. Please talk to me, honey, I think you'll feel better if you get it off your chest."

Charlotte squeezed Nancy's hand and, in a halting voice, managed to whisper, "I've been having an affair."

Nancy paused for a moment, "I suspected as much. I had a feeling you were trying to hide something when you went away for the weekend. You weren't with Jodi were you?"

"No, I wasn't with Jodi at the cottage. I was in Montreal."

Nancy released her hand and took a sip of her coffee, "Why don't you start at the beginning. How did you meet this person?"

Charlotte began to explain how Jodi's brother thought he saw Adam in New York with a woman and didn't stop until she'd told Nancy everything. Then, just as Nancy was about to respond, she put up her hand to stop her and said, "It's all over now, Mom; I won't be seeing him again."

"So you think he lied to you about being on an assignment?"

"Yes, and I wonder what other lies he's told me. In any case, I can't deal with this anymore. The time I've spent with him doesn't make up for all the times we've been apart. I've been utterly miserable and it's a wonder Adam hasn't noticed."

"This is all very curious. Does he really look that much like Adam?"

Charlotte got up from the table, took the photo of Julian out of her wallet and handed it to her mother. Nancy stared at it wide-eyed and then remarked, "Oh, my goodness, this is unbelievable. Are you absolutely sure they're not related?"

Charlotte sighed, "I can't be positive, Mom, they might be distant cousins or something like that."

Nancy shook her head, "I just find it really strange you were so attracted to someone who looks so much like Adam."

Charlotte picked Zoe up from the floor, where she had been brushing against her legs, and sat down, "I think I was intrigued at first and then I was flattered when he paid me so much attention. He told me I was beautiful and he made me feel desirable. I haven't felt that way in so long, Mom, and when I slept with him, I began to realize how naïve I'd been and how much I'd missed out on. I couldn't help myself; I started to fall in love with him. Now, I feel like such a fool but even though I know it's over, I'm really going to miss him."

Nancy's eyes started to well up, "I think I know how you feel, honey."

Charlotte looked at her and frowned, "How could you, Mom, I thought you and Daddy had a wonderful marriage?"

Nancy nodded, "We did but we were very young and, about a year after you were born, I felt as though I'd missed out on a lot. I saw a lot of my friends from school living this carefree life, travelling all over Europe and not having to worry about day to day things like paying the mortgage and bringing up a baby. Don't get me wrong, I loved you dearly and I never regretted having you but when I met this young man one day in the park, he brought a breath of fresh air into my life."

Charlotte was hanging onto every word, "What was so special about him?"

"First of all, he was one of the most handsome men I had ever met, very dark and exotic. He was born in Iran but came to Canada when he was a small child. His name was Yousef and he was an artist and quite successful. He invited me to an exhibition where some of his paintings were on display and that's how it all started."

"Did you sleep with him, Mom?"

Nancy smiled, "Yes, and when I did, I felt just as naïve as you did. He was a wonderful lover and he made me feel like the most desirable woman in the world."

"How long did this affair last and what ended it?"

Nancy thought for a moment, "It went on for about six months until it got to the point where I knew it had to stop or I would leave and run away with him. I couldn't leave you, I loved you too much, and taking you with me would have robbed you of your father. Daddy adored you and I couldn't do that to him."

"Did Daddy know about the affair?"

"No, he never did. It wasn't hard to keep it from him because he travelled a lot in his job. I'm glad he never found out because his family was important to him and he was a very sensitive man. When I think about how hurt he would have been, I thank heavens I stayed with him. Adam reminds me a lot of your father, he takes good care of his family and he's a good person, Charlotte. I know it's really hard right now, but you'll soon get over this Julian fellow and be relieved you didn't do anything rash."

"Did you ever see Yousef again?"

"Yes, after Daddy died, I ran into him in Yorkville. He was with a very attractive woman who he introduced as his fiancé. We chatted for a while, wished each other well and then said good-bye. It was all very civilized."

"Did it upset you running into him like that and seeing him with somebody else?"

Nancy paused while she took another sip of her coffee, "Honestly? I was a little hurt. Here he was moving on with his life and I was all alone."

Charlotte reached out and took her mother's hand, "You weren't alone. You had me, Mom."

Nancy smiled and gave her hand a squeeze, "Yes, that's true and you've brought nothing but joy to my life since the day you were born. I can't bear to see you hurting, honey."

"I'll be all right now, I promise, and thanks for listening to me. Now, how about another cup of coffee?"

Chapter Thirty-Three

Charlotte didn't expect to hear from Julian again. When she thought long and hard about the last time she saw him, she thought it had all been a little odd and then finding out he had lied to her about the assignment made her even more convinced he had just been using her. So, three days after confiding with Nancy, when her cell phone rang and she recognized the number, her hand shook as she put it to her ear and whispered, "Julian?"

"Bon jour, pretty lady, how are you? Did you miss me?" Julian responded, sounding in an upbeat mood.

"Where have you been?" Charlotte asked abruptly.

There was a moment of silence and then Julian replied, "In some godforsaken place up north. You know exactly where I've been, Charlotte."

"That's not what I was told."

"What are you going on about? Who were you talking to and what did they say exactly?"

"You didn't call me and I couldn't get hold of you so I called the paper and they told me you were on vacation."

Julian sounded angry, "That's a load of bull. Whoever you spoke to got it all wrong. I was on assignment just like I told you and anyway, what were you doing phoning the paper and checking up on me?"

Charlotte suddenly felt defensive, "I just wanted to talk to you, that's all. Why would they tell me you were on vacation?"

"How the hell do I know? Look, this is all nonsense. Either you believe me or you don't. If you don't then there's nothing more to say and we'll just go our separate ways."

Charlotte took a deep breath. This was her opportunity to tell him it was over but the words stuck in her throat and a moment later she was telling him how sorry she was for not trusting him and how much she desperately wanted to see him. By the time she got off the phone, she had promised him she would find a way to meet him the following week, no matter where it was, and he had promised he would try and make it to Toronto. That night she lay awake for hours staring at the ceiling wishing she'd had the courage to end it.

A week later, early in the afternoon, Julian arrived at the Island Airport and Charlotte was waiting at the ferry dock to meet him. They fell into each other's arms like long lost lovers and, two hours later, were lying in bed in the hotel room, after making passionate love, and sipping champagne, "I really missed you," Julian said.

"I missed you too," Charlotte responded. "I'm so glad you were able to come here this week."

"Well, it was easier than you trying to get away. I know we agreed it was risky meeting in Toronto but as long as we're careful, I'm sure nobody's going to see us together."

"Adam thinks I'm going shopping with a friend from work and then out to dinner, so I don't have to go home. I'll try and stay until at least nine tonight and then tomorrow we'll have all day."

Julian sighed, "I guess that's the most I can hope for. It's too bad I can't stay longer but I have to get back to Montreal. Maybe next time we can spend more time together."

Charlotte stroked Julian's hair, "If only this wasn't so difficult. I don't know how much longer I can go on making excuses to Adam before he suspects something's going on."

Julian sat up and swung his legs over the edge of the bed so Charlotte couldn't see his face, "Tell me about Adam," he said.

Charlotte felt uncomfortable talking about Adam, "What do you want to know?"

Julian shrugged, "Just where he grew up, what his family's like, that kind of thing."

Charlotte hesitated, "Well, he was brought up in Ottawa by a single mother and left home at nineteen."

Julian cut in before Charlotte could continue, "Does he have any brothers or sisters and how about his mother, is she still alive?"

Charlotte frowned wondering why Julian wanted to know, "He was an only child and yes, his mother's still alive. We don't see her very often because she's not an easy woman to get along with."

Julian stood up, walked naked over to the window, and looked down onto King Street below, "What's he like, your husband?"

Charlotte slipped off of the bed, came over to stand behind Julian and then slid her arms around his waist, "He's a really nice man. He's kind and very gentle. He hardly ever raises his voice and he adores the children."

Julian turned around so that he was facing her, "If he's so great, why are you with me?" he asked.

Charlotte smiled, "Because you're sexy and exciting," she replied as she slipped her hand between his legs.

"You're a wanton woman," Julian said scooping her up in his arms and depositing her back on the bed.

Days after Julian returned home, Charlotte found herself in a slump again and she almost regretted she had agreed to see him when she had the chance to end it. She considered writing him a letter and telling him their affair couldn't continue but the thought of giving him up literally made her feel sick to her stomach. How could she cut all ties with the one person in her life that made her feel truly alive?

Nancy picked up on her mood change within moments of meeting her for lunch the following weekend. She had spoken to her twice on the telephone since they last met but Charlotte had avoided talking about Julian. Nancy decided to come right out and ask the obvious question, "Have you spoken to Julian?"

Charlotte waited while they were interrupted by the waitress taking their orders and then said, "You asked me if I'd spoken to Julian and I have to be honest, Mom, I've not only spoken to him, I've seen him."

"Oh, dear," Nancy remarked, "I hope it was to tell him you wouldn't be seeing him again especially after he lied about where he was for two weeks."

Charlotte shook her head, "I just couldn't do it. As for the so called lie, he claimed it was all nonsense and he doesn't know why I was told he was on vacation. I believe him, Mom, and now I don't know how I'm ever going to give him up. I thought about what you told me about your affair but it was different, I was a baby and I really needed you so it was easier for you to walk away from Joseph."

"His name was Yousef,"

"What? Oh, sorry I mean Yousef."

"So what are you saying? Are you telling me you're considering leaving your family because you think Alexa and Tyler don't need you anymore?"

"No, I'm not saying that although Tyler certainly doesn't need me. I've never thought seriously about leaving."

"But it's crossed your mind. Has Julian asked you to leave?"

"He mentioned it once but I don't think he was serious."

"You are playing with fire, Charlotte. This is all going to end in disaster, I just know it."

Charlotte sighed, "I hope not, Mom, I really hope not but I don't know what to do."

"Just be careful, honey, and don't do anything stupid. Think about how much you can lose. I hope, with all my heart, you do the right thing."

"Yes, Mom, but your right thing might not be mine."

When Nancy returned home that afternoon she knew exactly what she had to do. From the moment she had seen the photograph of Julian, her suspicions had been aroused. Her intuition told her something wasn't right and if she could expose the truth and, by doing so, keep Charlotte's family together, then that's what she was going to do.

Chapter Thirty-Four

Like Charlotte, Nancy loved to read but her passion for reading far exceeded her daughter's. Not content to simply enjoy a book, particularly if it was based on the truth, she was compelled to learn more about the author and the people and places in every story. Because of her curiosity, as a gift to herself, on her fiftieth birthday, she purchased a computer and spent many hours researching on the internet. So, when she arrived home later that day, she wasted no time in her attempt to find out more about the man who threatened to turn Charlotte's life upside down.

Not wishing to arouse Charlotte's suspicions, she hadn't asked her for any details about Julian and even though she knew his age and where he worked, she didn't even know his last name. She decided to go on the Gazette's website to see if they listed the names of their employees but was disappointed to find only phone numbers for advertising personnel and newsroom editors. Then she googled *Gazette Photographers* and found several stories about individual photographers and their achievements, but none named Julian. Frustrated, she got up from her desk, paced while she considered her next move, and then returned to the computer to look up the Gazette's main number. A few minutes later, she sat smiling to herself, it had been so simple. She finally knew his name, Julian Richards.

Feeling excited, she googled the name and immediately discovered there were several Julian Richards but none who appeared to have any connection with the man she was looking for. She even clicked on Images, but again nobody remotely resembled Adam. Feeling a little discouraged, she sat staring at the monitor and then decided to see if his phone number was listed only to find there were several J. Richards but no Julian. Nevertheless she jotted down all the phone numbers and their addresses and then shut down the computer while she considered her next move. What if she called each number and asked for Julian and he actually answered? What would she say then? She needed time to think so she decided to wait until the evening before she continued her search. Walking into the kitchen, to make some coffee, she was followed by Gypsy and Luna looking for treats. Bending down, she petted them both gently and said with a grin, "They'll be calling me Nancy Drew next."

At eight o'clock that evening, assuming most people would be at home, she picked up the telephone and dialed the first number on the list. A woman, obviously elderly, with a heavy accent answered. Strike one, Nancy said to herself as she crossed out the number with a stroke of her pen. Finally, on the seventh call, she hit the jackpot. At least, the man who answered said he was indeed Julian Richards but did she have the right one?

"I'm sorry to bother you," Nancy said, "but I'm trying to find an old friend of mine and I was wondering if you might be related to her. I know she had a son named Julian but I lost track of her over the years. I'd love to get in touch with her."

"What was your friend's name?" Julian asked.

Nancy was prepared for this question, "Well, we always called her Franny because she didn't like her own name. It's been so long, I can't remember what it was now. That's the problem with getting old, the memory starts to go."

Julian chuckled, "I don't recall my mom ever answering to Franny. Her name was Fiona. Does that ring a bell with you?"

"It seems familiar but from your reply, it sounds like she's no longer with us. I hope that isn't the case," Nancy remarked, knowing full well his mother was deceased.

There was a moment of silence, "Mom died recently. She'd been sick for a number of years."

"Oh, I'm so sorry. I hope I haven't upset you calling like this."

"Not at all, in fact, it would be nice to talk to someone who knew her when she was younger. Maybe it was my mother. Did you meet your friend when she was single?"

"Yes, I never did get to meet her husband. I actually met Franny in Kingston and we roomed together for a year."

Julian sighed, "Then I don't think it could have been my mother because, as far as I know, she never lived in Kingston. She always lived in Laval after she came here from Scotland."

"Oh dear, that's too bad. I guess I'll have to keep on looking. Again, forgive me for bothering you like this. Thank you so much for your time and I'm so sorry for your loss."

"That's quite all right, I'm sorry I couldn't help. By the way, what's your name? You sound like a very nice lady."

Nancy couldn't help herself, "Its Nancy Drew," she replied, counting on the fact he'd never heard of the fictional teenage detective.

"Well Nancy Drew, it was a pleasure talking to you and good luck in finding Franny."

After they said their goodbyes, she put the phone down and sat staring into space. Her first thought was that he sounded like a charming man and maybe she should leave well enough alone. Then she remembered what it felt like to be caught up in an affair and how hard it was to walk away. She couldn't risk Charlotte doing anything rash and possibly ruining her life forever and causing heartbreak for Adam and the children. After a moment or two, she knew she had to find out more about this man and, if he was related to Adam in any way, then Charlotte needed to know that too. She was almost certain she had the right Julian Richards and now she had his mother's name and the place where he was brought up. How hard would it be to trace his birth certificate?

A week later, Nancy suspected Charlotte was already preparing to see Julian again. She had called to talk to her early on Thursday evening and Alexa had answered the phone. After they chatted for a few minutes, she discovered Charlotte was working late at the library and was going on a shopping expedition to Watertown on the weekend with Jodi. She immediately sensed the story Charlotte had told her family was merely a cover up for another rendezvous with Julian and realized she needed to try a little harder tracing his background. In the days since she had spoken to him, she had been unsuccessful in her attempt to locate any record confirming where and when he had been born and she knew, if she was to make any progress, she would need to get some help.

Later that evening she called the house again and Charlotte answered the phone, "Hi, Mom," she said, "I hear you called earlier."

"I certainly did," Nancy responded. "What's all this about you going off for the weekend?"

There was a pause before Charlotte answered, "I guess Alexa already told you. I'm going shopping with Jodi."

"And I still believe in the tooth fairy! You're seeing Julian aren't you?"

Charlotte was standing at the kitchen counter and looked around to make sure Adam and Alexa weren't nearby. "I can't talk to you now, Mom," she whispered.

"Then I suggest you make time to talk to me tomorrow. In fact, why don't you meet me for lunch?"

Charlotte sighed, "There's no point. You're not going to talk me out of going. Please don't give me a hard time, Mom."

Nancy softened her tone, "Oh, honey, I just want you to take a good hard look at what you're doing. If you're determined to go, then nothing I say is going to stop you but this has to end. Tell him you won't be seeing him again."

"I can't, I just can't. Look, I have to go but I'll call you on Monday, I promise and please don't be angry with me."

"I'm not angry, honey, I'm just disappointed but I still love you and I always will."

"I love you too, Mom," Charlotte whispered as she put the phone down.

Nancy walked out to the back garden and leaned against the wall of the house. There was a strong breeze blowing and she knew it was just a matter of weeks before the leaves started to turn. She shivered slightly, in her thin cotton dress, but it wasn't the thought of bare trees and the inevitable winter snow and icy roads, it was the thought of Charlotte making the biggest mistake of her life. She was convinced if she could find a connection between Julian and Adam, it would change everything. She needed to confide in someone who didn't know her family; somebody she could trust not to talk. Suddenly she thought of Tom, maybe he could help. After she met Tom Harper on the flight back from Vancouver, they had spoken several times by phone but had never actually seen each other again. Tom was a widower, living in Hamilton. He had been a lawyer, now retired, and usually only ventured into Toronto when he was attending the theatre or leaving from Pearson on vacation. He had been returning from a visit with his son and family in Burnaby when he first encountered Nancy. She had found him easy to talk to and the hours passed by so quickly, she was surprised when the announcement came that they would soon be landing. They had exchanged numbers and, a few days later, he called to see how she was and suggested they go to the theatre sometime but, so far, that hadn't happened. Maybe now she could persuade him to come into Toronto, even if it meant just going out to dinner and then she would have the opportunity to confide in him. With some trepidation, she picked up the phone and dialed his number. It rang four times before she heard him pick up and even before he spoke she could hear the barking of a dog in the background. That's when she remembered he owned a Jack Russell terrier. "Tom Harper here," he answered.

"Tom, how are you? It's Nancy calling."

Tom sounded pleased when he responded, "Nancy, how good to hear from you. I'm fine, how about yourself?"

"I've been healthy as a horse as usual, thank goodness. Is that your dog barking?"

"Yes, that's Badger. We were just going out for a walk so he's getting impatient."

"Oh dear, well I won't keep you but I was wondering if you would be coming into town soon. I'd really like to see you and to be quite honest I need your advice on a personal matter."

"Nothing I can help you with on the telephone?"

Nancy hesitated, "I would prefer to speak to you in person and I could even come to you if you like."

"No, it isn't necessary for you to come all this way. I can hop on the GO train and meet you at Union Station. You still drive don't you?"

"Yes, that's right. Did you give up driving?"

"No, but I find taking the train quite relaxing. That way I can read the paper or a magazine and not have to sit in traffic on the expressway. When would you like me to come?"

"How about this weekend? Would that be possible?"

"Yes, I can manage that. I'll come in on Sunday at around noon. I'll have to arrange for my neighbour to take Badger for a few hours but I don't think it will be a problem."

"That would be wonderful, Tom. I can't tell you how much I appreciate this."

"It's my pleasure, Nancy. I'll give you a call when I know the exact time I'll be arriving but I'd better go now before Badger starts making a racket again."

After they said goodbye, Nancy put the phone down and breathed a sigh of relief. She finally had someone to talk to.

Chapter Thirty-Five

Nancy left her house on Sunday morning to pick up Tom. On the drive down she thought about the telephone conversation she had earlier. Alexa had called to ask if she could come over that afternoon as she was at loose ends and Adam was busy getting ready for a meeting the next day. Nancy was upset that she had to turn her down but she couldn't possibly invite her over with Tom there. It wasn't a question of keeping her friendship with him a secret but the fact that she needed to speak to him in private. She chatted with Alexa for a while and got the impression she was feeling a little depressed. When she asked if anything was wrong, she was surprised when Alexa confessed she thought her mom and dad were having some problems. Nancy tried to get her to elaborate, even asking if she had heard them arguing, but Alexa was somewhat vague and responded that her mom seemed very distracted and didn't talk very much, plus the fact she was away from home a lot more than usual. Nancy was worried Alexa might suspect Charlotte of having an affair so she tried to make light of the whole situation. By the time she hung up the phone, Alexa seemed more like her usual self but it made Nancy even more determined to find out all she could about Julian.

Tom walked out of Union Station onto Front Street and stood on the sidewalk waiting for Nancy, who was circling the block rather than looking for a place to park. She noticed him immediately as she turned the corner and honked her horn loudly as she pulled to a stop at the curb. Tom glanced up, saw her waving frantically out of the car window, and dashed across the street while keeping an eye out for oncoming traffic. Nancy hadn't realized how tall he was, having spent most of the time seated near to him on the plane. It was obvious he had been a handsome man in his time and still had a good head of hair, now turned completely white. He was wearing jeans with a pale blue checkered shirt and carrying a light tan jacket but, even though casually dressed, he still had an air of affluence about him. As he reached the car Nancy waved him around to the other side, "Hi there," she said, "jump in before someone gives me a ticket."

Tom settled into the passenger seat, "Well, that was easy; I've only been waiting a couple of minutes."

Nancy grinned, "Good, because I just got here myself. I only had to go around once and there you were. How was the trip in?"

"Very relaxing. I started reading this novel last night in bed and I couldn't put it down. I decided to bring it with me and got so absorbed in it, before I knew it, we were pulling into the station."

"I love to read too. In fact, I can't go to sleep unless I've read a chapter or two. Even if I get home late, which isn't too often these days, I still need to read for a while."

Tom nodded, "I know exactly what you mean."

There was silence for a moment then Nancy said, "I thought we'd go out to lunch, my treat. There's a lovely little restaurant called the Pear Tree we can go to. Afterwards I can show you my house, if you like. What time is your train back to Hamilton?"

"It leaves at just after five. I need to go back early because I have to pick Badger up. My neighbours are going out later so they can only keep him until seven."

They continued to chat while Nancy drove in the direction of Cabbagetown and it was only when they were seated at their table, waiting for their lunch to be served, that Tom asked, "So, how can I help you Nancy? I gather this is a delicate matter."

Nancy nodded, "Yes, I'm afraid it is because it involves my daughter, Charlotte. I didn't feel I could confide in anyone who knew the family and that's why I thought of you. You may have some connections that can be of help."

"I see. Well, I'll certainly do my best to assist you if at all possible. Now, why don't you start at the beginning?"

Nancy attempted to tell Tom all she knew about Charlotte's affair with Julian and his uncanny resemblance to Adam. "If I found out they were related, I'm sure Charlotte would give up this relationship. That's why I've been trying to track down Julian's background but I'm hitting a brick wall. I thought you, having been a lawyer, might know somebody who investigates this type of thing."

Tom had been listening intently, "Have you ever met this fellow?" he asked.

Nancy shook her head, "No, but I've seen his photo and he could be Adam's double."

"So, are you assuming that maybe he's his twin?"

"Yes, I am, and if he is, then maybe Julian was adopted and Adam doesn't even know about him."

"Have you considered the fact maybe Adam is the one who was adopted?"

Nancy frowned, "It crossed my mind briefly but I know his mother and she dotes on him."

"That's no reason to believe she's his biological mother. Do you know her very well?"

"Not really. Personally, I find her very difficult to get along with and so does Charlotte but Adam won't hear a bad word about her."

Just then the waiter arrived with their lunch and they sat silently for a few minutes while they ate until Tom put his fork down, "Tell me what you've done so far to try and trace Julian's background."

"Well, I contacted a couple of the agencies in Quebec and spent a lot of time on the internet, even joining Ancestry dot com on a trial basis, but there are a few Julian Richards out there, none of whom seem to fit."

"I do know someone who can help, actually, Gary Norman. He's an investigator with my old law firm and he's an excellent man for a job like this. In my field of criminal law, we need all the information we can lay our hands on to ensure a positive outcome for our clients, so a good investigator is critical."

"Would I be able to hire him privately to look into Julian's background?"

"Yes, I'm almost certain he'd be willing to help. He was like a second son to me and I still keep in touch with him on a regular basis."

"Of course I'd pay him for his services but I hope it doesn't cost too much."

Tom smiled, "Don't you worry, I'll tell him it's for a dear friend of mine and he might even do it for nothing."

Nancy smiled back, "That's really generous of you, Tom, but I couldn't ask him to do that."

"Well, we'll see what happens. I'll contact him as soon as I get home and let you know what he has to say. Now, let's enjoy this lovely lunch and then afterwards you can show me your house."

Nancy drove Tom back to the train station, later that afternoon, after having spent some time at her home. Tom was interested in architecture and particularly enchanted by the Victorian style and the well-manicured gardens in both the front and back of the house. He was also enchanted by Gypsy and Luna who immediately took a fancy to him and kept circling his legs. "I'm glad you're not allergic to cats," Nancy remarked.

Tom leaned down and stroked Luna's white fur, "I think this one's my favourite," he whispered.

Nancy put her finger to her lips, "Don't let Gypsy hear you say that."

Tom laughed, "That would never do. She might get an inferiority complex."

"How long have you had Badger?"

"Six years. I got him when he was only eight weeks old, right after Helen died."

"It must have been really hard for you after being married for so long."

"Yes it was hard. I never expected her to go before me. Helen had always been healthy, in fact, she still worked out nearly every day up until the time she got sick and she was careful about what she ate. We'd never had any pets because she had allergies but I'd always wanted a dog since I left home to go to college. My parents had two beagles and a calico cat you could walk on a leash, so I was used to having animals around. It sounds rather trite but Badger made life worth living again. We both needed each other."

"I don't think it sounds trite at all. I would have liked a pet when I lost my husband but Charlotte was only six when he died and I had to work long hours."

Tom looked thoughtful, "Why didn't you ever marry again, Nancy? You're a very attractive woman. You must have had a lot of opportunities."

"Oh, I spent a lot of years dating but never found that special someone I thought I could live with again. Now, I'm way too old and set in my ways to share my life with anyone else. I'd probably drive them into an early grave."

"I feel the same way. I don't know how anyone would put up with me but it would be nice to have a female friend and I hope we can keep in touch."

"I'd like that very much," Nancy replied.

Chapter Thirty-Six

While Nancy was driving back from Union Station, after dropping Tom off, Charlotte was preparing to drive back from Jackson's Point. She had picked Julian up at the Island Airport on Saturday morning and then headed for The Briar's, a popular country inn, but not a place they expected to run into anyone they knew.

As it was between seasons, too late for summer activities and too early for winter, when they weren't holed up in their room making passionate love or taking time out to eat in one of the Briar's dining rooms, they were hiking the Lake Simcoe Trail. Julian had seemed especially attentive and by Sunday afternoon, Charlotte realized she was falling more and more in love with him. They were packing up their few belongings, just before leaving, when Charlotte sat down on the edge of the bed and sighed. Julian looked up from what he was doing and noticed tears in her eyes, "What's wrong?" he asked.

Charlotte dropped her head so he couldn't see her face, "I don't want to go home," she whispered.

Julian got down on one knee in front of her, "Then don't go. Come home with me."

Charlotte put her head in her hands, "You can't mean that."

Julian pulled her hands away, "Why wouldn't I mean it? I thought you wanted to be with me."

"I do want to be with you but how can I possibly leave my family? I'm not even sure you really want me to. You've never said you loved me or wanted a committed relationship."

Julian stood up, "Why does everything have to be about love and commitment? We enjoy being together, isn't that enough?"

Charlotte was shocked at his response, "No it isn't enough. You expect me to run off with you just like that when I have so much to lose."

Julian scowled, "What do you have to lose? Is Adam so wonderful that you can't bear to leave him? Is he able to satisfy you the way I do?"

Charlotte jumped to her feet, "This isn't all about sex," she answered angrily. "Adam loves me and you seem to forget, I have a daughter at home who needs me."

Julian smirked, "She's seventeen years old. How long before she takes off and then you'll be all alone with your precious Adam? Are you going to be content to stay with him for the rest of your life?"

Charlotte picked up her overnight bag and headed for the door, "I've had enough of this. I'll wait for you in the car."

On the drive back to Toronto, there was a stony silence until they crossed Highway 407 then Julian reached over and laid his hand on Charlotte's thigh, "I'm sorry," he said. "Will you forgive me?"

Charlotte glanced over at him and saw the sulky look on his face. She hesitated because she had been so hurt by his remarks but in an instant he was able to make her feel as though it was all her fault. "I'm sorry too but it doesn't change anything. I still can't go with you; not now, anyway."

Julian slid his hand further up her thigh and patted her gently, "It's okay, I can wait," he said.

Charlotte felt herself becoming aroused and chided herself inwardly for being so susceptible but at the same time she wanted things back the way they were so, at the next exit, she drove a few kilometers onto a secluded side road and parked the car. Julian had known exactly what he was doing, merely exerting more pressure on her thigh without proceeding any further. It was only after they came to a full stop that he reached over and pulled her towards him. Then, sliding his hand up under her skirt and pulling aside her panties, he thrust his fingers inside of her. At that moment, Charlotte forgot all about the harsh words and the tension between them. She was totally under his spell again.

Alexa was peering through the front room window when Charlotte stopped in the driveway at just after seven that evening. She waited until her mother walked through the door before she stepped into the hall and said in a low voice, "Hi, Mom."

Charlotte was surprised to see her there and even more surprised to see her hanging back rather than giving her the usual hug. "Hi, honey," she answered, "I wasn't sure if you'd be home. Where's your dad? I didn't see his car outside."

"He just went to pick up some milk. We're almost out." Then, looking down at the overnight bag Charlotte was carrying she asked, "Where were you, Mom?"

Charlotte started to walk past her to go upstairs, "You know where I was, Alexa. I went to Watertown with Jodi."

Alexa watched her climb the stairs and called after her, "You said you were going shopping. I want to see what you bought."

Charlotte glanced back over her shoulder, "Not now," she answered impatiently. "It was a long trip and I'm tired and need a bath. Tell your father I've had dinner and I'll be down soon."

The moment Charlotte disappeared into her bedroom; Alexa raced out to the garden and used her cell phone to call Nancy. "Nana, it's me," she said, "Mom just came home and I don't believe she's been shopping. She doesn't have any bags and when I asked her what she bought she ran upstairs and said she was having a bath."

Nancy was at a loss for words, "Where's your father?" she asked attempting to change the subject.

"He's at the store getting milk. Nana, did you hear what I said? I don't think Mom's telling the truth. Do you know where she really went?"

"Now, now, you mustn't jump to conclusions. Maybe she didn't buy anything. I've been on a couple of those shopping expeditions and came back empty handed."

"But she's acting strange like she's trying to avoid us. Maybe I should talk to Dad about it."

Nancy felt a growing sense of alarm, "No, I wouldn't do that, Alexa. There's no reason to make him think there's something wrong when there may be a perfectly good explanation for the way your mother is behaving."

Alexa sighed, "Okay, Nana, but will you talk to her? Maybe she's sick or something and doesn't want to tell us."

"I'm sure that's not the case but just to put your mind at rest, I promise I'll talk to her tomorrow. I'll call her early in the morning and see if she has time for lunch."

"That would be great. Can I call you when I get home from school to see what happened?"

"Of course but if your mother knows you're concerned about her she'll probably want to speak to you yourself."

There was a moment of silence and Nancy thought they'd been cut off, then Alexa said, "Dad's back. He's calling me wondering where I am. I'd better go."

"Okay, honey, and don't worry."

"Okay, I'll try not to," Alexa replied.

A half hour later, when Charlotte came downstairs, Alexa was sitting in the family room with Adam watching America's Funniest Videos. She was laughing so much she didn't see her mother come through the door. Adam sensed her standing behind them and got up immediately to give her a hug, "Good to see you back. How was your trip?"

Charlotte returned the hug, "Tiring, it was a long drive."

"Well, why don't you sit down and have a glass of wine. Alexa tells me you've already eaten."

Charlotte walked over and sat down on the recliner, adjacent to the sofa, "That would be lovely, thank you," she responded glancing over at Alexa.

Alexa kept her eyes glued to the television screen while Adam went to fetch some wine from the kitchen. "What did you get up to while I was away?" Charlotte asked.

Alexa looked sullen, "Nothing much, just hung out with Hildy yesterday and stayed around here today. Oh, and I spoke to Nana while you were upstairs," she said finally turning to look directly at her mother.

"How was she?"

"She was fine. She said she'd call you early in the morning to see if you could have lunch with her."

Charlotte sighed, "Maybe I should call her tonight."

Just then Adam walked back into the room carrying a glass of wine and a bottle of Molson's, "Who are you going to call?" he asked.

"I should call, Mom," she answered as she reached for the wine.

Adam nodded as he sat down and then started to get up again, "Alexa," he said, "sorry, honey. Did you want another coke?"

"No, Dad, I'm fine," she answered. "Why don't you ask Mom what she bought on her trip?"

Adam turned down the volume on the television and looked over at Charlotte, "Good idea. What did you buy, honey?"

Charlotte shrugged, "Just some lingerie," she lied, "there weren't any really good sales."

"What about Jodi? She must have bought something." Alexa asked, determined not to drop the subject.

"Not too much," Charlotte replied. "She bought a couple of tops that's all."

"Seems like a long way to go just for that," Alexa remarked abruptly.

Charlotte glanced at Adam, who appeared to be engrossed in the television, and then glared at Alexa, "Aren't you going out this evening?" she asked.

Alexa grinned, "No. Mom, I'm staying home so maybe later on you can show me your new lingerie."

"Maybe," Charlotte answered as she got up and walked out of the room.

A few minutes later, Adam found her sitting on one of the patio chairs in the garden, "What are you doing out here, honey?" he asked. "It's getting a bit cool. Would you like me to get you a sweater?"

Charlotte looked up at him, "No, I'm fine. I'm just not in the mood for watching TV. I thought I'd come out here and sit with Zoe for a while but I couldn't find her."

Adam chuckled, "She's probably in Tyler's room. She's suddenly taken to sleeping on his bed every night. Did you look in there?"

Charlotte shook her head, "No, I didn't. It's funny how she picks a different spot in the house every few weeks or so."

Adam sat down next to her, "I guess she gets bored being in the same place all the time. Speaking of which, honey, you seem a bit restless lately. Is anything bothering you?"

Charlotte stared straight ahead as she answered, "No, not really. It's probably the thought of winter coming on. It's a bit depressing when I look at the garden and imagine all the trees without their leaves."

Adam looked at the trees surrounding the large expanse of grass and the bordering flower beds, "I know what you mean. I guess I should think about covering the pool soon. I don't think we'll be swimming for a while."

Charlotte started to get up, "I think I'll go inside now," she said.

Adam reached out and grabbed her hand, "Don't go just yet," he said, "I haven't seen you all weekend."

Charlotte hesitated then started to pull away, "Sorry, Adam, but I'm really tired. I'm going upstairs to lie down and read for a while."

Adam released her hand and frowned, "We hardly ever talk anymore. Are you sure nothing's wrong."

Charlotte started to walk away, "I'm sure. I'm just tired, that's all."

Chapter Thirty-Seven

On Monday morning, after Adam had left for work and Alexa had gone to school, the phone rang in the kitchen. Charlotte knew it had to be Nancy, "Hi, Mom," she said waiting for the inevitable third degree.

"Good morning. I know it's early but I was wondering if you could meet me for lunch."

Charlotte paused, "I suppose I could as long as it's a little later. I have some errands to run this morning."

"That's perfectly fine, dear. Why don't we meet at Coquine's at one? Do you know where it is?"

"Yes, I've been there before. I'll park on one of the side streets."

"Okay, Charlotte, I'll see you later. Love you." And, with that Nancy hung up before Charlotte had a chance to respond.

She was already seated in the restaurant when Charlotte walked through the door at ten minutes after one. She was beginning to wonder if Charlotte would show up at all and was surprised to see her approach with a broad smile on her face. She got up to give her a hug, "Hello, dear, I hope you don't mind but I started without you," she said motioning towards the glass of wine on the table.

Charlotte shook her head as she sat down, "I'm glad you didn't wait, Mom," she replied. "I'm sorry I'm a bit late but I was almost out of gas so I had to stop."

"Guess you emptied the tank driving all the way to Watertown and back," Nancy countered.

The smile left Charlotte's face, "You know very well I didn't go to Watertown. Do we really have to have this conversation?"

"I think we do but why don't you order something to drink and then we can talk. We can wait a while to order lunch."

Charlotte nodded and beckoned to the waiter, "I'd like a glass of Chardonnay, please."

While they waited for the wine, both mother and daughter studied the menu in an effort to avoid speaking and when the waiter returned, a few minutes later, Nancy informed him they were in no hurry and would let him know when they were ready to order. She waited until Charlotte had taken a sip of her wine and then asked, "So where did you go for the weekend?"

"We drove up to Jackson's Point and stayed at the Briar's."

"That's a pretty popular spot. Weren't you concerned you might run into someone you knew?"

"Not at this time of year. There were very few people there."

"So I gather you enjoyed yourself and you're going to go on seeing him."

"He asked me to go home with him, Mom."

Nancy took in a deep breath, "I see, and what did you have to say to that?"

Charlotte decided to be truthful about her response and Julian's subsequent reaction. Nancy paused for a moment before asking, "It sounds like you had some harsh words but I gather you made up. How did that happen?"

Charlotte began to blush and couldn't look her mother in the eyes, "I'm not sure," she answered."

Nancy reached over and tipped up Charlotte's chin so that she could see her face, "I get it," she said. "You have a strong physical attraction for him and he knows it. That's how he's manipulating you."

Charlotte shook her head vehemently, "No, you've got it all wrong. He's not manipulating me. We don't spend all of our time in bed if that's what you're implying."

"You still didn't answer my question. Are you going to continue seeing him?"

"You didn't ask me, Mom, you just assumed and you were right. We're going to make plans to see each other again."

Nancy sighed, "Then you really need to know Alexa is concerned about the way you're behaving."

Charlotte cut in. "What do you mean? Have you been speaking to her about me?"

"As a matter of fact, she called me. She's worried because you hardly ever talk to her anymore and you're away so much lately. It's so out of character. Honestly, I think she suspects you're having an affair."

"Did she actually say that?" Charlotte asked frowning.

"No, but what else would she be thinking. She called me last night, right after you got home, to tell me she didn't believe you went shopping because you didn't have any shopping bags with you and, on top of that, you were avoiding her."

Charlotte looked annoyed, "So she called you soon after I got back. What did you tell her?"

Now it was Nancy's turn to look annoyed, "What do you think I told her? I tried to allay her suspicions. The last thing I want is to see my granddaughter torn apart because of what you are doing. I'm surprised Adam hasn't noticed what's going on and I suggest you stop right now before he does."

Charlotte put her glass down on the table and stood up, "I can't listen to this anymore," she said. "I'm a grown woman and you can't tell me what to do. I think I'll just skip lunch and go home."

Nancy looked up and very calmly said, "I'm sorry you feel that way, Charlotte. Have a nice afternoon."

Charlotte remained where she was for a few seconds staring down at her mother and not quite believing what she had just heard and then, with tears in her eyes, she walked out of the restaurant.

A week later, Nancy got a call from Tom. He suggested they get together as he had some information about Julian. Nancy was excited and wanted to drive to Hamilton immediately but was pleased when Tom invited her to his home the very next day.

Tom lived in a cozy two-bedroom bungalow on Baron's Avenue and Nancy was pleasantly surprised when she walked through the door. Tom proceeded to show her around but was hampered by the antics of Badger who insisted on running ahead and then running back to circle Nancy's legs. Tom was at his wits end trying to control him but Nancy thought he was adorable. "It's all right," she kept saying. "I don't mind."

After their tour of the house, Tom led Nancy back to his office, which he had set up in a corner of the finished basement. "Have a seat," he said, "while I get us some coffee. I'll put Badger out in the back yard so he won't disturb us."

Nancy was anxious to find out what information Tom had for her but waited patiently while she looked around the room. She hadn't noticed any photos in the living room or any of the other rooms of the house but there was one photo that sat predominantly on Tom's desk and it was obviously his wife, Helen. Nancy picked it up and couldn't help admiring the face looking back at her. Helen had been a very attractive woman, with deep green eyes and an abundance of dark curly hair that almost reached her shoulders. It made Nancy sad when she thought how difficult it must have been for Tom to lose her and she was still holding the photo when Tom walked back into the room carrying a tray with two mugs of steaming coffee and a small jug of cream. "I remembered, you don't take sugar," he said as he put the tray down.

"Yes, that's right, thank you," Nancy replied.

Tom handed her a mug just as she was replacing the photo on the desk, "That picture was taken about a year before Helen died."

"She looks like she was a lovely person," Nancy said quietly. "She must have been gorgeous when you first met her."

Tom smiled, "Yes, she was. I couldn't take my eyes off her. It was love at first sight."

Nancy smiled back, "Did she feel the same way?"

Tom chuckled, "Hardly. She didn't even like me. I must have asked her out about a dozen times before she agreed to go to a movie with me and, after that, I guess I grew on her."

"I suppose you have to be thankful for all the good years you had together."

"I am, I just wish there had been a few more," Tom said in such a low voice, Nancy could hardly hear him.

She sat quietly while he opened a drawer and removed a manila folder and then sat down beside her. "I think you'll find this rather enlightening," he said. "Gary came up with some interesting information but I still don't think it proves this Julian fellow is related to your son-in-law."

Nancy took the folder, opened it with some trepidation, and after reading through the papers inside, she looked over at Tom and said, "So, according to these papers he was adopted when he was about a year old by William and Fiona Richards. That seems clear enough but I don't understand his birth certificate. It shows he was born Julian Andrews at St. Andrews, Rockport, Ontario on July 2nd, 1967 but it doesn't show the name of his biological parents."

"That's because his parents are unknown. Julian was a foundling. I suspect he was left on the steps of St. Andrew's Church as a very young baby and in these cases; the place where a child is found is designated as the place of birth. Obviously they picked Andrews for his surname and I can only surmise he was named Julian because he was born in July, although no one can be sure of his exact date of birth."

"So then he was put in foster care and finally adopted by the Richards' who renamed him?"

"Yes, that's correct and I need to caution you, Nancy, he may not even know he was adopted."

"But he'd know from his birth certificate wouldn't he?"

Tom sighed, "Not if the Richards' had a new one made up. It's not hard to do if you can make the right connections."

Nancy tapped the folder, "What about the marriage certificate, is it real?"

"Yes, Julian was married when he was twenty-three and there's no evidence of a divorce. Seeing as Charlotte has been to his home, I suspect he no longer lives with his wife so they're probably just separated."

"What about children? Were there any?"

"Gary is still checking that out and still trying to trace what happened to the wife. She doesn't appear to be residing in Quebec unless she changed her name."

"He told Charlotte he'd never been married. Why would he do that?"

Tom shook his head, "Who knows? Maybe he's never been divorced and he doesn't want to expose himself to a lot of questions."

Nancy sat looking thoughtful for a moment, "Adam's birthday is June 12th, that's about three weeks before Julian's birthday. Do you think it's possible whoever examined Julian, when he was found, made a mistake about how old he was?"

Tom nodded slowly, "It's possible, I suppose, especially if he was very small. Are you still convinced they must be twins?"

Nancy leaned back in her chair, "There's only one way to find out," she answered.

Tom frowned, "Oh, oh, what are you proposing to do?"

"I'm proposing to pay a visit to Adam's mother."

Tom reached over and grabbed her arm, "Wait a minute. Are you seriously considering asking her outright if she had twins and left one on a doorstep?"

"Well, I'll try and be a little more subtle than that," Nancy protested.

"I think you may be opening up a whole can of worms."

"Maybe I am, but I'll do anything to protect Charlotte"

"How is it protecting her if what you believe happens to be true? Are you just going to hope Adam never finds out she's been having an affair with his twin?"

Nancy stood up, "I don't know but I have to do something."

Chapter Thirty-Eight

While Nancy was in Hamilton visiting Tom, she had no idea Charlotte was being confronted with a situation that seemed destined to put her whole future in jeopardy. She had only spoken to Julian once, since they returned from their weekend away, and it had left her upset and wondering what to do next. After he suggested she meet him in Montreal the following week and she was unable to make a commitment, his mood turned sullen and he cut her off rather abruptly without any indication he would call her again. She tried to be upbeat around Adam and Alexa, especially now that she knew Alexa was watching her every move, but it took an almost superhuman effort and, at the end of the day, left her drained.

By Tuesday, when Julian hadn't called back, she was anxious to hear his voice but not in the way she expected. Adam was in the family room watching the news and Alexa was helping her put away the dinner dishes when the telephone on the kitchen counter rang. Alexa immediately picked up the receiver and announced, "Hamilton residence, how may I help you?"

Charlotte watched while Alexa paused and then frowned as she passed her the phone, "It's for you," she said.

"Who is it?" Charlotte asked as she covered the mouthpiece with her hand.

Alexa shook her head, "I don't know. It's some man asking for Charlotte."

Charlotte felt her hand start to shake as she turned her back on Alexa and put the receiver to her ear, "Hello," she said in almost a whisper, "this is Charlotte."

The voice was unmistakable, "Is this the lady of the house?"

Charlotte could feel Alexa's eyes boring into her back as she answered, "Yes, what are you calling about?"

Julian chuckled, "Nice, Charlotte, keep up the charade. I gather that was your daughter who answered the phone. She sounds kind of sexy, just like her mother."

Charlotte was desperately trying to think on her feet, "I'm sorry," she said, "but I'm really not interested. Please don't call here again."

"Then meet me on the corner. I'm in my car at the end of the street."

Charlotte took a deep breath, "Thank you. I appreciate that." Then she hung up the phone and turned to face Alexa.

"Who was that, Mom? Alexa asked.

"Just a telemarketer," Charlotte lied. "He wanted to know if we wanted any renovating done."

"How come he asked for you by your first name?"

"I have no idea," Charlotte answered impatiently. "I don't know how these people operate."

Alexa started to walk out of the kitchen, "I think I'll go over to Hildy's, she may come back with me."

Charlotte was no longer paying attention. All she could think of was how she was going to get out of the house to meet Julian. She couldn't believe he had actually called her on the land line and he was sitting almost outside her front door. She waited until Alexa left and watched as she walked to the end of the street, hoping and praying she wouldn't notice Julian sitting parked at the corner, and then she walked back through the house and poked her head through the family room door, "I'm just going to run out and get some cereal for the morning."

Adam glanced around, "Do you want me to come with you?" he asked.

Charlotte shook her head, "No, you stay here. I won't be long."

A few minutes later, she backed out of the driveway and took off down the street to where Julian was parked. She pulled up alongside him and called out, "Follow me," and then drove around the corner onto Scholfield Avenue until she reached Rosedale Park. She pulled over and stopped the car beneath some trees on the edge of the park and waited until Julian's car pulled up behind her. She only hesitated for a second before jumping out and screaming at him through the open window, "What the hell do you think you're doing. How dare you phone me at home like that and then show up outside my door."

Julian stepped out of his car and held up both hands with palms facing towards her, "Whoa," he said, "I never heard you talk like that before. I like this feisty side of you."

Charlotte stepped back and scowled, "I'm waiting for an answer," she demanded. "What are you doing here?"

Julian reached out to grasp her arm, "I'm here to see my pretty lady. Why else would I be here?"

Charlotte shook her head and tried to pull away. She was angry and frightened and her voice rose as she looked around her to see if anyone was watching, "You should have called me. We could have arranged to meet somewhere but not here. Why are you doing this?"

Julian grasped her other arm and pulled her towards him, "Because I couldn't wait to see you. Come back to Montreal with me. Leave Adam and move in with me."

Charlotte struggled but as she looked into his eyes she felt her resolve start to weaken, "I told you, I can't leave my family."

Julian smiled, "But you said you loved me."

Charlotte reached up and touched his cheek, "I do love you and I don't want to lose you. I want to see you every chance I get but not here. Go home, Julian. I promise I'll call you tomorrow and see you next week."

Julian released his grip, stepped back and leaned casually against the side of his car, "What would happen if your husband found out about us? Would he throw you out? Would you come home with me then?"

Charlotte's hand flew to her throat, "Adam can't find out about us. Please, Julian, I'm begging you. You're scaring me."

Julian stepped forward again and took her in his arms, "No need to be scared, pretty lady," he said and kissed her gently on the lips.

She didn't resist, she didn't want to. Unable to help herself, she wrapped her arms around his neck and kissed him back while in her mind she was thinking, "I can't let him go."

Afterwards, Julian got back in his car and, without another word, drove away. Charlotte watched as he disappeared around the corner and then got back into her own car. She sat there for ten minutes and then started to drive home. She was so engrossed with her own thoughts she was shocked when she saw Alexa and Hildy standing on the front steps of the house. As she stepped out of the car onto the driveway, Alexa immediately asked, "Where did you go, Mom?"

Charlotte nodded at Hildy and then turned to Alexa, "To the store. I thought you were going out tonight."

Alexa ignored this remark, "Dad, said you'd gone for cereal. Where is it?"

Charlotte started to walk past her, "They didn't have the kind I like," she answered.

Alexa glowered back at her mother, "There's a whole box full in the cupboard."

Charlotte swung back around, "What? Are you spying on me now? How dare you."

Alexa shrugged and grabbed Hildy's hand, "Let's get out of here," she said.

When Charlotte went into the house, Adam was in the kitchen getting a beer out of the refrigerator. He looked up as she walked through the door, "Hi, honey," he said, "did you see Alexa?"

Charlotte nodded, "Yes, I did and that young lady is getting a little too big for her britches."

"She's a teenager, what do you expect? It's probably just a temporary phase."

"Well, I sure hope so. Why did she come back from Hildy's?"

"She wanted to ask my permission to stay out later tonight. They were going to a movie with a couple of friends."

"Girlfriends, I assume?"

Adam shook his head, "No, as a matter of fact, they were going with a couple of lads from Rosedale Heights."

"Did you give your permission?"

"Yes, I know it's a school night but she's seventeen, we have to start treating her like a grown up."

"Well, maybe you should tell her to treat me like a grown up."

"Why, what happened?"

Charlotte sighed, "Oh, nothing much. Let's just drop it."

Adam uncapped his beer and took a sip, "Okay. By the way, did she tell you there was cereal in the cupboard?"

Charlotte huffed, "Yes, she made a point of it."

Adam suddenly realized Charlotte had arrived home empty handed, "Didn't you buy some more when you were out?"

Charlotte just shook her head and walked past him. "Why don't you go and relax," she said. "I'm going to pour myself a glass of wine and then I'll join you."

Chapter Thirty-Nine

On Wednesday morning Adam left early to fly to Ottawa to meet with Howard and wasn't expected back until the next day. Charlotte was grateful to have the time to herself and as soon as she had cleared away the breakfast dishes and waved Alexa off to school, she tried contacting Julian. She had promised to call him and had to be sure he wouldn't show up on her doorstep again. She had no idea how she would manage to get away to see him the following week and she was beginning to realize her feelings for him were beginning to change. She knew he only had to hold her in his arms and she lost all sense of who she really was. He had a hold over her that was hard to break but she couldn't go on with the deception. She needed to make a decision. Time and time again, she tapped in the number on her cell phone but her attempts continually went to voice message. She begged him to call her back and even tried texting but to no avail. Where was he and why wasn't he answering her calls?

It was mid-afternoon when her cell phone rang and her heart started to race. It was Jodi. Although they hadn't spoken in a while, she couldn't afford to tie up the phone and attempted to put her off, telling her she was just leaving to go shopping. Jodi was persistent wanting to know what was going on with Julian and if she had come to her senses yet. Feeling pressured, Charlotte got angry and for the first time that she could remember, their conversation ended in an argument but Jodi had the last word. "What you're doing is wrong, Charlotte. You can't have it both ways. Either you leave Adam and take up with Julian or you go back to being the wife and mother you once were. I'll support you, no matter what you decide because you're my friend but I can't support what you're doing right now. Call me when you've made up your mind." Charlotte started to respond but Jodi had already hung up the phone.

Ten minutes later, the landline phone rang and Nancy's number showed up on the display. There was no way Charlotte wanted to talk to her mother. She let it ring and then listened to the message asking her to call her back but what could she say to her? She didn't want to talk about Julian.

The minutes seemed to drag on and Charlotte was almost at her wits end. She decided to make a casserole to fill the time while every fifteen minutes she placed another call to Julian. Alexa wasn't expected home until six o'clock. She was going to the library with some friends to study and although Charlotte was feeling desperately lonely she didn't want her to be there when Julian called her back.

By seven o'clock she began to worry. Where was Alexa? Now she was more concerned about her daughter than Julian. She attempted to call her but her cell phone was off and in utter frustration she started pacing the floor. At eight o'clock, she began contacting Alexa's friends but those who'd been with her at the library had last seen her when she left there just before six. Finally, she called Nancy hoping she had heard from her. "Mom, it's Charlotte," she said.

"Oh, hi dear, I was hoping you'd call me back tonight."

"Mom," Charlotte cut in, "have you heard from Alexa?"

"No. Why, is she supposed to be at home?"

"She was supposed to be here at six and I can't reach her. She was with some friends at the library but she left there to be here in time for dinner. I'm worried, Mom, where can she be?"

"Where's Adam?"

"He's in Ottawa and won't be back until tomorrow. I don't want to worry him."

Nancy didn't hesitate, "I'll be right there," she said and hung up the phone.

Charlotte was standing on the front step, with Zoe in her arms, when Nancy pulled into the driveway. As she stepped out of her car, she called out, "Any news?"

Charlotte just shook her head and Nancy could see the tears in her eyes. She climbed the steps and put her arm around her, "Come inside and we'll try and figure out where she can be."

Charlotte followed her mother into the kitchen and put Zoe down, "I think I know where she might be, Mom, and I'm terrified."

Nancy frowned, "Here sit down. What's this all about?"

"I think she's with Julian," Charlotte blurted out. "I think he's taken her."

"What? Why on earth would you think that? What's happened?"

Charlotte related everything that had happened the night before and the fact that she was unable to contact Julian all day. Nancy listened carefully, "That doesn't mean he's got Alexa."

"I think he does, Mom. I think he's trying to punish me because I won't leave Adam."

"Well, it's a bit of a stretch but I suppose it's possible. Do you think he's capable of harming Alexa?"

Charlotte began to shake her head vehemently, "I don't know, I just don't know. Maybe we should call the police."

Nancy reached over and grasped her arm, "If we do that, Adam's going to find out everything. Let me think for a minute." She sat perfectly still for a moment and then asked, "When you text somebody can they see the message right away?"

Charlotte nodded, "Yes if they hear the phone vibrate."

"Show me how to text on your phone."

"What are you going to say?"

"Never mind that, just show me."

It took Charlotte only a few seconds to show her mother what to do and then she watched while Nancy got up and walked out of the kitchen. "Where are you going?" she called out but Nancy didn't answer, she was too busy texting, "This is Nancy Drew. You may remember me. We need to talk."

Moments later as she walked back into the kitchen, the phone started to ring. Charlotte reached out to take it but Nancy shook her head. After the third ring she answered, "Julian," she said. "Thank you for calling me back."

"Who are you?" Julian asked without preamble.

"Surely you remember?" Nancy responded. "I spoke to you recently about a friend of mine named Franny who I was trying to trace."

"How did you get hold of that phone?" Julian replied impatiently.

"That's an easy question to answer. It's my daughter, Charlotte Hamilton's phone. My name is Nancy Fleming."

"You said your name was Drew. What are you playing at?"

"I think you may be the one who's playing games Mr. Richards, or is it Mr. Andrews? If you have any idea where my granddaughter is, then I suggest you tell me unless you would prefer me to call the police."

There was a deadly silence on the other end of the line while Charlotte stood with her mouth open, only understanding half of what was being said.

Nancy waited for a few seconds, "Would you like me to repeat myself?" she asked in a very imperious tone.

"I'm bringing Alexa back; I should be there within an hour."

Nancy drew in a breath, "Make sure you are or I promise you, you'll be spending the rest of your life in a cell. They don't take very kindly to kidnapping in this country."

Charlotte stepped forward and grasped her mother's arm. Nancy turned to her and nodded. "It's going to be all right," she whispered.

Julian cut in, "I told you I'm bringing her back. I'll drop her off on the street just down from Charlotte's house. I haven't hurt her. She came with me willingly. Promise me you won't call the police."

"You have my word," Nancy replied. "Please hurry."

Charlotte collapsed in Nancy's arms after she handed her back the phone, "When will they be here? I can't believe he took her."

"There, there, dear," Nancy murmured stroking Charlotte's hair. "He said within an hour."

"Perhaps we should still call the police."

"No, I don't think we should, provided Alexa's okay, but you will have to tell her the truth about Julian."

"How can I ask her to keep a secret like that from her father?"

"You can ask her because she won't want to see her father get hurt."

Charlotte shook her head, "It's not going to work, Mom. I know she'll hate me and I can't blame her. Look what I've put her through. She was probably scared out of her wits."

"Then you need to tell Adam before she gets the chance to."

"Oh, Mom, this is going to be the longest hour of my life."

Only half an hour had passed before Charlotte was compelled to open the front door and stand on the steps while she waited for Alexa to come home. Nancy soon joined her, after searching through the hall closet for a jacket. "Here," she said, "put this on. It's getting a bit cool."

Charlotte slipped into the jacket and then glanced back over her shoulder, "Thanks, Mom. Better close the door a bit so Zoe doesn't get out."

They waited in silence, tensing every time they heard a car coming down the street and then a neighbour walked by with his dog and waved at them, "Have a good night, ladies," he called out. Everything seemed so normal.

It had been exactly an hour since Nancy had spoken to Julian and she was beginning to wonder if she should have called the police after all when, suddenly, they heard a car in the distance and, a moment later, a slight figure came running down the street towards them. Charlotte began to race down the driveway and out onto the sidewalk. "Alexa," she called out, "it's Mom." Seconds later they were in each other's arms. Nancy watched while mother and daughter embraced and then walked slowly back to the house. She could hear Charlotte quietly sobbing and Alexa repeating over and over again, "It's all right, Mom. I'm okay."

Nancy waited until they reached her then hugged them both, "Let's go inside," she said, "and you can tell us what happened."

Chapter Forty

"I had just left the library," Alexa began after they were all settled in the family room, "and I was walking towards the bus stop when this red BMW pulled up beside me and the driver honked his horn. I thought it might be someone I knew but I wasn't sure. I was a few feet away when I bent down to look through the window. I was so surprised when I saw Dad in the driver's seat so, without a second thought; I opened the passenger door and jumped in. As I was closing the door, he started to pull away and when I turned back to look at him, I knew it wasn't Dad after all. I couldn't even speak for a moment because he looked so much like him except for the scar on his face. He said not to be scared because he wasn't going to hurt me; he was just taking me for a little ride. I asked him who he was and he said I could call him Julian."

"You must have been terrified," Charlotte said as she sat holding Alexa's hand.

"Actually, I wasn't frightened at all, Mom. I think because he looked so much like Dad, I figured he had to be nice and when I asked him if they were related, he just said that maybe they were."

"Didn't you ask him where he was taking you?" Nancy asked.

"Yes, and he just repeated we were going for a little ride and he would bring me back home later. He said he just wanted to find out more about me and my family."

"What did you tell him?"

"Well, he wanted to know all kinds of stuff like where Dad worked and what he did for a living then he asked me about school and if I had a boyfriend. Oh, and he asked me where my grandmother lived. I told him I had two grandmothers, my Nana Nancy and Grandma Mary."

"Did you tell him?" Nancy asked looking at Charlotte and frowning.

"Well, yes, but not exactly. I just said Nana lived in Cabbagetown and Grandma Mary lived in Napanee.

Nancy sighed with relief, "That's good dear. What else did he want to know?"

Alexa shrugged, "Nothing much. Oh, he did ask about Tyler." She suddenly stopped and looked at Charlotte. "It's funny, Mom, but he didn't ask anything about you."

Charlotte ignored the remark "Did he talk about himself at all?"

"He told me he was a photographer and he lived in Montreal but he didn't say much else. Most of the time he was really quiet and I was trying to figure out how to get away from him."

"So you were scared?"

"No, not really but it felt like we were driving farther and farther away from home and I was getting a little nervous."

"Did you stop anywhere?"

"Yes, we stopped at a MacDonalds and he bought me a hamburger and a coke. I saw a sign that said Davis Drive."

"That's in Newmarket," Nancy said. "Why didn't you tell someone you were there against your will?"

"Because he was right there with me, all the time. I was dying to go to the bathroom but he made me wait until he was sure nobody else was in there before he told me I could go. Then he waited right outside the door."

"Oh, honey," Charlotte cried putting her arm around Alexis. "We should have called the police."

Alexa pulled away from her mother, "What's going on, Mom. Who is Julian and why did he want me to go with him?"

Charlotte looked at Nancy and then back at Alexa, "I guess it's time to tell you the truth, honey, and I hope and pray you won't hate me because I am truly, truly sorry."

Charlotte then proceeded to tell Alexa how she had met Julian and how it had developed into an affair but she played down the intensity of it and the amount of time she had spent with him. When she'd finished, she took Alexa's hand and said, "I hope you'll forgive me."

Alexa had listened expressionless while her mother was speaking but now there were tears in her eyes, "You really cheated on Dad?" she whispered.

Charlotte nodded, "Yes, I'm ashamed to say I did and I can't ask you to keep it a secret."

Alexa turned to Nancy, "Did you know what was going on all along, Nana?"

Nancy shook her head, "No, dear, not all along but when I found out, there was nothing I could do except encourage your mother to end it." Her voice softened as she continued, "I know you're very young but you're old enough to understand people can't always be in control of their emotions. We all try to do the right thing but sometimes the temptations in life can be overwhelming."

"Have you ever had an affair, Nana?"

Nancy looked over at Charlotte and sighed, "Yes," she admitted. "When your mother was just a baby but your grandfather never found out about it."

"Did you love granddad?"

"Yes, with all my heart."

Alexa turned back to her mother, "Why do you think Julian took me and how did he know who I was?"

"I think he took you to punish me. He wanted to scare me because I wouldn't leave your father. As for how he knew who you were; I've been thinking about that. He may have seen you last night when you left the house to go to Hildy's. He was sitting in his car at the end of the street. He knew where you went to school so maybe he waited outside and then followed you to the library, then waited again until you were alone."

"I have another theory about why he really took you," Nancy said.

Charlotte frowned, "What is it, Mom?"

"Well, I always felt there was a connection between Adam and Julian and so I hired a private investigator to find out if they were really related."

Charlotte gasped and Alexa's eyes widened, "Really, Nana?"

"Yes, really; do you remember the nice man we met on the plane?"

"Yes, you were flirting with him."

"I was not," Nancy responded indignantly, "but we did exchange phone numbers. I knew he'd been a lawyer and had connections and when I called to ask him for help, he came here and met with me. It was through him I found an investigator."

"What did he find out?" Charlotte asked.

"That Julian was adopted when he was about a year old. He was a foundling."

"What's a foundling, Nana?"

"A baby who's been abandoned and nobody knows where he came from or who his real parents are."

"Where did they find him?"

"They found him on the steps of a church in Rockport."

"How sad, Nana."

"Yes, it is sad and I think that's why he asked you about Grandma Mary."

Charlotte frowned, "Are you suggesting he believes Adam might be his brother and that Mary is his biological mother?"

"That's exactly what I'm suggesting but, even though you told him where she lives, Alexa, he'll be searching for her under the name of Hamilton. He doesn't know she remarried."

"But why do you think he made me go with him, Nana?"

"Two reasons; I think he wanted to pump you for information about your family and I think he's jealous of your father."

"I don't understand, why would he be jealous, he's never even met him?"

"I don't understand either," Charlotte added.

"Just think about it. He was probably intrigued when he first found out how much he resembled Adam. Then, when his mother died, that's when he probably found out he'd been adopted and maybe the circumstances of his birth. Imagine what it must feel like to discover you'd literally been left abandoned and maybe you had a brother who'd been raised by two loving parents. It's not surprising that you'd feel resentment and maybe Charlotte, and I'm just speculating, the only reason he asked you to leave your family was for revenge."

Charlotte's hand flew to her chest, "Oh, how could I have been so stupid?"

Alexa reached over and pulled her hand away, "It's going to be all right, Mom. I'm not going to say anything to Dad."

Charlotte started to cry again, "I don't deserve you. I don't deserve anybody."

"Nonsense," Nancy said, "you made a mistake; rather a big one in the scheme of things but it's over now."

Charlotte wiped her eyes, "What if Julian comes back? What if he contacts Adam himself?"

Nancy shook her head, "We can't be sure he won't come back. Right now I think he's more interested in finding his real mother and we may have scared him off by threatening to call the police. I told Tom I intended to pay a visit to Mary. Maybe if I confront her, she'll break down and tell me Adam wasn't the only child she gave birth to."

"I hardly think she'd confess, Mom, you know what a difficult woman she can be and what about the fact they're at least a month apart in age?"

"That's easily explained, Julian could have been very small and they just miscalculated. He was found in July, so that's probably why he was named Julian. Oh, and there's something else the investigator discovered; he was married and there's no evidence he was ever divorced."

Charlotte drew in a breath, "He told me he'd never been married."

"I know, dear, but it's not really important now. The important thing now is to find out if Mary is his mother."

"But what then, are we all supposed to become one big happy family?"

"I don't know," Nancy replied, "I haven't figured that out yet but if I know all the facts maybe I can reason with Julian."

"Reason with him about what, Nana?'

"About this path of revenge, I'm sure he's on."

Alexa looked sad, "I feel kind of sorry for him."

Nancy smiled, "You're a lovely compassionate young lady and I'm proud of you."

"Me too," Charlotte whispered giving Alexa a hug.

Chapter Forty-One

When Nancy arrived home later that night, she was worried and immediately called Charlotte to make sure they remembered to lock all the doors and to call the police if they heard anyone snooping around the house or trying to break in. Charlotte assured her they would be extra careful and had already suggested Alexa sleep with her while Adam was away.

Nancy was taking care of Gypsy and Luna, who were pacing the kitchen floor looking for food, when she noticed the light on her telephone flashing. The message was from Tom asking her to call him back as he had more information on Julian. Nancy glanced up at the clock and decided it was too late to call so she would leave it until morning.

After a restless night, she came downstairs, just before seven, and looked out of the window onto Salisbury. It was raining heavily and didn't look like it was going to clear up for some time. She switched the radio on to CHFI and listened to the news while she made coffee and two slices of toast, liberally spread with peanut butter, then sat down at the kitchen table and thought about everything Alexa had told them. She was now even more determined to find out if Julian was not just related, but if he was Adam's twin but the thought of confronting Mary was not an encounter she was looking forward to.

Breakfast over, she called Charlotte to make sure everything was all right and Alexa had had a good night's sleep. "She went out like a light the moment her head hit the pillow," Charlotte said. "I wish I could say the same for myself but I couldn't stop going over everything in my mind. I was tossing and turning for hours, what about you, Mom?"

"I had a bad night too," Nancy replied. "But I feel fine this morning. Tom left me a message to call him. He has more news about Julian."

"Oh, I wonder what it is. You'll let me know when you find out, won't you?"

"Yes of course, dear. Is Alexa up yet?"

"She's in the shower. I'm going to be driving her to school and I'll pick her up when it's time for her to come home."

"It's Thursday, isn't this the day you have to work?"

"Yes, but I'll leave early to make sure I'm there on time."

"Okay, I'm going to call Tom in a little while and I'll call you at the library later."

When Nancy called Tom at eight o'clock, she got his answering machine so she left a message and stayed in the house waiting for him to call her back. It was almost nine when the phone rang. She was pleased to hear his voice. "Good morning, Tom," she said, "I'm glad you got my message."

"Sorry, Nancy," he said. "I was out walking Badger. I gather you were out last night."

"I was at Charlotte's. It was quite an evening," and she proceeded to tell him about Alexa's ordeal.

"I think you should still call the police," Tom remarked.

"I don't want to unless I have to. What did Gary find out?"

"Well, according to some neighbours who lived in the area at the time, Julian's wife walked out on him because their marriage broke down after they lost their daughter."

"So he had a child? What happened to her?"

"She had leukemia. She was only eight when she died."

Nancy gasped, "Oh, how awful. I can't imagine how any parent could cope with that."

"Well, from what we can gather, he started drinking heavily and even lost his job. His wife couldn't put up with it anymore and left but there's still no evidence of a divorce."

"Fancy having to deal with all that and then find out your mother abandoned you. Alexa said she felt sorry for him and I have to admit, I do too. It sounds like he's had a difficult life."

"I agree, but that doesn't give him the right to lure a young girl off the street. He's damn lucky he hasn't been charged with kidnapping"

"I know and I promise we'll be careful but I'm still going to visit his mother to see if there's any connection."

"When are you planning on going?"

"Tomorrow, I might as well get this over with."

"I remember you said she lived in Napanee. That's quite a drive back and forth in one day."

"It will take me about two and half hours to get there. I'll leave here around nine and after I see her, I'll have lunch somewhere and then just take my time coming back."

"Will you call me when you get home? I'd like to know how you got on."

"Yes of course," Nancy answered. "Enjoy the rest of the day."

Nancy waited until ten to call Charlotte. She wanted to make sure she had already arrived at the library. Charlotte was surprised and saddened to hear about Julian's daughter but was concerned her mother had already decided to leave for Napanee the next day and suggested she reconsider. When Nancy wouldn't back down, Charlotte offered to go with her but Nancy wouldn't allow it. She wanted to leave Charlotte completely out of the picture. She spent the morning doing chores around the house and, after lunch, shopped for groceries at St. Lawrence Market. She was looking forward to enjoying the fresh halibut she had just purchased and settling down to a relaxing evening in front of the TV.

It was close to eight o'clock and the sun had not long set when the doorbell rang. Nancy wasn't expecting anyone so, in order to be cautious, she peeked from behind the living room drapes and was surprised to see Adam standing on the front step. Her heart began to race, certain the only reason he was there was because he had found out about the affair. She took a deep breath then walked slowly down the hallway, trying to gather her thoughts, and opened the door. "Adam," she said, "what a sup . . . ." The words caught in her throat and her heart beat even faster when she realized it wasn't Adam. She stepped back and then froze in place.

Julian remained where he was and extended his hand, "Mrs. Fleming," he said. "It's a pleasure to meet you. I'm Julian Richards."

Nancy ignored the outstretched hand, "What are you doing here?" she asked in a shaky voice.

"Forgive me for intruding but I'd like to talk to you. May I come in?"

Every instinct told Nancy to shut the door in his face but her curiosity got the better of her. "What do you want to talk to me about?"

"Several things; I assure you I'm not here to cause any trouble. If you would feel more comfortable meeting me tomorrow in a public place, I'd find that perfectly understandable."

Nancy stared at him and then, in almost a trance like state, opened the door a little wider, "Perhaps, you'd better come in," she murmured.

Julian waited while she closed the door and then followed her as she led him into the living room. She motioned to one of the wing chairs near the fireplace, "Do sit down. May I get you something to drink; coffee or soda?"

Julian looked up at her, "Just some water please."

Nancy made her way to the kitchen. Her hand shook as she took a glass out of the cupboard and filled it with ice water. She glanced over at the set of knives sitting in the block on the counter. It crossed her mind to hide one under her cardigan but then Luna distracted her by jumping onto the kitchen table and, by the time she shooed her off, the thought had gone. She walked back into the living room, handed the glass to Julian and sat down in the chair opposite him. The likeness to Adam was startling except for the fact he was more muscular and then there was the scar just above his lip. "So tell me why you're here, Mr. Richards."

"Please call me Julian, Mrs. Fleming." He paused and then continued, "I do have to say it's obvious now where Charlotte gets her looks."

Nancy started to feel more in control "Well, that's all very flattering but you haven't answered my question."

"I'm sorry. First I want to apologize for last night. I know what I did was wrong and I'm grateful you didn't call the police."

"I'm not sure why you're apologizing to me. It's Charlotte who you scared out of her wits. How did you find out where I lived, anyway?"

"It was pretty simple after you told me your real name yesterday. I checked the phone book and made some phone calls; the same way you found me. I narrowed it down to two addresses and when I rang your doorbell I wasn't even sure I was at the right house but, when I saw you, I knew I had the right Nancy Fleming."

"How could you have been so sure?"

"Because you and Charlotte look so much alike, just the way Adam and I look so much alike. That's why you tracked me down isn't it?"

Nancy nodded, "The resemblance between you and my son-in-law is astonishing. I wanted to find out if you were related."

"So, that's why you made up a story about trying to find an old friend, Franny wasn't it? I realised later you very cleverly got me to tell you my mother's name. Why, were you so anxious to prove there was a connection between Adam and myself?"

Nancy sighed, "I didn't approve of Charlotte's relationship with you. I could tell she was getting in much too deep and it would end badly, not just for her but for the whole family. I figured she'd end the affair if she knew you were a close relative of Adam's."

Julian was silent for a moment then he took a deep breath, "I'm not in love with Charlotte, Mrs. Fleming. At first, I was infatuated and I didn't pay much attention to the fact I looked like her husband until after my mother died. When I moved her into a long term care home several years ago, I got rid of her furniture and kept any personal papers but I never bothered to look through them. Then about three days after

her death I decided I should get rid of the papers too. That's
when I found out I'd been adopted."

Nancy cut in, "So your mother never told you?"

Julian shook his head, "No. Aunt Beth assured me she
always had every intention of telling me but after she got ill,
it was too late. Naturally, when I found out, I was shocked
but I was even more shocked when I found my original birth
certificate and discovered the circumstances of my birth."

"You were a foundling," Nancy whispered.

Julian's eyes widened, "You knew; how?"

"I hired a private investigator to find out everything he
could about you. I needed to know the truth."

Julian slowly nodded, "I see. What else did you find out?"

"That you were married and had a daughter." Nancy
leaned forward as though she wanted to reach out to him,
"I'm so sorry."

Julian hung his head and when he looked up again there
were tears in his eyes, "Emma was the love of my life," he
said. "I'm not quite sure how I survived losing her. For years
afterwards I felt as though I had nothing left. I lost my wife
and my job and spent most days in a drunken stupor. I'm sure
you already know all this."

"It's hard to imagine having to cope with such a tragic
loss," Nancy said.

Suddenly Julian looked a little startled and Nancy looked
around to see Gypsy strolling into the room followed by Luna,
"Ah," she said, "here come the girls. I hope you're not allergic."

Julian smiled and reached out a hand as Luna came
towards him and plopped down at his feet while Gypsy sat,
sphinx like, two feet away staring at him. "I like all animals,"
he said.

Nancy smiled back, "I'm glad," she responded, "I've always
been suspicious of people who didn't."

Julian stroked Luna's head and then sat back, "I want
you to know I felt no anger towards my mother. She was an
amazing woman and she always supported me in everything I
did. I never knew my father. He left when I was about eighteen
months old. Mom was always vague about why he walked out
but I think I finally found the answer."

"You mean after your mother died?'

"Yes. I know he signed the adoption papers but I don't think he really wanted me."

"Why would you say something like that?"

Julian slipped his hand into the pocket of his jacket, pulled out a photograph, and handed it to Nancy, "Would you want a son who looked like that?"

Nancy looked down at the photo and gasped. It showed a baby with a severely disfiguring cleft palate. She laid the photo down on her lap and looked back up at Julian, "So that's why you have the scar," she said.

"Yes, my Aunt Beth told me I was about two when I was operated on at Sick Kids. My mother made sure I had the finest surgeon."

"The result is truly amazing," Nancy remarked.

Julian looked thoughtful, "The woman who gave birth to me dumped me like a piece of garbage on the steps of a church. She obviously couldn't stand to look at me."

"Maybe she was very young and very scared. Maybe her parents didn't even know she was pregnant. There could be so many explanations as to why she left you there. It may have been beyond her control."

"I thought so too, at first, but then I started to think about Adam and the way Charlotte reacted when she first saw me. It was then that I asked her to bring me a photograph of him and when I saw it, I knew."

"What did you know?"

"I knew he had to be my twin."

"You can't be sure of that."

"I felt it in my bones and I became enraged."

Nancy frowned, "I don't understand, I would think you'd be overjoyed to find out you had a brother."

"On the contrary; Adam was the baby they decided to keep. They fed him and clothed him and gave him a good education. He grew up to be a successful architect living in a big house with a beautiful wife and two great children. I was bitter and resentful and vowed to find the woman who abandoned me but, at the same time, I wanted to punish Adam for being the one they chose."

"It sounds so twisted, Julian."

"It is; I know that now. The only reason I asked Charlotte to leave him was to make him suffer the way I had."

"And now?"

"Two nights ago, I saw Alexa leaving the house. She walked right past my car and she reminded me of Emma. I figured that's what Emma would have looked like if she had lived; a typical teenager in a mini skirt rushing off to meet her friends. I wanted so desperately to talk to her but I knew Charlotte wouldn't allow it so I tricked her into going with me yesterday. I never ever meant to harm her and I always intended to bring her home. She's a lovely young lady. You must be very proud of her."

"I am, but didn't you have an ulterior motive for taking her?"

"Yes, I suppose I did. I wanted to find out where Adam's parents lived."

"It didn't do you any good did it?"

"No. She told me her grandmother's name was Mary and she lived in Napanee. I've spent most of the day trying to locate her."

"I'm not surprised you were unsuccessful."

"Why do you say that?"

"Mary was divorced from her first husband soon after Adam was born. She remarried a few years later and no longer goes under the name of Hamilton."

"So my real father left her too. I wonder why? Maybe it had something to do with me."

"That's mere speculation."

"Perhaps; I assume you're not about to tell me the name she goes under now?"

Nancy shook her head, "No, I can't do that. I'm beginning to think it might be better for everybody if you just went back to Montreal and went on with your life, Julian."

"It's too late for that now, Mrs. Fleming. If Mary is my biological mother, I want to know what happened when I was born and if Adam is my brother, I'd like to have a relationship with him."

"I don't know how that would be possible now that you've slept with his wife."

Adam paused, picked up his empty glass, and stood up, "May I have some more water please?"

"Of course," Nancy replied getting to her feet. "Are you sure you wouldn't like some coffee?"

"No, water would be fine," he said handing her the glass and sitting down again.

Nancy left the room with Gypsy trailing behind her. She no longer felt nervous having Julian in her house, in fact she found him rather intriguing and he had something about him that set him apart from Adam. She had always gotten along well with her son-in-law and although she considered him a good looking man, he lacked the sex appeal of Julian. It was hard to define what made the difference. Maybe it was the clothes. Adam had always been very conservative while Julian was dressed in jeans and a black leather jacket. Maybe it was the scar that gave his face more character or perhaps it was the eyes which, although similar to Adam's, were a softer shade of green. Nancy was still trying to figure it out when she walked back into the living room and found Julian with Luna on his lap. "I'm afraid Luna sheds a lot," she said as she placed the glass on the table beside him.

"It's fine," he replied stroking her fur. "I think she likes me."

Nancy smiled, "That's a good sign."

"You know, I've been thinking about what you said but I can't walk away now. Maybe Adam never has to find out."

"I don't see how that can be avoided. Alexa promised not to tell her father but if you suddenly show up as his long lost brother, I'm not sure she'll be able to keep her word."

Julian drew in a breath, "Are you telling me Charlotte told Alexa about our affair?"

"Yes. She really didn't have any choice. Alexa had already noticed her mother was acting strangely. She was very concerned and even confided in me. I wasn't certain how long I could assure her there was nothing wrong and then when you showed up last night, the truth had to come out."

"The poor kid, was she really angry with her mother?"

"Actually no, she wasn't."

"When did you find out about Charlotte and me?'

"I can't remember exactly but I knew something was going on and I kept pushing for answers until she finally broke down and told me."

Julian picked up Luna very gently, put her down on the floor, and then got up. He walked over to the fireplace and stared at a photograph of Adam and Charlotte taken on their anniversary a few years earlier. "I'm sorry, Mrs. Fleming," he said turning to look at her. "I regret all the trouble I've already caused but I really need to do this."

Nancy got up and walked over to him. Taking both of his hands in hers she looked directly into his eyes and said, "Then let me help you, Julian. I'm going to see Mary and we'll see what happens. If she's your real mother we'll take it from there, one step at a time."

Julian squeezed her hands, "Thank you. You're a special lady."

"Nonsense, I just want to be sure nobody gets hurt."

Julian took a step back, "I think I've taken up enough of your time so I'd better go. I'm needed in Montreal and I'll be driving back in the morning. Will you call me after you've visited this Mary person?"

"Yes, I might even see her tomorrow," Nancy said. She began to follow him out of the room then stopped abruptly, "Oh, one moment, Julian."

He turned and watched as she walked over to the table, near where she'd been sitting, and picked up the photograph, "You forgot this but, if you don't mind, I'd like to keep it."

Julian smiled, "Do you plan to shock her into a confession?"

"Something like that," Nancy answered smiling back.

Chapter Forty-Two

The next morning, Nancy got up early and began to prepare for her trip to Napanee. She dressed in a pair of cream coloured slacks, a white blouse and a lightweight caramel jacket then swept her hair up into a French roll. Checking herself out in the mirror, she felt very much in control, for the moment. A little later, after deciding not to call Charlotte about Julian's visit until she had spoken to Mary, she thought about the day ahead and began to feel anxious. She had no idea what the outcome would be and if Mary truly was Julian's mother, what then?

By nine o'clock she was already heading away from the city. As she approached Highway 401, it suddenly occurred to her that Julian might be following her and she nervously looked around trying to spot his red BMW. At that time in the morning, already past rush hour, and travelling in the opposite direction to most commuters, the traffic was very light and she began to relax as she continued on her journey. She had only visited the farm once before, when she had accompanied Adam and the children to visit their grandmother. She had never felt any connection with Mary whenever she'd come to Toronto and she understood why Charlotte avoided her mother-in-law whenever possible. She had a very abrupt manner, to the point of being rude at times, and it was difficult not to retaliate. She didn't expect a warm welcome showing up without an invitation and wasn't even sure how she was going to approach the subject of Julian. As she got closer and closer to Napanee, she began to have doubts. Was she really doing the right thing?

Maple Farm was located just north of the highway and spread over four hundred acres. Ray's father had owned the farm up until his death, almost twenty years before, at which time it was passed on to his son. Mary had lucked out when she met Ray McLeod. He was a mild mannered, kind and patient man and provided her with a good living. The farm housed upwards of fifty cattle and Ray had supplemented income from the sale of milk, with the harvesting of maple syrup. As Nancy drove onto the property, she could see most of the cattle were out grazing in the fields and there was one lone figure walking away from her towards one of the barns. She thought it looked like Ray but couldn't be sure. Hopefully, Mary would be alone in the house. She parked the car and glanced out of the side door window then noticed a movement on the porch. which wrapped around the front of the two story structure, and when she stepped out onto the driveway, a large dog came bounding towards her wagging its tail. She bent down, and instinctively reached out with her hand, holding it palm up below its mouth. The dog sniffed, licked her fingers and then slumped down at her feet, "Good boy," she whispered.

"Actually, it's a female," came a voice from nearby and Nancy looked up to see Mary standing over her. Short in stature and several pounds overweight, Mary was not an attractive woman. She had allowed her hair, which was drawn back in a ponytail, to turn completely grey and years of spending time outdoors had etched deep lines on her somewhat masculine face. She was wearing jeans, a checkered shirt and heavy workman type boots and had a sour expression.

Nancy rose to her feet, "Good morning, Mary," she said smiling. "It's good to see you."

Mary nodded, "I'm surprised you're here," she responded.

"Well, I was visiting some friends in Belleville, "Nancy lied, "and thought I'd drop by. I hope you don't mind."

"You'd better come inside," she said abruptly and turned to walk back into the house. Nancy began to follow her when suddenly she called out, "Maggie, get in here."

"What breed is she?" Nancy asked as the dog lumbered to her feet and nudged the back of her legs.

"Some kind of shepherd mix," Mary answered without looking back.

As Nancy continued to walk down the hallway she was still at a loss as to what she was going to say but she had to get Mary talking about her life before she met Ray.

When she entered the kitchen she was relieved to see they were alone but felt compelled to ask, "Where's Ray?"

Mary motioned to her to sit down at the table and reached for the kettle, "He's out in the barn. Don't expect him back before his dinner time."

"He's eaten lunch already?"

"Took it with him," Mary answered in her usual clipped manner.

Nancy looked around her and noticed Maggie was already curled up in a large doggie bed at the far end of the kitchen, "How long have you had Maggie? I don't remember seeing her when I was here before."

"Going on two years about," Mary replied as she put two tea bags in a teapot and took two mugs out of a cupboard.

Nancy sighed, thinking to herself; this is going to be harder than I thought.

There was silence while Mary waited for the kettle to boil then filled the teapot and brought it to the table along with a jug of milk and a bowl of sugar. As she returned to the counter to pick up the mugs, she glanced over her shoulder at Nancy, "How about a cookie? Got some fresh baked just out of the oven."

Nancy shook her head, "No thank you, Mary, I'm having lunch after I leave here."

"Won't hurt you, you know," Mary remarked looking her up and down. "You could do with more meat on your bones."

Nancy decided not to take the bait. "How have you been doing this year? Has the economy affected you at all?"

Mary sat down and started to pour the tea, "Not so's you'd notice; been busy as all get out as usual. Had a few setbacks like one of the laborers getting his foot injured. That left us short-handed and then the last two weeks we've had a lot of rain."

Nancy took the mug Mary handed her, "Really? It's hardly rained at all at home, except for yesterday."

Mary looked down at Nancy's shoes, "No, didn't think it had otherwise you wouldn't be wearing those."

Nancy held up one foot and examined her three inch tan pumps, "These old things," she said, "I wear them all the time."

Mary held up her own foot, "This is what you need out here. There's nothing like a good pair of boots."

Nancy decided to change the subject, "Have you spoken to Adam lately?"

"No. I haven't heard from him in a while. Last time he called, he didn't have much to say. I spoke to Alexa and she told me Charlotte was up at some cottage. I was surprised she went off like that."

Nancy felt compelled to come to Charlotte's defense, "Well, she's been feeling a little depressed lately and needed a break. It was only for a couple of days."

"Humph! What's she got to be depressed about? How many days does she work, two? It can't be that hard, she should try her hand at farming. Now that's a real job."

Nancy sat up straight in her chair, "It has nothing to do with working. I think she's really missing Tyler and the prospect of Alexa leaving home in the next few years is something she's not looking forward to."

Mary looked pensive, "I remember when Adam left home. It took me a while to adjust."

Nancy knew the moment had come, "I know just how you must have felt. I found it pretty lonesome when Charlotte left. Did you ever wish you had more than one child?"

Mary hesitated and lowered her eyes for just a moment but long enough for Nancy to notice, "No never did," she responded and then got up abruptly from the table.

Nancy looked up as Mary walked towards the counter and placed her mug in the sink, "Did I say something to upset you?" she asked.

Mary remained where she was with her back to Nancy, "No, I just haven't got time to socialize; maybe some other time."

Nancy rose from her chair, walked up behind Mary then, placing her hand gently on her shoulder, whispered, "It's not good to keep secrets, Mary."

Mary whipped around and pushed her away, "I haven't got any secrets."

"Oh no, I saw your reaction just now when I mentioned another child. Are you sure Adam is your only son?"

Mary gasped, "Get out," she yelled. "Don't come here and try to make trouble."

"I'm just trying to learn the truth, that's all."

"I don't know what you're trying to imply. Adam's my only son and I'll thank you to leave my house now or I'll call Ray to see you off the property."

Nancy smiled, "I don't think you really want to do that. You really are upset aren't you? Tell me, have you ever heard of a place called Rockport?"

Mary's eyes widened in surprise and she grasped the edge of the counter but her voice softened, "No, I've never heard of it. Now please leave."

"What about St. Andrews Church, surely you must be familiar with it?"

Nancy watched as Mary's hand flew to her throat and she looked as though she was about to faint. "Here, why don't you sit down," she suggested pulling out the nearest chair.

Mary took two steps forward and slumped down onto the seat, "What do you want from me?" she whispered.

Nancy took the chair opposite. "I told you I want the truth. Admit it Mary, you had another child and you abandoned it. You left it on the church steps and just walked away."

Mary shook her head vehemently, "No, no I didn't do it. It wasn't my fault."

"Then who's fault was it, Mary?"

"It was Jimmy. It was all Jimmy's fault."

Nancy reached out and took her hand, "Why don't you tell me all about it, Mary."

She tried to pull away but Nancy held on and Mary slumped down in her chair looking defeated, "Please, why don't you leave me alone."

"Because it's too late for that now; I know most of the story. I just need to hear what really happened."

"I told you it wasn't my fault. I wanted to keep both of my babies."

Nancy gripped Mary's hand even tighter, "I believe you and I'm here to help."

Mary took a deep breath and lowered her head, "I've always dreaded the day someone would find out the truth but somehow I'm almost relieved because I've never stopped thinking about it."

"Why don't you just start at the beginning, Mary? I assume Jimmy was your husband."

Mary nodded and began to talk in a faltering manner, "Yes, we were living in a rented house in Nepean and were having trouble making ends meet. Jimmy had just lost his job working at a feed store and I only had a part time job at the farmer's market so when I got pregnant, Jimmy was furious"

When Mary hesitated, Nancy whispered, "Go on, Mary."

"He wanted me to have an abortion but I just couldn't do it."

"You must have been very young. Where were your parents?"

"I was only nineteen; we'd only been married just over a year. My dad died when I was twelve and my mom had mental problems so she couldn't help."

"So you decided to go through with the pregnancy. How did your husband react?"

Nancy watched as she saw the woman she had always thought of as cold and unfeeling, crumple before her eyes, "He threatened to leave me," she managed to reply as tears began to stream down her face. "I begged him not to go and he agreed as long as I promised to give the baby up once it was born."

Nancy gasped, "But you didn't expect to have twins did you?"

Mary shook her head again, "No, we had no idea. They came early one night and so fast we didn't have time to go to the hospital. We didn't even have a telephone to call for help, so Jimmy ended up delivering them. He was as shocked as I was when the second baby started coming and that same night he told me he wasn't going to wait to have them adopted. He said he planned to take them and leave them outside the hospital but then he thought it would be too risky, so he decided to take them to Rockport and leave them on the church steps. I screamed and begged him not to do it. I said I'd kill myself if he took them away. Finally he agreed and put one of the babies in my arms. I pulled back the blanket he had wrapped the baby in and saw it was a boy. I was so taken with my son I didn't notice Jimmy creep out of the house with the other baby and when I realized he'd gone, I didn't know what to do. We had a beaten up old car that broke down all the time but I found out later he'd driven it all the way to Rockport and left the baby at St. Andrews. I pleaded with him to bring the baby back but he refused and threatened, if I ever told anyone, he'd take the other one away from me too. I didn't even know if it was a boy or a girl and he wouldn't tell me. I hated him after that and as soon as Adam was a year old, I took off. I got a job working as a companion to an elderly lady in Ottawa and she saved my life. I was able to have Adam with me all the time and when she died four years later, she left me some money. It wasn't a huge amount but enough to make sure Adam had a good education."

Nancy finally released Mary's hand, "Didn't you ever try to find out what happened to your other child?"

"I was too scared. I knew nobody would believe I was an innocent victim."

"What about Jimmy? Didn't he come after you?"

"No, he didn't want anything to do with me and seven years after we separated I got a divorce."

Suddenly Mary leaned forward and grasped Nancy's arm, "You knew all this didn't you? That's why you came here. You wanted to confront me. How did you find out?"

Nancy was prepared with her account of all of the events leading up to the moment when she was certain Julian was Adam's twin. She left out any reference to Charlotte and claimed to have run into Julian one day and being astounded at his resemblance to Adam. She also claimed to have withheld all knowledge of Julian from the family until she had spoken to her. "I have to admit," she said, "I did come here to confront you but I had no idea you were at the mercy of your husband. I can't imagine how you must have felt."

"I've never stopped thinking about what happened to my baby. At least, now I know it was a boy. I just wonder why Jimmy picked him to take away instead of Adam."

Reluctantly, Nancy picked her purse up from the table and pulled out the photo of Julian as an infant, "I'm sorry, Mary, but perhaps this might provide the answer."

Mary took the photo and, as she stared down at it, the tears started to fall again. "Oh, how dreadful; the poor baby."

"It's all right, the woman who adopted him made sure he was well taken care of. He had surgery to repair his palate and today he only has a scar. That's the one feature that really sets him apart from Adam."

"Does he know about me?"

"Yes, but he doesn't know where you live or even your last name. He knows we are related and that I was coming to see you today. It's up to you now, Mary."

"I have to see him, Nancy, but will he want to see me?"

"I'm sure he will after I tell him what happened when he was born. He didn't find out he was adopted until just recently so I expect it's all a little overwhelming for him. We also have to think about the effect on Adam."

Mary nodded, "Yes, you're right. How am I going to tell him he has a twin brother?"

"Maybe you need a little time to think about it. I'll be in touch with Julian when I get back to Toronto and try and arrange a meeting in a week or two. Will that give you enough time? You'll probably need to talk to Ray, or does he already know your story?"

"Yes, he already knows. I couldn't keep it to myself after I met him. I knew he'd understand."

Nancy stood up, "Good. Well, I'd better go. Thank you for being honest with me."

Mary stepped forward and grasped both of Nancy's hands, "No, it's me who should be thanking you. I'll talk it over with Ray and then I'll call you. Please leave me your telephone number."

Nancy wrote down her number on a slip of paper, handed it to Mary, and then headed for the door, "I'm so glad I came," she said as she stepped onto the porch.

As she drove away, she looked back and saw Mary, with Maggie beside her, feebly waving goodbye. She couldn't help thinking how wrong she had been about the woman she'd always considered aloof and unfeeling. Perhaps, she had just built a shell around herself, so that nobody could ever hurt her again.

Chapter Forty-Three

Rather than stopping for lunch. Nancy decided to drive straight home. She had a lot to think about and she wanted to talk to Tom. She was tired when she walked through the front door of her house and immediately headed for the kitchen for a cup of coffee and a bite to eat. She noticed the light flashing on her telephone and considered checking her messages later but something was telling her to pick up the receiver. She listened to the first message with growing alarm and when she finally put the phone down, she immediately picked it up again. She had to call Mary. Julian had followed her. Not in his own car but in a rented non-descript black model. He wanted to hear firsthand what Mary had to say.

A moment later, Nancy was punching in the number for Maple Farm. It rang, once, twice, three times and by the time the answering machine came on, she was in a state of panic. She decided to check her other messages and grew even more fearful when she heard Charlotte's voice. "Mom," she said, "Ray just called, Mary's been taken to the hospital; something about an intruder. I've called Adam and he's on his way there." As she continued, she began to sound almost hysterical. "Oh, Mom, did you go there? Did Julian follow you? Adam's going to find out. I don't know what I'm going to do." Then there was a moment of silence and a click as Charlotte hung up.

Nancy immediately called her back and when there was no answer she tried calling Julian but his phone was off. What had he done? Where was he? Fearful for Mary's condition she checked on-line for hospitals in Napanee and, seconds later, was punching in the number for the Lennox and Addington. Knowing that only a close relative could get information, she pretended to be Mary's sister and learned she had just been brought in by ambulance and was being assessed. Beyond that, she was unable to find out exactly what had happened so she decided to call Charlotte back. After getting no answer, and worrying about how Charlotte was reacting to the possibility of the truth coming out, she raced out to her car and took off for Highland Avenue, almost running a red light on the way.

Charlotte's car wasn't in the driveway and Nancy had no idea where she was. Now she had to worry about Alexa. School would soon be out and she'd be on her way home. Taking the key, she kept for emergencies from her purse, she entered the house and went straight to the kitchen to see if there were any messages on the phone, but there were none. A moment later, she noticed an envelope sitting on the kitchen table with 'Alexa' written on the outside. She knew immediately it was a note from Charlotte and unable to contain herself, she ripped open the envelope and pulled out the single piece of paper from inside. As she began to read what Charlotte had written, she slowly sank down onto a chair. Her daughter had been unable to face Adam.

My darling Alexa,

Please don't be alarmed but Grandma Mary had a heart attack and has been taken to the hospital. Dad is on his way there now.

I think Julian followed Nana when she went to the farm and, after she left, he did something to cause your grandmother to collapse.

I know I have put you in a terrible position asking you to keep my secret and now that the truth

*will come out, I want you to be sure to tell your father
that I begged you not to tell him about Julian.*

*Nana warned me nothing good would come of
what I was doing and she was right. I wish I could
go back in time and have everything the way it was
before I became so selfish with no thought of what I
was doing to my family.*

*I can't face your father right now so I'm going
away for a while. I want you to know I love you with
all my heart and I hope you will forgive me.*

*I don't want you to worry about me. I'll be in
touch with you soon but, right now, I need to spend
some time alone.*

Tell Nana not to worry.

With all my love,
Mom XXXXX

Nancy, although upset by the news, was relieved to learn
Mary had suffered a heart attack rather than being physically
harmed by Julian. Obviously his visit had been traumatic.
She assumed Ray must have called Charlotte back after they
reached the hospital but where was she now? Picking up the
kitchen phone, she tried reaching her on her cell phone but
it went straight to voice message. Pondering what to do next,
she was about to call Adam when she heard the front door
open and footsteps coming down the hall. Alexa appeared
in the doorway and looked surprised when she saw Nancy,
"Oh, hi Nana, I didn't know you were coming over today.
Where's Mom?"

Nancy reached out and grasped Alexa's hand, "I think
you'd better sit down, dear," she said. "Something's happened."

Alexa slowly sat down, "What is it? You're scaring me. Has
something happened to Mom?"

Nancy handed her the letter. "Your mother left you this
note. I apologize for reading it, Alexa, but I was worried. I was
already aware there had been some trouble."

Alexa's hand trembled as she took the letter and began to
read it. When she'd finished, she looked at Nancy with tears

in her eyes, "Where can Mom have gone? Is she ever coming back?"

Nancy shook her head, "I don't know where she's gone, dear. I tried calling her but there's no answer. I think she just needs some time to figure out how she's going to face your father."

Alexa suddenly looked angry, "Why did she have to go and hook up with Julian in the first place? Doesn't she love Dad anymore?"

"Life isn't that simple, Alexa. I told you before, sometimes our emotions take over. Your mom and dad have been married for a long time and it takes a lot of work to maintain a good relationship. Your dad's work takes him away a lot and now Tyler's left home, your mom's been feeling a little lost. When Julian came along and made her feel special, her heart began to rule her head. I've no doubt she loves your dad and the last thing in the world she wants is to be apart from him but it may take a lot for him to forgive her."

"So, you think he'll find out now?"

"I don't think there's any question about that. Ideally, your mother should be the one to tell him before he finds out from someone else. That way, she may have a chance of keeping the family together."

"What about Julian?"

"Well, your father is going to have to be told the truth about Julian and it will be up to him whether he can forgive him and accept him as his brother."

Alexa folded the note and put it back in the envelope, "Is Grandma Mary going to die?"

"I can't answer that, dear. She's in the hospital so I expect they're doing all they can for her. We'll just have to wait to hear from Ray or your father."

Alexa sighed, "Will you stay with me tonight please, Nana?"

Nancy got up and put her arm around her, "Of course. I'll just phone Mrs. Walker and ask her if she can pop in and feed Gypsy and Luna."

Alexa stood up, "That reminds me, where's Zoe?"

Nancy looked around the kitchen, "I'm sure she's somewhere in the house. Let's put some food in her bowl and I bet she'll be here in a flash."

Sure enough, minutes later, after filling her bowl with her favourite tuna and shrimp mix, Zoe appeared in the doorway. Alexa attempted to pick her up but, tempted by the food, she scurried right past her. Nancy laughed, "That's typical. All they think about is eating."

"Speaking of which, "Alexa responded. "What should we do about supper, although I'm not that hungry?"

"Well, we could go out but we need to be here in case anyone calls. Why don't we just order a pizza?"

Alexa went upstairs to change while Nancy telephoned her neighbour and then placed a call to Tom to tell him what had happened. He wasn't surprised Julian had followed her to the farm and was sorry he hadn't warned her of the possibility he might drive another car to mislead her. He asked if she wanted Gary to try and find Charlotte but Nancy preferred to wait, hoping Charlotte would be in touch.

Just before seven o'clock, after Nancy and Alexa had finished the pizza and were enjoying some chocolate fudge ice cream, they discovered in the freezer, Alexa's cell phone rang. They were sitting in the family room attempting to watch the news and both jumped when they heard the ring tone. Alexa tentatively picked up the phone and recognized the number, "It's Dad," she said.

Adam was at the hospital and had just been allowed to visit his mother who was in intensive care. She hadn't been able to speak to him but according to Ray, she had managed to utter a few words in the ambulance. Someone had come into the house and frightened her. She kept muttering something about a baby but Ray couldn't make head or tale of it. He had heard Maggie barking and knew something was wrong so he ran towards the house just in time to see a car pulling away but wasn't close enough to get the license number. He contacted the police and described the car but they had little to go on until Mary was able to tell them more. The doctor had little doubt she would fully recover and Adam had decided to stay at the farm overnight so that he could go back to the hospital in the morning. When he asked where Charlotte was, Alexa covered the phone and asked Nancy what to tell him. Nancy just shook her head and whispered, "Tell him she's gone to

pick up some milk." Adam seemed surprised Charlotte wasn't
at home and said he'd call back later but Alexa suggested
he wait until morning, once he'd seen Mary again, while
all the time she was praying her mother would be in touch
before then.

Chapter Forty-Four

Neither Nancy nor Alexa slept well. Both were up at the crack of dawn and sitting at the kitchen table cradling mugs of steaming hot coffee and waiting for the phone to ring. They were both in pajamas; Nancy having borrowed a pair of Charlotte's which she'd taken quite a fancy to.

"Where do you think Mom stayed last night?" Alexa asked.

Nancy sighed, "I don't know but maybe she went to stay with Jodi. I think we should call her later and see if she's heard from her."

"What if she's with Julian?"

Nancy looked surprised, "Oh, goodness no. I don't believe for a minute she's with him. Not after all that's happened."

"I hope your right, Nana," Alexa responded pausing to take a sip of coffee. "I'm so glad I don't have to go to school today. I don't think I'd be able to concentrate on anything and I don't want to leave the house in case Mom comes home."

Nancy glanced up at the calendar on the wall, "That's right it's Saturday. I've completely lost track of what day it is. Maybe I need some food to fuel my brain, how about some breakfast?"

Alexa volunteered to make some French toast while Nancy went upstairs to shower and get dressed. Fifteen minutes later, she was back downstairs and pouring more water into the Keurig coffee maker.

They had just finished eating when Alexa's phone rang and once again, after glancing at it, she said, "Its Dad."

Nancy reached out for the phone, "Why don't you let me speak to him?"

Without a moment's hesitation, Alexa tapped the screen and then thrust it into Nancy's hand, "Okay, Nana, thanks."

Nancy held it to her ear and tentatively said, "Hello."

Adam's voice came through loud and clear, "Nancy, what are you doing there at this time of the day. I tried calling Charlotte but there was no answer."

"Good morning, Adam," Nancy replied, trying to remain composed. "I've actually been here all night. How's your mother?"

"Ray and I are just heading to the hospital now but when we called earlier they said she was doing well and resting comfortably."

"That's wonderful news. Please give us an update after you've seen her."

"Of course, but how come you answered Alexa's phone? Isn't she there either?"

Nancy paused while Alexa stared at her intensely, "She's standing right beside me but I thought it would be better if I spoke to you. Charlotte isn't here, Adam. She hasn't been here all night and that's why I stayed over."

"What? I don't understand. Yesterday Alexa told me she'd just gone out for milk." His voice started to rise, "Didn't she come back? Is she missing? My goodness, what's happened to her?"

"I'm sure she's perfectly fine, Adam. Please try not to be alarmed. She decided to go away for a while. We didn't want to tell you last night because we knew you were upset about your mother and didn't want to make it worse."

"But where on earth would she have gone and why? She never said a word to me about this."

"She never said a word to anyone but she did leave Alexa a note. When you get home, Adam, we'll need to talk."

Adam sounded frustrated, "Talk about what? What the hell is going on?" He paused for a second and then continued, "I have to go, Ray's waiting in the car, but I'll be driving back to Toronto right after I've seen Mom and dropped Ray back at the farm."

"Alexa and I will both be here. Please try not to worry and tell Mary we're thinking about her."

After Nancy handed the phone back to Alexa, she put her arm around her, "I'm sorry, dear," she said, "but I don't think we have any choice. We have to tell your father what's happened."

Alexa looked alarmed, "Everything?"

"Well I'll try and play down the affair between your mom and Julian but I can't cover it up altogether. There has to be an explanation as to why your mom isn't here. As for the relationship between Julian and your dad, that has to come out."

"But how do we know they really are twins, just because they look so much alike?"

Nancy motioned to Alexa to sit down and then settled in the chair beside her, "There's just too much evidence for it not to be the case. I'm just wondering if your grandmother will be able to communicate with your dad when he gets to the hospital and tell him everything before he even gets here."

"Do you really think that's possible?"

Nancy looked thoughtful, "I'm not sure but maybe she'll disclose enough that Ray will be able to fill in the rest."

"Are you saying Grandpa knows all about Julian?"

"Yes, your grandmother told him what happened. She couldn't keep it a secret from everybody."

"Poor Grandma, I feel so bad for her. I wonder what she's going to say when she hears about Mom. I hope she comes home before Dad gets here. Maybe then we can come up with some other reason why she left."

"I don't think that's going to happen. My greatest wish is that your dad can forgive your mother and have a real relationship with Julian but that can only happen if everyone is brutally honest."

"But didn't you say you were going to play down the affair. Did you mean it?"

Nancy sighed, "I just don't want to make it sound like it was really serious and there's one other problem."

"What's that, Nana?"

"Well, if your dad finds out about Julian picking you up off the street, he's going to be furious. I'm not sure we can tell him about it."

"Let's not tell him then. I can always say I suspected something was going on with Mom and happened to see Julian near the house one day. That really isn't lying."

Nancy shook her head, "I think we're going to have to play that one by ear."

An hour later, Nancy phoned Jodi and left a message. She didn't mention Charlotte had been out all night; she merely asked if they were meeting for lunch as she had her dates mixed up. Just fifteen minutes after she placed the call, Jodi called back to say she hadn't spoken to Charlotte in over a week but was planning to get in touch with her in a few days. Nancy decided not to fill her in on what was going on, thanked her, and then phoned Tom to give him an update.

The hours seemed to drag by waiting for Adam to arrive home and, at the same time, desperately wishing for Charlotte to show up. Nancy occupied herself by washing her car, which was covered in dirt after her visit to the farm, while Alexa stayed in her room playing video games. At noon, Nancy made grilled cheese sandwiches and a garden salad and they sat out on the backyard patio trying to enjoy the day, which was unusually warm for September. They watched while Zoe prowled through the grass looking for some unsuspecting prey and they both smiled but their minds were elsewhere. What would the afternoon bring?

At two o'clock, Nancy heard the sound of a car pulling into the driveway and, a moment later, Adam was striding through the front door. "Nancy," he called out, "are you still here?"

Nancy walked out of the kitchen into the hallway and placed her hand on Adam's arm. "Come into the kitchen," she said.

He followed her and looked around, "Where's Alexa?"

"She's up in her room. I thought it would be best if I talked to you alone. Why don't you sit down?"

Adam pulled out a chair and slumped down onto it, "What's going on?"

"First let me get you something to drink. How about something cold? What about lemonade or maybe a beer?"

Adam nodded, "A beer would be good. Thanks."

"Have you eaten? Would you like me to make you a sandwich?"

"No, I'm fine thanks. I stopped at a drive-through on the way back and picked up a hamburger."

There was a moment of silence as Nancy took a beer from the refrigerator and handed it to Adam, then sat down opposite him. "Tell me about your mother. How was she today?"

Adam shrugged off his jacket and wrapped his hands around the bottle of Heineken, "She seemed a lot better but she's still not talking. The doctor expects her to make a good recovery but she needs to lose some weight and she'll be on blood pressure medication from now on."

"I'm so glad to hear that, Adam. You must have been really worried. Did Ray know any more about what caused her to have the attack?"

Adam shook his head, "No, I don't understand it. Some guy walks into the house, doesn't take anything and doesn't physically hurt her but obviously scares her enough that she has a heart attack."

Nancy sat silently for a few seconds, not even sure where to begin when Adam continued, "And now this thing with Charlotte. Where has she gone and why? Tell me what you know, Nancy."

Nancy took a deep breath and then, for the next ten minutes, told Adam everything. She didn't leave out any details except for playing down the affair and omitting the episode with Alexa.

Adam sat quietly taking it all in, his eyes widening in surprise at times and occasionally shaking his head. Then when Nancy finally stopped talking, he responded in almost a whisper, "Is that all?"

Nancy hesitated, unable to determine what Adam was feeling, "I don't know what else to tell you. I do know it's an awful lot to digest and you'll need some time to get your head around it."

Adam stood up abruptly, walked over to the kitchen counter and gazed out of the window then turned with eyes blazing, "You're damned right it's a lot to take in. You're telling me after forty-five years, I've suddenly acquired a twin brother and my wife's been sleeping with him."

Nancy slowly nodded, "I'm so sorry, Adam."

"How long have you known about all this," he asked, his voice rising in anger.

"A little while but I didn't think it was serious," Nancy lied. "I thought Charlotte was just having a fling and you'd never have to know about it."

"Hmmmm. Then you found out Charlotte's lover was my twin. How did you feel about it then?"

"I didn't know what to think," Nancy replied beginning to feel defensive. "I encouraged Charlotte to end it. I just knew it would end in heartbreak."

Adam walked back to the table and sat down again, "What about Alexa? How much does she know?"

"Well, she suspected her mother was seeing someone then she happened to see Julian one day and persuaded Charlotte to tell her the truth,"

"Do you know where Charlotte is now? Is she with him?"

"No, I honestly don't know where she is but I'm certain she's not with Julian. She was devastated when she realized the truth was going to come out and couldn't face you, not yet anyway."

"How do you know that?"

"I told you, she left Alexa a note. She has it in her room and I'm sure she'll show it to you if you ask her."

"What about Tyler, does he know what's been going on?"

"Thankfully, no; it's a good thing he's in London because I dread to think how he'd react."

"Well at least now I can figure out what happened to my mother. If this guy looks as much like me as you say he does, she must have had quite a shock."

Nancy decided to ignore the fact that Adam wouldn't even acknowledge Julian by name. "Yes, well even though I'd just finished speaking to her and she expected to see him soon, she didn't expect him to walk through the door right after I left. I can't imagine how she must have felt seeing the child she had taken away from her, all grown up and looking exactly like you."

"You claim Ray knew all about what my father did?"

"That's true but he couldn't have known the man he saw leaving the house was Julian. I think maybe the best thing you can do, Adam, is go back and tell your mother you know the whole story. She may be feeling terribly guilty and you need to assure her she has nothing to feel guilty about. None of this was her fault and she would probably want, more than anything, for you and Julian to have a real relationship. Of course, she doesn't know about Charlotte's role in this and it might be a good idea for her not to know about it for now."

Adam suddenly leaned both elbows on the table and placed both hands over his face. "I don't think I'll ever be able to forgive her," he murmured.

Nancy looked up when she heard a noise near the door and then watched as Alexa tiptoed into the room. She crept up behind her father and placed a small slim hand gently on his shoulder, "Daddy, you have to," she whispered.

Chapter Forty-Five

While Adam had been driving back to Toronto, Charlotte had been heading along the Queen Elizabeth Way towards the Peace Bridge. After she left the house, with a small suitcase and a large tote bag, she checked into the Marriott downtown and spent the next few hours trying to figure out where to go. She had no idea what was going on at home but she was certain the truth would come out and she couldn't face Adam. He would have so much to deal with and she dreaded to think what his reaction would be. He had always been a reasonable man and willing to give anyone the benefit of the doubt but he was human and she had no doubt he would be angry and terribly hurt. As soon as she'd settled in her room, she was tempted to call her mother but then decided against it and shut her phone off to avoid any calls.

Feeling drained from the stress of everything she was feeling, she stripped down to her underwear and lay down on the bed, then promptly fell asleep. When she woke up, it was already growing dark and she was hungry. After enjoying a club sandwich and a glass of Chardonnay from room service, she tried to occupy her mind by watching a remake of Wuthering Heights on the movie channel. At just after ten, she shut off the television and glanced at her phone. There were six messages,

two from Nancy begging her to call, one from Adam asking
where she was and three from Julian desperately wanting to
see her. She gasped when she heard Julian's first message, she
hadn't expected to hear from him again. Her head told her to
run and keep running but her heart was telling her otherwise.
She forced herself to put the phone on top of the dresser and
decided to take a bath and try to relax. Sinking down into the
warm water, her body started to unwind but her mind kept
darting from one thought to another. Maybe, if she called
Julian, he'd tell her what happened at the farm? Perhaps if she
went home now and begged for Adam's forgiveness, she could
save their marriage. Maybe, she didn't really want to save her
marriage? What would life be like if she was single again and
could do whatever she wanted?

When she finally got out of the tub and exited the
bathroom, wrapped in one of the hotel's heavy white robes,
it was just in time to hear her phone ringing. She thought she
had turned it off and tried to ignore it but curiosity got the
better of her and she picked it up. It was Julian. She put the
phone down again and walked away only to hear it ring again
a moment later. This time, her anger surfaced and in the heat
of the moment, she answered the call. "What do you want,
Julian?" she yelled. "Haven't you done enough damage?"

There was silence at the end of the line and then Julian
replied in a very gentle voice, "Please don't be angry, Charlotte.
I need to see you and explain."

"There's no excuse for what you did. Because of you Mary
suffered a heart attack. You're lucky she didn't die."

"I know you won't believe me but I didn't do anything.
Please meet me somewhere so we can talk."

"No, I don't want to talk to you. Please leave me alone."

"But I need . . . ."

Charlotte ended the call and turned the phone off. The
sound of Julian's voice brought back too many emotions. She
really thought she had been in love with him and she couldn't
risk seeing him again.

The next morning, after breakfast in the hotel coffee shop,
she took a second cup of coffee up to her room and checked
her phone again. There was another message from Nancy

and two more from Julian. It was time to move on. She had
even considered flying to London and surprising Tyler but she
wouldn't have been able to pull it off. She had never been good
at play-acting and having to pretend she was on vacation and
spend most of the time sightseeing, wasn't a possibility. In the
end, she decided to just drive and see where her journey took
her and the more she thought about it, the more she began
to feel a sense of adventure. She had never done anything
like it before and the anticipation of what might lie ahead was
intriguing.

She reached the Peace Bridge at noon and was relieved
she'd had the presence of mind to bring her passport. It was
Sunday and there were a lot of tourists crossing the border
looking for bargains but it didn't deter her and she passed
through customs and immigration without incident. She had
just taken the ramp onto the New York State Freeway when
her cell phone rang again. She was too busy concentrating on
her driving to even glance at the screen to see who it was and
ignored it but, she was sure it was Julian. It occurred to her,
he was never going to take her seriously and after the incident
with Mary, she wondered if he might pose a danger to her or
her family. It was then she realized she may be making a big
mistake by running away and needed to think about what she
was doing. A few minutes later, she was exiting to get onto I90
and heading towards downtown Buffalo. It had been many
years since she driven through the downtown area and had
no idea which direction to take. Parking on a side street, she
asked a passerby where the best hotels were and he directed
her to an area close to the river near La Salle Park. Before
she drove away she checked the message on her phone and
discovered she had been right. It was Julian again, begging
her to call him.

Checking into the Hyatt Regency, she settled into her
room, changed into a pair of tan slacks and a lightweight
turquoise sweater and decided to go down to the Atrium
Bistro. Once there, she ordered a chicken quesadilla with fries
and a glass of zinfandel. It was three o'clock in the afternoon,
but not having eaten since breakfast, she was hungry and
felt less conspicuous eating alone when the restaurant

wasn't busy. She was determined to enjoy her meal and had deliberately left her phone in her room so she wouldn't be interrupted. Now she had to decide whether she was going to keep on driving south or whether she was going back to face the music.

Once back in her room, she discovered there were two more messages from Julian and one from Nancy. Obviously her mother was really worried about her and she needed to let her know she was all right. She sat down on the edge of the bed and tapped in Nancy's number. It only rang twice before she heard her mother's voice, "Hello."

"Mom, it's me,"

Nancy let out a sigh of relief, "Oh, Charlotte, thank goodness. I've been so worried about you. Are you okay?"

"Yes, I'm fine, Mom. I just couldn't stay there and face Adam. Have you seen him?"

"Yes, he stayed overnight at the farm so that he could see Mary again this morning, then he came home."

"How is Mary?"

"She's doing a lot better and the doctors think she'll fully recover. She hasn't said exactly what happened yet so we're none the wiser. Anyway, I'm more concerned about you right now. Where are you?"

"If I tell you, you have to promise not to tell Adam. I suppose he knows everything by now? What did you tell him exactly? He's probably pretty angry anyway and isn't likely to want to see me."

"Well, I had no choice, dear. I had to tell him why you left so suddenly. I did try to make the affair between you and Julian appear like it was just a fling, but I'm not sure he believed me and finding out he has a twin brother came as quite a shock. Listen to me, I promise I won't tell anyone where you are, dear, but I do wish you'd come home or at least come and stay with me for a while until you've figured things out."

"No I can't do that, Mom. I'm staying at the Hyatt regency in Buffalo for the night and I promise I'll call you in the morning. What about Alexa, did she get my note?"

"Yes, and she showed it to Adam. She's worried about you and as for Adam, well it's hard to know what he's really thinking. He was very withdrawn when I left there this morning and he told me he was taking Alexa to see her grandmother."

"Oh, I'm glad; at least it will keep her occupied. You will keep an eye on her won't you, Mom?"

"Yes, of course I will. By the way, has Julian tried to contact you? I tried calling him but he's not answering his phone."

"He's called me a number of times and left messages. I spoke to him once and told him to leave me alone but I don't think he's paying any attention. That's another reason I'm nervous about coming back. Do you think he could be dangerous?"

Nancy didn't hesitate, "No, I don't think so. I'm surprised he's still trying to chase after you though."

"Why do you say that?"

"It doesn't matter, dear, just come home."

"Like I said, Mom, I'll call you in the morning after I've had more time to think."

"All right, I'll be waiting to hear from you. I love you, Charlotte."

"I love you too, Mom. Take care of yourself."

A few minutes later, after talking to Nancy, she spent the next two hours lying on the bed trying to figure out what to do. She knew, sooner or later, she had to face the truth and running away was not the answer. She had to go back. She started packing up her belongings and was just about to exit the room when her cell phone rang again. It was Julian. She tried to ignore it but if she didn't convince him, once and for all, that their affair was over, he would never leave her alone. She dropped her suitcase beside the door and went back to sit on the bed, "What do you want, Julian?" she asked abruptly.

"I want to see you, Charlotte" he replied without hesitation. "Can't we talk about this?"

"No, we can't. There's nothing more to talk about. I made the worst mistake of my life when I got involved with you."

"You don't mean that. We had something special and you can't just give it all up and go back to the mundane life you were living."

Charlotte's voice rose as she responded, "You don't have any idea what my life was really like. I have a wonderful family and I've let them down. I have to make it up to them somehow."

Julian hesitated then in almost a whisper said, "Why don't you meet me one last time? I think you owe me that and then I'll leave you alone."

"What about Adam? Will you leave him alone too; after all he's your brother?"

Julian's voice hardened, "I've done without a brother for forty-five years. I don't need one now."

"I wish I could believe you, Julian."

"Adam probably hates my guts anyway so it won't be hard to stay away. I'll just go back to Montreal and he can forget I ever existed."

"That may not be possible and, in any case, how do I know I can trust you?"

"Meet with me and I'll convince you. Please, Charlotte."

Charlotte began to feel less resistant. Maybe it wouldn't hurt to see Julian one last time. "I'll be back in Toronto this evening," she whispered. "Meet me in the bar at the Thompson at six."

"Where are you now?"

"It doesn't matter."

"I'll be there," Julian replied and ended the call.

Charlotte sat staring at the phone for a few minutes and then slowly walked towards the door, retrieved her suitcase, and headed to the lobby to check out.

She took her time driving back to Toronto and as she approached Grimsby, she decided to get off the expressway and find a place where she could get coffee and a bite to eat. The first place she noticed was a MacDonalds and it was exactly the kind of place she needed. She had no desire to eat in another fancy restaurant alone. She ordered a chicken wrap and a milk shake and sat in a corner noticing how many families were seated at the other tables, all appearing to be enjoying themselves. She began to ache to have the days back when she and Adam and the children would all spend time together. She could never get those days back and her life seemed empty now. No wonder she had succumbed to Julian's charm. The more she thought about the time she had spent with him, the more she began to think about what she had been missing in her life and, suddenly, her heart beat a little faster. Was she really over him?

Chapter Forty-Six

Charlotte arrived at the hotel at five-thirty and, after parking her car, took the elevator to the Rooftop Lounge. She sat in one of the banquettes, where she could easily see anyone entering the room, and ordered a glass of Chardonnay. Being Sunday, there were only a few other people in the bar and Charlotte felt conspicuous. A middle-aged man seated alone, a few yards away, was staring at her and made her feel even more uncomfortable. She wished Julian would arrive. She still hadn't decided if she would go straight home after seeing him or if she would spend the night in the hotel. Then it occurred to her that maybe she should go and stay with her mother so, in order to keep occupied while she waited for Julian, she took out her cell phone and called Nancy.

"Hi, Mom," she said after Nancy answered, "it's me again."

"Oh, honey. Is everything all right?" Nancy asked anxiously.

"Yes, I'm fine. I decided to come back to Toronto but I'm not ready to go home yet. I was wondering if I could come and stay with you."

Nancy didn't hesitate, "Of course you can stay with me. Maybe it will be for the best then Adam and Alexa won't be worrying about where you are."

"I doubt Adam's worrying about me at all after everything that's happened."

"That's not true. He called me again about an hour ago to see if I'd heard from you."

"You didn't tell him where I was, did you?"

"No, I told him you'd telephoned and you were staying at a hotel but wouldn't tell me where."

Charlotte sighed, "Thanks, Mom. Please don't let him know I'm coming to your place. I'll see you in a couple of hours."

"Okay, dear, please be careful driving back."

"I will, don't worry."

After Charlotte ended the call she realized Nancy thought she was still in Buffalo just about to leave to drive to Toronto. It didn't really matter. As long as she showed up by about eight; Nancy would have no reason to worry.

She had just slipped her phone back into her purse when she noticed the elevator doors open and Julian stepped into the room. He noticed her immediately and began walking towards her with a smile on his face. Charlotte picked up her glass but her hand began to tremble. It wasn't fear that caused her reaction on seeing him again: it was excitement. He still had a hold on her. She remembered the time she first met him, right here in the same place, and the shock when he turned around and she saw his face. Now, in her eyes, he no longer resembled Adam, even though their features were almost identical. He was Julian, someone who made her feel alive again. No matter what happened, this time, she had to resist him.

Slipping into the banquette beside her, he lifted her hand, drew it to his lips and kissed it gently. "Hello, pretty lady," he whispered.

Charlotte withdrew her hand, "What do you want, Julian, I haven't got much time?"

Julian beckoned to the waiter, "Surely you can spare me a few minutes. I'd like to explain what happened when I went to the farm. I didn't touch that woman."

"That woman happens to be your mother."

Julian shook his head, "Maybe, maybe not. I never even got a chance to speak to her. She took one look at me and started clutching at her chest then that damn dog started barking and I took off."

The waiter interrupted them and Julian ordered a Heineken. Charlotte waited until they were alone again, "Why didn't you call 911? You were lucky she didn't die."

"What happened to her? Has she said anything?"

"Not yet, as far as I know. It was her heart, she was still in intensive care but they expect her to recover."

Julian nodded, "I see. I guess when she does start talking the truth will come out."

Charlotte looked somber, "It's already come out. When I didn't come home last night, my mother told Adam everything."

"So are you telling me you've left him?" Julian asked reaching for her hand.

"Please don't touch me." Charlotte responded, her voice rising slightly.

Julian smirked, "You've never minded before."

"Well I do now. I'm going back home and I'm going to tell Adam how sorry I am and hope he can forgive me."

"So it's all over between the two of us. Is that what you're telling me?"

Charlotte started to get up, "Yes it's over and I want you to leave me alone. Go back to Montreal and forget you ever met me."

Julian pulled her back down, "It's not quite that simple. What about the fact Adam is my brother? Am I supposed to forget all about that too?"

Charlotte shrugged, "I don't know. I can't answer that. I just know I need to go home now so please don't try and stop me."

Julian waved his hand in the air, "Go!" he said and remained seated as Charlotte slowly got up and started to walk away from the table. Just before the elevator doors opened, she turned back and he was still sitting there watching her. It all seemed too easy.

Within minutes she was in the underground parking area, about to open the car door, when she heard a footstep behind her. She whirled around and came face to face with Julian, "What are you doing here?" she yelled out. "Why are you following me?"

"Get in the car," he answered abruptly.

Charlotte glanced around but there was no sign of anybody. Her instinct told her to run but Julian must have read her mind because he grabbed her arm and repeated, "Get in the car."

Once in the driver's seat, she thought of turning the key, stepping on the accelerator and racing for the exit but again, Julian must have read her mind. He leaned through the window and said, "Don't even think about taking off if you care about your family. You wouldn't want any of them to get hurt, would you?"

Charlotte stared straight ahead, expressionless. She had to play along. She couldn't let him know she was terrified. She should have known he wouldn't let her go so easily.

Julian slipped into the passenger seat, "Okay, drive," he demanded.

Charlotte began to slowly ascend to street level and just before they exited onto Wellington, she asked, "Which way now?"

"Go to Spadina, then head down to the Lake Shore and take the Gardiner going east."

"Where are we going?"

"Somewhere; where we can be alone."

"My mother's expecting me. If I don't show up she's going to know something's wrong."

"Just keep on driving. We have a long way to go."

Charlotte continued to stare straight ahead, desperately thinking of how to escape, "My mother will call the police if I'm not there by morning."

Julian roared with laughter, "Ha! Do you really think the police are going to come looking for you? They'll just think you've run off. You're an adult, not a child."

"Not if Mary tells them it was you who walked in on her at the farm. Once they hear the whole story, they won't be so quick to believe I just ran off."

Julian scowled, "Who's going to believe the ranting of some old woman and there's no proof it was me? Sorry, Charlotte, but no one's going to come looking for you for a long, long time."

Charlotte kept driving in silence until they were on the Don Valley Parkway heading north towards Highway 401. "Why are you doing this?" she asked.

"I was wondering when you'd get around to that," Julian responded. "If you think it's because I'm obsessed with you, you're dead wrong. That's not what this is about?"

"What is it about? Charlotte whispered.

"Revenge; pure and simple. Payback for everything that was taken away from me"

"Revenge against who; I don't understand?"

"Adam, of course, he got everything and I got nothing."

"But he didn't even know you existed. If anyone was to blame, it was your father."

Julian tapped her on the shoulder and she glanced over to see his eyes blazing, "Shut up and just drive."

Charlotte's hands tightened on the steering wheel. She suddenly realized she might be in grave danger and she had to find a way out.

Chapter Forty-Seven

At nine o'clock, Nancy tried calling Charlotte on her cell phone but there was no response and she was becoming alarmed. Next she called Adam, who picked up after the first ring. "Nancy, what is it? Have you heard from Charlotte?" he asked.

"Yes, she called earlier to say she was going to be here at eight and she'd be staying over but she hasn't shown up. I'm worried, Adam."

"Why didn't you tell me you were expecting her?"

Nancy paused, "Because she wanted to be back with the family but didn't know if you could ever forgive her. She needed more time before she could face you."

"Have you tried calling her back?"

"Yes, but her phone's off. I don't know what to do."

"I'm coming over," Adam said. "We need to talk."

Nancy was surprised at Adam's reaction. "What about Alexa? Where is she?"

"She's staying at Hildy's for the night. It's better she's not involved. I've been trying to keep her distracted because she's been pretty upset."

"I see. Well, I guess I'll see you in a little while."

"Okay, it should only take me about fifteen minutes and, don't worry; I'll make sure Zoe gets fed before I leave."

Nancy couldn't help chuckling, "You took the thought right out of my head," she said.

While Nancy was waiting for Adam, she made a quick call to Tom and told him what was going on. When she mentioned calling the police, he confirmed what she already suspected, there was no way the police would get involved this early and maybe never, considering Charlotte had already left once on her own accord. After she put the phone down, she put on a pot of coffee and sat down at the kitchen table with Gypsy on her lap. Where on earth was Charlotte?

Adam arrived twenty minutes later and they spent the next hour talking about everything that had happened and where they suspected Charlotte might be. Adam felt sure she'd just gotten cold feet and changed her mind about coming back but Nancy was convinced something more sinister was going on. "I think Julian's got her," she said.

"What do you mean? Are you suggesting he's kidnapped her? Aren't you being a little dramatic?"

"That's exactly what I'm suggesting. I never told Charlotte this but he told me he wasn't in love with her, he just wanted to take her away from you. I think he's manipulative and he may have convinced her to go with him."

"Okay, so she goes with him, what then?"

Nancy sighed, "I don't know. I really don't. I'm just concerned he may be dangerous."

Adam got up and started pacing the room, "I think we have no choice but to wait for her to contact you again. She could be anywhere by now."

Nancy looked up at him and, at that moment, he seemed to have aged beyond his years. He had dark circles under his eyes and his shoulders were hunched forward. "Adam," she said in a gentle voice. "Do you think you can forgive her?"

He shook his head, "I don't know, Nancy. I always thought we had a good marriage. I know my work's taken me away a lot but she's never complained. She always seemed content and she's never wanted for anything. We live in a great house, have two very special kids and she enjoyed her job at the library."

"Maybe it just wasn't enough," Nancy remarked.

Adam hesitated, "If you're referring to our sex life; we've been married for over twenty years. It's not what it used to be but not so bad that I had to jump into bed with someone else."

Nancy got up and laid a hand on Adam's arm, "I understand, Adam, and I can't blame you for being angry but I truly believe Charlotte has never stopped loving you."

"She's your daughter. I know you only want what's best for her and she's lucky to have you on her side, Nancy, because, right now, I don't think I can be. In fact, I think I'll go home now and try to get some sleep. I'm going back to the hospital tomorrow to see my mother and I'll call you when I get back."

Nancy slowly nodded, "I'm sorry you feel that way," she said. "Please tell Mary she's in my prayers."

Adam started to head for the door, "I will, and you try and get a good night's sleep too. I'm sure wherever Charlotte is, she's all right."

After Adam left, Nancy sat for a while thinking about their conversation and decided to call Tom back. "Sorry to bother you so late," she said. "Adam was here and I think he really believes Charlotte has just run off but I'm convinced Julian has her. I know we can't get the police involved but do you think there's anything Gary might be able to do?"

Tom told her he'd call Gary and get back to her right away and, true to his word, the phone rang less than ten minutes later. "Gary tells me you caught him at the right time because he has a few days off. He figures the only chance he has of finding Charlotte, if she's with Julian, is to find out where he might be likely to take her, where nobody would find them."

"Where would he even begin to look?" Nancy asked anxiously

"Well, for a start, he suggested the best way would be to make contact with someone Julian works with. Maybe that individual knows if Julian owns any property, other than where he lives."

"Are you suggesting he might have taken her to Montreal?"

"Yes, and Gary will need to go there. This can't be done over the phone. He needs photos of Julian and Charlotte.

Obviously you don't have one of Julian so you'd better send Adam's photo. Can you e-mail those to me tonight?"

"Yes, of course, I have lots of photos. I'll try and find some that are close ups. Don't forget to remind Gary that Julian looks just like Adam."

Tom chuckled, "I think he's already aware of that. Listen, Nancy, he's willing to leave first thing in the morning and he'll have to drive because he'll need his car once he gets there. I have to warn you, this could turn out to be very expensive."

Nancy didn't hesitate, "I don't care what it costs; we just need to find Charlotte."

Chapter Forty-Eight

Charlotte had just turned onto the Highway 401 when Julian demanded she hand over her phone. She shook her head vehemently but Julian ignored her and reached over to grab her purse, which was lying in her lap. Instinctively, Charlotte tried to stop him but, as she lifted her hand off the steering wheel, she lost control and the car veered over into the next lane. Julian seized the wheel to regain control, "You stupid bitch. What are you doing; trying to get us killed?" he screamed.

Tears began to stream down Charlotte's face. "Please, let me go," she begged. "I told you, my mother's waiting for me."

Julian smirked, "Tough," he said and, after opening the window, tossed Charlotte's phone, as far as he could, so that it landed in a grassy area off the highway.

Charlotte knew then her only hope was to play along, so for the next two hours she kept silent. Every now and again she would glance over at Julian but he sat stone faced staring out of the window. Soon, the road signs showed they were approaching Kingston and Julian ordered her to take the next exit ramp so they could go into town. Charlotte asked meekly, "Are we staying here?"

"Maybe, for the night," Julian answered. "I haven't decided yet but we need to get some food."

"I need to go to the bathroom," Charlotte whispered.

"Well, that's a bit of a problem because I don't want to let you out of my sight." He hesitated for a moment then told her to pull over onto the shoulder and, as soon as they came to a stop, he told her to get out. Once she was out of the car, he jumped out from the passenger side and motioned to some bushes set back a few feet from the highway. "Be my guest," he said.

Charlotte was desperate to relieve herself and slowly walked away, thankful it was already dark but, as she distanced herself from Julian, she glanced about wondering if there was any way she could escape. As she drew closer to the bushes, she realized that, behind them, there was a solid brick wall and nowhere for her to go. She looked back over her shoulder and could see Julian, half hidden behind the rear end of the car, obviously relieving himself too.

When Charlotte returned, Julian walked around to the driver's side and ordered her to get into the passenger's seat, "I'm driving from now on," he said.

"Aren't we stopping in Kingston?" Charlotte asked.

"No, I've changed my mind. There's a truck stop a few kilometers on where we'll get something to eat but I'm warning you now, don't even consider trying to get away. Think about your family."

When they reached the truck stop, he escorted Charlotte inside and ordered two cheeseburgers and two large coffees. They sat in silence at one of the tables and Charlotte surveyed the room while her mind was racing. There was only one other woman there but she didn't look out of place. She was dressed in overalls and fit right in with the dozens of truckers, mostly big burly men who could have overpowered Julian in a heartbeat but Charlotte knew she couldn't risk raising the alarm. What would he do to her family? Maybe he would be arrested for kidnapping but one day he'd get out of prison and what then? She looked over at him wondering what was going through his head, but he seemed perfectly relaxed as though he knew she wouldn't dare to expose him.

By this time Charlotte was emotionally drained and all she wanted to do was lie down and go to sleep but Julian had other

ideas and, less than fifteen minutes later, they were back on
the highway. They kept heading east and eventually Charlotte
asked again, "Where are we going?"

"Never mind," Julian responded. "Just sit back and relax,
we should be there in about three hours."

Charlotte sighed and sank down in her seat. At first she
assumed he was taking her to his place in Montreal but, then
again, it would be risky. There would be too many people
around. He had to be taking her somewhere else, but where?
After a while, she could no longer keep her eyes open and fell
into a deep sleep.

Charlotte realized she must have dozed off for some
time because, when she woke up, she noticed the road signs
indicated they were on Highway 34. As she stretched her legs,
Julian looked over at her and said, "You were really out of it for
a while."

"Where are we?" she asked, ignoring his remark. "Aren't
we going to Montreal?"

"No, we're not going to Montreal," he replied. "You'll soon find
out where we're going. We should be there in less than an hour."

About twenty minutes later, Charlotte began seeing signs
in French and she knew they had crossed the border into
Quebec and were heading north. She glanced down at her
watch and saw it was now two o'clock in the morning. They
had left Toronto almost seven hours ago. When was this
nightmare going to end? Soon after this thought crossed her
mind, they turned onto a road with a sign pointing to a place
called Harrington. It didn't sound French and she has no idea
where they were. "Are we still in Quebec?" she asked.

Julian nodded, "Yes, we're about a hundred and twenty
kilometers northwest of Montreal."

"Have you been here before?"

Julian chuckled, "Getting really curious aren't you?" he
teased.

Charlotte took a deep breath and remained silent. It
probably wouldn't be long before she found out exactly where
he was taking her.

It was eerily dark as Julian guided the car down a deserted road bordered by trees on either side. Charlotte peered through the front window fearful a deer or some other animal might leap into their path. It had happened before when she was returning home from a week's vacation in Algonquin Park, with Adam and the children, and it was only Adam's skillful driving that saved them from colliding with a deer that had raced across road in front of them. Now, she was gripping the sides of her seat waiting for the inevitable crash, but it never came. Instead, Julian began to slow down and then turned into a clearing and stopped. "We're here," he said.

Charlotte didn't wait for him to tell her to get out of the car, she just opened the door, stepped out onto a grassy area, and looked up at a structure situated directly in front of her, on a slight elevation. It was a simple wooden cottage, looking more like a large hut, but with an external staircase leading up to a second floor with a wooden railing creating a balcony, which appeared to circle the building. She looked at Julian, "What place is this?" she asked.

Julian had exited the car and was standing just behind her, "It belongs to my Aunt Beth. She usually comes here for a few weeks each summer. When I was a kid, my mother used to bring me here every year to stay with her for a week or two." His voice suddenly dropped to almost a whisper. "We used to come here with Emma too."

Charlotte couldn't help feeling sad. There was no doubt he had loved his daughter very much. That was one thing they had in common and maybe it would help her to convince him to let her go. "Let's go in," he said.

Charlotte looked back at the car. "Can I get my suitcase; I need to change my clothes?"

"Wait here," Julian ordered as he went to retrieve her suitcase and tote bag from the back seat.

In those few moments, Charlotte turned full circle but it was so dark, all she could see were tall trees and shadows and she thought she heard the haunting sound of a loon. Whatever it was, it made her begin to tremble and she was grateful when Julian returned and motioned to her to follow him up the stairs. Once inside, he dropped her belongings near the entryway, turned on the lights and proceeded to give her a guided tour of the cottage. Charlotte soon realized the exterior was deceiving. The kitchen was surprisingly modern with an electric stove and refrigerator and a washer/dryer combination. One half of the kitchen was taken up with a wooden table, oval in shape, and four ladder back chairs and there was a set of sliding doors which led out to the balcony. When Charlotte stepped outside, she was surprised to see a patio table with four more chairs and directly in front of her she could tell the trees gave way to a large clearing. "Is that a lake out there?" she asked.

Julian took a breath of the fresh air that surrounded them, "Yes, it's called Green Lake. There's a dock and a small boat. You can see it all in the morning."

"It's morning now," Charlotte remarked.

"Yes, well, I'll show you the downstairs and then I'll show you the bedroom."

Charlotte followed him down a flight of stairs and was surprised to find the lower half of the cottage consisted of a large living area with one small window but no obvious exit to the outside, and a small powder room. It looked comfortable enough, with a well upholstered, chintz covered sofa, a bookcase, housing an eclectic selection of novels, both classic and modern and a small flat screen television. "The reception isn't too good out here," Julian said, "but most of the stations are in French anyway." He then led her back upstairs where, to her surprise, there were two bedrooms and a bathroom complete with a shower and tub. "You'll be sleeping in this room," he said as he led her into the second bedroom which had a double bed, covered with a light green duvet, a small dresser with a mirror, an armoire and a window, but no exit to the balcony.

"Where will you be sleeping?" Charlotte asked, holding her breath.

"In the other room," Julian replied abruptly, "I'll get your things and bring them in. You can use the bathroom and then get some sleep."

Charlotte stared straight into his eyes, "What makes you think I won't run?"

Julian stared straight back, "Because, I'm locking the door from the inside and I don't think you're the type to attempt to climb over the balcony. In any case, where will you go in the dark? The forest can be pretty creepy at night. There are a lot of strange creatures out there."

"And when daylight comes?" Charlotte said lifting her chin defiantly.

"We'll cross that bridge when we come to it," Julian shot back and walked away.

Charlotte waited until he brought her belongings and then rifled through her suitcase for a pair of cotton pajamas before locking herself in the bathroom. She would have loved to soak in the tub but she was too tired. All she wanted now was to lie down on the bed and sleep.

Ten minutes later, having scrubbed the make-up from her face and showered long enough to feel refreshed after such a long trip, she finally slipped under the duvet and closed her eyes. It took a while before she fell asleep because she kept wondering what her family was doing. Were they already looking for her? Just before her brain finally shut down, she realized she didn't remember seeing a telephone anywhere in the cottage. Maybe there wasn't one.

Chapter Forty-Nine

Nancy spent most of the night cuddled up with Luna and Gypsy next to her. She found some comfort having her pets close by but it didn't help her to sleep. She was awake for hours worrying about where Charlotte was. She kept going over the conversation she had with Julian when he was sitting in her living room. There were times when she could sense his vulnerability and even felt sorry for him but she couldn't be certain he wouldn't harm Charlotte. In the morning she was up at dawn and sitting at the kitchen table, her hand wrapped around a cup of coffee. She wasn't sure how she was going to get through the day.

At noon, after hours of puttering around the house and trying to keep busy, Adam telephoned to tell her he had been to see his mother and she was doing a lot better and had been moved out of ICU. When Nancy asked him if she'd spoken about what happened to cause the attack, he claimed that when he asked her about it, she'd shaken her head and refused to answer. Not wanting to upset her, he quickly changed the subject. Not even Ray had been able to get a word out of her about what had occurred. Nancy wasn't sure whether to tell him she'd hired Gary to find Charlotte but when she did, he tried to assure her he still thought she was wrong about Julian taking her against her will but understood why, as a mother, she felt the need to do something.

Right after speaking to Adam, Tom called to say Gary had set out for Montreal at five o'clock. His plan was to try and gain entry to the Gazette's offices and locate the area where Julian worked. He then intended to see if he could make contact with one of Julian's colleagues and hopefully get more information about him.

"How exactly is he going to do that without anyone getting suspicious?" Nancy asked.

Tom chuckled, "He's got his methods. Don't worry. I'm sure he'll find out something helpful. He said he'd be calling you directly when he has some news."

Nancy suddenly had a thought, "What if Julian's actually there working?"

"I'm sure Gary's already considered that possibility."

"But that would mean Charlotte isn't with him," Nancy remarked hopefully.

"Are you having second thoughts?" Tom asked.

Nancy paused, "Not really, but if he's there what would he have done with Charlotte?"

"We'll worry about that later. Let's not speculate any more. Let's just wait until Gary gets in touch."

"I guess you're right," Nancy responded. "I'll let you know after I hear from him. I'd better get off the line."

By two o'clock, Nancy was ready to climb the walls. She had made herself a sandwich but it was sitting half eaten on a plate. She then poured herself a glass of wine, hoping it would calm her nerves, but it didn't seem to be working. Fifteen minutes later, her telephone rang and she pounced on it. It was Gary. "I have some news, Mrs. Fleming."

"What is it? Have you found Charlotte?" Nancy blurted out knowing full well it would be too much to hope for.

"Sorry, ma'am, I haven't tracked her down yet. I've only been here a couple of hours but I did get some information."

"Oh, I didn't mean to pressure you, I know you're doing your best. What did you find out?"

"Well, apparently a relative of Julian's, an aunt I think, owns some property north of here. Maybe that's where they are."

"How did you find that out? I'd be curious to know."

"I got lucky. I spotted this guy with a camera exiting one of the Gazette's news vans. I followed him to a coffee shop, less than a block away, and started chatting with him. I asked him where he worked, although I already knew. I told him I'd met Julian when he was on an assignment in Toronto and was wondering if he was around. The guy's name was Claude and he said he hadn't seen Julian for about a week and assumed he was on vacation. I commented what a lucky dog he must be, probably lazing around on a beach somewhere with some babe. That's when he told me he thought he may have gone up to the cottage. I acted surprised and said I didn't know he owned a cottage and he mentioned he thought it belonged to an aunt or some family member."

"Did you manage to find out where the cottage was?"

"No, I'm afraid not. I suggested it would be a surprise if I took a run up there and dropped in on him but Claude couldn't remember the location. He knew it was on a lake and the place had an English sounding name and he remembered Julian telling him it was only a hundred and fifty kilometers northwest of the city, but that's all."

"So, what can we do now?"

"Have you ever heard him mention an aunt?"

Nancy paused for a moment, "Yes, he has an Aunt Beth but I don't think you'll be able to find her."

"Why's that?"

"Because she's his mother's sister, so she wouldn't have the same last name."

"Mmm . . . . that's too bad. Well, ma'am I'm going to see if I can do a bit more digging here but if I can't get any more information I may need to take a little road trip. First I'm going to do some research to find out if there are any spots with English names northwest of the city. I have the photos with me and the make and model of Charlotte's car. Maybe somebody's seen them."

"Maybe they're driving Julian's car."

"I doubt that, it's too conspicuous but it's a possibility."

"Isn't this all a bit of a long shot, Gary? What if they're still in Toronto or somewhere else in Ontario?"

"It's your call ma'am. Do you want me to keep on looking or would you like me to quit?"

Again, Nancy didn't hesitate, "Please, keep on looking," she replied.

It was six o'clock before Nancy heard from Gary again. He had spent an hour in an internet café surfing the internet and gathering as much information as he could about vacation areas northwest of Montreal. He had decided to drive to Piedmont, the first name on his list but on returning to his car, it wouldn't start and had to be towed to a garage. It turned out to be a problem with the ignition. They promised to have it ready for him by five but now they were unable to get it back to him until the morning. "Sorry, ma'am," he said, "but I'm going to have to check into a hotel for the night. I've found a cheap place to stay in old Montreal and I hope to be back on the road by nine."

Nancy was upset but realized there was nothing she could do. Charlotte would have to spend another night with Julian. "Please call me as soon as you can tomorrow." she said.

An hour later, Adam called to tell her he had to go out of town in the morning for a couple of days and wondered if she could possibly come over to stay with Alexa. He added that Alexa was adamant she could look after herself but he wasn't comfortable leaving her alone under the circumstances. Nancy said she'd be glad to help and would make sure she was there by the time Alexa got home from school. While on the phone, she gave Adam an update on what was happening with Gary but he seemed distracted as though he didn't really want to hear it. Maybe he thought it was all a waste of time and money.

After making sure her neighbour was able to cat sit, Nancy sat down in front of the television and tried to concentrate on a movie playing on HBO but her mind kept wandering. Eventually she gave up, went to bed, and picked up the latest book she was reading: an inspiring true story of a woman who survived a life threatening disease, but it couldn't hold her attention either. Exhausted, she turned out the light and closed her eyes but sleep wouldn't come. This was going to be a long night.

Chapter Fifty

Early that same morning, several hundred kilometers away, Charlotte woke up with a start. For a moment, she had no idea where she was and then it all came flooding back. She glanced over at the clock on the bedside table and saw it was just after eight o'clock. She had not expected to wake up so late and wondered where Julian was. Cautiously she crawled out of bed, slipped on a robe, and poked her head out of the door. The hallway was clear so she quickly gathered up the toiletries she needed and raced next door to the bathroom, locking the door behind her. She brushed her teeth and piled her hair on top of her head while she ran a bath and then stepped into the tub. She would love to have stayed there for a long time, relaxing in the warm water, but she was too anxious and expecting Julian to knock on the door at any moment. Just, five minutes later, she was hastily drying herself off and slipping back into her robe. She applied some make up and brushed her hair vigorously before stepping out into the hall and tip toeing back to her room. While she was rummaging through her suitcase for a pair of jeans and lightweight sweater, she suddenly smelled the aroma of coffee and knew Julian had to be in the kitchen. She couldn't imagine what the day would bring.

A minute later she heard a noise behind her and turned to see Julian peeking around the door frame. His hair was tousled, he had stubble on his chin and he looked a lot younger than his forty-five years. "Good morning," he said, "I heard the water running in the bathroom. Did you find everything you needed?"

Charlotte merely nodded and then turned back to continue looking through her suitcase. "I'd like to get dressed now," she said.

"Of course, I'll leave you to it but why don't you hang up your clothes in the armoire?"

Charlotte glanced over her shoulder, "I don't expect to be staying that long."

Julian didn't react to her remark. "I've got fresh coffee and there were some frozen waffles in the freezer. I can pop them in the toaster when you're ready," he said as he started to walk away.

As soon as Charlotte heard his footsteps receding, she ran over and closed the door. Quickly, she slipped on the jeans, a long-sleeved white tee shirt and a pair of sneakers and then sat down on the edge of the bed. What was Julian playing at? How long did he expect to keep her there? When she finally got up and made her way to the kitchen the thoughts were still tumbling through her head.

Julian was standing at the kitchen counter, barefoot, in a pair of light coloured chinos and a black sweatshirt. He was ripping open a package of waffles and didn't turn around but had obviously heard her come in. "Have a seat," he said. "I'll just toast these up. There's some syrup on the table. Coffee will be ready in a moment."

Charlotte sat down and stared at Julian's back. "What are you planning to do all day?" she asked.

Julian took two mugs out of a cupboard and put them on the counter, "We don't have any milk," he said. "After breakfast we'll have to go into the village and get some supplies. I hope you don't mind your coffee black for now."

"And after that, what do you propose to do for the rest of the day?" Charlotte persisted.

Julian began pouring the coffee into the mugs, "Maybe we'll go for a boat ride."

"How lovely," Charlotte responded sarcastically.

Julian placed one of the mugs in front of Charlotte and smiled, "I think it will be," he said. "It's a beautiful morning and I hear it's warming up later."

Charlotte scowled at him, "I asked you before and I'm asking you again. How long do you think you can keep me here?"

"As long as I want to," Julian replied still smiling.

A half hour later, they were driving along a tree lined roadway headed for the town. Charlotte tried her best to figure out which way they were going and how long it took to get there. She was already planning her escape. If she could get out of the cottage, she could make her way into town and get help but then she remembered Julian's warning. What would he do to her family if she managed to get away?

Julian parked the car outside a large wooden structure. It looked like the typical country store that sold almost everything one could think of. He ordered Charlotte out of the car and steered her by the elbow through the open door, at the same time whispering in her ear, "Remember to keep your mouth shut."

There were three other people in the store, apart from the woman behind the counter, and they all greeted Julian in French, "Bon jour!" to which he responded in kind while Charlotte just lowered her head. Then Julian walked over to the counter and said in English, "Good morning, Alice, good to see you again."

The woman was just under five feet tall and very slight with shoulder length grey hair and a pair of wire rimmed spectacles perched on the tip of her nose. "Good morning, Julian," she replied with a pronounced English accent. "How long are you here for this time?"

"I'm not sure yet," he answered. "This is my friend Charlotte. We haven't decided how long we're staying."

Alice surveyed Charlotte over the top of her glasses, "It's nice to meet you."

Charlotte mumbled, "Thank you, nice to meet you too," then turned to look around the store.

Alice looked at Julian and raised her eyebrows. "How's your aunt? Isn't she with you?"

"She's fine and no, she's not here. Charlotte and I just wanted some time to ourselves."

"I see, so I guess you'll need some supplies?"

"Yes, we'll just browse around and get a few things. Like I said, we're not sure how long we'll be staying so we'll just get enough for a couple of days for now."

Charlotte's heart skipped a beat when she heard what he'd said. Maybe this would soon all be over and she'd be back with her family.

They returned to the cottage with three bags full of groceries and four bottles of wine. Julian had decided they would have a barbecue that night but instead of steak, they would have to make do with hamburger. Food was the last thing on Charlotte's mind but she felt the only way she could survive this ordeal would be to play along until Julian decided to let her go.

After putting the groceries away, Julian told her he was going down to the dock to make sure the boat was okay and suggested she sit out on the balcony and read the Gazette which he'd picked up at the store. When he left the cottage, Charlotte was well aware he'd locked the door behind him and as he walked down towards the lake, he glanced up at her and waved, "See you soon," he called out.

Charlotte sighed. He was acting as though they were on vacation. Two perfectly normal people enjoying the countryside but there was nothing normal about it. Once he was out of sight, she leaned over the balcony to see how far the drop was to the ground below and, although she was scared of heights, she knew she could make it but would she be able to find her way to the village after that? Maybe it would be better to take the chance. Perhaps Julian was bluffing and had no intention of hurting her family.

Just to keep busy, even for a brief time, Charlotte offered to prepare lunch for the two of them. She slathered Kaiser rolls with butter and mayonnaise and piled on layers of ham, cheddar and cucumber then poured two glasses of Chardonnay. Julian looked up in surprise when she walked out onto the balcony with the tray and laid it on the table. "Well, this is very nice," he said smiling. "I think you're beginning to like it here."

Charlotte sat down and picked up her wine, "Do I have any choice?" she responded without looking at him.

Julian chuckled, "Think of it as a mini vacation. You'll be back home soon enough."

Charlotte put her glass down and stared at him intently, "What is the point of all this? Really, Julian, please answer me?"

Julian frowned, "How many times do I have to tell you? Are you stupid? I've told you before; I want Adam to know what it's like to be deprived. Is that so hard to understand? Frankly, Charlotte, I'm sick of your whining. Why don't you just shut the hell up and eat?"

Charlotte recoiled at his change in tone and spent the next half hour picking at her food and sipping on her wine in silence while Julian read the paper.

After lunch, he told her to grab a jacket because they were going out on the lake and they might be gone for some time. Charlotte had no idea what this meant but she was grateful to get out of the cottage just to escape the boredom she was beginning to experience. She followed Julian down a pathway leading to a small shed and a dock where a rather derelict looking rowboat was tied up. He opened up the shed and pulled out two fishing rods and a covered container, helped her climb into the boat, then untied the rope and pushed away from the dock. "Is this thing safe?" Charlotte asked, noticing what looked like cracks in the wood under her feet.

Julian began to row out onto the lake, "It's perfectly safe. You have nothing to worry about. You're not going to drown."

"I assume that you expect me to fish," Charlotte remarked nodding at the rods.

"That's the plan," Julian replied. "There's a lot of trout in this lake. Who knows, we may end up having fish instead of hamburger tonight."

Chapter Fifty-One

After spending almost three hours on the lake, Charlotte was beginning to feel exhausted and her rear end was numb from sitting on the hard wooden bench. She had always considered fishing a rather boring pastime and now she was convinced of it. Julian, on the other hand, seemed perfectly content waiting patiently for some innocent fish to take the bait and he had been rewarded several times while Charlotte had only managed to catch one pint size trout. Finally, Julian announced it was time to go back and they arrived at the dock at just after five o'clock. "I'll show you how to prepare the fish for dinner," he said as they were walking back up to the cottage.

Charlotte had no desire to learn how to debone and descale and, worst of all, how to chop off the heads but she watched quietly while Julian expertly went through the whole process and persuaded her to try it. It wasn't quite as difficult as she had imagined and she was quite proud of herself when Julian laid her very own fish on the barbecue. She had already put together a salad and warmed up some croissants when Julian brought the trout inside on a large platter. "I think we should eat inside," he said, "it's getting a bit cool out."

"What do you think?" he asked, after Charlotte had taken her first bite.

Charlotte nodded, "It's very good. I don't think I've ever eaten fish as fresh as this before."

Julian was quiet for a moment and then he put down his fork and gazed towards the open sliding doors. "Emma used to love going out on the lake," he said wistfully. "She had this little rod and one day she caught this rather large bass and nearly got pulled into the water. I was scared to death but she thought it was great fun."

"Why didn't you tell me about your daughter before?"

Julian sighed, "Because then I'd have to have told you about how she died. I wasn't ready to do that before but being here brings back some precious memories."

Once again, Charlotte saw Julian's vulnerable side, "You must miss her terribly."

Julian sighed, "That's an understatement." Then he got up abruptly and walked out onto the balcony. Charlotte didn't know whether to follow him or not.

After a few minutes, she got up, started to clear the dishes from the table and placed them in the sink. Suddenly Julian appeared beside her and picked up the tea towel, "You wash and I'll dry," he said.

"That's not necessary," Charlotte responded, "I can just leave them in the dish rack."

Julian shook his head, "My mother always insisted on drying them right away and then putting them back where they belonged."

"I see." Charlotte said, all the while thinking that anyone coming upon this scene would think they were a perfectly normal couple occupied in a perfectly normal activity. It was all very bizarre.

After Julian put away the last dish, he poured them both another glass of wine and suggested they sit out on the balcony in spite of the cool night. Charlotte excused herself while she went to her room and changed into a heavier sweater. While she was alone, she realized Julian appeared to be in a mellow mood and had mentioned his family on two occasions. She decided to take advantage of the situation and hoped to get him to open up about the effect of Emma's death on his life and the close relationship with his mother. Maybe then he would understand how desperately she needed to return to her own family.

Encouraging Julian to tell her about his daughter was easier than Charlotte had anticipated and she was surprised when he left her for a moment and came back with an album filled with photographs of Emma from the time she was an infant. Charlotte could see why Julian had been so proud of her. She was an adorable looking child and, at the age of four, had masses of dark curly hair and huge eyes, the same colour as her father's. Then, as he continued to turn the pages, it was evident Emma was no longer a happy, healthy little girl and finally Julian closed the album and said, "I think that's enough."

Charlotte laid her hand on his arm, "She was a beautiful child, Julian. I am so sorry."

Julian got up abruptly and took the album back inside. "I'll be right back," he said.

Charlotte could no longer talk about her own family. She realized it might upset him even more and she had no idea what his reaction would be. She had to think of some other way to get out of this situation.

Later that evening, they sat in the downstairs area watching an English language programme although Charlotte's mind was elsewhere. She was concentrating on the small window situated high up at one end of the room and wondering if she could squeeze her way through it. She had no idea if it was locked and she had no opportunity to find out while Julian was awake. She had considered climbing over the balcony but it was over ten feet to the ground and she was worried she might get injured if she attempted it. At one point she was so lost in thought Julian turned to her and said, "Are you watching this?"

Charlotte immediately focused on the television screen. "I was," she said, "but I'm not finding it too interesting. I think I'll go to bed."

Julian glanced at his watch, "It's only nine o'clock."

"I think the fresh air got to me," Charlotte responded and stood up.

Julian stood up too, "I'll need to lock up," he said and followed her up the stairs then watched her go into her room. She heard the sound of the key turning in the lock and Julian's footsteps as he went back downstairs. How long would it be before he finally went to bed and how long before he actually fell asleep?

After getting ready for bed, Charlotte decided to read for a while in an attempt to stay awake but soon found her eyes were no longer able to focus and she turned out the light hoping she would wake up sometime during the night.

It was dark when she eventually woke up and peered at the clock. It was almost three in the morning and the ideal time to make a move. Quietly slipping out of bed, she changed into jeans, a thick sweater, heavy socks and sneakers and, without bothering to wash her face or comb her hair; grabbed her purse and tiptoed out into the hall. Holding her breath, as she crept past Julian's room, she went down the stairs but, when she reached the bottom step, she thought she saw a movement beside her and gasped, only to realize it was her own shadow. She stood still for several seconds before making her way across to the window and staring up at it. There was an old leather ottoman near the couch and she dragged it over beneath the window hoping she'd be able to reach up and try the latch but she never got that far. Suddenly she felt a hand on her shoulder and Julian's voice, "Where do you think you're going, Charlotte?"

Her hand flew to her throat as she turned to face him and cowered back against the wall, "Please, let me go," she begged.

She watched as he took a step backward and then in the half-light saw him grin, "You look like a scared little rabbit. I like that."

"What are you going to do?" she asked beginning to tremble.

Julian thrust out his hand and grabbed her wrist, "I'm going to give you what you deserve," he answered and proceeded to drag her across the room to the bottom of the stairs.

Charlotte began to scream but Julian just laughed and slapped her with the back of his hand, "You stupid cow," he said. "Do you really think anyone can hear you way out here?"

Charlotte tried desperately to pull away but he was too strong for her and, grabbing her by the hair, forced her up the stairs and into her room where he threw her onto the bed. "Take your clothes off," he demanded.

"Go to hell," she yelled and spat in his face.

At that, he became enraged and forcing himself on top of her, pinned both of her arms above her head with one hand while pulling at her jeans with the other. She began to scream again, at the same time trying to twist from side to side to push him off but it was useless. There was no doubt in her mind; he was going to rape her, but it didn't happen. At the last moment, just as he was about to enter her, he suddenly stopped and rolled away. Charlotte lay sobbing on top of the bed while Julian pulled up his pants then picked her jeans off of the floor and tossed them to her. "Put these on," he said.

Charlotte sat up and pulled the comforter over to cover herself, "You almost raped me, you bastard. I thought you had some decency in you but I was wrong. I must have been crazy to ever have gotten involved with you. You're not even half the man Adam is."

Julian took a step forward, "I think you'd better stop before I make you," he said.

"I'll say it again, go to hell!" Charlotte screamed even though she knew she was provoking him but he merely walked out of the room leaving her lying there.

She was wondering what his next move would be and she didn't have to wait long because, a moment later, he was back carrying a roll of twine. "What are you going to do with that," she asked attempting to jump off of the bed.

"This will teach you not to try and get away," Julian replied grabbing her arm before she could get a foot on the floor.

Charlotte struggled with as much strength as she could but once he had secured one of her wrists to the bedpost it was impossible to fight him anymore. Minutes later she was lying spread eagle on the bed with both wrists tied and feeling totally helpless. "This is how you're going to have to sleep at night," Julian told her. "Tomorrow I'll let you loose because I'll be able to keep an eye on you but as long as you're here this is how your nights are going to be."

Charlotte just stared at him, refusing to react as he left the room. Now she had to find another way out.

Chapter Fifty-Two

By the next morning, not only was Charlotte exhausted from lack of sleep but, in Montreal, Gary had been up most of the night too. He was frustrated about his car breaking down and it didn't help that some guests in the next room were obviously having a party and, at four in the morning, a drunken brawl had broken out in the hallway right outside his door. At seven o'clock he had already showered and shaved ready to head out to look for a spot open for breakfast. After walking for a while, he found himself on Rue Notre Dame and noticed a small café which had already opened its doors. He sat down at one of the small tables and ordered scrambled eggs with smoked meat, a croissant and dark roast coffee then took out his notebook so that he could review the route he was going to take to his first stop, Piedmont. On doing a little more research the night before, he realized Piedmont was not particularly English sounding and the language spoken there was mainly French. In addition, the population numbered close to three thousand so he didn't expect to have much success but it was located on a river and if he concentrated on the area with vacation cottages, maybe somebody would recognize Julian. He figured it would only take an hour to get there but he still had to wait for his car to be ready so, after exiting the café, he spent the next hour walking the narrow streets of Old Montreal.

Meanwhile back in Toronto, at the Hamilton house, Nancy had just seen Alexa off to school and was wondering what to do for the rest of the day. She had done her best not to alarm Alexa by suggesting her mother might be in harm's way but the alternative meant she had just run off and abandoned the family, and Adam had not been helpful. The evening before, Alexa had left right after supper to go to Hildy's and hadn't arrived home by eleven. Being a school night and concerned about her walking back in the dark, Nancy eventually telephoned and spoke to Hildy's father who assured her he would bring Alexa back himself. When she arrived, she seemed detached, hardly saying a word except to say goodnight and immediately took herself up to bed. Even in the morning, after Nancy made her a special breakfast of French toast, she was tight lipped. Not wanting to pressure her, Nancy simply put her arms around her as she was leaving and said, "Don't worry, darling, Mom will be back soon."

Alexa pulled away and Nancy could see tears in her eyes as she turned to walk away and whispered, "Maybe, maybe not, Nana."

At the same time Alexa was leaving for school, Charlotte was still lying in bed at the cottage staring at the marks on her wrists being left by the twine. She had managed to doze off once or twice but by seven o'clock she was desperate to relieve herself and when she smelled the aroma of coffee and knew Julian was up, she called out to him. A minute later, he poked his head around the door and smiled, "Good morning, I see you're awake."

"Please, let me up," she begged, "I need to use the bathroom."

He didn't hesitate in coming forward and untying her, "Of course, you're free to move around now."

Charlotte ignored him and rushed to the bathroom, slamming the door behind her, but a few moments later there was a knock on the door and she heard Julian's voice, "Why don't you have a bath and get dressed. After breakfast we're going to take a little trip."

Charlotte's hopes began to rise as she sank down into the tub. Maybe he was taking her home. The more she thought about it, the more excited she became and, unable to relax, she quickly went through the motions of bathing and then toweled herself off, threw on her robe, and ran to her room to dress. As she slipped into a pair of cargo pants and a yellow sweat shirt, she wondered if she should start packing up her belongings but then she could be entirely mistaken about Julian letting her go and she didn't want to enrage him by assuming too much. When she went into the kitchen he was scrambling some eggs and had just put some bread in the toaster. He glanced at her as she came through the door, "We'll have to pick up more milk on the way back," he said. "We're running out."

Charlotte's heart sank as she sat down. She wasn't going home after all. "Where are we going?" she asked.

Julian slid some eggs onto a plate and brought them to the table, "To a place that's very important to me," he said.

"Is that all you're going to tell me?"

"That's all you need to know. We'll be gone for most of the day so maybe you can help me make some sandwiches to take with us once you've finished breakfast."

Charlotte picked up her fork and, without looking up, responded, "How cozy. I guess this is your idea of a family picnic."

Julian immediately grabbed her arm and the fork dropped from her fingers onto the floor with a clatter, "There's no need to be sarcastic."

Charlotte pulled back her arm and pushed the plate away, "I'm not hungry."

Julian walked back to the counter and poured two mugs full of coffee, "Suit yourself but we have a long way to go before lunch."

In that moment Charlotte knew she had to figure out how to escape. Even if it meant Julian would come after her family she had to take the chance the police would protect them and he would be arrested and put away for a long time. Once they were on the road and closer to civilization she would have to alert someone about the situation she was in, but how without arousing Julian's suspicion and putting her in immediate danger?

An idea began to take place while she stood beside him at the kitchen counter silently making sandwiches and packing them up for the journey. When he suggested she get her jacket in case it turned a lot cooler, she went to her room to collect it and then picked up her purse and locked herself in the bathroom. She fished in her purse for a pen then hunted for something to write on. She had two or three business cards in her wallet but that was all and she actually smiled as she imagined calmly handing a card to a stranger with the word 'Help' on the back. Suddenly she realized she didn't have to look much further and tore off a few sheets of toilet tissue. Now all she had to do was write something to get somebody's attention so she jotted down her license plate number and three words, 'Call the police.' By now, she hoped her family had reported her missing and were already looking for her car. This way, they would have some idea where she was. She had just tucked the tissue into the pocket of her jacket when there was a knock on the door. "Come on, Charlotte, it's time to get going."

She didn't answer but, a moment later, when she came out into the hall; Julian was standing a foot away waiting for her. "What's the hurry?" she asked with her chin in the air.

"I told you," he replied grabbing her by the arm, "we have a long drive ahead of us."

They had only been on the road a short time when Charlotte realized they were heading towards Montreal and her hopes began to rise. Maybe they would be going west and closer to home but, just north of the city, Julian took a road going eastward and Charlotte knew she was being taken further and further away. "Where are we going?" she asked again.

Julian glanced over at her and frowned, "Why don't you just relax. You'll find out when we get there."

Charlotte patted her pocket to make sure the tissue was still there and wondered when she would get the opportunity to leave it where someone might pick it up. They weren't stopping anywhere for lunch because they had brought food with them. Were they really going on a picnic somewhere? If so, why so far away from the cottage? None of it made any sense.

An hour later, not long after they passed some road signs leading to a place called Louisville, Charlotte noticed another sign indicating there was a gas station ahead. She wasn't particularly adept in understanding French but it was obvious there was also a rest area and refreshments available. Maybe this was her chance. "I'd like to stop," she said, "I need to go to the bathroom."

Julian shook his head, "No, we're not stopping here. You'll have to wait for a while and we'll find a place somewhere else along the road."

"What about gas, don't we need gas?"

"Already taken care of; my aunt always kept a couple of cans at the cottage. I put them in the trunk."

Charlotte sighed, "But why won't you let me out? We're in the middle of nowhere. What do you think I'm going to do?"

"Don't argue. I told you I'd find a place and I will."

Charlotte sat with her lips pressed together trying to figure out what her next move would be. If he expected her to go in some bushes again, what about her plan to leave her message for someone to see?

A few minutes later, Julian turned on the radio and was obviously listening to what sounded like a newscast but Charlotte couldn't understand a word. Then, when the station started playing classical music, he turned the radio off and pulled over to the side of the road in an area close to some trees and heavy undergrowth. "Here you are," he announced abruptly. "Make it quick."

Charlotte jumped out of the car, disappeared behind some bushes and crouched down. Maybe another car would come by and she could run out and flag it down but perhaps Julian would try and run her over or cut off the other driver. It was much too risky. Reluctantly she returned to the car and climbed into the passenger seat. The tissue was still in her pocket.

Chapter Fifty-Three

It was close to noon and, at the Hamilton house, Nancy had just finished two loads of laundry. She wasn't exactly fond of household chores but it gave her something to do and helped take her mind off of Charlotte for a brief time. She was considering making herself a sandwich then decided to call Tom first to see if he'd heard from Gary, but her call went straight to voice mail. She then thought she'd run over to her own house instead, have lunch, and at the same time check on Gypsy and Luna and see if Gary had tried to contact her there. One way or another she had to find out what was going on.

When she arrived home, both cats greeted her at the door and after petting each one briefly she went straight to the kitchen to see if there were any messages. She could see the light flashing on the phone as soon as she walked through the door and immediately ran over and picked up the receiver hoping the message was from Gary but praying it was from Charlotte. There had been two calls while she had been at Charlotte's house, one from Tom, from the evening before and the other from Gary, just an hour earlier. He had already passed through Piedmont after spending most of the morning driving back and forth through the cottage area showing the photographs to storekeepers and vacationers but with no success. He intended to get a bite to eat and then drive to Morin Heights, about twelve kilometers further west and would report back again later. Nancy now had to figure out how she was going to keep herself occupied all afternoon.

It was just after one o'clock when Charlotte sensed they were nearing their destination. She knew from the road signs, they were about fifty kilometers north of Quebec City and had just left the highway, heading towards a place called Saint Raymond. "Are we almost there?" she asked.

Julian merely nodded and kept staring straight ahead. He looked really solemn and Charlotte couldn't help feeling that, wherever they were going, it was not going to be a pleasant experience. Soon they were entering the village of Saint Raymond itself and, as Julian began to slow down, Charlotte saw a number of people strolling along the sidewalk. She thought about opening the car door and jumping out. Then again, maybe he would chase after her and a lot of innocent people could get hurt. She couldn't risk it.

Eventually they pulled up outside a church and parked near the front gate. Julian ordered her to get out and, as she did so, she looked around and realized they were alone. Her mind suddenly flew to the story of Julian's birth and his abandonment on the church steps but that was some other town and she struggled to remember the name. She didn't have long to wait to find out the real reason for the journey. After walking through the gate, instead of going into the church, Julian grasped her elbow, guiding her behind the building and into an area which was obviously a cemetery. Without a word, he took her along a pathway and then, after crossing a few feet of grassy area, stopped in front of a tomb stone and let go of her arm. "We're here," he whispered.

Charlotte noticed the angel carved into the rose coloured granite and read the inscription. It simply read, *'Emma Renee Richards—taken by the angels far too soon. She was only 8 years old.'*

Charlotte didn't know what to say so she knelt down and started plucking out the weeds springing up around the grave site. Julian reached down and put his hand on her shoulder, "Don't do that."

"I'm sorry," she said as she slowly stood up. "I was just trying to tidy up."

"Emma liked things just the way they were," Julian responded. "She thought all living things should be given a chance to grow. It didn't matter what it was. She would even pick up insects that came into the house and carry them outside. She would never dream of killing them."

"Why didn't you bring any flowers?" Charlotte asked in a gentle tone.

"For the same reason; Emma didn't believe in picking flowers. She loved to watch them bloom and she would go into the garden, stroke the petals and talk to them."

"She sounds like she was really special."

"She was," Julian replied bowing his head.

"Is this the anniversary of the day she died? There isn't any date on the tombstone."

Julian shook his head, "I don't need anything to remind me of that day. No, today would have been her birthday. I come here every year."

"Did she live here with her mother?"

She watched as his face hardened, "Yes, this is where she brought Emma when she walked out on me. She even tried to keep me from seeing her when she was dying but she couldn't keep me away. I was with her when she took her last breath."

Charlotte suddenly felt a deep sense of sadness come over her and she reached out and took Julian's hand, "I'm so sorry, I really am."

He turned to her, "I just need a few moments."

Charlotte nodded, released his hand, and took one step away from him. "I'll be right here," she said.

While Julian stood with his hands clasped in front of him staring at the tombstone, Charlotte began to think about slipping away and just driving off but she realized he had her car keys in his pocket. Maybe if she just started running she could find a place to hide and then, when the coast was clear, she could find someone to help her. So many thoughts were running around in her head but when she glanced back at Julian and saw tears running down his face, all thoughts of escape evaporated. Perhaps, in his vulnerable state, she could appeal to him to let her go.

After a few more minutes, Julian began to walk away from the gravesite and motioned to Charlotte to follow him. When they reached the car, she settled in the passenger seat and waited until he was ready to drive away. Then, she said, "I'm not really hungry and I know it's been a long drive but I'd just like to go back now."

"You mean back to the cottage?"

Charlotte hesitated, "No, I'd like to go back home. Hasn't this gone far enough, Julian? I promise I won't call the police. I'll make up a story that I went off somewhere by myself for a few days. I won't even implicate you at all but I need to get back to my family."

Julian shook his head, "That isn't happening. Not yet anyway. I'm not ready to let you go yet."

"But what's the point? You think you're punishing Adam but I'm sure he's not pining away for me. I'm certain he thinks I've run off with you and if you knew anything about him, you'd know he's a proud man and not likely to fall apart."

Julian paused, "Maybe tomorrow I'll let you go, maybe the next day. Right now, whether you're hungry or not, I need something to eat so let's not talk about this anymore."

As they started to pull away from the front of the church, Charlotte said, "Does your wife still live here?"

Julian scowled, "She's not my wife anymore and no, she doesn't live here. She remarried about a year ago and moved somewhere out east. Good riddance is all I have to say."

"Does she ever come back to visit Emma's grave?"

"I don't know and I really don't care. I just hope I don't run into her; anyway, why all the questions?"

Charlotte shrugged, "No reason."

"Well, let's just drop the subject and find a place where we can get something to drink to go with the sandwiches. I think there's a drive-thru near here."

Charlotte suddenly remembered the tissue in her pocket. Why on earth hadn't she thought of it when she was in the cemetery? It would have stood out like a sore thumb against all that green grass. Now she'd have little chance to toss it any place where it wouldn't look like just a piece of litter.

They had been driving for about twenty minutes and were approaching a town called St. Gilbert when Julian pulled into a drive-thru just off of the highway. He didn't bother asking Charlotte what she wanted; he just went ahead and ordered two root beers. Charlotte never liked root beer but decided not to say anything. After all she didn't have to drink it and, at that moment, she was too engrossed in thinking about what would happen if she tried to escape. They were situated in a space barely wide enough for the car and if she could manage to slip out through the door and run away from the rear of the car, there was no way Julian could chase after her without driving forward first, and then circling the building. She knew he'd forgotten to lock the doors when they left the church and this may be her only chance but just as she extended her hand to grasp the door handle, she heard the familiar click and knew it was too late.

Chapter Fifty-Four

Nancy was reluctant to return to Charlotte's house in case she missed the call from Gary. To keep busy and be near the phone, she decided to do some baking. It wasn't something she especially liked to do and wasn't very good at it but it would help to kill time. It was exactly two o'clock and she had just finished mixing the ingredients for a gingerbread cake when there was a knock at the front door. She immediately stopped what she was doing and ran down the hall praying she'd find Charlotte standing there but it was Mrs. Walker.

"Hi, Carol," she said. "Do come in."

Her neighbour followed her into the kitchen, "I knocked because I saw your car in the driveway. I didn't want to just walk in. Do you still need me to cat sit?"

Nancy nodded, "Yes. I'm afraid I have to go back to stay with Alexa tonight but I should be back late tomorrow afternoon. Adam will be home at five and I'll be able to leave."

Carol Walker frowned, "Can't Alexa look after herself? Isn't she seventeen now?"

Nancy hadn't told Carol what had been going on because she didn't want to start any gossip. "There have been a couple of break-ins recently and only a few houses away. Adam doesn't feel comfortable leaving her alone."

"I see. Well that makes sense. You can't be too careful nowadays."

Nancy motioned for her to sit down, "Why don't you stay for a cup of coffee, or tea if you prefer."

Carol remained standing, "No I think I'll leave you to your baking. I suppose you'll feed Gypsy and Luna before you go so I'll pop in just before I go to bed and check on them."

"And give them a treat," Nancy said smiling.

"Yes, of course," Carol replied as she turned on her heel and started to walk away. "Good luck with the cake and save a piece for me."

Nancy sighed when she heard the front door close. She was relieved Carol had decided not to stay. She didn't want her there if Gary called but she didn't want to be rude. Ten minutes later, just as she was popping the cake into the oven, the phone rang.

"Hello," she answered in almost a whisper.

"It's Gary, Mrs. Fleming. I thought I'd just touch base in case you were worrying."

"I haven't stopped worrying since Charlotte went missing. Have you found any clue as to where she might be?"

"Not exactly but I think I might be on the right trail."

"What do you mean?"

"Well, I met someone in a fish tackle store here in Morin Heights who thought he recognized Julian's photo. He said he hadn't seen him in a few years but he was pretty sure it was him. He remembered he wasn't from around there but, if his memory served him right, he sometimes spent time in Harrington. He even recalled seeing him with a small girl who he assumed was his daughter. She looked to be about seven or eight."

Nancy's heart started to race, "Oh, my goodness. How far away is this place? Are you on your way there now?"

"It's only about thirty-five kilometers west of here and I'll be on my way there right after I get off the phone but I don't want you to get your hopes up."

"Why? Don't you think you'll be able to find them?"

"I feel pretty sure I'll be able to find the aunt's cottage, if that's where it is, but that doesn't mean they'll be there. They could be anywhere."

"But wouldn't you think that's where Julian would take her if he didn't want her to be found?"

"Possibly and we have to rule it out before we start looking anywhere else."

"If you do find them, what are you planning to do?"

"Well, if there's evidence they're in the cottage I'll have to try and determine if your daughter's there of her free will."

"How do you propose to do that?"

"Just by observing any activity; if she's able to come in and out of the cottage by herself, then I have to believe she's there because she wants to be."

Nancy shook her head vehemently even though she knew Gary couldn't see her, "No, I'll never accept that. There's no way she'd just go off and not get in touch with her family and she'd never tell me she was coming here and not show up."

"I'm sure you're right Mrs. Fleming," Gary said gently. "Let's assume he's actually keeping her confined there. If that's the case, I'll need to involve the police. I don't want to alarm you but Julian could be dangerous."

"Please be careful, Gary, and don't do anything to put Charlotte in harm's way."

"Don't worry, ma'am, I'll take every precaution."

Before hanging up Nancy gave him the number at Charlotte's house and told him she'd be back there by five. Now she had to clean up the kitchen while the cake was baking and then lie down for a while. All of the stress was beginning to get to her.

Gary had failed to notice, while talking on the phone, that black clouds had formed overhead and just as he was about to turn the key in the ignition, rain began to fall. Ignoring the fact it looked like a storm was coming, he drove west for several kilometers before he realized the rain was getting heavier and he could see lightning flashes and hear the rumbling of thunder. He turned on the radio but only got French language programmes and a lot of static, so he pulled over to the side of the road and checked his phone to pull up the weather news. It looked like that area of Quebec was in for some severe storms but he decided to take his chance and head onto Harrington and stop at the closest bar. Twenty minutes later, he was entering the town and looking for somewhere to stop and take cover when he noticed a sign over a large wooden building, Alice's General Store. After parking his car at the curb, he entered through the main door and made his way towards the counter. The diminutive woman, almost hidden behind the cash register, looked up at him in surprise and with a little apprehension. Gary was not only a stranger but he was an imposing figure, over six feet tall and almost two hundred and fifty pounds. "Yes, sir, what can I do for you?" she asked meekly.

Gary smiled, "You must be Alice," he responded. "My name's Gary Norman, ma'am. I was just passing through and noticed your shop."

"I see. Is there something you wish to purchase Mr. Norman?"

"No ma'am. I'd just like to ask you a couple of questions?"

"What kind of questions," Alice asked as she noticed him reaching into the pocket of his jacket.

Gary laid the photograph of Adam on the counter. "I was wondering if you'd ever seen this man."

Alice picked up the photo, took it closer to the lamp behind her, and then handed it back to Gary, "That's Julian, I've known him since he was a youngster. He used to come in here with his mother and his Aunt Beth. Why are you looking for him?"

Gary responded by sliding the photo of Charlotte towards her. "I'm actually looking for this woman. Have you seen her with him?"

Alice glanced down and then up again, "Yes, they were either here yesterday or the day before. My memory isn't as good as it used to be. He said she was a friend. I think her name was Charlene or something like that."

"Thank you, that's very helpful," Gary said picking up the photo. "Perhaps you can tell me where they're staying."

"Not unless you tell me what this is all about."

"I'm afraid it's a personal matter. I need to contact them."

Alice shook her head, "Well, I can only tell you Julian's aunt owns a cottage on Green Lake. You'll have to find your own way but I wouldn't suggest it in this weather. I hear they're expecting some trees to be down by the time this is over and the road may not be passable."

Gary nodded, "I think I'll take your advice ma'am and hole up somewhere for a while."

"I suggest you go to Remy's. It's a couple of doors down and you can get a bite to eat and even a beer, if that's what you're looking for."

"I'm much obliged, ma'am," Gary said extending his hand.

Alice shook his hand and then studied him as he walked out into the rain. Why was he looking for Julian's lady friend?

Chapter Fifty-Five

Almost two hours later, Julian arrived at the general store after driving from just north of Montreal, in blinding rain. Warning Charlotte to keep quiet before he dragged her inside, he ran through the door holding onto her arm. "Hi, Alice," he called out. "It's pretty bad out there. I guess business is slow this afternoon."

Alice was spooning some candy into a large jar and looked up from behind the counter in surprise, "Oh, Julian, it's you. I didn't expect anyone to come out in this storm."

Julian walked up to the counter with Charlotte in tow, "We've been out for most of the day and need to get more milk before we head up to the cottage."

"I don't think you should chance it. I heard there were some trees down."

"Where did you hear that?"

"Fred Babbs was just in here. He lives up the road a bit and heard it on his CB."

Julian turned to look out of the window, "It's been raining pretty heavily for a while but I'm sure we'll be able to get through."

"Well, it's up to you but don't blame me if you get stuck. By the way," Alice continued glancing at Charlotte, "someone's been here looking for you."

Charlotte gasped and Julian dug his fingers into her arm, "Who was here?" he asked sharply.

"A man; he said his name was Gary Norman. I wrote it down so I wouldn't forget. He showed me a photograph of you and then one of the young lady."

"What did he look like and when was this?"

Alice frowned as she tried to remember, "He was awful tall and big and he had red hair and a mustache. That was just after my programme finished on the radio, so it was about two-thirty."

"What else, Alice? What did he want?"

"He didn't really tell me. He said it was personal and he was looking for her," she responded as she inclined her head towards Charlotte.

Julian began to grow agitated, "What did you tell him? Did you tell him where to find us?"

Alice stepped back from the counter as she sensed Julian's obvious discomfort, "I just told him that your aunt owned a place on Green Lake and I warned him not to try and drive up there in this storm. I sent him over to Remy's to wait it out."

Julian turned and started to walk away while steering Charlotte ahead of him, "Let's go," he said abruptly.

Alice called out after him, "What about the milk?" But Julian ignored her.

A moment later he shoved Charlotte roughly into the passenger's seat and was soon driving away from the store towards the road leading to the cottage. "Aren't you going to see if he's still here in town?" Charlotte asked, desperately hoping he would stop and turn back.

"No chance. He's probably well ahead of us by now, whoever he is. Perhaps you can fill me in. Who is this guy?"

"I have no idea. I've never heard the name before and I don't know anybody who looks like the man she described."

"Well, right now I don't really give a damn. If there's no sign of him, we're going to pick up some things and be on our way but if he's tracked us down already I'll just have to take care of him."

Charlotte shuddered as she imagined all kinds of scenarios. Did Julian mean to do the man harm? Maybe they'd never even reach the cottage. She could hardly see out of the front window, the rain was coming down so hard. "Please, Julian," she begged. "Let's go back. It's too dangerous driving on this road and we have no idea who this person is. He could be dangerous too."

Julian merely laughed, "You're not very convincing, Charlotte. There's only one reason he's here. He's trying to rescue you and I'm going to make sure that doesn't happen."

Gary had been biding his time in Remy's for over two hours and was getting impatient. He'd eaten a plate of poutine, a slice of sugar pie and downed two bottles of beer but it hadn't slowed him down. His gut was telling him Charlotte was there against her will and the longer he waited, the less chance he might have of catching up with her. What if Julian found out someone was looking for them? He would be gone in an instant. He felt Alice had been reluctant to tell him exactly where to find the cottage but that's why the time he'd spent at Remy's hadn't been a total waste. He was on his second beer when the door opened and a man came in wearing an oilskin jacket and a baseball cap. He called out something in French to the woman behind the counter and, after shrugging out of his jacket and hanging it up near the door, sat down at the table next to Gary's and nodded. "Tempête méchante là aujourd'hui," he said.

Gary shrugged, "Sorry, I don't speak French."

The man grinned and extended his hand, "That's okay," he answered, "I don't speak it too well either. Fred Babb's the name, originally from Liverpool."

Gary shook his hand, "Gary Norman, pleased to meet you, Fred."

"What brings you to these parts? I guess that's your car parked outside Alice's. I noticed the Ontario plates."

Gary decided this might be the break he was looking for, "I'm chasing down a friend of mine. He's staying at his aunt's cottage at Green Lake. He invited me up for a few days but I'm not sure how to get there from here."

"Who's your friend; I know most of the people around here?"

"Julian Richards."

"Ah, Beth's nephew, sure I know him. Nice chap and too bad about his little one. She was a real sweetheart. Used to come up here and go swimming with my granddaughter. Did you ever meet her?"

Gary decided to play it safe, "No, I met Julian about a year after she died. He's come a long way since those days."

They proceeded to chat and Gary gradually gained Fred's confidence to the point where he had no problem getting him to reveal the exact location of the cottage.

When Gary finally left Remi's, Julian was well ahead of him. Charlotte had begged him not to drive through the storm but he was determined to get to Green Lake to retrieve their belongings and take off to some place where they wouldn't be found. "This is madness," Charlotte said, almost in tears. "Where are you planning on going? You can't make me stay with you forever. Please, Julian, let me out of the car. I'll walk back into town."

Julian was hunched over the steering wheel peering through the front window while the rain made it almost impossible to see and it was as dark as night. "Shut up," he yelled. "I'm trying to drive. You're not going anywhere."

Charlotte didn't respond. She knew it was useless trying to talk any sense into him. He was determined to keep her with him until he figured Adam had been punished enough, or until he got tired of her. There was no reasoning with him and, at that moment, she decided when the next opportunity came, she would escape. Maybe when they got to the cottage, she'd just open the car door and start running. Because it was so dark and raining so heavily, she might have a chance. As long as she could reach the trees before he caught up with her, she could make it. She wouldn't have any idea which way to go to get help but she might be able to double back to the dock and take the boat across the lake to where she knew there were other cottages. She was deep in thought when suddenly Julian screamed, "Hang on," and she felt the car veer sharply to the left and then straighten out again.

She felt her heart begin to race, "What was it?" she yelled back.

"I'm not sure. It must have been an animal of some kind. I just missed hitting it, whatever it was."

There was a flash, as lightning lit up the sky, immediately followed by the sound of thunder. The storm was getting worse. "Please, Julian, we have to stop and wait it out", Charlotte pleaded as she grasped the sides of her seat, her body tense and fearing the worst.

"We'll be there soon; stop worrying."

Charlotte tried taking deep breaths to calm herself but she was terrified. She knew something ominous was going to happen and there was nothing she could do about it. Seconds later, she saw it; a huge shape looming up ahead of them and she heard Julian cry out, "Jesus Christ." Then, there was a screeching sound as he hit the brakes and everything went black.

Gary came upon the scene fifteen minutes later. He had left Remy's just a minute or two after Julian pulled away from Alice's but unlike Julian, he had taken his time. At one point, he even considered going back but he was too keyed up and anxious to locate Charlotte so, with extreme caution, he kept on going. If it hadn't been for the lightning, he might never have seen the massive tree lying right across the roadway and the crumpled vehicle almost hidden beneath one of its enormous branches. Breaking quickly, he managed to stop in time and seconds later, after grabbing his flashlight from the glove compartment, he was racing to see if anyone was injured. It was only when he was a foot away from the rear of the car he recognized the make, it was an Acura. It was too dark to tell the colour but he knew it had to be Charlotte's. He reached the passenger side and shone a light through the window which was still intact. He could see a woman slumped forward. She had blond hair but he couldn't see her face. Part of the door was barred by a branch and he used every ounce of his strength to pull it away before he finally gained access. Looking over towards the driver's seat, he saw the whole area, plus part of the passenger side, had been crushed and the windshield had shattered leaving a hole, large enough for the driver to be ejected through it. If the woman was Charlotte then the driver had to be Julian. Maybe he'd managed to survive the impact and had conveniently vanished.

Gently, Gary reached down and felt the woman's pulse. It was weak but she was alive. He didn't think he'd be able to move her and, if she had a serious injury, he could do her more harm. He had to get her to a hospital. Pulling his cell phone from the inside of his jacket he tried calling 911 but couldn't get a signal. He had no choice, he would have to drive back into town and get help. As he was running back to his car he remembered his notes with Charlotte's license number. He seized a blanket from the trunk and raced back, stopping briefly to shine a light on the license plate. It was a match so now he knew it really was Charlotte and he had even more reason to keep her alive. He draped the blanket over her head and shoulders to protect her from the rain pelting through the shattered windshield, gently closed the door and took a quick look around. He was just about to leave when something caught his eye and he looked up. He couldn't quite make it out so he shone his flashlight up into the tree. He had been involved in a lot of cases and seen things no human should ever be exposed to but, at that moment, what he saw took his breath away. A man was swinging in the wind like a rag doll, the broken end of a branch piercing his back and exiting his chest. It was Julian and there was no doubt; he was dead.

Gary started to drive towards town, no longer cautious but frantic to get there. The rain had let up a little but visibility was still poor and he had only gone about five kilometers when he saw another vehicle coming in the other direction. He immediately stopped and jumped into the middle of the road waving his arms and praying the driver would see him. He wasn't sure if it was luck or fate when he saw it was a truck and when it stopped, a few feet in front of him, Fred Babbs climbed down from the cab. "Had a feeling you'd get yourself in trouble," he said. "You got car problems?"

"No," Gary blurted out, "there's been an accident and someone's been hurt. They need to get to a hospital but my cell phone isn't working. I didn't want to move them so I decided to race back to town."

"Well, I've got a CB so I'll call it in. How far is it from here?"

"I don't know exactly, maybe five or six kilometers. There's a huge tree down and I guess they didn't see it."

"They; you mean there's more than one person hurt?"

"No. The woman passenger's hurt but the driver's dead. It's not a pretty sight. He must have got catapulted through the windshield and skewered on a branch."

"Jesus, you have to be kidding."

"I'm afraid not. We'd better make that call, I'm concerned the woman won't make it."

"I'm right on it," Fred replied as he climbed back into his cab.

After Fred had notified the police on his CB, Gary jumped into the truck and they drove back to the scene of the accident. Fred glanced up as he approached the mangled car then stopped and made the sign of the cross. "Christ, it's Julian Richards, poor bugger," he whispered then turned his attention to Charlotte who hadn't moved. He opened the door and, like Gary, felt for her pulse. "Well, she's still alive. Let's hope they get here soon."

It seemed like an eternity but it was less than fifteen minutes later when the police arrived along with emergency services and they managed to extricate Charlotte from the car and place her on a backboard. She was unconscious and barely breathing. Gary walked back to Fred's truck after seeing her face and slammed his fist into the door, then yelled out, "Damn it, why did it have to end this way?"

Chapter Fifty-Six

Nancy and Alexa arrived at Hawkesbury General at ten-thirty that evening, after taking a Porter Airlines flight to Dorval and renting a car for the hour long drive to the hospital. When Gary had called a few minutes before six, Nancy had just finished making a salad to go along with the lasagne they were having for dinner and Alexa was filling Zoe's water bowl. Fifteen minutes later, they were both frantically throwing clothes into suitcases and waiting for the taxi to arrive to take them to the island airport.

On the way downtown, Alexa tried calling her father but he wasn't answering and she had to leave a message. "Dad," she said, "Mom's been in an accident. Nana and I are flying out tonight to be with her. I'll have to call you back because you won't be able to reach me on the plane. We should be in Montreal at about nine, I'll call you then. Love you."

Nancy reached over and took Alexa's hand, "Everything will be all right, honey. I'm sure once your dad knows what's going on he'll be on the first flight out of Halifax."

Alexa nodded and tried to put on a brave face but Nancy could see the tears in her eyes.

Nancy squeezed her hand and stared out of the window. Everything looked so normal. People were strolling along the sidewalks talking and laughing while Charlotte was lying in a hospital bed in critical condition. "Darn you, Julian," she said under her breath.

Gary met Nancy and Alexa at the front entrance of the hospital and accompanied them to the emergency ward but they weren't allowed to see Charlotte until after they had spoken to the doctor. While they sat in the waiting room, Gary filled them in on everything that had happened after he arrived in Harrington. The police had already taken a statement from him and requested that Nancy come to the station the next day to give credence to his account that Charlotte had been abducted by Julian. "I can drive you to Harrington in the morning," Gary said.

Nancy nodded, "That's very kind of you but I think Adam will be here by then and he may want to go with me."

"In that case, I can take him too. It wouldn't be any trouble."

"I think you've done quite enough thank you, Gary. You found Charlotte and even though it's not the way I wanted it to happen, I'm really grateful."

"Suit yourself, Mrs. Fleming, but the offer still stands if you change your mind."

Nancy turned to Alexa, who was flipping through a magazine, "What time did your dad say he'd be here, dear?"

"He was catching the latest flight and expects to arrive in Montreal just before midnight. He said he'd rent a car and drive straight here."

"Well, I don't expect he'll get here until close to two o'clock. Was he really upset when you told him what had happened?"

Alexa hesitated, "It was hard to tell. He wanted to know how bad Mom was but I couldn't really tell him. I just told him it was critical and he should come right away."

Nancy was about to respond when the doctor walked through the door. "Mrs. Fleming?" he asked, extending his hand. "I'm Doctor Graham. I believe you're Charlotte Hamilton's mother."

Nancy shook his hand, "Yes, I am and this is her daughter, Alexa."

The doctor nodded at Alexa, "I'm sorry you had to wait so long. Mr. Norman told me earlier that you were flying in from Toronto."

"Yes, we came straight here when we heard," Nancy replied, beginning to feel impatient. "Please, doctor, is Charlotte going to be all right?"

The doctor sat down opposite her and glanced at the chart in his hand, "Right now, she's in critical condition and we need to take her to surgery; in fact they're prepping her now."

Nancy heard Alexa gasp and she reached over to rub her shoulder, "Why do you need to operate?"

"She's had a traumatic brain injury. We need to relieve the pressure inside the skull. She also has a broken leg and some broken ribs. We'll set the leg while she's under anaesthetic and strap up the ribs."

"What are the chances for her recovery, doctor?" Nancy asked

"I'm afraid we won't know that until we know the extent of the trauma to the brain. The effect of this type of injury is hard to predict. Sometimes a patient will fully recover with only minor physical or mental issues and sometimes there can be more long-term or permanent conditions."

"Is my mom going to die, doctor?" Alexa whispered.

The doctor smiled, "Not if I can help it, young lady. There's always a slight risk when we have to operate but I don't usually lose any of my patients." He then turned back to Nancy, "I understand Mrs. Hamilton's husband is on his way here but I'm afraid we need to go to surgery right away, so I'd like you to sign the consent form, Mrs. Fleming."

Nancy took a deep breath, "Of course, I'll do that right now but I need to ask one more thing?"

"Yes, what's that?

"Would you please take good care of my daughter, doctor?"

At two-thirty in the morning, Nancy was watching Alexa curled up on a couch in the waiting room fast asleep, when Adam walked through the door. She immediately put her finger to her lips then jumped up, gave him a hug, and ushered him into the hallway. "Oh, Adam I'm so glad you're here," she said.

"I just managed to get the last flight out. How's Charlotte?"

"Come," Nancy replied leading him by the hand away from the waiting room. "Let's go down the hall a ways so we don't wake Alexa up. Poor girl, she's exhausted."

"Did she get to see her mother?"

Nancy shook her head and glanced at her watch, "No, neither of us has seen her. They took her into surgery about three hours ago. I expect the doctor will be back to talk to us soon."

"Alexa said it was a car accident. If she's critical, it can't just be some broken bones. What is it, Nancy?"

"I'm afraid it's a head injury and they have to relieve the pressure on her brain. She does have some broken bones but those can be fixed. It may take some time before we know how serious the head injury is."

Adam sighed, "How did this happen. Was she driving?"

Nancy looked down, "No, Julian was driving."

Adam clenched his teeth and took a deep breath, "Where is the bastard?"

Nancy put her hand on his arm, "He's dead."

Adam turned and started to walk back towards the waiting room. "I'll tell you everything I know," Nancy called out, "as soon as we hear from the doctor."

Adam kept walking and made his way to Alexa who was still sleeping. He sat down beside her, gently stroking her head and she began to stir. Seconds later, she opened her eyes, looked up and smiled, "Daddy, it's you."

Adam smiled back, "It's a long time since you've called me that."

Alexa sat up and laid her head on his shoulder, "Mom's not going to die, is she?"

Nancy watched from the doorway as Adam put his arm around her, "No, she's going to be as right as rain."

Half an hour later, Dr. Graham walked into the room. He was still wearing his green scrubs and a mask was dangling from around his neck. Nancy immediately sprang to her feet, "How is she, doctor?"

He looked over as Adam rose and walked towards him, "I assume you're Charlotte's husband?"

Adam nodded, "Yes, I am. What can you tell us doctor?"

"Well, you're wife came through the operation without any problem. We had to remove part of the skull to repair the fracture and excise the haematoma."

Alexa jumped up, "Oh goodness, does that mean my mom's got a hole in her head?"

Dr. Graham smiled, "Not any more. We put the bone back with a few screws and once it knits together we can take the screws out."

"What about her other injuries? Is she going to make a full recovery?" Nancy asked.

"We've set her broken leg so she's in a cast and we've strapped up the ribs but those are the least of our concerns. She isn't out of the woods yet. Any time we operate on the brain there can be issues concerning memory or speech. These issues are usually temporary and rarely permanent. In most cases, the patient recovers without any after effects. Only time will tell."

"Where is my wife now?" Adam asked.

"She's in recovery and she'll stay there until her blood pressure and breathing are stable, then she'll be moved to ICU."

Alexa took hold of Adam's hand, "When can my mom come home?"

Dr. Graham smiled again, "She'll be here for at least a week and even then, she has to be well enough to be transported back to Toronto."

Nancy looked anxious, "Can we see her, doctor?"

"Not for a while, I'm afraid. Once she's in ICU we'll let you know and then you can see her."

Adam shook his hand, "Thank you, doctor."

"Yes, thank you," Nancy repeated. "We'll be here waiting."

Dr. Graham nodded at Nancy and Alexa then turned to leave the room, "Try not to worry, Charlotte's in good hands."

Chapter Fifty-Seven

After Dr. Graham left, Adam suggested Nancy take Alexa and check into a hotel but she wouldn't hear of it. "It's only a few hours until daylight and maybe we'll be able to see Charlotte. Alexa will be all right sleeping here and I'm not going anywhere."

Once Adam realized Nancy wasn't leaving, he settled in a chair and picked up a magazine. Meanwhile, Nancy excused herself to get coffee from the vending machine and Alexa went back to her position on the couch. By the time Nancy returned, Alexa was already asleep, "I brought you a Pepsi," she said to Adam, "I didn't think you'd appreciate the coffee they have here."

Adam reached out and took the can from her hand, then set it on the table beside him, "I see it didn't take long for Alexa to drop off. Maybe this will give us a chance to talk."

"I think it would be a perfect time," Nancy responded.

"What I'd like to know is; how did you find out Charlotte was here?"

"Gary Norman called me. He was the one who found her."

"So your hunch paid off. I have to hand it to you, Nancy, you're pretty determined when you set your mind on something."

Nancy looked annoyed, "Charlotte isn't just something; she's my daughter. I was willing to do anything knowing she might be in danger."

Adam didn't react, "Where's this Gary chap now?" he asked.

"I sent him off to get some sleep and then suggested he go home. He's already given his statement to the police and, by the way, they need to talk to me in the morning so I'll need you to drive me to Harrington."

Adam frowned, "How far away is this place and why do they need to see you?"

"Gary told me it was about forty minutes north of here. He reported a possible abduction to the police. Even though Julian is dead, they still need to investigate and I can fill them in on a lot of the details."

"So you still maintain Charlotte went with him against her will?"

"Yes, I'm certain of it. Why don't I tell you everything I've learned?"

"Go right ahead," Adam responded, "I've got all night."

At seven o'clock, after both Adam and Nancy had managed to nod off for a few minutes and Alexa continued to sleep undisturbed, a very young looking man in a white coat, with distinctly Asian features, walked into the room. "Good morning," he said, "I'm Dr. Tanaka. Mrs. Hamilton has just been moved to ICU so you should be able to see her in about thirty minutes."

Nancy stood up, "Does this mean she's stable now, doctor."

Dr. Tanaka nodded, "Yes, but her levels of oxygen are still low and she isn't fully awake yet. A nurse will be here later to tell you when you can go in."

Alexa started to stir as the doctor left the room. Still half asleep, she mumbled, "Can we see Mom now?"

Nancy went over to sit beside her, "Soon, honey; very soon."

It was another hour before a nurse appeared and directed them to ICU, "I have to warn you," she said looking directly at Alexa, "she's got a lot of bandages and a breathing tube but I'm sure she's going to be fine."

"Thank you," Nancy said, touching her lightly on the arm and bracing herself as they entered the ICU.

There were three patients in the room but it was easy to identify Charlotte. She was the only one with a breathing tube, her head covered in bandages, and her leg encased in a cast and elevated in a sling. Alexa stopped just inside the door when she saw her and grabbed hold of her grandmother's hand, "Oh, Nana, I'm scared."

Nancy put her arm around her shoulders and guided her forward while Adam followed a step behind, "It's going to be all right, honey. Just let your mom know you're here. I'm sure she'll be able to hear you."

Alexa let go of her hand, stopped beside the bed, and stared down at her mother's face. Although it was partially covered by a mask she could see several bruises and small cuts on the left side. She reached out and gently touched the right cheek with her fingertips, "Mom, it's me, Alexa. Please wake up."

Nancy looked up at Adam but his face was expressionless and she had no idea what he was thinking. "Maybe you should let her know you're here too," she said. "I think it would mean a lot to her."

Adam merely nodded then took a step forward to stand beside Alexa, "Charlotte," he said gently, "it's Adam. You've been in an accident and you're in the hospital but you'll be okay. Your mother's here too."

He glanced over his shoulder at Nancy and shrugged, "She can't hear me."

Nancy shook her head, "You don't know that. Let me talk to her," and she almost pushed him out of the way while Alexa moved to the foot of the bed. "Charlotte darling," she whispered as she gently took hold of one of her hands, "its Mom. You have to get better, do you understand? Alexa and Adam need you and I do too. I love you so much and I'm not going to leave you."

At that, Alexa started to cry and Nancy released Charlotte's hand to go and comfort her while Adam stood awkwardly a few feet away. When a nurse appeared to check Charlotte's vital signs, Nancy suggested they should leave to drive to Harrington and come back later and, without another word, they left the room and walked out to a cool but sunny September morning.

"How did you get here from the airport?" Adam asked when they reached the parking lot.

"I rented a car," Nancy replied, "in fact it's the blue Nissan over there."

"I rented a car too; we might as well take mine."

Once they were heading north, Nancy was shocked when Adam suddenly announced he would be dropping her back at the hospital after they had talked to the police and then he and Alexa would be driving to Montreal and taking a flight back to Toronto. When Alexa heard this she raised her voice in anger, "No, Dad. I'm not going. I want to stay with Nana"

"You'll do exactly as I say," Adam shot back. "I need to go back to work and you need to go to school."

"But Mom's really ill," Alexa cried. "I want to be with her. What if something happens to her?"

"Nothing's going to happen to her. She's in good hands. I'm not going to argue with you, Alexa, and I don't want to hear any more about it."

"I hate you. You're just punishing, Mom. I'll never ever forgive you if she goes and dies."

Nancy, who had been sitting staring straight ahead and biting her lip, turned to look back at Alexa and gave a slight shake of her head. She needed to have a private talk with Adam.

When they arrived at the police station in Harrington they were ushered into a small room and offered coffee. It was only then, all three of them realized they hadn't had breakfast, but food had been the furthest thing from their minds. They sat in silence until an officer brought them giant mugs of coffee and, a few minutes later, another officer arrived and introduced himself. He suggested Adam and Alexa wait outside while he questioned Nancy about the relationship between Charlotte and Julian but after Adam refused to budge he turned to Alexa and said, "Go sit on the bench in the hall."

Alexa flounced out of the room, slamming the door behind her, and Nancy recounted everything she knew from the time Charlotte and Julian first met. When she had finished, the officer looked at Adam and asked, "What do you think, Mr. Hamilton? Do you believe your wife was abducted?"

Adam shook his head, "No, I don't. I think she went with him willingly."

The officer nodded and then opened the file sitting on the desk in front of him. He took out, what looked like, a crumpled piece of tissue. "Perhaps you had better look at this," he said and passed it to Adam.

Adam frowned as he looked down at the paper in his hands and was just able to make out the number and words written on it. "Where did you find this?"

"In your wife's jacket pocket; we suspect she had every intention of leaving it where someone would find it."

"What is it? Please may I see it?" Nancy asked.

Adam handed it to her and her eyes widened in surprise, "Oh my goodness, that's her license number. She was trying to alert us."

"Yes, and that's not all," the officer continued. When we checked out the cottage we found evidence that she'd been forcibly confined. It appears she'd been tied up at some point."

Nancy looked at Adam, "Now do you believe me?" she said accusingly.

Adam didn't answer her, "What happens now?" he said directing his question to the officer.

"Nothing of any consequence; Julian Richards is dead so obviously no charges can be laid. Your wife's belongings were gathered up and we can sign them over to you when you leave here."

"I see," Adam said as he stood up, "then I guess we're through here."

"Not quite, Mr. Hamilton. Your wife's car is a total write off. You'll need to contact the insurance company. I'll give you the police report and you can proceed with a claim."

Nancy started to rise from her seat, "What happened to Julian's body?" she asked.

She heard Adam sigh as she waited for a reply. The officer got up and came around the desk, "He was taken to the morgue. His aunt is on her way there now to identify him."

Nancy shook her head, "What a terrible way to die," she said.

Before they left the room Nancy asked if she could have a private moment with Adam and she did her best to persuade him to allow Alexa to stay but he was adamant. She had never known him to be so cold and suspected that, even though he had proof Charlotte had not intentionally run off with Julian, he still couldn't forgive her for the affair. Maybe she was asking too much, after all Julian was his brother. It was only then she realized Adam had never even got to meet him and, for some reason, it made her terribly sad.

Chapter Fifty-Eight

When Adam dropped Nancy off at the hospital, Alexa begged him to let her go and see her mother one more time before they left and he relented. He left her with Nancy while he drove over to Tim Horton's to pick up some muffins and coffee for all three of them. Charlotte was in exactly the same state as when they were last in the ICU, and Alexa felt awkward. Deep down she was beginning to think it might be best if she went home especially when Nancy told her she was staying in Hawkesbury until she knew Charlotte was completely out of the woods, or until they could transport her to Toronto. When Adam returned, there were a lot of tears as Alexa said goodbye to her grandmother, "Please look after Mom," she said.

Nancy took her in her arms and held her close, "I will, honey, and I'll call you every day; maybe even twice a day. I'm going to find a place to stay and then you can always call me there if you need to and leave a message. I'm going to phone Mrs. Walker later and ask her to continue cat-sitting but I'd really be grateful if you could go over every couple of days to check on them. I'll tell Mrs. Walker to let you in so you can just knock on her door." She released Alexa while she pulled her wallet out of her purse and took out a number of twenty

dollar bills. She handed them to Alexa, "Here take this money
so you can take a cab back and forth to my house."

"That isn't necessary," Adam intervened, "I can drive her."

Nancy smiled at him, "That's kind of you Adam, but you
might be busy."

Adam shrugged, "Suit yourself but if you need a ride,
Alexa, just ask."

Alexa nodded and hugged her grandmother again, "Bye,
Nana, call me tonight."

"Okay, dear, I will. Love you."

"Love you too," Alexa whispered and then turned to follow
her father.

They were just steps away when Adam looked back and
said, "Thanks for staying, Nancy, and if you need me you know
where to reach me."

Nancy waved her hand, "Bye, Adam, drive carefully."

Late in the afternoon after a constant vigil at Charlotte's
bedside, Nancy drove to The Netherdale, a small bed and
breakfast about fifteen minutes from the hospital. She
would have preferred to have been closer but, after speaking
to two of the ICU nurses, she decided to go to a place they
both recommended. She found it located in a lovely area in
an original carriage house and surrounded by acres of flower
gardens. After she settled in her room, she checked with
reception for a decent place to eat and ended up at L'Escale
where she ordered a simple dinner of halibut and frites
followed by a slice of apple pie. She hadn't realized how hungry
she was until she sat down at the table and looked at the menu
but she'd only had a muffin and two cups of coffee all day.
After dinner she went back to The Netherdale and called
Carol Walker who was very surprised to hear the news about
Charlotte, but more than willing to look after Gypsy and Luna
for as long as Nancy needed her to. Nancy apologized for not
telling her she was leaving town the night before, "Everything
happened so quickly, "she explained, "the minute I got the call
about the accident, Alexa and I were on our way to the airport."

After hanging up, Nancy tried to decide whether to go
back to the hospital or just call it a night. She was exhausted,

not only from lack of sleep but because she was an emotional wreck and putting on a brave face for Alexa was especially difficult. She sat down on the edge of the bed, kicked off her shoes, then picked up the phone again. The phone only rang once at the Hamilton house before Alexa picked it up, "Hello," she said, "Nana, is that you?"

"Yes, dear, it's me. How was the flight back?"

"It was okay. We just got here a little while ago. A lot of the flights were fully booked and we had to wait. I got so bored hanging around the airport but guess what?"

"What, dear?"

"I saw this newspaper, the Gazette, and there was a photo of Julian on the front page."

"Oh, goodness, that's the paper Julian worked for. What did it say?"

"I only saw the headline. It said something like **Gazette Cameraman Julian Richards Killed in Storm.** Dad saw it too and he pulled me away and wouldn't let me read any more. I saw his face, Nana. When he noticed the photo, he went kind of pale."

"I'm not surprised. I'll have to see if I can pick up a copy somewhere. I hope they haven't mentioned your mother."

"How's Mom? Is she any better?"

"There hadn't been any change when I left before dinner. I'm not sure if I'm going back tonight. I found a place to stay and right now I'm sitting on the bed. It looks very inviting and I may just lie down for a little while."

"You should, Nana, you must be really tired."

"I am, but I might just take a nap and then see how I feel."

They continued to chat for a while and Nancy gave Alexa the telephone number where she could be reached. When she asked where Adam was, Alexa told her he was on his phone in the family room talking to Ray. Someone had to tell Mary that Julian was dead.

When Nancy woke up, she couldn't figure out where she was for a few seconds. Suddenly she realized it was already dark and, after glancing at the clock, saw it was just after ten. She still considered going back to the hospital but decided to call first to see if there had been any change. The nurse on duty suggested it would be better if she came back in the morning as Charlotte was still not awake but her vital signs were stable. Nancy was relieved and after she put the phone down, she stripped off her clothes, removed her make-up, and crawled back into bed.

By eight the next morning, she had already bathed, dressed, eaten breakfast in the charming dining room and was on her way back to the hospital. When she arrived at the door to the ICU she was a little alarmed when she was intercepted by one of the nurses who had been attending Charlotte the day before. "Good morning," she said, trying to maintain her composure, "how's my daughter?"

The nurse smiled, "Good morning, Mrs. Fleming. Charlotte's awake and we're just waiting for Dr. Tanaka to come and check on her."

Nancy breathed a sigh of relief, "May I see her?"

"Yes, of course but don't expect too much. She's feeling a bit nauseous but that's pretty common after the type of surgery she had. Why don't you just go ahead, I'm sure she'll be happy to see a familiar face?"

"Thank you, nurse," Nancy said, putting on a big smile, as she headed towards Charlotte's bed. When she got there, she found her lying with her eyes closed and she looked exactly as she had last seen her, except the breathing tube had been removed. Not sure what to do, she looked around for the nurse but suddenly thought she heard a movement. She quickly whipped back around and noticed Charlotte's eyes were now open and she was looking up at her. Before she had a chance to speak, Charlotte whispered, "Mom?" and a tear ran down her face.

Nancy leaned over and gently wiped the tear away, "Yes, it's me darling. Everything's going to be all right."

Charlotte's eyes darted from side to side and she started to lift her hand towards her head but Nancy stopped her, "Where am I, Mom, what happened?"

Nancy drew up a chair and sat down beside her holding onto her hand, "You're in the hospital. You were in a car accident and you were injured but everything's okay now and you're going to recover."

"My head hurts, Mom. Did I hurt my head?"

Nancy sighed, "Yes, dear, you fractured your skull and they had to operate and I'm afraid you broke your leg and a few ribs but you're alive and you're going to get better."

"How did the accident happen? Was I driving? Was anyone else in the car?"

Nancy shook her head, "You don't need to know all the details now, Charlotte; you just need to concentrate on your recovery."

Charlotte started to speak and then began clutching her throat, "I'm going to be sick."

Nancy immediately called for the nurse who came running with a bowl and Charlotte proceeded to retch while she looked on helplessly. It wasn't easy seeing Charlotte like this. She had seldom been ill, even as a child and Nancy wanted, more than anything, to comfort her and assure her she was going to get better.

A few minutes later, Dr. Tanaka arrived and performed a series of tests to ensure there were no complications from the surgery. He had her wiggling her fingers and toes, checked her eyes and asked her questions to make sure her speech had not been impaired in any way. After he was finished, he turned to Nancy and said, "All looks well, Mrs. Fleming. If Mrs. Hamilton continues to improve, we will probably be moving her to a regular room tomorrow."

Nancy smiled, "Thank you, doctor." Then she turned to Charlotte, "Did you hear that, dear; you may be moved tomorrow?"

Charlotte gave a weak grin, "Yes, I heard, Mom, but when can I go home?"

Chapter Fifty-Nine

The next day passed without incident. Charlotte was taken from ICU to a semi-private room on the fourth floor and Nancy spent most of the day with her. At night she left the hospital, stopped for a bite to eat, and fell into bed exhausted. All day she had been expecting Charlotte to be alert enough to start asking questions but most of the time she had drifted in and out of sleep. In the evening, she called Adam to report on Charlotte's progress and was able to speak to Alexa who was thrilled to hear her mother was out of ICU and anxious to know when she would be coming home. Meanwhile, it was still difficult to know what Adam was really thinking.

The next morning, before returning to the hospital, Nancy drove across the bridge to Quebec and stopped in Grenville to see if she could find a back copy of the Gazette. She was anxious to see what the article said about Julian and got lucky when she stopped for breakfast in a café and found out the owner had about a week's worth of old newspapers stored in a back room. He invited her to take whatever she liked. There were several copies of Le Devoir, all in French which she immediately discarded, and then suddenly there it was, a copy of the Gazette with Julian's face staring back at her. She ordered a second cup of coffee and could hardly wait to get back to her table to read through the article. She was surprised to discover Julian had a reputation for producing some memorable photographs for the paper and had also been a volunteer for a charitable organization called the Leukemia and Lymphoma Society for many years. There was some mention of his marriage and divorce and that his only child, a girl, had died at the age of eight. There were no gory details about the accident, just that he was killed after the car he was driving hit a downed tree and he was thrown through the front window. The article also referred to an unidentified female companion who was with him at the time, who had suffered some critical injuries and had been taken to hospital. No arrangements had yet been made for his burial but they expected his aunt, Mrs. Elizabeth Moss, to make an announcement within a day or two.

Nancy put down the paper and breathed a sigh of relief. There was no evidence linking Charlotte to Julian and no reference to the horrendous way in which he died. Now, she felt comfortable being able to tell Charlotte that Julian was killed outright in the head on collision, and that was all. Somehow, deep down, although she was certain he had changed from lover to abductor, she was also certain there was no way Charlotte would have taken pleasure in the way he died.

It was close to ten o'clock when she made it back to the hospital and, after she parked the car, she raced up to Charlotte's room to see if there was any improvement. When she got to the floor and walked quickly down the hallway, she was stopped by a nurse, "Mrs. Hamilton," she said in a gentle voice, "please don't be alarmed but we had to take your daughter back to ICU."

Nancy's hand flew to her throat, "Oh, no. What happened; is she going to be all right?"

The nurse nodded, "She had a seizure and we had her moved back to ICU as a precautionary measure. It's fairly common after a craniotomy but we need to keep a close eye on the situation at this early stage in her recovery."

"Is this likely to happen again?"

"Possibly. Every patient is different and it often depends on which area of the brain was operated on. Some can go for months after surgery before experiencing a seizure and it may only happen once but it could be a condition that needs to be controlled by medication."

"May I see Charlotte now?"

"You can check with the ICU nurse but you may have to wait for a while because they only just took her up to the floor."

Nancy sighed, "Thank you, nurse. Maybe I'll go to the cafeteria and have a coffee before I go there."

The nurse reached out and laid her hand on Nancy's arm, "That's a good idea."

Instead of going to the cafeteria, Nancy took the elevator down to the ground floor, walked outside to get a breath of fresh air, then went back inside to look for a telephone so she could call Adam. She just had to talk to somebody. She managed to get hold of him at his office and gave him the latest news and this time he seemed a little more concerned. "Maybe I should fly out there if you think it's serious," he suggested.

"Well, apparently it happens often after brain surgery but I'm still worried. I'll have to see how she is as the day goes on and I'll call you around dinner time."

"Okay, but if you need me before that, I'll be here in the office all day," Adam responded and Nancy began to believe he was starting to come around. Maybe he would be able to forgive Charlotte after all.

Nancy spent the rest of the day at Charlotte's bedside. Most of the time she just watched while she slept and, when she did wake up, she wasn't completely coherent. At four o'clock, Dr. Tanaka returned to perform the same tests he had done before and when he left he was satisfied the seizure had not had any ill effects but was still cautious about whether there would be a recurrence. After he left, Charlotte was more alert but still somewhat confused about where she was and why. Nancy repeated that she had been in a car accident and assured her she was going to be all right but when Charlotte didn't ask about the family or about Julian, Nancy thought maybe it was just as well. She left the hospital at five to find a place to eat and intended to go back to her room to get some rest but she was too wound up. It was a warm September evening, without even the hint of a breeze, so she decided to drive down to the marina, where she could park, and take a short walk along the riverbank. For a while she was able to clear her head and by the time she got to The Netherdale at just after eight she felt relaxed and ready to settle down and read or watch a little television. She had just taken off her clothes and slipped into a nightgown when the telephone rang. It was Alexa. "Hi, Nana," she said, "didn't you get my message?"

Nancy glanced down at the phone, "Oh, I'm sorry, honey," she replied, "I didn't know there was one. I didn't see any light flashing. Actually, I only got here about five minutes ago."

"Well, you told Dad you were going to call tonight and when we didn't hear from you we were worried. How's Mom?"

Nancy sat down on the edge of the bed, "She seems to be doing better. I guess your father told you she had a seizure. The doctor did some more tests and he got the same results as before so that was good news. She has to be on medication for now to alleviate the chance of any more seizures but they can't guarantee anything."

There was a pause before Alexa spoke, "Nana," she said haltingly, "has Mom asked about me?"

Nancy paused too before she replied. "I have to be honest with you, dear. She hasn't asked about anybody in the family. I think she just needs a little more time. Please don't be upset."

"I want to come back but Dad won't let me. I could come and stay with you in your room, Nana."

"I don't think that's a good idea, Alexa. There's nothing to do but just sit in the hospital all day. Your mom wouldn't want that; she'd prefer you stayed in school."

Alexa sighed, "I suppose you're right but I'm really, really worried about her."

"You need to stop worrying, young lady. I'm sure it won't bc long before she comes home."

"Maybe Dad won't want her to come here."

"I'm afraid that's a bridge we'll have to cross when the time comes. In the meantime, you're the lady of the house now and I hope you're helping out with some of the chores and preparing some meals."

"Yes, I am but I don't really like doing it. It's so boring, Nana."

Nancy laughed, "Tell me about it, I've been doing it for over fifty years. By the way, dear, have you checked on Gypsy and Luna yet?"

"No, but I'm going over tomorrow. I did call Mrs. Walker so she's expecting me."

"Good girl; and what about Zoe?"

"She's fine. She's actually sitting on my lap right now purring away."

"Where's your dad?"

"He's in the family room working on his lap top. Do you want me to get him?"

"No, dear, just pass on my message. I'm going to hang up now and get a little rest."

"Okay, Nana, love you."

"Love you too and I'll call you tomorrow."

Nancy put the phone down and then stretched out on the bed. She had no intention of falling asleep but ten minutes later, a herd of wild horses wouldn't have woken her up.

Hours later, in the middle of the night, Charlotte woke up with a start. At first, she had no idea where she was and then remembered her mother being there and telling her she was in the hospital. She tried to move but realized something was weighing her left leg down. With great effort, she lifted her head from the pillow and, in the low light from a wall lamp near her bed; she could see her leg was in a cast. She looked around helplessly to see if anyone was nearby and could see there were other beds, some occupied and some empty. Just at that moment, a nurse passed through the room and she called out to her. The nurse turned and approached her bed. "Mrs. Hamilton," she whispered, "I'm surprised to see you awake. How are you feeling, is there something you need?"

"Yes, please. I'd like some water."

"Of course, I'll get you some but first I need to check your vital signs." She proceeded to take Charlotte's temperature and blood pressure and then adjusted her pillow. "There, is that better?" she asked.

"Yes, thank you," Charlotte responded.

"I'll get you some water now," the nurse said and started to turn away.

"Wait," Charlotte said. "I think my mother was here. Do you know where she's gone?"

The nurse smiled, "Mrs. Fleming was here all day but I'm sure she's fast asleep in bed by now. It's three o'clock in the morning, dear."

Charlotte looked a little sheepish, "Oh, goodness, I didn't realize. I don't even know what day it is. Am I in a special ward?"

"You're in ICU but I expect you'll be back in your room soon after breakfast."

"Back in my room; do you mean I was there and then brought back?"

"Yes, I'm afraid you had a seizure. It's fairly common after brain surgery but we need to be cautious. You're on medication now so it should help."

Charlotte looked shocked and raised her arm to try and touch the side of her head. "What kind of brain surgery?" she asked.

The nurse patted her hand, "I'll let the doctor explain it to you in the morning. Right now you just need to get more rest. I'll be back in a moment with the water."

Charlotte closed her eyes and tried to take it all in. She vaguely remembered her mother and some man talking to her about an operation but it was all very fuzzy. She didn't even know which hospital she was in and thought she would ask the nurse when she returned but, minutes later, she had fallen asleep again.

At just after six, she was being woken up and transported back to a room where she noticed she was the only patient. Once she was settled she was brought a bland breakfast of oatmeal, toast and tea and told the doctor would be visiting her shortly. It was only then that she asked, "Which hospital am I in?" and was surprised to learn she was in Hawkesbury, a place she knew was somewhere close to the Quebec border. Shortly afterwards, bits and pieces came flooding back. She remembered being with Julian and driving back through a storm after visiting a graveyard. She remembered going into the general store and Julian's desperate dash to get to the cottage and how scared she had been and then suddenly, there was nothing. Where was Julian now? Was he hurt? Was he in the hospital somewhere? She had to find out and she had to warn somebody he could be dangerous. Her heart started to beat a little faster and when Dr. Tanaka walked into the room it was obvious she was agitated. "Mrs. Hamilton," he said in a gentle voice "is something troubling you?"

"Yes, doctor. I know I must have been in an accident. Was anyone else brought here with me?

Dr. Tanaka shook his head, "No. I was on duty in emergency when you were brought in and you were the only accident victim admitted. Was your mother driving, because she's been here but she doesn't have any injuries?"

"No my mother wasn't driving. It was a male friend. So, you don't know what happened to him?"

"I'm afraid not but I can probably find out. Then again, I'm sure your mother will be able to answer your question. I expect she'll be here soon."

Charlotte nodded and lay back while he took yet another series of tests and assured her that her condition was improving. Then she asked about her leg, "How bad is it, doctor?"

"You had a clean break of the femur and we had to insert a titanium rod. It will probably be about two months before you will be able to do any walking and at least another two months after that before you are able to get around without any aid."

Charlotte sighed, "I guess I'm a bit of a mess, doctor."

Dr. Tanaka smiled, "It could have been a lot worse," he said, "at least you're alive and you're going to get better."

Chapter Sixty

Nancy arrived at Charlotte's bedside an hour later and was surprised to see her awake and alert. She kissed her on the cheek and took hold of her hand, "Charlotte, darling, how are you feeling?"

Charlotte squeezed Nancy's hand, "Hi, Mom, I feel pretty good this morning. My leg hurts a bit but the nurse just told me they're going to give me more pain medication."

"Oh, I'm pleased to hear that," Nancy responded pulling up a chair and sitting down. "You look a lot better. You've even got a bit of colour in your cheeks."

Charlotte reached up and felt the bandage above her right ear, "Did they shave off all my hair, Mom?"

"I'm not sure, dear, but it will grow back. That's the least thing you should be worrying about."

"What else should I be worrying about?"

Nancy realized she'd opened a can of worms and hesitated before she replied, "Well, you have to concentrate on your recovery."

Charlotte frowned, "That isn't what you meant. I started to remember everything right up until the accident. What happened to Julian, Mom? Tell me the truth? Did he get hurt? Is he here in this hospital?"

Nancy looked down for a moment and then up again, "Julian's dead, dear. He was killed instantly."

Charlotte took a deep breath, "Oh, no. I didn't expect that. I don't know whether to laugh or cry."

"It's only natural you have mixed emotions. Now you need to tell me the truth, Charlotte, did you just run away or did he make you go with him. When you didn't show up at my house, I was so worried."

"He made me go with him. I agreed to meet him one more time and it was a big mistake. There's so much to tell you, Mom, but not now. I'll tell you everything that happened later."

Nancy patted her hand, "It's all right; we'll wait until you get better. I'm just happy you're safe."

"The nurse told me I was in Hawkesbury. Am I going to be staying here?"

"I don't know. I could try and see if we can get you moved to Toronto. Is that what you'd like?"

"Is it what Adam would like?"

Nancy was taken aback by Charlotte's question and wasn't sure how to answer so she decided to skirt around it, "I know it's what Alexa would like. She wanted to come back to stay with me but we thought it would be better if she remained in school instead of sitting around a hospital every day."

"You said she wanted to come back. Are you saying she was already here?"

Nancy nodded, "Yes, the minute I heard about the accident, I flew out with her. Adam was out of town but he flew in too and they both stayed until they knew you were no longer critical. Alexa didn't want to leave but I'm afraid Adam insisted."

"How did you find out about the accident?"

Nancy took in a deep breath and then let it out, "I got a call from a private detective I hired to find you. I just knew in my heart Julian was up to no good. His name's Gary Norman and he used to work for Tom. He managed to trace you to Harrington and was on the same road when the accident happened. Thankfully, he was able to get help and get you to the hospital. I hate to think what would have happened if you'd been trapped inside your car for hours."

"You said Julian was killed instantly. How do you know that?"

"He was thrown through the windshield. That's all I really know," Nancy lied. "I guess the paramedics, or whoever found him, must have told Gary."

"I can't believe you hired a private detective, Mom. You may have saved my life. Why were you so sure I hadn't just run off with Julian?"

Nancy smiled, "Because I know my daughter, that's why. You wouldn't have not just showed up. You would have left a message of some kind."

Charlotte was quiet for a moment, "I wrote a message, Mom, but I don't remember what happened to it."

"You must be thinking about the note you wrote the police found in your pocket. It was written on a scrap of toilet tissue."

Charlotte's eyes lit up, "Yes, I remember now. I never got the chance to leave it anywhere."

"Well, it left no doubt you'd been abducted."

"Did Adam see the note?"

"Yes. I'm sure he accepts the truth now about what happened but I'm afraid it doesn't eliminate the fact you had an affair."

"I guess he knows every detail by now?"

"You have to understand, it's a lot for him to process. Suddenly he's faced with the fact he had a twin brother and you'd been involved in an intimate relationship with him."

"Do you think he'll ever be able to forgive me?"

"I don't know but I hope so. It's just so sad it couldn't have turned out differently. Putting aside the issue of the affair, imagine finding out you have a twin and then never getting to meet him. I can't imagine what must be going through Adam's head."

They continued to talk for a while until Nancy could tell Charlotte was beginning to tire. She left her to get some sleep while she spoke to the nurse about moving Charlotte to Toronto. The nurse suggested she speak directly to Dr. Tanaka when he made his rounds in mid-afternoon. Feeling a little frustrated, she went down to the cafeteria to get some coffee and sat thinking about her conversation with Charlotte then she began to wonder about Julian and if arrangements had been made for his funeral. The more she thought about it, the more she thought about actually attending; after all he had been Adam's twin. She figured the best way to find out about the funeral was to check on the internet and she asked a man sitting at the next table if he knew of any internet café's nearby. He didn't have any idea but suggested she try the public library so, soon afterwards, she found herself driving down Hugginson Street and, minutes later, she was seated in front of a monitor staring at the obituary columns in the Gazette. Many of the notices had photographs and it only took a moment to recognize Julian. It was the same picture that had been on the front page. There was to be a visitation at the Blythe Bernier funeral home in Montreal the next day and the burial was on the following day in Saint Raymond. Nancy had no idea where Saint Raymond was and decided to try and locate it on a map. She was surprised to learn it was over two hundred kilometers from Montreal and wondered what the connection was. Maybe she would ask Charlotte if she knew. She printed out the page with the obituary and after leaving the library, stopped for a sandwich in a nearby café and then returned to the hospital. Charlotte was still sleeping so she wandered down to the main visitors lounge to read for a while before returning to intercept Dr. Tanaka on his rounds. At just before three, she took the elevator back up to Charlotte's room and noticed the doctor had just come out and was headed down the hall in the opposite direction. She hurried after him, "Doctor," she called out, "please, do you have a moment?"

Dr. Tanaka turned and smiled, "Good afternoon, Mrs. Fleming," he said, "we were wondering where you were. Your daughter seems to be a lot better today. We've given her more pain medication and she's much more comfortable."

"That's what I wanted to talk to you about, doctor. Is there any possibility we could get her transferred to a hospital in Toronto?"

"Well, she is doing a lot better but we have to make sure she's completely stable before we can move her. I would say it might be possible in a couple of days. I'd have to see if there's a bed available at St. Mike's or maybe Sunnybrook but the transport itself can be fairly expensive unless Mrs. Hamilton had private insurance coverage."

"How would she be transported?"

"Voyageur has a non-emergency service. I'll have one of the nurses get you some literature."

"Thank you so much. You've been so kind."

Dr. Tanaka did a quick nod of the head, "My pleasure, Mrs. Fleming," and with that he turned on his heel and proceeded down the hallway.

At five o'clock Nancy had spent almost another two hours talking to Charlotte. She didn't show her the printout from the Gazette but managed to discover Saint Raymond was where Julian's daughter had been buried. She also learned about the time Charlotte had been held captive at the cottage. She had not had any intention of letting Charlotte live through it all again while in such a fragile state but, once she began telling Nancy what had happened, she couldn't seem to stop. Nancy sat quietly listening and watching Charlotte's face intently. She appeared to be unemotional as she recounted the events except when it came to the part where she had almost been raped. That's when she began to tear up and Nancy reached out to hold her hand. When she had finished, Nancy got up and put her arms around her, "I'm so sorry you had to go through all that, darling, thank goodness he never really physically assaulted you."

Charlotte was just about to respond when they heard footsteps and she looked past Nancy and reached out for the bed rail. She looked terrified. Nancy released her and turned around. She had expected to see the nurse or someone bringing Charlotte's tray but she was wrong on both counts. Her eyes widened in shock because, in the dim light, she thought it was Julian. Then, when the man stepped forward she let out a cry, "Tyler, oh honey, is it really you?"

The tall young man, looking more and more like his father, grinned, "Yes, it's me, Nana."

He stopped when he reached her and gathered her into his arms, "Hi, how are you?"

Nancy kissed him on the cheek and held him at arm's length, "I'm all the better for seeing you but what on earth are you doing here?"

He leaned over the bed and rubbed Charlotte's shoulder, who had visibly relaxed, "I had to come and see Mom; I heard she was in the hospital."

Charlotte looked up at him, "You have no idea how happy I am to see you. When did you arrive?"

"I flew into Montreal a couple of hours ago and then came straight here."

"Who told you about the accident?"

"Alexa, of course, you know she can't keep anything to herself."

"I'm not so sure about that," Nancy remarked looking at Charlotte knowingly. "Anyway, did you come alone or did you bring Shelby with you?"

"I came alone as soon as I heard. I had to make sure you were all right, Mom. Alexa told me you were in a car accident and you had to have brain surgery. She said they cut out a piece of your skull."

Charlotte managed to grin, "Don't worry, honey, they put it back. I don't have a hole in my head."

"What were you doing here so far away from home?"

Nancy laid a hand on his arm, "Let's not tire your mother out, I can fill you in on all the details later. Where were you planning on staying tonight?"

"I hadn't really thought about it. I took a bus directly from the airport."

"Well, I suggest you go with me when I leave and we'll see if they have a vacant room where I'm staying. Were you planning on going home from here for a few days?"

"Yes, I want to see Dad and Alexa. I'm surprised they aren't here. Alexa said they were only here for one night."

Nancy glanced at Charlotte who looked back at her helplessly, "We'll talk about that later," she said. "We can go and get some dinner soon and I'll fill you in."

Tyler frowned, "It all sounds a bit mysterious."

"I know, dear, just try to be patient and let your mother get some rest. They should be bringing her something to eat soon and then we can leave."

Nancy hardly got the words out of her mouth when Charlotte's dinner arrived. Tyler stood quietly watching while his grandmother made sure his mother had everything she needed then remarked, "You're not really going to eat that are you, Mom."

Charlotte wrinkled her nose, "It doesn't look very appetizing, does it?"

"Yuk, no it doesn't."

"Now, now," Nancy intervened, "don't put your mom off her meal. She needs to eat to get her strength back."

Tyler shrugged, "Okay, sorry, Mom. Enjoy your dinner and Nana and I will go and get a hamburger or something."

Nancy rolled her eyes at Charlotte, "We'll see you tomorrow, bright and early. Try and get a good night's sleep."

"I will, Mom. Here, Tyler, come and give me a hug and take care of Nana."

Tyler chuckled, "I think Nana does a pretty good job of looking after herself."

After they left the hospital, they drove to Stephanie's, where Tyler ordered a cheeseburger and fries and Nancy ordered a club sandwich. When Tyler bit into his cheeseburger he let out a big sigh, "Wow," he mumbled with his mouth full, "I've been waiting for this."

Nancy grinned, "What do they feed you in London?"

"Fish and chips, shepherd's pie, bangers and mash; it's not that bad really, I just craved a good old Canadian hamburger."

They continued to chat about the Lewiston family and Shelby in particular and their plans for the future until Tyler finally said, "Okay, Nana, now we've exhausted that subject, how about telling me what's going on."

Nancy took a sip of water and cleared her throat, "I've been considering just how much to tell you and I realize you need to know the truth before you find out from someone else. I also think you're old enough to handle it but you'll need to think carefully before you pass judgement."

Tyler frowned, "It sounds rather ominous. I could tell Alexa was upset about more than mom's accident. What happened, Nana?"

Nancy opened her purse, pulled out the page from the Gazette and handed it to him, "I think you should read this first and then I'll explain."

Tyler scanned down the page and immediately noticed the photo of Julian. He gasped and started to shake, "It's Dad, and it's an obituary." He glanced up at his grandmother in shock.

Nancy reached over and took his hand, "It's not your dad, honey, read the name."

Tyler looked down again, "It says it's Julian Richards. I don't understand, he looks exactly like my dad."

"That's because he's your dad's twin brother. I think I'd better start at the beginning."

After half an hour, Tyler knew all, but the most intimate details, of the last few months. "I told you to think carefully before you pass judgement," she said. "Sometimes people make terrible mistakes in their lives and now you've suddenly become aware your mother isn't perfect. That doesn't mean she doesn't love you any less."

Tyler was quiet for a moment, "You know how I feel about Mom, Nana. She's always been there for me and now it's time for me to be there for her, but it's a lot to take in."

"I know, honey, and if you have any questions, I'll try and answer them."

"How does Alexa feel about all this?"

"She's upset but supportive. I think you both have to be."

"What about my dad?"

"Your dad's struggling. I'm not sure what he's thinking or feeling. I'm just praying he's able to forgive your mother and you can all come together as a family again."

Tyler shook his head, "I can't get over the fact he had a twin brother he didn't even know about. Come to think of it, he would have been my uncle. Poor Grandma Mary, is she doing any better now?"

"The last I heard, she was being sent home but she's still very weak. I believe Ray has already told her about Julian being killed. I just hope the news doesn't affect her recovery."

"I think I'll go and visit her when I get back to Toronto."

"That's a nice idea, Tyler. Actually, I want to be honest with you, I intended to go to the visitation for Julian tomorrow, just out of respect. Would you like to go with me?"

"Are you going to tell, Mom?"

"No, I don't think I should. She may not understand."

"I'm not sure I do either."

"Well, if I tell Mary I was there, it just might bring her some closure. As for Julian, I believe deep down he was a good person but he lost his way after his daughter died. When he found out about your dad, he felt he'd gotten the short end of the stick. He never really found out the true circumstances surrounding his birth."

Tyler looked deep in thought for a moment and then nodded, "Okay, Nana, I'd like to come with you but what will we tell Mom?"

"If you mean, how do we explain our absence? First of all, when were you planning on going to Toronto?"

"Well, I was thinking of going tomorrow afternoon if I can get a flight."

"That's perfect, honey. You shouldn't have any problem booking a flight with Porter for the early evening. The visitation is at three so we could visit Mom in the morning and then I'll drive you to Montreal. Once we get there, we can pay our respects and then I'll take you to Dorval."

"That's sounds like a good plan. I'll call the airline tonight."

Nancy motioned for the waitress, "We need to get out of here and see if there's a vacant room for you. If not, you may have to sleep on the floor in my room."

Tyler grinned, "I've slept in worse places, Nana."

Chapter Sixty-One

The next day, Nancy and Tyler spent most of the morning with Charlotte. She seemed apprehensive when her son walked into the room. She was aware her mother must have told him about the affair and wondered how he had reacted. When he walked up to the bed and kissed her gently on the cheek and then asked how she was, she reached out and grasped his hand, "I hope you don't think badly of me, Tyler."

"Mom," he responded squeezing her hand, "I love you. Nothing can change that. I'm not saying I condone what you did but Nana helped me to understand it."

Charlotte glanced up at Nancy and sighed, "Thanks, Mom."

"What I'm really concerned about," Tyler continued, "is what Dad's going to do now."

Charlotte shook her head, "I'm not sure. I think he's really hurting and he may not be able to forgive me. As for what will happen when I leave here, I can't even think about that right now."

Nancy stepped forward, "You shouldn't have to think about it, dear. You need to concentrate on getting well. I'm going to do my best to get you transferred out of here as soon as possible so, at least, you can be close to home and Alexa will be able to visit."

"That would be wonderful, Mom. I miss her so much but I'm so grateful you're here."

"Where else would I be?"

Tyler put his arm around his grandmother, "Nana is driving me to Montreal this afternoon. I'll be arriving in Toronto this evening and Dad's picking me up."

Charlotte frowned, "What did your father say when you called?"

"He said he was surprised when Alexa told him I was coming to see you but he also thought it would probably help a lot in your recovery. He seemed really pleased I'm able to spend time with him and my sister. He's planning to take a day off work tomorrow so we can do something special."

"I'm so glad, Tyler. How long do you think you'll be staying?"

"Probably only a few days but I hope I'll still be at home when you get moved back to Toronto."

"I hope so too. I've missed you a lot."

"Well, when you get better, Mom, maybe you should come and visit me in London."

Charlotte nodded, "I'd like that and Nana can come with me."

Tyler smiled, "Of course, you two would have a great time."

By two o'clock, after a quick lunch in the hospital cafeteria, Nancy and Tyler were well on their way to Montreal. It was only when they were approaching the outskirts of the city that Nancy realized it wouldn't be possible for Tyler to accompany her to the visitation. "I've just thought of something," she said. "You can't go inside the funeral home with me. Julian's aunt doesn't know anything about him being a twin and, if she sees you, your resemblance to her nephew is likely to raise all sorts of questions."

"Well, that's fine Nana, but won't she ask you who you are?"

Nancy hesitated for a moment, "I expect there'll be a lot of people from the Gazette there and obviously I can't fit in with that crowd. Maybe I can pretend I'm an old friend of Julian's mother. I don't expect his aunt would have known all of her friends."

"I suppose that sounds plausible. Perhaps I can do a little sightseeing while you're there."

"Do you have your license? If so, you can take the car and take a spin around Old Montreal for an hour or so."

"Hey, I like that idea, Nana. Yes, I have my license."

"Okay, that's the plan then. We should be at the funeral home by just after three and you can come back to pick me up at four."

When Nancy entered Blythe Bernier's, she was surprised at the number of people there. Nobody stopped her until she entered the actual viewing room, where she expected to see a closed casket but the casket was open. There were three men standing just inside the door and two women seated on chairs along one wall. One woman was quite young while the other looked to be in her seventies. She was tiny and dressed in black from head to toe with a string of pearls around her neck. She looked up as Nancy crossed over to the casket and stared down at Julian's face. He looked peaceful with no evidence of the violent death he had encountered. Nancy only hoped it had been instant. She had never been a religious person but she said a silent prayer asking God to let his soul rest in peace and then she stood silently thinking about the evening she had spent with him at her house. Suddenly she felt a movement beside her and turned to see the elderly woman smiling up at her, "Excuse me," she said in a whisper, "but I don't think we've ever met. I'm Elizabeth Ross, Julian's aunt."

Nancy extended her hand, "I'm pleased to meet you, Mrs. Ross," she said. "I'm Nancy Fleming, an old friend of your sister's."

The woman frowned, "I thought I knew all of Fiona's friends.

"Actually we were neighbours in Laval for a short time and then later we lost touch," Nancy lied. "I saw the obituary in the paper and I just had to come."

The woman smiled, "That's very kind of you. I'm afraid most of the other people here are from the Gazette and they only knew Julian as an adult. I suppose you must have known him when he was a child. He was such a special boy, so thoughtful and loving and he adored his mother."

Nancy was grateful when Julian's aunt began rambling on because she wasn't sure how she could continue with the deception. She had just begun to tune her out when she realized she had asked her a question, "I'm sorry. What did you say?" she said.

"I asked you if you would like a cup of tea. You must be tired of standing. There are refreshments in the other room."

"Thank you, I would like to sit down and tea would be lovely. Please accept my condolences, Mrs. Ross. It's been such a pleasure to meet you. Fiona used to talk about you a lot."

The woman beamed from ear to ear, "That's so nice to hear." She then turned to look back at Julian and her expression changed, "My only consolation is that he will be with her now."

Nancy reached over and patted her hand, "That's a sweet thought and I hope it's true." She then took one last glance at Julian and walked out of the room.

Three days later, Nancy watched as Charlotte was wheeled out of the front doors of the hospital on a stretcher and loaded into a Voyageur patient transfer vehicle. Dr. Tanaka had pronounced her medically stable and likely to remain so during the journey to Toronto. Nancy had the option of accompanying her but she needed to drive herself back home so she decided to leave immediately after collecting her belongings from The Netherdale. She hoped to arrive within an hour after Charlotte reached St. John's Rehab, where she was expected to remain for three to four weeks.

After all arrangements had been made for the transfer, Nancy had called Adam to let him know when Charlotte would be there but he seemed distant and more concerned with ensuring Nancy be reimbursed for any costs incurred. When she asked him if he intended to visit Charlotte, he was evasive but assured her both Tyler and Alexa were anxiously waiting to see their mother.

By the time Nancy arrived at St. John's, Charlotte was already settled in a bright sunny room overlooking a large green space surrounded by trees. "Hello, dear" she said, kissing Charlotte on the cheek, "how was the ride? Did they make you comfortable?"

Charlotte smiled, "I slept most of the way, Mom. What about you? You must be really tired."

Nancy pulled up a chair beside the bed, "I am a little but I have plenty of time to sleep later." Then, looking around her, she continued, "This is a very nice room and I see the only other bed is empty. Let's hope it stays that way so that you're able to get some peace and quiet."

"How long did you say I was going to be here?"

"Well, they told me it could be up to four weeks. You just need to work with the rehabilitation people and you'll be up and about in no time. I expect someone will be in to see you soon to tell you what to expect."

Charlotte sighed, "I wish I could just go home."

Nancy took hold of her hand, "Oh, honey, I wish you could too but I'm worried about what's going to happen between you and Adam."

"Does he know I'm here?"

"Yes, but I have a feeling he isn't coming to see you. I need to have a talk with him but he might tell me to mind my own business."

"What about Tyler and Alexa? Will they be here?"

Nancy's eyes lit up, "Yes, and I'm sure they'll be walking through the door any minute. I told them what time you'd be here but suggested they give you a couple of hours to settle"

"I don't know how to thank you for everything you've done for me, Mom. Why don't you go on home now? I bet you're dying to see Gypsy and Luna."

Nancy grinned, "Yes, I've missed those two little critters but I don't regret one moment I spent with you. Nothing is more important to me."

Tears began to well up in Charlotte's eyes, "Stop it," she said, "you're making me cry."

Nancy started to get up, "Well, that won't do will it? I'll take off before Tyler and Alexa arrive so you can have a nice visit with them. I'll just jot down the phone number here and then I can call you this evening."

Charlotte's rehabilitation lasted for just over three weeks. During that time, Nancy visited her every day and Alexa accompanied her on several occasions. Meanwhile, Tyler only managed to visit twice and then, after a tearful farewell, he returned to London. During the first week, Nancy had appeared unannounced at the Hamilton house and approached Adam about his intentions towards Charlotte. She was discouraged to learn he didn't feel able to deal with her betrayal but was concerned that she make a complete recovery for the sake of the children. "Are you saying you want a separation?" Nancy asked.

Adam shook his head, "I haven't considered a legal separation at this point but when Charlotte is ready to leave the rehab centre, I'll be moving out of here."

"Are you sure that's what you really want?"

"Hmm . . . . I never wanted any of this. I thought Charlotte and I had a solid marriage but I was wrong. Don't worry, Nancy, I'll make sure she's well looked after financially. She can stay in the house with Alexa and I'll just find somewhere else to live."

Nancy laid a hand on his arm, "I'm so sorry, Adam, I really am. You've been a good husband and no one can fault you for feeling the way you do but I wish you would reconsider."

Adam shook off her hand and walked towards the window. He gazed out at the garden and said in a gentle voice, "I can't do that. Tell Charlotte, when she comes home, I won't be here."

Nancy waited a week before relaying the conversation to Charlotte and discussing it with Alexa. Charlotte reacted with little emotion while Alexa was upset and bordering on the verge of anger. "Why can't Dad forgive her? Why does he have to move out?"

"Please don't be angry with your father, Alexa. This has been really hard on him. He didn't expect anything like this to happen. Maybe, one day, he'll feel differently but right now he can't even bring himself to speak to your mom."

Alexa made a sour face, "I think it sucks!"

Nancy chuckled, "I couldn't have said it better myself."

Charlotte did well in the rehab programme. There had been no more seizures and she progressed to walking with crutches by the time she was ready to go home. Nancy was committed to taking her back to St. John's for their out-patient back-on-track programme but she was worried about her spending most of the day alone. When she suggested moving in with her for a while, Charlotte was all for it but concerned about her mother's cats. "That would be lovely, Mom," she said, "but what about Gypsy and Luna? Perhaps you can bring them with you."

Nancy laughed, "Oh, sure, I can just see Zoe when those two show up on her territory. No, it's not a good idea. I'll just ask Carol to look after them and I'll drop over once a day to spend some time with them."

When they arrived at the house, it was eerily quiet. The only sign of life was Zoe, who darted down the hallway when she heard Charlotte awkwardly making her way through the front door on her crutches. Charlotte instinctively opened the closet door where the family always hung their coats and noticed everything belonging to Adam was missing, "I guess Adam's really moved out," she whispered.

Nancy took her arm, "Well, you were expecting it dear. Now let's get you settled. Would you like to go and lie down or would you prefer to sit up for a while in the family room."

"I think I'll sit up for a while," she answered. "Can you stay until Alexa gets home?"

"I can do better than that," Nancy replied guiding her towards the family room and settling her on the couch with her leg elevated. "I told you I was moving in and I hope you haven't changed your mind because all my stuff is in the car."

Charlotte raised her hand to her forehead, "Oh, dear, I think my memory is going. I'd forgotten all about that."

"Nonsense, you're just tired. I'm just going to stay until you're able to manage on your own. I'll be here day and night except for an hour every morning when I'd like to pop home and check on things."

Charlotte patted the seat beside her, "Sit down, Mom, I need to talk."

Nancy sat down and took Charlotte's hand, "What is it, dear? What can I do to help?"

"Well I've thought a lot about why I was so attracted to Julian. It wasn't because he looked like Adam; it was because he made me feel so special. I know now it wasn't real and he fooled me into thinking he was in love with me but I needed someone to pay attention to me. I used to love being a wife and mother but after Tyler left home and Alexa became more and more independent, I felt as though I wasn't needed any more. Even Adam seemed to grow a little more distant. He started working away from home a lot more and I spent so much time alone. Now, it looks like I'm really going to be alone and I have to find something to fill my life; something that gives me a purpose. I just don't know what that is, Mom."

"Being alone isn't all bad, Charlotte. You get to do anything you like, anytime you like and as for getting involved with something worthwhile, you need to think about the kinds of things you like to do. You love to read and you've enjoyed your job at the library. Maybe you can work there full time now."

Charlotte shook her head, "No, that isn't what I want to do."

"Well what about cooking? You're really good at baking and perhaps if you took a course and got some credits, maybe you could land a job as a chef in some fancy restaurant."

Charlotte couldn't help chuckling, "Oh boy, you've got a vivid imagination. Can you imagine me in one of those tall white hats and an apron?"

Nancy grinned, "As a matter of fact I can, but there are other areas you can explore. You like interior decorating, party planning and gardening. There are all sorts of areas you could get involved in."

Charlotte paused, "I do like party planning. Remember all the parties I planned for Tyler and Alexa and even some of the neighbours' children?"

"Yes, I do and there's no reason why you can't start charging people for your services. Come to think of it, Jodi is exposed to a lot of wealthy people in her job and she may be able to help get you started."

"Did I tell you she called me when I was at St. John's? She was on vacation with Rick in Italy for a month and just got back. She wants to come and see me this week."

When Alexa got home, she told Charlotte her father was staying with Sam and Eleanor until he found a place to rent and he would be in touch in the next few days. Nancy shrugged and muttered, "Too bad he couldn't tell you himself."

Later, after Nancy managed to put together a decent meal and both Alexa and Charlotte had even complimented her on her cooking, Alexa left to go to Hildy's house. It was then that Nancy decided to approach Charlotte about her financial position. Even though the house had been mortgage free for many years, she was concerned Adam was committed to providing her with enough money to pay all the bills and take care of Alexa's education. "As you know, I haven't spoken to Adam yet," Charlotte said, "but he's always been very generous so I don't think that will change. When I first started working at the library, he suggested I should keep every penny I earned and put it in a savings account in case I ever wanted to spend it on something really special. I know it's only been two days a week and they don't pay too much but over the last ten years I've saved a nice little nest egg. If there is a problem, I do have some funds to fall back on."

"I hope that isn't going to be necessary, Charlotte. This would be the opportune time to invest money in some kind of business. If you really want to break out on your own then you have a lot to consider. For example, if you want to be a party planner, then you're going to have to advertise, purchase supplies and so on. It will take a lot of organizing."

"It sounds a bit overwhelming, Mom, I'm not sure I can do it on my own."

"You don't have to, dear, I'm sure Jodi will help and I can help too. Not only can I invest a few dollars but in case you've forgotten, I was a graphic artist so I can do a lot of the advertising design for you."

Charlotte picked up Zoe, who had just appeared and was sniffing at her injured leg. "Well, as long as I have your support

I'd like to start making some plans. I could write down a list of ideas to start with."

Nancy felt elated as she watched Charlotte's face light up. She so desperately wanted her to feel she had a purpose in life beyond being a wife and mother and maybe she could even become a successful business woman.

Chapter Sixty-Two

The following weekend, Charlotte finally heard from Adam. It was Nancy who picked up the phone. "Good morning, Adam," she said cheerfully when she heard his voice. "It's good to hear from you. Would you like to speak to Charlotte, she's right here." She turned to Charlotte who was sitting at the kitchen table nursing a cup of coffee and looking at her uneasily. "It's for you."

Charlotte took the phone and, in almost a whisper, said, "Hello, Adam."

Nancy watched Charlotte's face as she listened, finally said, "Thank you, I'll see you tomorrow," and then seemed to crumple with her face in her hands.

Nancy put her arm around her shoulders, "What on earth did he say, dear?"

Charlotte shook her head and then looked up at her mother with tears in her eyes, "He just said he was staying at Sam's but would be moving into his own place next week. He wanted to sort out some financial arrangement and suggested he come here tomorrow at eleven to discuss it. It was like listening to a stranger, Mom."

Nancy sighed, "Adam's always been a proud man, dear. He's having a difficult time coming to terms with everything that's happened. I'm sure he feels he's been deceived by both you and his mother. He might be beginning to realize Mary was not to blame for depriving him of his brother but your affair with Julian is something he may never be able to forgive. I think it would be better if I wasn't here tomorrow when he arrives. It will give you two a chance to talk."

"I don't think Adam really wants to talk, Mom, he's probably going to come here with a list of what he is or isn't prepared to pay for."

"Maybe and maybe not but you need to be civil to one another. Try not to get too emotional, dear, even if he says something to upset you. I'll be at home so, as soon as he leaves, you can call me and I'll come back. Remember Jodie will be coming for dinner so I'll pick up some groceries on the way."

"I don't know what I'd do without you, Mom."

"Yes, and you're stuck with me until you can manage on your own."

The next morning, Nancy picked out an outfit for Charlotte, in preparation for Adam's visit. She came downstairs to the spare guest bedroom on the main floor where Charlotte had been sleeping and held out a long powder blue jersey skirt and a lacy white top. "I think this will be perfect," she said.

Charlotte rolled her eyes, "Mom, I don't need to get all dressed up."

Nancy stood with her hands on her hips and surveyed Charlotte in a pair of old grey sweat pants and matching top, "Nonsense. You can't see him looking like that and you need to put on some make-up."

Charlotte grudgingly agreed to change her clothes and apply some foundation and a little lipstick. Later, she had to admit she felt a lot better and when Alexa finally appeared close to ten o'clock, looking for something to eat, and told her she looked really cool she was pleased she had made the effort.

Nancy rushed Alexa through her breakfast, "Eat up young lady we don't want to be here when your father arrives."

Alexa frowned, "But I want to see my dad."

"Well you can see him some other time. Your mother needs some private time with him."

Alexa stared at her mother hoping she'd come to her defense but Charlotte just shook her head. Looking back at Nancy, she said, "Where am I supposed to go?"

"That's simple; you can come home with me. You can help me put some of my patio furniture away and spend some time with Gypsy and Luna. Later, we'll have some lunch and then go grocery shopping for dinner tonight with Jodie."

Alex's eyes lit up, "Jodie's coming here for dinner?"

"Yes, but after dinner, you'll have to make yourself scarce again so your mom can spend some alone time with her."

"That's no problem. Hildy and I are going to a movie tonight. Do you want to come with us?"

"Not if you're going to see one of your usual comedies or one of those awful sci-fi films."

Alexa giggled, "Sorry, Nana, but there are some aliens in this one."

"Hmmm . . . . That's what I thought. No thank you, dear, I'll find something else more interesting to do. Now hurry up and help me clear away the dishes and then we'll be leaving."

After Nancy and Alexa left, it was deathly quiet in the house. Nancy had left the front door unlocked so Charlotte wouldn't have to get up to open it. "I don't expect Adam will walk right in," she said. "When he knocks, just call out to him. He should be able to hear you."

Sure enough, at just after eleven there was a knock on the door and Charlotte, who was sitting on the couch in the living room at the front of the house, called out, "Come in." She held her breath as she heard the door open and close and then the sound of footsteps. A moment later, Adam peeked into the room, "Oh, there you are," he said without smiling.

Charlotte looked up at him and couldn't help thinking about Julian, "I won't get up if you don't mind," she said.

Adam glanced at the crutches leaning against the arm of the couch, "That's quite all right," he responded as he walked towards a wing chair near the window, "I'll just sit over here."

Charlotte waited until he was seated, "You're looking well," she said.

"You too, how is the physio coming along?"

"It's hard but I'm making progress. I'll be on crutches for a while but at least I can get around."

There was an awkward silence as Adam looked towards the door, "Where's Alexa?"

"She's gone with my mother to her house. Mom thought we should meet in private."

"I see. Well there isn't too much to talk about, Charlotte. I just wanted to apprise you of the financial arrangements."

Charlotte suddenly felt annoyed, "Apprise? Have you been discussing this with a lawyer, Adam? Why so formal?"

Adam stood up, "Look if we're going to get into an argument, I might as well leave. I can e-mail you the details."

Charlotte reached a hand out towards him, "I'm sorry. Please stay, I'd like to talk to you."

Adam ignored her hand but sat down again. "I'm going to be depositing money in our joint account every month and I won't be touching any of those funds. They are strictly for you to spend on food, clothes, gas or anything else you need. All of the other bills that come in, like hydro, insurance etc. I'd like you to send to Diane at the office. They'll all be taken care of."

"That's really generous of you, Adam, and I'm really grateful but now can we talk about us?"

Adam got up again, "There is no us, Charlotte, not any more. I don't want to talk about anything that's happened. I'm going to move on and I think you should too."

Tears started to well up in Charlotte's eyes, "I'm so sorry, I didn't mean to hurt you. I'll do anything to make it up to you."

Adam shook his head and started towards the door, "It's too late for that. I came to say what I had to say. Now I've done that, I'm leaving."

"Wait," Charlotte called out, "you could have told me all this on the phone. What did you really come here for?"

Adam turned back, "Honestly? I came to see for myself that you were all right. After all you are the mother of my children. I was also hoping to see Alexa but as she's not here I guess I'll see her one night next week."

Charlotte paused and then hung her head, "I suppose there's nothing else to say."

"No there isn't. I'm going now. If you need anything you can let me know. Goodbye, Charlotte."

"Goodbye, Adam," Charlotte whispered without looking up.

When Nancy and Alexa returned to the house at three o'clock, they found Charlotte fast asleep on the couch. They didn't want to wake her but Nancy was concerned she'd been there since they left and hadn't had anything to eat. Gently she shook her shoulder, "Charlotte dear, wake up its Mom."

She began to stir and slowly opened her eyes, "Oh, what time is it?" she muttered.

"It's just about three and I bet you haven't had lunch."

"I'm not hungry."

"You have to eat something to keep your strength up." Nancy turned to Alexa, who was watching from the doorway. "Alexa, please make your mom a sandwich and put the coffee pot on. Just make something simple because we'll be having dinner at six."

Alexa advanced into the room, "What did Dad say, Mom."

Charlotte looked at Nancy helplessly and then back at Alexa, "He just came to talk to me about our finances."

"Is he coming back home?"

Charlotte sighed, "No, I'm sorry, honey."

Alexa flounced out of the room, "This really sucks," she called out.

Nancy sat down beside Charlotte, "What happened, dear?"

Charlotte shifted awkwardly attempting to sit up straight, "He was all business just like I thought he would be. When I tried to talk about what happened, he just cut me off. I think he was here all of five minutes."

Nancy patted her hand, "What about the house and all the bills?"

"I don't have anything to worry about there. He's putting money in an account every month and I have to send all the bills to his office to be paid."

"Maybe you won't need to go back to the library when you've completely recovered and you'll be able to devote all your time to starting your own business. Much as I hate to say this, you really need to start thinking about your future without Adam."

"I know. I was thinking about it before I dozed off and I'd like to talk to Jodie about it later."

Nancy got up, "Great idea. Now, you sit tight and try and eat the sandwich Alexa's supposed to be making. We bought some potato gnocchi and I'm going to make a mushroom sauce with cream and white wine. With a simple salad, I think it will be a nice dinner."

Alexa walked into the room carrying a sandwich on a plate, "What about dessert, Nana?"

Nancy smiled, "Oh, I'm sure we can find something," she replied winking at Charlotte.

When Jodi walked into the living room, looking particularly attractive in a black sweater dress offset by a large silver pendant, she took one look at Charlotte and immediately ran over and threw her arms around her. During dinner, most of the talk centered round the trip she had just taken with Rick to Italy and when Charlotte mentioned starting her own business, Jodi was full of helpful ideas and even thought she might invest some of her own funds. Adam's name wasn't mentioned, that is, until Nancy and Alexa left them alone for the evening.

Charlotte confided every detail of her affair with Julian and ended up crying on Jodi's shoulder when she told her about Adam's visit earlier. Jodi was sympathetic but, like Nancy, tried to put everything in perspective. "You have to look at it from his point of view, Charlotte. It must have been quite a blow to his ego and then to find out Julian was his twin; that must have been pretty devastating."

"I know," Charlotte responded wiping her eyes. "Mom said the same thing."

Jodi smiled, "Thank goodness for your mom. How much longer will she be staying with you?"

"I'm not sure. She insists I have to be able to look after myself before she goes back home."

"What about Alexa, can't she help?"

"She's at school all day and it's still a bit difficult hobbling around on these crutches, plus I need Mom to drive me back and forth to physio."

"Well, considering what you've been through I think you're doing really well and while you're not very mobile, you can still work on this new venture you've been considering."

Charlotte brightened up, "It sounds really exciting, Jodi. I think I can make it work but there's so much to think about. I thought I'd just start off with children's parties and if I'm successful, I can branch out a bit."

"Whoa, slow down," Jodi cautioned, "let's just concentrate on one thing at a time. I've already given you a few ideas and I can come back one day during the week, when it's not so late, and we can make a list of everything you'll need."

"That would be wonderful. I'm not going anywhere except to physio. Phone me tomorrow and in the meantime I'll find out when my appointments are."

Jodi stood up from the table, "Done, my friend, I'll call and be back in a day or two." Charlotte began to rise from her chair but Jodi motioned to her to sit back down, "Don't get up, I can see myself out. Tell your mom again, it was a lovely dinner." She leaned over and gave Charlotte a hug, "Take care of yourself and try not to worry. Everything's going to be okay."

Charlotte held onto her for a moment, "Thank you, you're a good friend. I love you."

"Love you too," Jodi answered as she pulled away then blew a kiss as she left the room.

Chapter Sixty-Three

Later that night, Nancy arrived back just before Alexa. Finding Charlotte already on her way to bed, she asked about her visit with Jodi and then mentioned she would like some time for herself the next day. Being Sunday, Alexa would be there to look after her.

"I really don't need looking after," Charlotte remarked. "Is there something special you wanted to do?"

Nancy had been reluctant to tell her but decided truth was better than a lie, "I want to go and see Mary," she said.

"Why, I thought she was at home and a lot better?"

Nancy sighed, "I want to tell her about Julian. I think she deserves to hear all about the child she lost."

Charlotte's face clouded over, "Are you going to tell her how he abducted me and almost raped me too?"

"No, I'm not," Nancy answered emphatically. "For all I know, she may have already heard about the abduction from Adam or Ray. I want to let her know about the other side of Julian. I want her to know about the love he had for his daughter and the woman who adopted him. I want her to know her son wasn't all evil."

Charlotte shook her head vehemently, "Why do you have to do this, Mom, after what he did to me?"

Nancy took both of Charlotte's hands in her own, "Think about your own son, Charlotte. Think how you would feel if everyone was telling you Tyler was no good. Wouldn't you desperately want to hear something positive about him; after all you gave birth to him?"

Charlotte paused before responding and then, as she felt the tension start to leave her body, she said, "I guess you're right, Mom. I keep forgetting how Julian was taken away from Mary. I'll make sure Alexa is home with me tomorrow."

The next morning, before leaving for Napanee, Nancy called Tom to update him and tell him she was on her way to visit Mary. Tom understood why she wanted to go but was concerned about her driving all that way and back in the rain. "It's coming down pretty heavily here," he remarked. "Maybe you should wait until it clears up."

Nancy laughed, "I've been driving in a lot worse than this," she replied. "You worry too much."

It was almost three hours later, when Nancy arrived at the farm. There had been an accident on the 401 which held her up for a while but the rain finally stopped just as she passed through Belleville. Ray was coming out of the house when he saw her pull into the driveway and came forward to greet her with Maggie running behind him, her tail wagging with excitement.

Nancy got out of the car, greeted Ray with a hug and then bent down to pet Maggie. "I probably should have called before I came out, I hope you don't mind me just showing up," she said.

"Not at all, it's good to see you and I know Mary will be glad of some company."

"How is she?" Nancy asked as she followed him into the house.

"She's doing quite well. She's a bit tired but that's to be expected and she's not too happy about the diet she's on but she needs to lose a bit of weight."

Ray motioned Nancy into the living room where Mary was lying on a couch dressed in a robe and partially covered with a blanket. Despite the fact she was still overweight, she looked frail but when she saw Nancy her face lit up and she attempted to get off the couch. Nancy rushed over to stop her and kissed her on the cheek. "Hello, Mary," she said, "I thought it was time I came to visit you."

Mary took Nancy's hand, "I wish I'd known you were coming, I would have gotten dressed."

"Nonsense, you're fine just the way you are. How are you feeling?"

"Oh, I'm a bit weary but getting stronger every day. I was hoping to take a little walk this morning but it was raining."

Ray, who was standing in the doorway, interrupted, "Excuse me ladies but I have some work to do so, if you don't mind, I'll leave you to chat."

"Take Maggie with you," Mary called out as Ray turned to leave. She waited until he had gone and said, "He's been a godsend. He's been waiting on me hand and foot."

"That's lovely to hear," Nancy remarked as she sat down opposite Mary.

"How have you been?" Mary asked.

"Me? Oh, I'm fine but things have been a little difficult because of Charlotte's accident."

"Yes, I heard all about it. Adam called Ray right after it happened and then he came here himself two days ago. He told me he'd moved out of the house."

Nancy nodded, "I wish that wasn't the case but it is. Maybe you don't want to talk about it, Mary, but how much did he tell you?"

Mary bowed her head and then looked up again. Nancy could see the tears beginning to form in her eyes, "I don't think I do want to talk about it, if you don't mind."

"That's all right, I understand, at least I think I do. You lost your son twice didn't you?"

At that, Mary seemed to crumple and started to sob uncontrollably. Nancy got up, squeezed in beside her and put her arm around her. "Go ahead," she said, "let it all out."

Mary continued to cry for a moment but finally pulled herself together, "I never really even saw him," she whispered. "Now he's dead and I'll never get the chance."

"I know. I'm so sorry, Mary. I can't imagine what you must be feeling."

Mary looked Nancy straight in the eyes, "Is it true what Adam told me about him. Did he really have an affair with Charlotte?"

"Yes, I'm afraid it's true but let's not talk about that. I want to tell you about the son you would have been proud of."

Mary frowned, "What do you know about him?"

"Well, he came to my home once and I learned quite a bit about his life and, I haven't mentioned this to anyone else except Tyler, who happened to be with me; I went to the visitation after he died."

Mary gasped, "You mean you actually went to his funeral?"

"No, not the burial; it was a little too far away but I went to the funeral home and I met his Aunt Beth. I believe she was the only close living relative. I learned a lot from her too."

Mary grasped Nancy's hand, "Tell me about my son," she said.

Nancy decided it was time to tell her about Emma and, when she'd finished, Mary began to cry all over again, "So, I had a granddaughter and now she's gone too. Damn that Jimmy I hope, wherever he is, he rots in hell for what he did."

Nancy managed to calm her down and, while fetching her some water from the kitchen, she bumped into Ray and Maggie again. "I was getting a bit peckish," Ray said. "How about I make us all lunch?"

Nancy graciously declined claiming she had to get back to Toronto and ten minutes later she was on the highway heading towards the nearest diner. She just needed a break from all the drama.

Chapter Sixty-Four

By mid-November, Charlotte was free of her cast and a lot more mobile, but still having to use crutches. Nancy, although having moved back to her own house, was still popping in every weekday, when Alexa was in school. She needed to make sure Charlotte was managing and she continued to drive her to her physio appointments. At least once a week, Jodie joined them and they slowly began to prepare a business plan for their new venture. It was Nancy who came up with the name, Rainbow Dreams Party Planners, and she was full of ideas on marketing, including setting up a web site. Charlotte wasn't comfortable with her mother investing any money; she felt she had done enough without taking any risk with her savings. Meanwhile, Jodi had made a significant loan at a very low interest rate, with no strings attached, to ensure Charlotte had enough start-up capital.

One week before Christmas, prior to the launch of Rainbow Dreams, strictly by word-of-mouth, Charlotte got a call from the mother of one of Alexa's friends asking if she could plan a reception for her son Isaac's bar mitzvah at the end of January. Charlotte had never even attended a bar mitzvah and had no idea what was expected or how much to charge but with Nancy's help, and a lot of research, she managed to develop several ideas that were not only acceptable to her very first client but so impressive, she told Charlotte, if all went well she could expect to be hearing from some of her friends and neighbours.

Charlotte's preoccupation with starting up her business, as well as planning her first party, helped to take her mind off her physical limitations. Occasionally, as a result of her head injury, she would get a dull, persistent headache but she continued to work through it knowing it was not uncommon and might be a condition she would have to deal with for several years. She had also managed to put the upcoming holiday season out of her mind, mostly because she had no idea how to handle it.

Adam had moved into a one bedroom rental unit on Queen's Quay with a view of the lake. Alexa had been there a number of times and thought it was cool, while Charlotte had only heard from Adam once since the time he had been to see her. He wanted to get Tyler's address in London so he could send him a package. Charlotte didn't even ask him what the package was for; she just assumed it was an early Christmas gift. It was Alexa who brought up the subject of the holidays one morning when Nancy was there, "What are we doing this year?" she asked.

Charlotte looked at her mother and shrugged, "I don't know, honey, has your father mentioned anything to you."

"Yes, he said he was spending Christmas Day with Ray and Grandma Mary and then on Boxing Day he's coming back to visit with Sam and Eleanor. He did ask me if I wanted to go to the farm with him but I told him I wanted to stay with you."

"That's lovely to hear, Alexa, but if you'd really like to go with your father and see Grandma Mary, I won't be upset. Your Nana and I will just go out somewhere for dinner."

"No, Mom, I'd rather stay here. Hildy wants me to go over there in the afternoon for an hour or two but we can still go out later if you like."

Nancy nodded, "It sounds perfectly fine to me. It will be nice to have a simple holiday without all the fuss and bother. Your mother isn't up to cooking a fancy dinner and you know

I'm not so great in the kitchen. I'll find us a really good place to eat and we'll have an enjoyable time, just the three of us."

"Don't you have any plans at all to see your father over the holiday?" Charlotte asked.

"Yes he wants to take me to lunch at Canoe on Christmas Eve. Hildy's been there and she says it's really great. You can see right across the lake on a clear day."

"I've been there," Nancy remarked. "I think you'll enjoy it."

Right at that moment Charlotte's cell phone rang and she was surprised to see the caller was Adam. She answered with some hesitation, "Hello, Adam, how are you?"

Nancy and Alexa stood staring at her while she sat listening to whatever Adam was saying, nodding her head and eventually saying, "Thank you, I appreciate you thinking of me. I'll ask Mom if she can drive me over to see it. I have Sam's number here so I can call and find out when it's convenient." There was more silence until she continued. "Yes, I hope you have a good holiday too. Alexa is looking forward to having lunch with you. As a matter of fact, she's right here. Would you like to speak to her?" After she said goodbye, a moment later, she handed the phone to Alexa who immediately exited the room.

"What was that all about?" Nancy asked.

"Well, Alexa told him all about the business venture and he knew I needed another car so he thought he had a really good deal for me. Apparently, Sam's getting Eleanor a brand new Trailblazer and she's selling off her three-year-old Ford Explorer. It would have enough room to transport the party supplies and she only wants about twelve-thousand for it. Adam said it was in immaculate condition and a real bargain."

"He's right, it is a bargain. I wonder why she's selling it."

Charlotte chuckled, "I don't think you've ever met Eleanor. It's a good thing Sam and Adam have been successful because I don't think Sam would have been able to satisfy Eleanor's expensive tastes. Don't get me wrong, she's a nice enough person but a little extravagant."

"Then why isn't she driving something a little flashier?"

"Oh, she has another car. I think it's an Audi or something similar. Anyway it was good of Adam to think of me."

Nancy nodded, "Yes it was. He seems to be coming around. At least the two of you can be civil to each other."

Unlike past holidays when Charlotte was always busy decorating the house, baking and shopping for gifts, Christmas almost seemed like any other time of the year. Just a dusting of snow fell on Christmas Eve causing a thin blanket on trees and rooftops and enough to show the imprint of Zoe's paws on the lawn but not enough to remain on the streets overnight.

At lunch, on Christmas Eve, Adam presented Alexa with a Pandora bracelet and later Nancy gave her gift certificates to Cineplex, Chapters and Sephora's. She had long ago given up traipsing around the stores looking for gifts and even preferred receiving gift certificates herself. Meanwhile Charlotte promised, once she was back to normal, she would make up for not being able to shop for presents during the holiday and still feeling somewhat guilty, she insisted on paying for Christmas Day dinner at the Windsor Arms.

New Year's was another quiet affair, especially for Charlotte. Tom had invited Nancy to a dinner and dance at the Hamilton Convention Centre. At first, she was reluctant to go because it meant staying overnight but Tom graciously offered to put her up at the Holiday Inn and she had no need to feel compromised. Alexa would also be away from home as she had been invited to a party at her friend Sunny's house along with Hildy and some other schoolmates. She hadn't seen Sunny since her family had moved north of the city to Aurora. Hildy's father was driving them there and picking them up the next morning. This left Charlotte completely alone, except for Zoe and both Nancy and Alexa were concerned about leaving her. She insisted they go and enjoy themselves and claimed Jodi and Rick were popping in for a quick drink before heading out to celebrate with Rick's friends.

That night when the clock struck twelve, Charlotte was already in bed thinking about everything that had happened in the last few months and contemplating the future. Where would she be at the same time next year?

Chapter Sixty-Five

By mid-March, Rainbow Dreams was already becoming well known in the Rosedale area and Charlotte was apprehensive about the amount of promotional material Nancy was planning. She wasn't sure how much business she would be able to handle. The bar mitzvah had been such a success that, the following week, she received requests for three birthday parties and a baby shower. She had still not fully recovered from her accident and even though she'd dispensed with her crutches, she was not free of pain in her leg and tired easily. Jodi tried to help out whenever she had a spare hour or two and Alexa even did her best to help when she wasn't out with her friends, but it was Nancy who was there for her every step of the way and who seemed to be enjoying the challenge.

Once Charlotte was able to start driving, she began to feel independent again. The Explorer had proved to be exactly what she needed to shop for, and transport, all of the various items she needed. Soon one corner of the garage was filled with boxes of balloons, decorations and party favours. With Nancy's help, she began to develop themes such as a Cinderella party or a Sesame Street party and for older children, a Rock Star party. For the first time in her life, except for her experiments in the kitchen, she suddenly realized she had imagination and it was exciting despite the toll it took on her physically.

She only had one more face-to-face interaction with Adam. They talked on the phone two or three times about issues concerning Alexa or financial matters, such as minor repairs needed in the house, but anything personal was off-limits. One evening he called to ask if he could come over the next morning to pick up his golf equipment as he was planning a four-day trip to Myrtle Beach with Sam and a client. Charlotte had trouble sleeping that night and was anxious when she got up at just after seven. She took extra care with her make-up, put on a pair of jeans and a blue mohair sweater, which complimented her colouring, and used a curling iron to turn her usually straight hair into a mass of loose waves. Looking in the mirror, she felt a lot more confident and began to think about what Nancy had suggested on a number of occasions. She needed to update her wardrobe and take more care with her appearance. Throughout her marriage, the only time she'd spent a lot of money on herself was when she was seeing Julian. As soon as the thought came into her head, she felt guilty but she also realized how good it had made her feel to dress up in some of the latest fashions and she decided to go shopping the very next day.

When Adam arrived, she noticed a distinct change in him. He was wearing a tan leather jacket over a polo neck sweater, his hair was longer and he had a trace of stubble on his chin. Again her thoughts immediately turned to Julian and she felt as though she had a lump stuck in her throat when she opened the door. It was all she could do to say, "Good morning, come in. I just made coffee."

Adam hesitated before replying, "Well I was just planning on picking up my golf bag but I guess I can stay for a few minutes."

Charlotte was conscious of his eyes studying her as she walked down the hallway into the kitchen and she needed to break the tension. "Is it very cold out?" she asked.

"No actually it's quite comfortable. It's supposed to rain later but I think they've got it all wrong again."

When they entered the kitchen, Charlotte motioned for him to sit down and then poured some coffee into a mug and handed it to him. "There's cream on the table," she said.

"Yes, I can see that," he remarked, making her feel foolish.

Charlotte remained standing with her back against the kitchen counter, "When are you going to Myrtle Beach?"

"On Saturday, we'll be gone until Wednesday morning."

"Who's looking after the office with both you and Sam away?"

"Diane's more than capable of taking care of things."

"I see; it's nice that you're able to get away for a few days."

There was an awkward silence for a few moments and then Adam said, "You look nice, Charlotte, how are you feeling?"

Charlotte nodded, "I feel good except for a bit of pain in my leg and I get tired easily."

"Alexa tells me your party planning business if really taking off. I'm pleased for you."

"Thank you. It's been a lot of hard work but my mom's really helped me a lot. I couldn't have done it without her."

"You're lucky to have her."

"What about your mom, how's Mary?"

"She's a lot better considering what she's been through both physically and emotionally."

Charlotte sensed a change in Adam's mood and she was afraid of what he might say next so she decided to change the subject. "Aren't you going into work today?"

Adam glanced at his watch and stood up, "Yes, as a matter of fact I am and I should get going."

A few minutes later, she breathed a sigh of relief as she watched him load his golf clubs into the trunk of his car, back out of the driveway, and turn onto Highland. Why did she feel like she had been given a reprieve?

The very next day, Charlotte walked through the doors of Holt Renfrew with every intention of buying a new wardrobe but she hadn't considered the cost of shopping in such a high end store. After checking the price tags on several articles of clothing, she was just about to leave when a red wool jacket, in one of the in-store boutiques, caught her eye. Just for fun, she decided to try it on and immediately fell in love with it. The saleswoman took full advantage of her prospective client and by the time Charlotte walked back out onto Bloor Street she was carrying two very large shopping bags containing, the red jacket, a pair of tan leather pants, a cream angora sweater and a jersey dress in a shade of green she just couldn't resist. She didn't even want to think about the moment she saw the final bill and she still needed shoes and a new purse. That evening, after she had modelled her new clothes and was showered with compliments by both Nancy and Alexa, she remarked, "Thank you, but I have no idea when and where I'm going to wear them."

It was ironic that, two weeks later, just before the end of March, Charlotte received a phone call from Tyler giving her the perfect opportunity to show off her new clothes. He started off the conversation with his usual banter and then, just as she thought he was running out of news, he said, "Mom, I've got something to tell you and I know it will be a bit of a shock but I hope you'll be happy for me."

Charlotte felt her hand start to tremble, "What is it, Tyler?"

"Shelby and I are getting married, Mom."

Charlotte sank down onto the nearest chair, "What do you mean? You're way too young to get married."

There was silence on the other end of the line and Charlotte was just about to speak again when Tyler whispered, "Shelby's pregnant."

Charlotte took in a deep breath and then exhaled, "Oh, my goodness. How far along is she?"

"She's only six-weeks but we want to get married right away before she really starts to show."

"Are you sure this is what you want, honey?"

"Yes, Mom, I love her. We always planned to get married one day. It's just going to happen earlier than expected,"

"Do you think you're ready to take on the responsibility of a family? What about Shelby's parents; what do they think about this situation?"

"I know I'm ready; the Lewistons' aren't exactly thrilled but they're coming around and they've given us their blessing. We're already planning the wedding for the end of next month. We're getting married on April 30th at Gibson Hall and I want you to be there with Alexa and Nana."

Charlotte could hardly believe what she was hearing, "Tyler, that's just four weeks from now. Why didn't you let us know sooner?"

"We only found out ten days ago that Shelby was pregnant and when we decided to get married right away, Mrs. Lewiston wanted it to be in a church but at such short notice it was impossible. Dr. Lewiston managed to book us into the Garden Room at Gibson Hall for the ceremony and we'll be having the reception there too. Please say you'll come, Mom."

Charlotte sighed, "What about your father are you inviting him too; and what about Grandma Mary and Ray?"

"Of course I want Dad to come. I know it might be a bit awkward for you but I want you both there. As for Grandma, if she's well enough I'd like her to come, and Ray as well."

Charlotte hesitated, "This is all a bit of a shock, Tyler. I think you're too young to get married but I don't suppose there's anything I can do to change your mind."

"No, there isn't. I told you, I love Shelby and I can't wait for you to meet her."

They continued to chat about all the arrangements that had been made for the wedding and Tyler suggested a number of places where the family could stay in London. When Charlotte finally put the phone down, she remained sitting for several minutes. Eventually she had to admit she was excited about seeing Tyler get married and finally visiting the city he had chosen to make his home.

Chapter Sixty-Six

Two days before the wedding, Charlotte found herself transfixed by the sight below her. They were coming in for a landing at Heathrow and she could just make out Tower Bridge and the Houses of Parliament. Nancy was almost draped across her and craning her neck to look out of the window, "Oh, my," she remarked, "look at that. There's the London Eye."

Alexa was sitting with Adam, three rows behind them and both just as mesmerized by the view. "Dad, can you see the palace?" Alexa asked excitedly. "We have to go there. Maybe the Queen will be home."

Adam chuckled, "Sure, we can go and take a look but I don't think you'll be seeing the Queen."

It had been awkward when he met up with Charlotte at the airport in Toronto but he helped with the luggage and spent most of the time talking to Nancy, while they were waiting to board. "It's too bad your mother and Ray couldn't come," she remarked.

"Yes, it is," he replied, "but she gets tired easily and she's nervous about flying. By the way, why didn't you ask that gentleman friend of yours to come along?"

Nancy frowned, "He's just that; a friend and nothing more. Besides that he doesn't know the family."

Adam nodded, "I understand. You're really much better off on your own."

"I hope that's not how you feel, Adam," she said but didn't get to hear his response because, in the next instant, their flight was called.

Despite, taking the express train to Paddington Station which only took fifteen minutes, it was almost eleven at night by the time they stepped down onto the platform and walked out through the gates. With the time change, they had no reason to be tired but it had still been a long day and they were anxious to get to the hotel. Dr. Lewiston had suggested to Tyler that it would make more sense to allow his family a chance to unpack and get some rest. Although Tyler was itching to pick them up, he reluctantly agreed it would be better if they all met the next day for brunch. Charlotte was a little disappointed when he called her a week earlier and told her he wouldn't be at the station but, once they arrived, she was grateful they were able to settle in for the night and not have to socialize. They took a taxi to the Marriott on Grosvenor Square, where Dr. Lewiston had arranged accommodation for them. Adam was booked into a single room while Charlotte, Alexa and Nancy were booked into a large suite with two four-poster beds and a pull-out couch. When they walked through the door, Alexa gasped, "Oh, my goodness, look. How cool is this?" she exclaimed and proceeded to run around looking into the closet and the bathroom and eventually exiting through a pair of patio doors leading to an outdoor terrace.

Charlotte grinned at Nancy as she watched her daughter, "I think she's going to like it here," she said.

Nancy looked around the room, "It's pretty nice, to say the least. I'm glad Shelby's father's footing the bill. This must cost a fortune."

"I know, but he insisted so let's just be grateful and enjoy it." She started to place her suitcase on one of the luggage racks and called out to Alexa, "Come on in, Alexa, and start unpacking. We need to get some sleep."

Less than an hour later, Nancy was tucked under the covers in one of the beds while Charlotte and Alexa were in the other. They had already said goodnight to each other when Alexa whispered, "I hope Zoe's okay, Mom."

Nancy didn't wait for Charlotte to respond, "She'll be fine," she called out. "When I took her over to my place, Gypsy and Luna just sniffed at her and then walked away. Mrs. Walker will be checking on them three times a day so don't you worry about her."

Alexa rolled over into a fetal position, "Okay, Nana, sleep well."

"You too, honey," Nancy replied and closed her eyes but it was a long time before she fell asleep. She couldn't believe she was actually in London.

The next morning, they were all waiting in the lobby of the hotel when Tyler walked through the door. After much hugging and kissing, he walked them out to the street where Dr. Lewiston was sitting curbside in his silver Bentley. He jumped out when he saw them approaching and shook everyone's hand, welcoming them to London and ushering them into the car. Nancy was especially impressed by his exceptional manners and rather taken with his looks. He reminded her of Jeremy Irons, her favourite actor. Charlotte noticed how her mother kept staring at the doctor and she couldn't help smiling and wondering what his wife was like. When they arrived at the terraced house on Granville Square, it didn't take long to find out. Diana Lewiston was tall and slim with almost white hair swept back into a French twist. She was what most people would describe as a handsome woman and usually attracted attention when she walked into a room. She welcomed the visitors with open arms and was anxious to introduce them to Shelby. Tyler went to fetch her from her room where she was nervously waiting and when he returned, Charlotte was enchanted. She looked almost exactly like the girl she had seen in the photograph except that she had curled her long ash blond hair and was even prettier. Within five minutes of meeting each other, Shelby and Alexa were off in a far corner of the living room chattering away as though they were old friends while

David Lewiston was mixing cocktails to serve to his guests and his wife was taking them on a tour of the house.

Brunch was served by a housekeeper and consisted of lobster bisque soup, salad Nicoise and Dover sole accompanied by new roast potatoes and asparagus. As each course was placed before her, Alexa looked at Nancy and rolled her eyes and Nancy looked back, with a slight shake of her head. None of them were used to the formality and Alexa, in particular, was feeling a little uncomfortable.

Tyler was very much aware of the situation between his parents and had gone out of his way to ease any awkwardness. After brunch, along with Dr. Lewiston, he took his father on a sightseeing tour of the city, concentrating on the architecture which he knew would be of the most interest. Meanwhile, Diana Lewiston, had arranged to take Charlotte, Nancy and Alexa on a Thames river cruise and suggested that, on the following day, they might like to take the hop-on-hop-off bus and tour several of the historic landmarks, such as The Tower, St. Paul's, and Buckingham Palace. "You mean we can really go inside the palace?" Alexa asked.

"Yes, but only to see the state rooms. No one is allowed in the private quarters."

"Oh, that sucks," Alexa remarked.

Diana frowned, "Excuse me?"

Nancy grinned, "She means that's not so good."

"I see," Diana responded, "I don't think I've heard the expression before."

Alexa shrugged, "I thought everyone knew what it meant. By the way, can Shelby come with us tomorrow?"

"No, I'm afraid not. She's too busy getting ready for the wedding. You won't see her now until the rehearsal dinner tomorrow night."

"Will the dinner be at your house?" Alexa asked.

"No, it's being held at the St. James Club. My husband is a member. Only family are invited, so you'll be meeting my brother Gerald, his wife Karen, my nephew Reid and also my sister Cynthia. David's parents will be joining us too. Oh, and there will be one more guest, Shelby's closest friend, Caroline. She's Shelby's maid-of-honour."

"We'll look forward to meeting them all," Nancy said graciously.

The next day, after visiting all the places Diana had suggested as well as two or three others, the three women were exhausted and happy to rest up for an hour before taking a shower and getting ready for the rehearsal dinner. "I wonder where Dad was all day," Alexa remarked.

"Tyler said they were going to go to the Old Bailey and then they were driving to Canterbury. Your dad wanted to see the cathedral; I think Tyler said it was originally built sometime in the six hundreds."

"You're kidding, that's pretty old." Alexa remarked.

"Yes," Nancy responded, "and if you don't let me have a nap, I'll be feeling pretty old too."

Chapter Sixty-Seven

The rehearsal dinner went off without a hitch. Charlotte was especially pleased because she was seated next to Shelby and it didn't take long for her to understand why Tyler had fallen in love with her. She only wished they wouldn't be living so far away. Meanwhile Nancy was in her element talking to Shelby's father and Alexa had obviously taken a shine to Shelby's cousin, Reid. Every now and again, Charlotte would glance over at Adam, who was seated at the other end of the table, but most of the evening, he was engrossed in a conversation with Diana's brother. It was obvious that Tyler had a hand in the seating arrangements and she knew he meant well but she would have liked to have been closer to Adam. Maybe, at the wedding reception, things would be different.

The ceremony in the Garden Room at Gibson Hall brought tears to Charlotte's eyes. Tyler looked especially handsome in his charcoal grey suit and silver tie while Shelby almost took her breath away when she appeared in the doorway, on the arm of her father, in a strapless tulle wedding gown with lace embroidery and a single gardenia in her hair. Tyler stood transfixed as his best man, Reid, stood beside him while Caroline, wearing a simple rose chiffon gown stood smiling as Shelby approached. Several other family members had driven into the city to attend the wedding, along with friends and colleagues of Dr. Lewiston but, in all, Nancy figured the guests only numbered about fifty. She found it to be a refreshing change after the numerous over-the-top weddings she had attended in her lifetime and remarked on it to Charlotte as they were seated at a table adjacent to that of the wedding party. It was close to six o'clock after all the formal photographs had been taken and Alexa was complaining that her stomach was rumbling. Charlotte was just about to make a comment when she noticed Adam walking towards the table. He paused for a brief moment and then said, "I guess I'm sitting here."

Nancy leaned over and picked up the place card to her left, "Yes, I guess you are, Adam."

Alexa grinned, "Hi, Dad, did you see Tyler? He looked really cool."

Adam sat down, "He sure did but he kind of mumbled his vows."

"He was probably real nervous. I know I will be when the time comes."

"Well, I hope that's a long way off, young lady."

Alexa chuckled, "Don't worry, Dad, I may never get married. Looks like a lot of hard work to me."

Charlotte began to feel uncomfortable and wanted to change the subject. She looked around her to see if any of the other tables were being served with food or wine, "I wish I could get a drink," she said.

"Me too," Alexa remarked, "and I wouldn't mind a cheeseburger right now."

Nancy shook her head in disgust, "You are not going to get a cheeseburger here. I already saw the menu and I know they're having lamb."

Alexa groaned, "Oh no, is that all they're having? Maybe I'll get drunk first. Can I have a glass of wine, Dad?"

Adam looked over at Charlotte who merely shrugged her shoulders, "I guess it's okay but only one glass. Do you hear me?"

Alexa looked like the cat that had swallowed the canary, "Awesome, Dad, thanks."

Later, after the traditional first dance by the bride and groom, Shelby pulled her father onto the dance floor and Tyler graciously led Diana onto the floor too. Charlotte had no idea what was about to happen next but, moments later, both couples split apart and she found herself in Tyler's arms while Adam was just a few steps away with Shelby. She felt very conspicuous dancing in front of so many people and was relieved when Tyler released her, but her relief was short lived because suddenly she found herself in Adam's arms and she couldn't even look at him. She didn't realize it at first but they were playing, Lady in Red, a song that had special meaning to both of them. Why did she suspect this had all been planned? They navigated the dance floor from one end to the other twice then Adam leaned back so that he could look her in the eyes, "Do you remember this song?" he asked.

She nodded, "Yes, of course."

"You were wearing a red dress the night I met you."

"Actually it was on our second date."

Adam frowned, "Was it? Anyway, you looked beautiful, just like you do tonight. I like your gown, that shade of blue really suits you."

Charlotte had no idea how to react except to say, "Thank you."

They continued to dance until the music stopped and then Adam led her back to the table and excused himself. Nancy was just returning from dancing with David Lewiston and was anxious to know what had transpired between them. She didn't even get the chance to sit down before Charlotte shook her finger at her, "Did you set that up, Mom?"

Nancy looked taken aback, "Certainly not, I don't know what you're talking about."

"Charlotte sighed, "Never mind. Where's Alexa?"

"She's talking with Reid. I think she's taken a shine to him. If we're not careful, she'll want to be moving to England too."

"Over my dead body," Charlotte muttered.

At midnight, Tyler and Shelby began the rounds of saying goodbye to family and friends. They were taking a limousine to the Radisson at Heathrow and flying out first thing in the morning to Ibizia. "It's not Egypt," Tyler remarked to Nancy, "but I'm sure we'll get there someday."

Nancy nodded, "I'm sure you will too. Don't give up your dream, honey."

In the early hours of the morning, after finally getting into bed, Alexa said, "I wish we weren't leaving tomorrow."

"Actually it's today we're leaving," Charlotte remarked.

"I know that, Mom. Do we really have to go?"

"Yes, I'm afraid so. I committed to the Greenberg twin's birthday party weeks ago and I only have two days to prepare for it."

"Well I'm ready to go home," Nancy said. "I want to make sure the cats are all okay."

"I thought you said not to worry about them, Nana."

"You're right, I did, but I still miss them."

"Mmmm it will be nice to see Zoe," Alexa muttered as her eyes began to close.

"Go to sleep, Alexa," Charlotte said. "It's awfully late and we don't want to get up too late because we have to get ready to leave. That means we still have to pack."

"Okay, Mom, night," Alexa whispered.

"Goodnight, honey. Goodnight, Mom."

Nancy didn't answer, she was already almost asleep.

Chapter Sixty-Eight

It was a few minutes after one in the afternoon when the Air Canada flight lifted off from Heathrow. It was expected to arrive in Toronto at about two o'clock. Dr. Lewiston had insisted on driving them to the airport and Charlotte was grateful because, with the time difference, she knew it was going to be a very long and tiring day.

Having pre-booked, they were seated in the same places as before with Alexa next to Adam, three rows behind Charlotte and Nancy. Alexa was sad as she stared out of the window and watched the city drop away below her. "I wish we weren't going home," she moaned.

Adam chuckled, "Is it London you're going to miss or Shelby's cousin?"

Alexa pouted, "Both," she answered adamantly. "I loved seeing all those old buildings especially the Tower where they cut off people's heads and Reid was really cool."

Adam shook his head, "I'm having trouble connecting one to the other."

"Oh, Dad, don't be such a dork. You know what I mean. Reid gave me his phone number and his e-mail address. He said he might even come to Toronto next year."

"Wow, you must have made quite an impression on him."

Alexa looked smug, "He said I was pretty, Dad, and not only that, he thought I was smart too."

"I've been telling you that all your life, young lady."

"Yes but you're my dad. It's not the same."

Their conversation was cut off by one of the attendants handing out earphones and after that, Alexa settled down to watch a movie while Adam began to read the John Grisham novel he'd picked up at the airport.

They were half way through the flight and had just finished eating when Alexa noticed Charlotte get up and walk towards the front of the plane. She assumed she was going to the bathroom and suddenly had an idea. Pulling off her earphones, she jumped up, walked forward a few steps, and then sank down into the seat beside Nancy. "Hi, Nana," she said grasping her grandmother's arm.

Nancy was startled for a moment, then smiled, "Hello, honey, what are you doing here?"

"I thought I'd come and sit with you for a while. I just finished watching a movie and Dad's got his nose stuck in some book."

"Well, I'd love to have your company but your mom will be back in a minute."

"That's okay, she can sit with Dad."

Nancy looked at her suspiciously, "It sounds like you're up to something."

Alexa shrugged her shoulders, "Maybe. Did you see them dancing together last night? They looked pretty cozy to me."

"Hmmm. I would hardly have called it cozy. What if your mother doesn't want to change seats?"

Alexa chuckled, "She will, don't worry."

"You seem pretty sure of yourself so just leave me out of this."

Alexa patted Nancy's hand as she watched Charlotte exit the bathroom and make her way towards them. She stopped when she reached Alexa and motioned to her to get up, "What are you doing?" she asked.

Alexa remained where she was, "I wanted to spend some time with Nana. Why don't you go and sit in my seat?"

"You mean next to your father?"

Alexa merely nodded and turned her head away to stare out of the window. Charlotte looked at Nancy, who was pretending to be absorbed in a magazine, then proceeded down the aisle and stopped where Adam was sitting. He looked up in surprise when he saw her, "Is everything okay?" he asked.

"Yes, but your daughter has commandeered my seat. Would you mind if I sat here?"

Adam closed his book, "Of course not. Would you prefer to sit by the window?"

"No I'll be fine here," she replied and sat down.

They were both silent for a few minutes then Adam opened his book again and pointed to the earphones Alexa had stuffed into the pocket of the seat in front of her. "You can watch a movie if you like."

"No, I'd rather not. I may just try and close my eyes for a little while."

"I don't blame you. I'm feeling a bit weary myself after the late night."

"What did you think of the wedding?"

"I thought it was perfect. Tyler made me proud. I have to say, he's matured a lot. I think he'll manage the responsibility of a family well and I think Shelby will make a good partner. I really liked her."

"I liked her too but I still think they're too young and I wish they weren't living so far away."

They talked some more about the wedding, the Lewistons' and the sights they had seen and, when the attendant approached them for the second time with the offer of a beverage, Adam ordered a glass of white wine for Charlotte and a Coors Light for himself. By the time the announcement came that they would be arriving at Pearson in half an hour, Charlotte no longer felt awkward, in fact, she felt very comfortable and was reluctant to move when Alexa decided she wanted to sit next to her father again.

Passing through customs and waiting for their luggage seemed to take forever but eventually they made it to the arrivals area. "Did you take a taxi to get here?" Adam asked.

"No, a limousine," Nancy replied. "What about you?"

"Sam gave me a lift. Why don't we share a limousine going back? If we take the Gardiner, you can drop me off at Queen's

Quay and then continue on from there. Don't worry I'll put it on my credit card."

Nancy looked at Charlotte who nodded, "Thank you Adam, that's very generous of you."

The traffic was light on the expressway and they reached Adam's building in just over twenty minutes. When the limousine came to a stop, he turned around from his seat, next to the driver, said goodbye to Nancy and Charlotte, blew a kiss to Alexa and stepped out onto the driveway. At the same time that the driver got out to help him retrieve his suitcase from the trunk and settle the bill, Charlotte exited the back of the limo. "I think I'll sit in the front," she said.

"Wait," Adam called out. "Can I have a word with you, Charlotte?"

Charlotte looked at the driver, "I'll just be a moment," she said.

The driver tipped his hat, "No problem, ma'am. Take your time."

Alexa's face could be seen pressed up against the window as Adam motioned for Charlotte to step away from the limo. She walked tentatively towards him. "What is it?" she asked.

Adam hesitated, looked down at the ground and then up again, "Will you have dinner with me one night next week?"

Charlotte hesitated, "You mean, like a date?"

Adam nodded, "Yes, like a date. I've missed you, Charlotte."

Charlotte reached out and lightly touched his hand, "I've missed you too, Adam."

"So, you'll go to dinner with me?"

"I'd like that very much."

Adam smiled, "I'll call you."

Charlotte watched as he walked away and, when she turned around, she noticed Alexa had opened the window. "What's happening, Mom?" she called out.

Charlotte grinned and gave her the thumbs up, "Your dad asked me out on a date."

Alexa's head whipped around, "Did you hear that, Nana?" Then she turned back, smiling from ear to ear, "That's cool, Mom, really cool."